A Perilous Situation

The phone in Phaedra's reticule vibrated with a text and she pulled it out. Marisol. The new lit prof arrives tomorrow.

Phaedra frowned and texted, Okay. So?

You agreed to give him a tour. Remember?

She groaned. I forgot. Thanks.

"Everything okay?" Charlene wondered.

"Yes, fine." She returned her phone to her reticule. "That was my teaching assistant, reminding me that our new English professor arrives from Oxford tomorrow. He's a Shakespearean scholar. I volunteered to give him a tour of the campus." Phaedra was already regretting her offer.

"I'm sure he'll be an asset to the faculty."

Privately, Phaedra suspected he'd be more of an ass than an asset. He'd postponed his start date twice. Not a surprise, she surmised, given his superior Oxford education.

As everyone in the drawing room conversed in small, convivial groups, drinking sherry and doing their best to ignore the grumble of thunder and flashes of lightning, Tinsley excused herself to get another glass of sherry.

A gust of wind howled down the chimney and a log slipped, sending out a shower of sparks. Conversation ceased as the lights flickered.

"Hope we don't lose power." Scott, the director, made his way to a window, glass in hand, and peered out.

"It's like being in one of those murder mysteries," Renee, another bachelorette, said as she eyed the antique furnishings and tall windows with trepidation. "Stuck in an old house, in the middle of a storm—"

"And someone gets murdered," Scott finished.

A crack of lightning split the air, eliciting a small scream from the girl, and gasps from several others.

"That was close," Kyle said, and let out a nervous laugh. "Talk about drama! I love a good electrical storm as much as anyone, but this is a bit much, even for me."

"I'll go fetch some candles," Finch announced. "Best to be prepared in the event we do lose power."

"If this keeps up it'll put us behind schedule," Karolina fretted.

Scott frowned. "We'll have to shelve tomorrow's shoot and move it indoors. The ground's already saturated—"

A sizzling sound drowned out the rest of his words as the power wavered, flickered, and went out, plunging the drawing room into darkness.

"There should be candles around here somewhere," Scott said. "An old place like this." There was a bang and a muttered curse as he bumped into a table.

"Anyone have a lighter?" Kyle said.

The scriptwriter did. "Smoker," he admitted. "Trying to quit, but it's tough." He withdrew a Bic and thumbed it, and a flare of light cast a feeble nimbus around him.

"You look like a vampire, Monty," Kyle joked.

Monty held the lighter under his chin and intoned, "Who vants to marry Mr. Darcy now?"

"Finch!" Collier bellowed, his voice ringing out in the darkness from the entry hall. "It's black as pitch in here! Where the devil are those candles?"

Before the butler could reply, a scream pierced the darkness.

Pride, Prejudice, and Peril

A Jane Austen Tea Society Mystery

Katie Oliver

BERKLEY PRIME CRIME
New York

BERKLEY PRIME CRIME
Published by Berkley
An imprint of Penguin Random House LLC
penguinrandomhouse.com

ISBN: 9780593337615

First Edition: December 2021

Printed in the United States of America
1   3   5   7   9   10   8   6   4   2

Book design by Alison Cnockaert

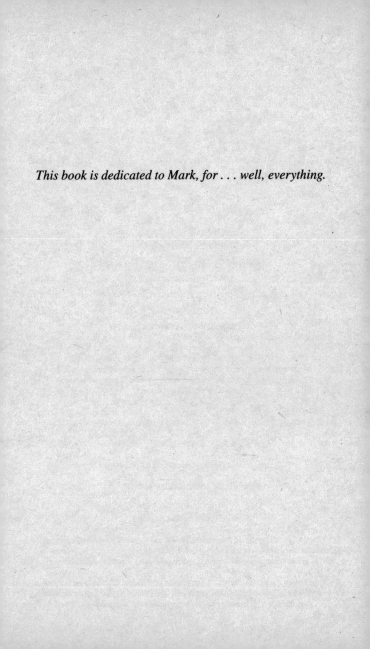

This book is dedicated to Mark, for . . . well, everything.

A large income is the best recipe for happiness I ever heard of.

JANE AUSTEN
MANSFIELD PARK (1814)

One

Spend the night with Mr. Darcy again, Phaedra?"

Professor Phaedra Brighton ignored the comment as she entered the faculty lounge. Not only because she was in imminent danger of dropping the briefcase and umbrella thrust under her arm, but because she no longer found Darcy jokes particularly funny.

"I know I'm late," she acknowledged, dumping her briefcase on the conference table. "And yes, before you ask, I stayed up to finish rereading *Pride and Prejudice*."

"There *are* other books out there, you know." Lucy Liang, professor of modern and postmodernist literature, barely looked up from texting. Black hair framed her face in a short, angular style that, on anyone else, would've looked severe, but suited her sharp edges perfectly. "Admit it. You're obsessed with Mr. Darcy."

Phaedra touched her hair, pinned up in a dark blond topknot. She'd spent ten minutes in front of the bathroom mirror with a curling iron to create a cluster of ringlets on each side of her face, with debatable success. "What can I say? I like socially awkward older men."

"The ringlets look great, by the way. Very Carey Mulligan in *Northanger Abbey*."

"Thanks." Phaedra glanced down at her Empire waist gown. She'd made it years ago for a summer job as a docent at Monticello, former president Thomas Jefferson's home in Charlottesville, Virginia. Dressing in historically appropriate clothing was important to her.

Even now, her students at Somerset University enjoyed seeing her deliver lectures in full Regency attire.

She gave her umbrella a brisk shake and set it aside. "At least I won't miss the Thursday morning staff meeting."

"You say that like it's a good thing." Lucy glanced at the clock. "Ten minutes more, and you'd have avoided Dean Carmichael's justification for slashing the Humanities budget yet again. Not to mention finding out how much, or more to the point, how little he's giving the English department for the Jane Austen lit fest."

Removing her soggy sneakers, Phaedra retrieved a pair of ballet flats from her briefcase, slipped them on, and withdrew a reticule, lecture notes, and a Moleskine planner. "I can still leave. You can pretend you never saw me."

"No deal. If I have to suffer, you have to suffer." Lucy laid her cell phone aside as Phaedra sat next to her. "When are you joining the rest of us and going electronic? I mean, I get the reticule—a Regency lady can't be without her tiny drawstring purse—but no one uses notepads or planners anymore."

"I do. And the reticule not only lends authenticity to my outfit, it's practical. I keep my cell phone in there."

"Sorry I'm late." Marisol Dubois, resident advisor, graduate student, and Phaedra's high-energy, part-time assistant, sailed into the lounge with a stack of essays clutched against her chest and put them on the table in front of Phaedra. "I would've been on time, but the copier jammed again."

"I just got here myself. And thanks for making my point," Phaedra said.

"Point?"

"Copiers jam, electronic files disappear, and when the server's down, which it invariably is, we can't access anything. Paper may be old-school, but it's dependable."

"Paper burns," Lucy pointed out. "Or gets lost. Ink fades."

"Like old love letters." Marisol ran a hand absently through her glossy, shoulder-length brown hair. "The ink may fade, but the sentiment remains forever."

Lucy rolled her eyes. "Spare me. Romance is a myth."

"Speaking of romance," Marisol said, "I swear I just saw Nick Ross in the express line at the IGA."

"Nick Ross." Lucy raised one dark brow skeptically. "As in, the famous Welsh actor?"

"Yep." Marisol sat down across from Phaedra. "He bought a candy bar and a bottle of kombucha." She frowned. "Kind of a weird combination, now that I think about it."

Phaedra barely looked up from her notes. "The kombucha was for himself. The candy bar was for someone else."

"And you know this how?" Lucy asked.

"The tabloids say he's fanatical about eating healthy. No sugar, no unrefined carbs. And they're filming *Who Wants to Marry Mr. Darcy?* nearby, which means he's on a strict diet. The candy bar was obviously for a cast member."

"Obviously." Marisol and Lucy exchanged glances. They were used to Phaedra's idiosyncrasies.

"Thank you, Sherlock Brighton, for your incisive deductive reasoning." Lucy frowned. "Isn't that Mr. Darcy thing you just mentioned a new reality show? I thought it was called something else."

"Filming nearby, as in where?" Marisol asked.

Phaedra glanced up. "Marling. You know, the historic mansion that sits on a rise halfway between Laurel Springs and Crozet. And you're right, Lu. The pilot was called *Who Wants to Marry a Fortune?*"

"I remember. But the network pulled the plug."

"I'm not surprised." Marisol fished out a hair elastic from her handbag and pulled her hair into a low ponytail. "Harold Fortune died a billionaire, but he left his wife and five daughters broke and gave every penny to his nephew instead. No one wants to marry a Fortune now."

"They still have money," Phaedra pointed out. "The papers say he left them enough to live on comfortably."

"Comfortably. As in, no more chauffeured Bentleys or cruises to Iceland or custom-made designer clothes." Marisol glanced at her Chanel twinset and jeans. "I prefer vintage. It's timeless. And far more budget friendly."

"Longbourn Pharmaceutical is worth millions," Lucy said. "It's one of the top five pharmaceuticals in the country."

"He must've been furious to cut them out." Marisol frowned. "I mean . . . who does that? It's cost the Fortune girls big bucks. Not to mention their TV show."

"Actually," Phaedra said, "the show's still happening."

Lucy leaned back in her chair, arms crossed. "Okay, clarification, please. You just said—"

"I said the network canceled the pilot. But they're producing a new version—"

"*Who Wants to Marry Mr. Darcy?*" Lucy finished.

"Who doesn't?" Marisol said. "After all, he's the perfect man. Brooding, handsome, fabulously rich . . . not to mention he's a real gentleman, too."

"And fictional," Lucy reminded her. "He doesn't exist. Besides, the 'perfect man' is an oxymoron. There is no such animal. I should know; I've dated enough losers to confirm it." Her glance returned to Phaedra. "How will this program work, exactly?"

"Eight bachelorettes will compete for the bachelor, Mr. Darcy, in hopes of receiving a marriage proposal by the end of the season. He'll be handsome, wealthy—"

"And in need of a wife?" Marisol clapped her hands together in excitement. "It's like *The Bachelor* meets *Pride and Prejudice*. Will there be lots of betrayals and backstabbing and off-camera sobbing?"

"I'm sure there'll be plenty of drama," Phaedra assured her, and glanced at the door before lowering her voice. She'd saved the best for last. "I'm consulting on the show. I start today."

"Congratulations!" Marisol jumped up from her seat and threw her arms around Phaedra. Lucy remained seated.

"That's amazing," she said. "Truly. But what about your academic schedule?"

"I'll work around my classes. I'm headed for the set after the meeting. And please," Phaedra added, "don't breathe a word to anyone. This stays between the three of us. Karolina—the producer—swore me to secrecy."

"And we see how well *that* worked." Lucy set her coffee aside and stood up.

"What else did Karolina tell you?" Marisol asked.

"Only that the network loves the idea."

"Of course they do," Lucy said dryly as she headed for the door. "Because it's a truth universally acknowledged that a single man in search of a wife must eventually star in a reality show."

Two

An hour later, Phaedra grabbed her notepad and essays and stalked out of the conference room.

"Carmichael not only slashed our budget," she seethed as she and Lucy emerged into the hall, "he cut funding for the Jane Austen literary festival to the bone. Instead, big surprise, he's increasing the Economics budget."

Lucy shrugged. "Econ attracts more students and more financial support . . . unlike us redheaded Humanities stepchildren. That won't change anytime soon. But, hey," she added with faux brightness, "at least we'll have a new English professor. He'll be here tomorrow. The cuts to our Humanities budget are probably helping to fund his educated-at-Oxford salary."

"I'm sure he'll be insufferable."

"An Oxford fellow, a professor of English and comparative literature, and a Shakespearean scholar? Of course he'll be insufferable."

Phaedra didn't reply.

"Don't worry." Lucy stopped and touched Phaedra's arm. "You'll figure out a way to raise the money. The only other option is shelving the lit fest altogether."

"No." Phaedra pressed her lips together. "People come from Charlottesville and D.C. for the festival. We've always sponsored it, and this year will be no exception."

"So, are you headed to Marl . . ." Seeing Phaedra's frown, followed by a lip-zipping motion, she said, "The place?"

"Yes. I'll see you at the meeting tonight."

"Wouldn't miss it."

"Good. Because it's your turn to feed us."

"Then I hope you and Mari like stale chips and leftover sushi with your pinot gris."

"We're the Jane Austen *Tea* Society, Lu. As in cucumber sandwiches and Darjeeling."

"I'm out of both. So, wine it is. See you later."

She went into her office, and Phaedra returned to the teachers' lounge to retrieve her umbrella and glanced at the clock. Half-past eleven. Karolina expected her at Marling at noon, and if she didn't get a move on, she'd be late. And rumor had it that Karolina *despised* tardiness.

Thankfully, she had no lectures scheduled today. She'd be cutting it close to get to the set on time.

Wind whipped at her skirts and clouds lowered overhead as she emerged from the Humanities building and hurried across the parking lot. A spring storm, typical of Virginia's capricious mountain weather, promised to make for an unpleasant drive out to the Marling estate. A distant rumble of thunder confirmed it.

Not a promising day for an outdoor location shoot.

Phaedra reached her bright blue convertible Mini Cooper and took out her key fob. Would they cancel filming? Move it inside?

The first drops of rain began to fall. She slid behind the wheel, never easy in an Empire gown, and closed the convertible top as the shower became a deluge.

A glance in the rearview mirror confirmed that in her present damp, bedraggled state, she looked less like a Regency lady and more like Elizabeth Bennet after walking three miles in the rain to visit her sister at Netherfield.

Mr. Darcy would not approve.

She untied her sodden bonnet and tossed it on the seat beside her when her cell phone rang. The phone, along with her laptop and car, was a reluctant concession to modernity. Although she did her best to stay in character while in costume—verisimilitude was everything, after all—her phone was a necessary evil. The bass line of Queen's "Under Pressure" filled the cabin.

"Mom," she said, switching the phone to speaker as she backed out of the space. "I'm just leaving."

"Just leaving? But you'll be late. You shouldn't be late on your first day."

"We had a faculty meeting." Phaedra turned out of the parking lot. "I stayed behind to answer a question from one of my first-year lit students."

"You're dedicated to a fault."

"And you're the only person I know who can make a compliment sound like a criticism."

"No criticism intended. I simply wanted to wish you good luck on your first day as a reality show consultant. But if you'd prefer I hang up—"

"No, of course not." Phaedra knew that injured tone all too well. Smoothing her mother's ruffled feathers required a diversionary tactic. "What are you up to today?"

"Nothing much." Mollified, Nan Prescott Brighton, former Richmond, Virginia, socialite and reigning queen of the Laurel Springs Historical Society, added, "I stopped by the carriage house to drop off your mail this morning, but you'd already gone."

"Sorry. I overslept and barely made it to the meeting on time."

"Dreaming of Mr. Darcy again, no doubt."

Phaedra heard the note of disapproval but chose, as she often did with her mother, to ignore it. "Did you lock the door when you left?" she asked.

"Of course I did. I only forgot the one time."

"You forget every time."

"The kitchen smelled divine, by the way," Nan added, adroitly changing the subject. "A new scented candle?"

"Bath buns. I brought some to the set." She glanced at the back seat to reassure herself that the bakery boxes, filled with several dozen sweet rolls topped with crunchy demerara sugar and studded with candied citrus, were there.

"Karolina will be pleased." There was a beat of silence. "I understand that Nick Ross is the bachelor."

"How did you know that? You're not supposed to know that."

"Millie Peters saw him at the IGA this morning buying kombucha and a candy bar. It's a small town. You know how it is. And just think—you're the historical consultant on the show! Lucky girl."

Rain lashed at the windshield as the wiper blades struggled valiantly to keep up. "Luck had nothing to do with it."

As a Jane Austen scholar and a professor of English literature at Somerset University, Phaedra was often sought out by educators, documentary filmmakers, and writers for her Austen expertise. Her Regency teaching attire attracted the attention of the local news station, and the piece proved so popular the affiliate network broadcast the story.

But none of that mattered to her mother as much as Phaedra's regrettably single status.

"You're eminently qualified," Nan agreed. "With Nick on board and those silly Fortune girls out of the picture, the show will attract higher ratings."

"That's what Karolina's banking on."

"Marling belongs to Harold's nephew now, doesn't it?"

"He inherited everything. He's allowing the Fortunes to stay in the caretaker's cottage for the time being."

"Kind of him." Her mother's voice dripped with sarcasm. "I do hope you can talk some sense into Charlene."

"It's a little too late for that."

"Oh, and before I forget, your father says to stop by the bookstore tonight. He put a few mysteries aside."

"I'll swing by after the Tea Society meeting."

Nan let out an impatient breath. "What do you girls do at those meetings, anyway? Besides drink tea and gossip."

"We discuss books, Mother. And we talk about local current events."

"I can't imagine there's much to discuss, then. Nothing ever happens in Laurel Springs."

Phaedra slowed the car to avoid a pothole and turned onto Route 250. At least the rain was letting up. "Listen, I have to go. I just got here and I see Charlene," she added, mentally crossing her fingers at the fib.

"Tell her I said hello, and for goodness' sake, try to find out what's going on." She paused. "I will say one thing for Charlene, though. At least she's *married*."

Phaedra bit back a sharp retort and ended the call.

The road wound past horse farms, wineries, and fences before giving way to the gentle slope of the Blue Ridge foothills, and Phaedra's tensions eased with each passing mile. The landscape never failed to relax and rejuvenate her. She lowered her window, breathing in the clean scent of rain-washed air as she caught sight of Marling.

Built in the Georgian style of aged Virginia brick, with a hipped roof and tall windows, Marling overlooked the foothills of the Blue Ridge just as it had for two hundred and fifty years. Wings added on either side in the early nineteenth century only enhanced its singular beauty.

Phaedra slowed and turned onto Rolling Hill Road, following it until she reached a pair of stone pillars flanking the private, tree-lined drive that led to Marling. An earlier rain had left the dirt lane rutted and muddy. A glance at the sky revealed more clouds in the distance.

She pulled into the unit location and parked on a grassy area crowded with film crew vehicles, a catering truck, and trailers. Retrieving the bakery boxes and setting them atop the car, Phaedra searched the faces of the cast and crew but didn't see Karolina.

She locked the car with a chirp of the key fob and eyed

the muddy lot with misgivings. So much for keeping her hem and slippers clean.

An intimidating collection of cameras, dollies, and lights confronted her, and crew sporting clipped-on microphones and wireless packs navigated a snarl of cables crisscrossing the lawn. Golf carts zipped back and forth.

Phaedra suddenly wanted nothing so much as to turn around, go home, make a nice pot of Earl Grey, and bury her nose in an Austen novel. This . . . this was way out of her comfort zone. But she'd promised Karolina she could do this, and she wouldn't let her down.

She picked up the bakery boxes, drew in a deep, calming breath, and headed onto the set.

"Excuse me," she called out to a passing woman with a wireless mic clipped to her hip. "I'm Phaedra Brighton, the historical consultant. Can someone take these to Karolina? They're Bath buns. I made them for the cast and crew."

"Sure." She took the boxes and indicated a group of canvas-backed chairs by the house. "You're over there."

"Ms. Brighton?"

Phaedra saw a young man with a clipboard in hand approaching. "Professor Brighton," she corrected.

"You're a professor?" He eyed her sprigged green muslin gown and ballet flats doubtfully.

His confusion was understandable. Like him, everyone else wore jeans and T-shirts, sported wireless packs or clipped-on mics, and held a script or a clipboard. Or both.

"My students are used to seeing me dressed like this." She smiled. "I like to say I'm the height of fashion . . . circa 1811."

"But you're not a bachelorette."

"No." She paused to admire the loping, confident stride of Nick Ross as he joined the young women gathered on Marling's front steps. In colorful Empire gowns, their hair pinned up in curls and Grecian knots, they resembled a collection of exotic butterflies. "I'm not a bachelorette."

But she suddenly wished she were.

Nick was certainly swoon-worthy. With his dark hair and eyes, sporting a frock coat and buckskin trousers tucked into shiny Hessian boots, Ross was the embodiment of Mr. Fitzwilliam Darcy.

Plenty of giggling, eyelash batting, and whispering went on as Nick took his place among the bachelorettes.

Was I that man-crazy at twenty-one? Phaedra wondered, but she knew the answer was no. Even then, her nerdy little heart belonged firmly to Mr. Darcy of Pemberley.

She dragged her attention back to the man in front of her. "I'm the historical consultant."

"Kyle Columbus, production runner." He thrust out a bound document and a sheet of paper. "Here's today's script and the call sheet for tomorrow."

He left to run copies to other members of the crew.

She tucked the script under her arm and cast an uneasy glance overhead. The wind had increased, turning the leaves a silvery green and sending the clouds scudding.

"This is a travesty, do you hear me? A travesty!"

Drawn by a commotion nearby, Phaedra made her way to the front of the house. The cast and crew stared, transfixed, as a middle-aged woman hurtled up the front steps to the producer and jabbed her finger in her chest.

"You tell William Collier he won't get away with this!" she shouted. "I'll see him in hell first!"

Three

Phaedra found a canvas-backed chair with her name stenciled on it and sat down. A quick glance confirmed she wasn't the only one listening to the woman's rant. Every member of the crew avidly drank in the unfolding drama.

Mrs. Dorothy Fortune didn't care. Her green eyes snapped as she snatched off her cat's-eye sunglasses and gestured at the eight young women ranged around her on the front steps.

Phaedra recognized Harold Fortune's widow from newspaper photos. From her dark auburn French twist to her stylish high heels, she quivered with indignation.

"You've replaced my girls, my beautiful, *famous* girls, with this collection of costumed nobodies." She glared at the producer. "I won't have it! I won't!"

A slim young woman in jeans and a crop top charged up the steps after her. "Mother, stop. Let it go."

Mrs. Fortune didn't turn around. "I can't do that, Patsy. This was meant to be *your* show. You and your sisters, on national television."

"Well, it didn't happen," Patsy said. "It's over. And who cares about a stupid reality show, anyway?"

Just before she flounced away, she glanced at Nick Ross,

and the tense line of her lips eased. He inclined his head slightly. Regretfully.

Interesting, Phaedra mused as Patsy left. Did she and Nick know each other?

"I'm sorry." Karolina Dalton, the show's producer and subject of Mrs. Fortune's ire, plainly wasn't. She wore yoga pants, a T-shirt, and a harried expression as she tugged her reddish-blond ponytail through the back of her baseball cap. "But Patsy's right. With no money, no one wants to marry your girls now. Which means *Who Wants to Marry a Fortune?* is out and *Who Wants to Marry Mr. Darcy?* is in."

Phaedra winced at her bluntness. Typical Karolina.

"You gave your word," Dorothy accused. "You have no right to change the entire concept—"

"The network pulled the plug. Their decision, not mine. Now, you're wasting my time. And time," Karolina added, encompassing the collection of cameras, lights, and crew with a sweep of her hand, "is money." She signaled to a security guard. "Escort Mrs. Fortune off the property."

"This is outrageous," she sputtered. "I won't be thrown off my own property like some kind of riffraff!"

Karolina walked away as the security guard arrived.

"It's not your property any longer, ma'am. Come along, please." He reached for her arm.

She jerked away and began to weep, great, wrenching sobs, and Phaedra felt an unexpected surge of sympathy for her. Although Dorothy Fortune had shamelessly traded on her daughters' good looks and social media notoriety for years, she didn't deserve to be left penniless by her recently deceased husband. Yet that's exactly what Harold Fortune did when he left everything to his nephew, William Collier.

"What seems to be the trouble here?"

As if her thoughts had summoned him, Bill Collier, CEO of Longbourn Pharmaceuticals, her friend Charlene's new husband, and the current owner of Marling, appeared. Self-importance radiated from him like heat from a wood-burning stove.

Wearing a royal blue blazer over a white polo, with Italian leather loafers encasing his sockless feet, he would've been at home on the bridge of a yacht. At barely five foot seven, he looked less like a newly minted millionaire and more like Napoleon in khakis.

"I'll tell you what the trouble is," Dorothy snapped. "You've turned my beautiful home into a circus."

"We're filming a reality show, Dottie." He brushed a speck from the lapel of his blazer. "And it's not your home any longer."

"Yes, a reality show meant for my daughters. Which you stole, along with my husband's estate."

"Harold left his estate to me. I stole nothing." His lips stretched thin over his teeth as he produced a smile devoid of either warmth or sincerity. "Contest the will if you like, but it's ironclad."

"How did you manage it, I wonder?"

"I'm sure I don't know what you mean."

"It's obvious you coerced my husband into handing everything over to you. What I don't understand is how you did it. Did you threaten him? Blackmail him?"

"Careful," he warned. "Persist with these wild accusations and I'll evict you and your daughters from the caretaker's cottage. Which, may I remind you, I'm graciously allowing you to use. Don't push me."

"I'd like to push you," she hissed, "right out a window. You may have our money and live in our house. I can't change that. But I *can* wish you a long and miserable existence. And I do. Death is too good for you."

She stalked away, casting a dark look over her shoulder as she went.

Collier spotted Phaedra. "Professor Brighton!" He greeted her with false bonhomie. "My pardon for Dottie's outburst. I'm sure she didn't mean what she said."

Phaedra had no doubt Dorothy Fortune meant every word. "She recently lost her husband, and her daughters lost their father, and their home. Of course she's upset."

If he registered the rebuke, he gave no sign. "Indeed. Poor woman. Dreadful business." He focused a polite smile on her. "It's such a pleasure to meet you. Charlene tells me you're a consultant on the program."

"Yes. Karolina felt my expertise as an Austen scholar might prove useful."

"As I have no doubt it will. Speaking of my wife, have you seen her?" He glanced at the Chopard watch on his wrist. "We have an early dinner reservation at that new French place."

"I haven't, but if I do, I'll certainly tell her you're looking for her."

"Places, everyone," the assistant director called out. "The weather's sketchy, so let's try to get this in one take."

Marling presented a dramatic backdrop as the cameramen set up the shot. The skies added a brooding background, while the lights focused on the steps bathed Nick and the bachelorettes in bright, faux sunshine.

"Professor Brighton?"

Karolina Dalton, wearing a headset and a determined expression, approached. "I'd like some of those Bath buns for a scene we're filming next week. They'll be perfect to serve with tea."

"I used an authentic Regency recipe." Warming to the subject, Phaedra added, "Did you know Solange Luyon created the first Bath bun in 1780? She was a Huguenot refugee. No one could pronounce her name, so everyone called her Sally Lunn—"

"Fascinating." Karolina glanced at her wristwatch, making no secret of her disinterest. "Can you do it? I need four dozen."

"Well . . . I only have one class scheduled tomorrow, so I suppose I could—"

"Good. No, I don't know where Monty is," she barked into her headset. "Try Fiona's dressing room."

And she strode off.

The wind tugged at Phaedra's skirts and chased leaves

across the lawn. Thunder growled, followed by a fork of lightning in the distance.

"Okay, that's a wrap!" the director, Scott Zussman, shouted. "Let's get this equipment put away."

The words barely left his mouth when thunder rumbled overhead, closer now, chased by a zigzag of lightning.

"Everyone, come inside, please," William Collier called out from the front steps of the house. "This promises to be a nasty storm."

As crew gathered and secured equipment, another flash of lightning lit the sky, closer this time. Phaedra sprinted toward the house as a heavy rain began to fall.

Her dress was soaked through, and she looked like a shipwreck survivor. And lightning wasn't exactly her favorite thing.

The temperature had dropped, too. Shivering, she rubbed her arms and followed the cast and crew up the wide brick steps to the front door, and into Marling.

Four

P hae!"

Phaedra broke into a wide grin as Charlene Collier, née Lucas, rushed across the black-and-white-tiled entryway and gathered her into a tight hug. She smelled distinctly of horse.

"It's so good to see you!" Charlene drew back. "I've missed you."

"It's been too long." Phaedra's gaze went to the flying staircase, its balusters and treads made of mahogany, and she could almost imagine the former ladies of the house, skirts rustling and candles flickering as they descended in their Georgian finery. "What a beautiful home."

"Isn't it? I'm afraid to touch anything for fear I'll spill coffee on the upholstery or break something priceless." Charlene glanced down at her jeans and muddy, booted feet. "I didn't have time to change."

"You still like to ride, I see."

"I do." Charlene smiled. "Some things never change. At least now," she added lightly, "I don't have to muck out the stables anymore."

They'd met at the Barnett stables during freshman year at

Laurel Springs High. Phaedra's family had recently relocated, and she knew no one. And Charlene's after-school job, mucking out the stables on Saturdays and working part-time at Bertie's Café, left her little time for extracurricular activities, or friends.

Fourteen-year-old Phaedra, attired in jodhpurs and a riding jacket, recognized the girl in baggy jeans and mud-caked rubber boots from her first-period English class and offered a friendly hello. Charlene ignored her.

A week later, as she tried and failed once again to engage Charlene in conversation, Phaedra lost her temper and snapped, "Why won't you talk to me?"

"Because I have work to do. I don't have time to prance around on a horse like Lady Muck."

Phaedra dismounted and flung the reins aside. "You're the one who acts like a snob. Not me. What's your problem, anyway?"

Charlene didn't answer, only glared at her and brushed past. Phaedra reached out to grab her shoulder and spun her around. But her foot slid out from under her in the mud and she suddenly found herself sprawled on the ground.

For a moment, neither spoke. "Well," Charlene said finally, eyeing her with a smirk, "now you really *are* Lady Muck."

Phaedra laughed, the nickname stuck, and despite their very different backgrounds, the two became fast friends. Charlene devoted her time to her disabled mother and worked two jobs to help out. Studious Phaedra was obsessed with Jane Austen and the Brontës. Both clung to the life raft of their newly found friendship.

"How does it feel to be lady of the manor?" Phaedra asked her now.

"I still can't believe I'm married." She held out her hand to admire the gold band encircling her finger, nestled below a marquise-cut diamond engagement ring. "Bill is such a wonderful, kindhearted man."

Wonderful? Kindhearted? She suspected Dorothy Fortune might disagree.

"Would you like a tour before we join the others?" Charlene indicated a drawing room to the left where everyone gathered to wait out the storm. Nick Ross stood by the fireplace, one booted foot resting on the hearth. His dark good looks and Welsh accent riveted the bachelorettes.

She nodded, and Charlene led her past the stairs and down a long hallway, pausing before a set of double doors on the left. "This is where the cast and crew have lunch and dinner."

Phaedra glimpsed a pair of tall windows and a Georgian chandelier suspended above a table the length of an airport runway. Perfectly aligned china, silverware, and folded cloth napkins marched down both sides of the table.

Roberta Walsh, caterer for the production team and local owner of Bertie's Café, entered with a covered tray. She was a stocky, no-nonsense woman of late middle age with short gray hair and deep lines bracketing her mouth.

Her café had a loyal following, along with a reputation for satisfying, if uninspired, diner fare. She gave them a sharp glance but said nothing.

They arrived at a small room around the corner on the opposite side of the hall. A pair of French doors led out to a terrace, and a Sheraton desk and chair stood near the fireplace, where flames flickered behind the grate. Figured blue wallpaper gave the room a feminine yet dramatic feel.

"The morning room," Charlene explained. "Where the lady of the house handled her correspondence."

"It's lovely. Who painted your husband's portrait?" Phaedra crossed the room to stand before a painting hung over the fireplace mantel. "It's very . . . striking."

Strikingly awful, more like. William Collier's likeness was painted in dark, somber colors. He'd posed in the manner of one of the aristocratic subjects in the portraits hung in the hallway.

She wondered idly whose ancestors they were. Harold Fortune was a self-made man who made no secret of his humble background. And to her knowledge, Collier didn't have a drop of blue blood running in his veins.

"You don't like him, do you?"

Charlene's question was quiet but direct.

"I don't really know him." Phaedra turned to face her friend. "But neither do you. And that's what I don't understand. You married a man you barely know."

"And you've made no secret of your disapproval." Charlene crossed her arms and eyed her combatively. "Not everyone's had the advantages you have."

Phaedra stiffened. "That isn't fair. And this isn't about me." She sighed. "I'm just saying you have choices, Charl. You didn't have to marry a virtual stranger."

"Choices?" She shook her head. "No, I don't. I have to be practical. Bill wanted to marry me, plain old Charlene, a waitress at Bertie's Café . . . and he took my mother in as well. Not many men would."

Phaedra imagined such generosity came easily to a man who'd just inherited the Fortune wealth.

"I'm sure he's a good person," she ventured, choosing her words with care. "But he was implicated in illegal activities. He served time for tax fraud and embezzlement."

"Ten years ago," Charlene said, a trace defensively. "He paid his debt to society. For two years."

"Charlene, he broke the law. He scammed innocent people who trusted him, some of whom lost their life's savings. I just . . . I don't want to see you hurt."

"We've all made mistakes, Phaedra." Hectic spots of color flushed her cheeks. "You have no right to judge Bill. He's a good person. He's not the man he once was."

"I'm sorry." Phaedra laid a reassuring hand on her friend's arm. "You're right. I apologize."

Charlene gave her a fleeting smile. "I'm sorry, too. Water under the bridge. Let's go and join the others."

They returned to the drawing room and took seats on a Biedermeier sofa by the fireplace.

Bertie entered through an arched doorway that led into the dining room and set a large silver tray down. A young man and woman bearing identical trays followed behind.

"Help yourselves to wine, coffee, tea, sherry—whatever you prefer."

"Perhaps some sparkling water?" Charlene suggested.

Bertie pressed her lips into a thin line. "Don't know as we have any. I'll see what I can do."

"Well, she's a charmer," Phaedra observed as she left. "Who's managing the café while she's here?"

"Sue Tilden. Washed-out blond hair, calls everyone 'hon'? Sweet, but a little nosy."

Phaedra nodded. "I noticed a 'For Lease' sign in the window. Is Bertie selling the business?"

"She doesn't have much choice. The new owner refuses to honor her lease." Charlene stood. "Would you like a glass of wine?"

"I'll stick to tea. I'm driving home when the storm ends. Wickham gets grouchy if he can't go out."

"Did I hear you say 'Wickham'?" A young woman sitting nearby leaned forward. "The handsome cad in *Pride and Prejudice*?"

"Yes. But he's not a cad, he's my cat. A Himalayan." As Charlene crossed the room to get her a cup of tea, Phaedra dug out her phone and scrolled until she found a photo of Wickham. "He's a bit of a ladies' man, too."

"He's gorgeous." The young woman, a blonde in an aquamarine silk gown, admired the cat's silvery fur and blue eyes set in a dark gray face. She handed the phone back. "Tinsley Prentiss. I'm a bachelorette."

"Phaedra Brighton. Historical consultant."

"She's much more than a consultant," Charlene informed Tinsley as she returned with Phaedra's tea. "She's a Jane Austen scholar and an English professor at Somerset University."

"A professor? Impressive. I'm a cardiologist. When I'm not competing on a reality show, that is," Tinsley added.

Phaedra raised her brow. "It's my turn to be impressed. What brought you here?"

"I love my career," Tinsley said. "But I have almost no time to meet men. So I decided to give this reality show thing a try." Her hand strayed to a choker tied around her neck by a delicate blue ribbon. Aquamarines, diamonds, and seed pearls gleamed in the soft firelight.

"What a beautiful choker." Phaedra set her cup aside and leaned forward to study it. "Late Georgian, if I had to guess. Is it real?"

"It's real," Charlene said. "It was a wedding gift from Bill. Just be careful," she warned Tinsley. "One of the stones is loose. I need to have it repaired."

"It's stunning." Phaedra leaned closer to marvel at the delicate workmanship and the square-cut aquamarine centered on Tinsley's neck. "It must be quite valuable."

"I agree. It's beautiful." Nick Ross sauntered up and smiled at Tinsley. "Almost as beautiful as Ms. Prentiss."

A deep flush crept up her neck. "Thank you, Mr. Ross. Or should I say, Mr. Darcy?"

"Call me Nick," he replied with an easy smile.

The butler appeared and began switching on lamps. Despite encroaching middle age, he had a certain boyish appeal. He glided around the room in an unobtrusive yet efficient manner.

Charlene followed her gaze. "That's Finch. He was Harold Fortune's butler, before . . ." She took a quick sip of sherry. "Before things changed."

"So he's been here at Marling for some time."

"Years. We're lucky to have him. After the Fortunes left I didn't think he'd stay on. But he did."

Phaedra stood and went to the window. "Things are getting bad out there." The sky was black. Wind lashed at the trees, sending branches flying, and squalls of rain pummeled the house.

"The latest news bulletin says they've closed Rolling Hill Road," Finch said. "There's a tree down."

"But that's the only route into town. How will I get home?" Phaedra stared out into the inky darkness in dismay.

"Good question." Nick joined her and peered out. "I won't make it back to my hotel if this keeps up."

"You're both welcome to stay the night," Charlene said. "We have plenty of guest rooms."

With a polite nod of thanks, Nick strode away into the dining room, cell phone clapped to his ear.

"At least he gets to keep his phone," Tinsley said as her eyes followed him. "We don't."

"No?" Phaedra returned to her seat on the sofa. "What if you have a family emergency?"

"The producers relay any messages. Which is bad enough. They also keep us separated from Nick, and chaperone every move we make." Tinsley sighed. "No phones, no Internet, no contact with the outside world."

"Doing without modern amenities lends the program more authenticity." William Collier, glass of sherry in hand, joined them. "After all, that *is* the point. Wouldn't you agree, Professor Brighton?"

Before she could reply, Collier's gaze went to the choker at Tinsley's neck. A frown puckered his forehead. "Isn't that my wife's Georgian choker?"

"Yes." Tinsley touched the square-cut aquamarine nestled at the base of her throat. "Mrs. Collier was kind enough to lend it to me to film a scene earlier this afternoon."

He turned to Charlene. "Is this true?"

"Yes. Karolina wanted to borrow it for Tinsley's scene with Nick. It goes so beautifully with her gown."

Phaedra had to agree. Tinsley's dress, of watered aquamarine silk, complemented the choker to perfection, and the jewels emphasized the green of her eyes.

But William plainly did not share their admiration. "Do you mean to say you loaned my wedding gift, a priceless family heirloom, to this . . . this *stranger* to wear?"

"I'm hardly a stranger. I'm one of the bachelorettes." Tinsley spoke in a low but firm voice.

"And a cardiologist," Nick added, rejoining them. "I think you can trust her with the family heirloom."

Collier ignored Ross to glare at Charlene. "What if the choker was lost, or, God forbid, stolen?"

"But it wasn't. And it's insured."

"That's hardly the point!"

"Bill, please. There's no need to cause a scene—"

"I disagree. You loaned out a priceless heirloom as cavalierly as if it were a dollar store trinket."

"I'm sorry if I've upset you. I did try to ask you about it earlier, if you recall. At any rate, it doesn't matter. The choker is fine. I'll make sure it's returned to the safe before I go to bed tonight. I promise."

"Very well. See that you do."

He drained his sherry, set the glass down with a thump, and left. Phaedra's gaze followed him as he paused by the door to exchange a few curt words with Bertie, and her brow puckered in a frown.

Collier's reaction puzzled her. Why such a fuss? After all, as Charlene pointed out, the choker was fine.

The phone in Phaedra's reticule vibrated with a text and she pulled it out. Marisol. The new lit prof arrives tomorrow.

Phaedra frowned and texted, Okay. So?

You agreed to give him a tour. Remember?

She groaned. I forgot. Thanks.

"Everything okay?" Charlene wondered.

"Yes, fine." She returned her phone to her reticule. "That was my teaching assistant, reminding me that our new English professor arrives from Oxford tomorrow. He's a Shakespearean scholar. I volunteered to give him a tour of the campus." Phaedra was already regretting her offer.

"I'm sure he'll be an asset to the faculty."

Privately, Phaedra suspected he'd be more of an ass than an asset. He'd postponed his start date twice. Not a surprise, she surmised, given his superior Oxford education.

As everyone in the drawing room conversed in small, convivial groups, drinking sherry and doing their best to ignore the grumble of thunder and flashes of lightning, Tinsley excused herself to get another glass of sherry.

A gust of wind howled down the chimney and a log slipped, sending out a shower of sparks. Conversation ceased as the lights flickered.

"Hope we don't lose power." Scott, the director, made his way to a window, glass in hand, and peered out.

"It's like being in one of those murder mysteries," Renee, another bachelorette, said as she eyed the antique furnishings and tall windows with trepidation. "Stuck in an old house, in the middle of a storm—"

"And someone gets murdered," Scott finished.

A crack of lightning split the air, eliciting a small scream from the girl, and gasps from several others.

"That was close," Kyle said, and let out a nervous laugh. "Talk about drama! I love a good electrical storm as much as anyone, but this is a bit much, even for me."

"I'll go fetch some candles," Finch announced. "Best to be prepared in the event we do lose power."

"If this keeps up it'll put us behind schedule," Karolina fretted.

Scott frowned. "We'll have to shelve tomorrow's shoot and move it indoors. The ground's already saturated—"

A sizzling sound drowned out the rest of his words as the power wavered, flickered, and went out, plunging the drawing room into darkness.

"There should be candles around here somewhere," Scott said. "An old place like this." There was a bang and a muttered curse as he bumped into a table.

"Anyone have a lighter?" Kyle said.

The scriptwriter did. "Smoker," he admitted. "Trying to quit, but it's tough." He withdrew a Bic and thumbed it, and a flare of light cast a feeble nimbus around him.

"You look like a vampire, Monty," Kyle joked.

Monty held the lighter under his chin and intoned, "Who vants to marry Mr. Darcy now?"

"Finch!" Collier bellowed, his voice ringing out in the darkness from the entry hall. "It's black as pitch in here! Where the devil are those candles?"

Before the butler could reply, a scream pierced the darkness.

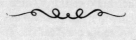

Five

Tinsley, Phaedra realized, and shot to her feet.

She couldn't see much, only the vague, hulking shapes of furniture, but the scream came from the arched doorway connecting the dining and drawing rooms, where the bachelorette had stood only a moment ago. "Tinsley? Are you all right? What's happened?"

"The choker!" she cried, her voice bordering on hysterical. "Someone yanked it right off my neck."

"This is your fault," Collier erupted, returning to focus his ire on Charlene. "If you hadn't loaned the blasted thing out, that choker would be in the safe right now, where it belongs."

"What's happened?" Bertie appeared, wiping her hands on her apron. "I heard someone scream."

"Charlene's choker's been stolen," Phaedra said. She made her way through the darkened room to join Tinsley and slipped her arm around the bachelorette's trembling shoulders. "Are you okay?"

"F-fine. Just a little rattled."

"Did you get a look at the thief?"

"No. Whoever it was came up behind me."

"You know what this means," Kyle mused, and gave a dramatic pause. "There's a thief among us."

"Oh, shut up, Kyle," Scott snapped. "We're not in the mood."

"All right, everyone." Phaedra's words were calm but firm. "If someone's playing a prank, having a bit of fun at Tinsley's expense, then well done. You've succeeded. Now, it's time to come clean." She paused. "Anyone care to fess up?"

Silence greeted her.

"Perhaps we should search for the necklace," Renee suggested.

"Kind of hard, in the dark," Kyle pointed out.

"That's an excellent idea, Renee." Phaedra glanced around the room. "But we need candles first. Or a flashlight."

Bertie turned to one of her staff hovering nearby. "Don't gawp, Jen. Go and find the professor some candles!"

Jen returned shortly with a couple of flashlights, and they began to search the room, overturning cushions, peering in dark corners, and opening drawers.

"This is ridiculous." Karolina returned to her chair. "It's gone. The necklace isn't here because someone took it. We should call the police."

"If someone took it," Scott said reasonably, "then it has to be here. Somewhere."

"Unless you plan to search the entire house," Karolina retorted, "or turn out our pockets and pat us all down, I guarantee you won't find it."

Phaedra returned to the sofa and took the phone from her reticule. Karolina was right. "I'll call the police."

"If we haven't lost cell service," Scott said. "The signal's not great out here, even on a clear day."

"I have to try." Only two bars showed on her screen, but the call went through. "Yes, there's been a robbery, at Marling," Phaedra said into her phone. "An antique necklace has been stolen."

The dispatcher promised to send someone as soon as possible. "But with accidents everywhere, might be a while."

She ended the call. "The police will be here as soon as they can. In the meantime, we should remain in the drawing room until they arrive."

"But that could be hours," Karolina protested.

"We should've stayed in L.A." Scott made no effort to hide his displeasure. "This is costing us time and money."

"I need to get back to my hotel," Nick said. "I'm supposed to meet someone for an interview."

"You heard the professor." Bertie crossed her arms. "Everyone stay put."

Finch returned with a candelabrum and set it down on a side table. A warm glow suffused the drawing room as he lit each taper, chasing the shadows away and sending a palpable wave of relief through the room.

"How could this happen?" Collier raged. "The choker's gone. Gone!"

"I'm sorry." Charlene's face, visible now in the candlelight, was stricken. "I didn't think—"

"No, you didn't *think*." He spat out the word. "Do you know how much that choker is worth? It's irreplaceable!"

By now he was shouting, his embarrassed wife trying valiantly not to cry in the face of his anger.

"Bill, please—"

"I shouldn't be surprised. After all, you're not accustomed to having nice things. You grew up with nothing. Why on earth did I entrust you with something so valuable?"

As Charlene choked back a sob, Nick rounded on him. "That's uncalled for, sir."

Phaedra surged to her feet. "I agree. That's quite enough, Mr. Collier."

"This is none of your concern, Professor," he snapped.

"I disagree." Her words were cool but firm. "It's my concern when you speak to my friend with such blatant disrespect. She's done nothing to deserve it."

"Here's a bit of unsolicited advice, dear lady." His eyes steeled. "Stick to Jane Austen and mind your own business." He turned back to Charlene. "I suggest you get upstairs and change." His eyes cut to her muddy boots and jeans. "We have standards to uphold."

With another withering glare at Phaedra, Collier turned to go. "Finch!" he bellowed. "Get upstairs and run my bath. God knows I pay you enough, you worthless toady."

"But, sir, the power's out, and the storm isn't over—"

"I'll take a flashlight."

"With respect, sir, the wiring in the east wing is dicey at best. Perhaps another bathroom?"

"Just do as I say, damn you."

"Yes, sir," the butler replied. "Right away, sir."

If his employer's harsh words bothered him, he gave no sign, merely inclined his head and followed Collier out of the drawing room and across the entrance hall.

Phaedra pressed her lips together as he left. Stick to Jane Austen, indeed.

"The man's an ass," Nick muttered, echoing her thoughts as he knelt beside Charlene. "Are you all right, Mrs. Collier?"

"I'm fine. Thank you." She fished a tissue out of her pocket with a trembling hand. "I'm sorry you all had to witness that. I apologize." She sniffled and blew her nose. "I should apologize to Bill, as well."

Phaedra touched her hand. "This wasn't your fault."

Tinsley's green eyes blazed. "She's right. Your husband's manners leave a lot to be desired. Someone ought to take him down a peg."

"I'm sorry he was rude to you."

"*He* was rude, not you." Tinsley sighed. "And I'm the one who's sorry. I'm a guest in your home. I have no right to criticize your husband."

"He's not usually like this." Charlene crumpled the tissue in her hand. "I can't blame him for being upset."

She stood and set her glass aside. "Now, if you'll all excuse me, I need to change, and check on Mother. I'll look for candles while I'm upstairs. The power may be out for quite some time."

"You won't be going anywhere in this weather." Phaedra

glanced at the rain-sheeted windows. "Finch is right. This isn't the best time to be outdoors. Or to take a bath."

"I agree. But arguing with Bill is useless."

"Surely he can bathe in another bathroom," Phaedra said.

She shook her head. "There's an old claw-foot tub in the east wing. The wiring hasn't been updated since the 1930s, but he likes the privacy. He reads the newspapers there every morning. I'll be back in a few minutes."

"Don't forget the candles," Phaedra said as Charlene grabbed a flashlight and left.

Joining a few of the others in front of the window, she peered outside. The rain had pummeled the flowers in the front beds, and tree branches were strewn across the lawn. The far end of the drive was obscured by water, and the ground had become a muddy morass.

"There's no salvaging tomorrow's shoot." Karolina took out her phone. "We'll have to film indoors."

"We could do an establishing shot," Scott said. "Stormy weather outside, stormy relationships inside . . ."

He'd barely finished speaking when Finch returned. "Would anyone like another glass of sherry?"

"Got anything stronger?" Monty asked. "No offense, but this stuff tastes like cooking wine."

"There's bourbon in the dining room, if that suits."

Monty rubbed his palms together. "That suits just fine."

Phaedra returned to the sofa. Poor Wickham! He'd want to go out, and he'd probably emptied his food and water dishes.

"Any news on the road closure?" she asked Finch as he returned with Monty's bourbon. "Is the tree still down?"

"The crews are out, so it shouldn't be much longer before the road reopens and power is restored, one hopes."

"Yes," she sighed. "One hopes."

Another flare of lightning illuminated the room, followed by a crack, and a deafening crash. The entire house shuddered on impact.

"What the hell was that?" Nick demanded. "Sounded like a tree fell on the roof."

"I should go upstairs and take a look," Phaedra said.

"I'll go with you," Nick said.

They looked up as Charlene returned, her face ashen. "A tree's just hit the back corner of the house. I was halfway down the stairs when I heard it fall."

"Nick and I were about to go up and investigate," Phaedra said.

Charlene glanced at the actor. "No need for both of you to go. Stay, Nick, and have another drink. You can come with me, Phaedra." She set down a box of candles. "I need to see if there's any damage. And Mother needs a sherry. To calm her nerves."

"Is she all right?"

"She's fine. Storms always make her jumpy. It doesn't help that she insists she saw the Marling ghost just now."

"The Marling ghost?" Phaedra followed her to the table where Finch had set out a decanter and glasses. "Sounds intriguing."

Charlene poured a sherry. "Josiah Marling built the house in 1770. He was a prosperous landowner and breeder of horses. Elizabeth was his daughter and his only child."

"And his wife?"

"She died in childbirth, and Elizabeth did, too. Legend has it the appearance of her ghost presages a death in the family."

"Do you think Violet really saw something?"

"I doubt it. Whatever she saw was at the far end of the hall, and her eyesight isn't what it once was. The storm, her nerves . . ." Charlene shrugged. "Nothing a little sherry won't fix."

"Did you and Bill work things out?" Phaedra asked.

"I didn't actually get a chance to talk to him."

Before Phaedra could ask why, or why she hadn't changed her clothes, Jen appeared with more candles . . . and a tiny bundle of dark, wet fur cradled in the crook of her arm.

"Who's this?" Phaedra asked, her voice softening as she reached out to stroke the kitten's damp fur.

"He was crying outside the kitchen door." Jen glanced down at him. "Poor thing's hungry. Finch lit the pilot on the gas range, and I'm warming some milk for him now." She giggled. "For Kitty, I mean. Not Finch."

Someone banged on the front door.

Finch went to answer it, holding a candlestick aloft, and returned a moment later. "There's a gentleman in the front hall, Mrs. Collier. His car's run out of gas and he wishes to speak to you."

"Very well. I'll deal with it." She produced a flashlight from her pocket and handed it to Phaedra. "Looks like you're on your own. I'll be up with Mother's sherry in a moment."

As Charlene followed Finch into the entrance hall to talk to the stranded motorist, Phaedra crossed the tiled floor to the staircase. Uneasiness tightened her stomach at the prospect of climbing those shadowy steps.

It was her sister Hannah's fault, insisting they watch a horror movie when they were home alone one night. Thirteen-year-old Phaedra had agreed, and gained a lifelong phobia of staircases when the murderer crept up a set of stairs and waited in the shadows to strangle his unsuspecting victim.

Charlene's talk of the Marling ghost did nothing to allay her fears.

With an unsteady hand, she lifted the hem of her gown and forced herself to ascend the stairs.

At the landing, she turned to the right, sweeping her flashlight beam over the Oriental runner, her senses alert. The sound of the wind and rain grew louder and she followed it into the west wing. Charlene was right. If a tree had fallen on the house, it must've crashed into one of the far corner bedrooms.

She only hoped it hadn't damaged the roof.

As she neared the last door on her right she hesitated. This should be the master bedroom. "Mr. Collier?" she called out tentatively. She was fairly certain he wasn't here; Charlene said the bathroom he favored was located in the east wing, on the opposite side of the house. Nonetheless, she knocked twice on the door. "Are you in here? Are you all right?"

No answer.

She hesitated and tried the doorknob. It opened easily.

A thick tree branch had crashed through the far bedroom window. The old oak at the back corner of the house must've sustained a lightning strike.

Broken glass littered the floor, and rain soaked the rug and darkened the silk upholstery of a Chippendale love seat. The roof appeared to be intact, with no evidence of damage or leaking.

There was no sign of William Collier.

Next stop, the east wing, she decided, and returned to the landing, still gripping her flashlight. She proceeded down the hall, opening each door she encountered. Bedrooms. And every one was empty.

One door remained at the far end of the hallway. It had to be the bathroom. It, too, was closed.

Phaedra's ballet slippers moved without a sound over the faded Oriental runner as she knocked on the door. "Mr. Collier? Are you in there?"

Once again, there was no answer.

Hesitantly, she reached for the doorknob and turned it. "Mr. Collier?" She pushed the door wider and peered inside. "Hello?"

Lightning flashed through the only window, illuminating a vintage black-and-white-tiled floor. A fluffy white towel was folded in readiness on a bench nearby, and a robe hung on the back of the far door. But it was the claw-foot tub standing several feet away that drew her attention. Water seeped over the sides and pooled in puddles on the tile.

Bill Collier lay sprawled in the tub, one arm hanging lifelessly over the side. A pink blow-dryer floated atop the water. It was plugged in.

Phaedra drew in a sharp breath and sagged back against the doorjamb as her hand flew to her lips.

He was dead.

His skin was puckered slightly from the water but otherwise appeared normal. But his eyes, open and staring sightlessly up at the ceiling, filled her with horror.

Surely not even Collier, as awful as he was, deserved to die like this.

She stepped away from the door, scarcely aware of what she was doing, careful not to touch anything or tread on the wet tile. She groped in her pocket for her phone with a trembling hand. The police. She had to call the police.

"Please send someone to Marling right away," she said when the 911 dispatcher answered. "There—there's a body."

"Can you give me more details, ma'am? What's your location?"

She opened her mouth but nothing came out. A merry-go-round of shock and revulsion gripped her as she dragged her gaze back to the bathtub. "A m-man's been electrocuted. In the bath upstairs."

"Do you know who he is?"

Haltingly, her words stumbling over themselves, Phaedra provided his name and his determination to bathe in the claw-foot tub in the middle of an electrical storm.

"I see there's already a responding officer on the way," the dispatcher said. "You called in a robbery earlier?"

"Yes. An antique choker was stolen."

The woman instructed her not to touch anything, to remain where she was, and to stay on the line until the police and the paramedics arrived.

It's too late for an ambulance, Phaedra thought, still numb with shock. She thanked the dispatcher and waited, the phone still gripped to her ear.

Poor Charlene. What a horrible thing.

It looked as if her new husband's fondness for soaking in the bathtub had proven to be the death of him.

Six

"Your husband is dead, Mrs. Collier," the sheriff's deputy said as the coroner departed. "I'm sorry."

Charlene, leaning heavily on Phaedra's arm, let out a moan. Her legs buckled, and she would have crumpled to the floor if Phaedra hadn't slipped her arm around her waist.

"She needs to lie down," Phaedra told the deputy. "This is very upsetting, as I'm sure you can understand."

"Of course. Just don't go anywhere. We'll need to question everyone in the house and get statements."

She hesitated. "You're considering this a murder, then." It wasn't a question; she already knew the answer.

He glanced at Charlene and away again. "A homicide detective is on the way."

"Who would do this?" Charlene mumbled as he turned away and Phaedra led her into one of the empty guest bedrooms. "Who would want to kill my husband?"

Phaedra could think of a number of people, but she kept the thought to herself.

"Please don't upset yourself. The police will find whoever did this, I promise you." She waited as Charlene stretched out atop the bed before taking a seat beside her. "Would you like a sedative to help you sleep? I can call your doctor. Perhaps a soothing cup of chamomile tea?"

"No. I don't want a sedative or a cup of tea. I just want some time alone." A tear leaked out from the corner of one eye and streaked slowly down her cheek. "Time to try and make sense of this. Because it makes no sense at all."

"We'll get to the bottom of it," Phaedra promised, her words firm. "Whoever did this will be found."

"What if they think I did it?" Charlene turned frightened eyes to hers. "The police. Oh, Phaedra—they'll think I killed my husband. For the money."

"I'm sure they won't think any such thing. You were in the drawing room when it happened, after all. There's no possible way you could've done it."

"I left," she whispered, her voice catching in her throat. "To check on my mother. And to get candles."

"You were only gone for a few minutes. For now, let the police do their job. They'll find whoever did this."

"Thank you, Phae. You're a good friend. You always have been."

"And I always will be. Lady Muck to the rescue." She gave Charlene's hand a reassuring squeeze and stood up. "Now, try and rest. I'll be downstairs if you need me."

Closing the guest room door quietly behind her, Phaedra returned to the landing at the top of the stairs. Her glance strayed to the east wing hallway. Although power had been restored shortly before the police arrived, the hallway leading to the scene of Bill's death remained shrouded in darkness.

She frowned. The power was out when Collier stormed out of the drawing room and came upstairs. Had it been out up here, as well? If so, how could Charlene's husband have been electrocuted?

The coroner emerged from Collier's bathroom and returned downstairs, interrupting her thoughts and letting in a blast of wind and rain as he left. The deputy took up a post outside the bathroom door to await the arrival of the homicide detective . . . and, Phaedra presumed, to guard the crime scene.

She took out her phone to make the first of two calls.

The first went straight to voice mail. *This is Lucy Liang. You know what to do.*

"Hey, Lu, it's Phaedra. Please call Mari and tell her tonight's Tea Society meeting is canceled. Something's come up. Talk soon. Bye."

One more call. She drew in a breath and pressed the pre-programmed number.

"Brighton residence, Nan speaking."

"Mom, hi. Listen, will you do me a huge favor and let Wickham out? And he'll need fresh water and kibble."

"Oh, Phaedra . . . of all times to ask me to go out! The roads are flooded and the rain is coming down in torrents."

"I know. I'm sorry. But I'll be late getting home, and I'm worried about Wickham."

"Of course you are. I'll leave right now," her mother assured her, following up with a heavy sigh. "Even though that cat of yours has no use for me. Are you sure he isn't part llama? He spits at me."

"You're exaggerating. He doesn't spit. He hisses."

"Spits, hisses . . . either way, he makes no secret of his dislike for me. And shouldn't you be heading home soon? Last time we spoke you were on your way to Marling. That was ages ago. Surely you're finished by now."

"I am. We are. But . . . something's happened. We lost power, and a tree fell on the roof."

"Oh my goodness! Was anyone hurt?"

"No. The power came back on a few minutes ago. But there's been an . . . incident, and I can't leave."

"An incident? What kind of incident?"

"I really can't say—"

"If there's been an incident," Nan said, "and you can't leave, it stands to reason the police are involved. Tell me what's going on, Phaedra."

She knew her mother wouldn't let it go. There was no point in prevaricating.

"You can't tell anyone this, but . . ." Phaedra hesitated. "There's been a murder."

"A *murder*?" Her mother's voice sharpened. "Oh my goodness. Who?"

She lowered her voice. "William Collier, Charlene's husband."

"Oh, how awful. Poor Charlene. A new bride, and now a widow! What *happened*?"

"It's not official yet; the medical examiner's still on his way. But it looks like Collier was electrocuted. In the bath."

For once, Nan Brighton was stunned into silence.

"But," Phaedra added firmly, "you can't share that information with anyone."

"Oh, sweetie . . . I don't like you being in a house where someone was murdered! Can't they question you first and cut you loose? Tell them you're a professor at the university. Tell them you're a Jane Austen scholar. Tell them your mother is Nan Prescott Brighton."

"I doubt your name or mine will carry any weight with the police, Mom." She suppressed a sigh. "I probably shouldn't even be on the phone right now."

"You're right. You shouldn't."

She whirled around, phone pressed against her bodice as her skirts swirled around her ankles.

A man stood on the top step, one hand resting on the banister. He wore jeans and a pale blue polo shirt, and she put his age at mid-thirties.

"Who are you?" she asked, meeting his eyes. They were a dark espresso brown, like his hair.

"Detective Morelli, Robbery and Homicide, Somerset County PD." He held up his credentials, and as he did she glimpsed his holster, a standard issue Glock pistol thrust inside. "Someone called in a robbery earlier. A stolen necklace."

"Choker," Phaedra corrected. "A Georgian choker. I'm the one who called."

"And you are?"

"Phaedra Brighton." She noted the arch of his eyebrow as he took in her gown. "I'm a historical consultant for the show."

"You're not a contestant?"

"I have to go, Mom," she said into the phone, and ended the call. "I'm a professor of English literature at Somerset University."

"Phaedra," he said, drawing the word out as he returned the ID badge to his back pocket. "Unusual name. What do they normally call you?"

"Phaedra." Her words were cool. "But you can call me Professor Brighton."

He cocked his brow. His face, attractive despite his tensed jawline and serious demeanor, betrayed the grim nature of his occupation.

She was willing to bet he didn't smile very often.

He glanced past her down the hall as he took out a small notepad. "What can you tell me about Mr. Collier? How did you find his body?"

"I found him by accident. It started when the power went out."

"And what time was that?"

"Around one thirty. We were all downstairs."

"'All' meaning you and the cast and crew, and who else?"

"The head caterer, Roberta Walsh; her staff; Mr. Collier's butler, Finch . . . and a few servants. I don't know their names."

He nodded. "Go on."

"Someone grabbed the choker from Tinsley's neck, and she screamed. A short time later, maybe twenty or thirty minutes, we heard a crash upstairs, and I realized lightning must've struck the oak tree behind the house. I went upstairs to investigate."

"Was anyone else with you?"

"No, I was alone."

"And you found William Collier's body."

"Yes, but not right away. A tree fell on the roof, and a

branch crashed through the Colliers' bedroom window. That was the first room I checked. I saw glass everywhere, but the bedroom was empty."

"How did you find Collier?"

"His wife, Charlene, was worried after the tree fell and wanted to make sure he was all right. But someone knocked on the front door, and she stayed behind to take care of it. I came up by myself."

"Why was her husband up here?"

"To take a bath before dinner. He apparently preferred to use an old claw-foot tub in the east wing. The butler, Finch, suggested he use another bathroom."

"Why would he do that?"

"He said the wiring in that wing of the house is old." She paused. "And it goes without saying that bathing during an electrical storm is never a good idea."

"So that's where you found Collier? In a bathroom in the east wing?"

Her glance strayed to the far end of the hallway, and she suppressed a shudder. "Yes."

"Yet you've just said the power was out."

"Yes." She frowned. "I did find that odd. Perhaps the east wing wasn't affected because it's wired differently."

"It's possible. We'll check into it. What time did you arrive at Marling?"

"Just before noon."

"And what was your relationship to the deceased, Professor Brighton?"

"No relationship. I barely knew the man. In fact, I only met him today. I'm a friend of his wife, Charlene."

"Did he have any known health issues? Take any medications for depression?"

"Not that I'm aware of." She paused. "And before you ask, he wasn't suicidal, at least not so far as I know. He'd just inherited this house and a pile of money. It's obvious his electrocution was either a bizarre accident or murder."

His gaze sharpened. "What makes you say that?"

"There's a towel folded on a bench near the bathtub, and his razor is on the sink. Which tells me he planned to get out of the tub, dry off, and shave. Hardly the actions of someone about to commit suicide."

"The razor could've been anyone's. Mrs. Collier's, for instance."

She shook her head. "Charlene told me herself she doesn't use that bathroom. Which makes me wonder why her blow-dryer was there in the first place. If I were conducting an investigation, that's what I'd want to know."

"Thank you, but I've got it." He took out his cell phone. "Stick around. I'll need a statement from you and Mrs. Collier and anyone else in the house. In the meantime, don't speak to the press or post anything online." He pressed the phone to his ear and said, "Morelli here. Secure the property and collect everyone's cell phones until we get their statements. Is the ME here yet?"

Phaedra left him to it and headed for the stairs. Halfway down, she saw Finch open the front door to a heavyset man hunched inside a rain slicker.

"Yes?" Finch inquired.

"Dr. Kessler, consulting pathologist, Somerset General." He didn't wait for an invitation but stepped inside and removed his fedora, revealing a cherubic face more suited to distributing gifts from a jolly red sack than determining cause of death.

"I'll take that, sir." Finch held out his hand.

He shrugged off his dripping slicker and handed it, along with his hat, to the butler. "Where's the body?"

"The east wing," Phaedra jumped in. "I'll take you."

He glanced up. "Thanks."

After leading him upstairs to the bathroom, she lingered, hoping to learn more, but Detective Morelli showed her the door.

"The crime scene guys should be here any minute. Why don't you go downstairs and direct them up here when they arrive? If you wouldn't mind," he added as he met her eyes.

She'd been dismissed. "Of course." She remained coolly polite in the face of his condescension. At least he hadn't asked her to brew a pot of coffee.

"Thank you, Professor Brighton. Oh—and if you could rustle me up a cup of coffee, I'd really appreciate it."

"Anything else?" she asked, inwardly seething. "Perhaps some cookies to go along with that coffee?"

"Nah, just the coffee. Thanks." He turned back to the pathologist and greeted him like an old friend. "Hey, Doc. How goes it?"

Phaedra made a show of leaving but hovered just outside the door. Any information she could glean might prove useful. Particularly since it was clear that Detective Morelli wasn't prone to sharing. Or sensitivity.

"—looks like a textbook case of electrocution," Kessler was saying. She heard the snap of latex as he pulled on a pair of surgical gloves. "Pretty uncommon nowadays, thanks to GFCI outlets. Ground Fault Circuit Interrupters," he added.

"I'm told the wiring in this wing of the house is old. Pre–World War II," Morelli said. "For some reason, the victim preferred to use this particular bathtub."

"And someone obviously knew it. Poor bastard. How long has the power been out up here?"

"Since one thirty."

Phaedra strained to hear more, but all was silent as the doctor conducted his exam. She was about to turn away when he spoke, his voice sharpening.

"Take a look. There's a bruise on the back of the vic's neck."

The detective grunted as he knelt down.

"See this tiny mark in the middle? Looks like a puncture wound," the pathologist said.

"Sure does," Morelli agreed. "What do you make of it?"

"I'd say he's been injected with something. Note the excessive sweating on his forehead and arm. And his pupils are dilated."

"Is that normal for someone who's been electrocuted?"

"No. There are no visible marks or burns on his skin, but in a case like this, that's not unusual. Diagnosing death by electrocution is difficult at best. I can't be certain until I conduct the postmortem, but the victim's symptoms lead me to question the cause of death."

Phaedra's eyes widened. The pathologist believed Collier might have died not by electrocution, but as a result of an injection of some kind.

"I'm inclined to rule out misadventure," the doctor went on. "This was no accident. Possibly a suicide, but the angle and location of the injection, and the fact there's no syringe to be seen, lead me to conclude that this man was murdered."

Seven

The conversation ceased as the ME concluded his examination of the body. Not wanting Detective Morelli to catch her lurking by the door, Phaedra left and returned downstairs.

Everyone had gathered in groups in the drawing room, talking in low voices as they waited to give their statements to a sheriff's deputy.

She paused in the doorway. Someone in this room was a thief. Could one of them be a murderer as well?

"How long are we expected to stay here?" one of the male servers demanded. "I have another job, you know."

"As long as it takes," the deputy replied.

Good thing Phaedra had called her mother earlier. Wickham would not approve of being deprived of either his evening meal or his customary prowl around the backyard. Phaedra settled herself in an armchair near the door to wait and found her thoughts drifting to possible suspects.

Who hated William Collier enough to kill him? And why?

He certainly had his share of enemies. She recalled Dorothy Fortune's exchange with Collier earlier that day.

Had Dorothy's fury provoked her to turn her veiled threat

to Collier into reality? Did she slip into Marling afterward and lie in wait for him? With so many people in the house and on the grounds, from film crew and craft services to caterers and servants, it would've been a simple matter to steal upstairs unnoticed and wait for an opportunity to kill him. And after losing her home and her husband's fortune to Collier, she certainly had motive.

Who else stood to gain from Collier's death? Charlene did, certainly. As his wife and only living relative, the estate would go to her. Which gave her an admittedly damning motive. And Phaedra and Tinsley and several others had overheard Charlene and Bill exchanging heated words over the antique choker.

And she couldn't ignore the fact that Charlene had disappeared for fifteen minutes.

Had she gone to check on her mother and change clothes, as she'd claimed? Phaedra's eyes widened as a sudden thought occurred. Charlene still wore her riding clothes when she'd returned to the drawing room. She hadn't changed.

Why? Had she slipped upstairs and seized the opportunity to murder her husband?

Phaedra pushed her doubts aside.

Charlene hadn't done this. Charlene *wouldn't* do this. Aside from the fact that she'd been in the drawing room during the time frame of Bill's murder, save for the few minutes she'd left to locate candles, why would she use her personal blow-dryer to electrocute him and knowingly incriminate herself? And what was the dryer doing in his bathroom, a room that Charlene claimed only her husband used, in the first place?

None of it made sense.

Of course, Collier's death could be an accident, or suicide. Charlene herself said the wiring in that wing of the house hadn't been updated since the 1930s. But knowing that, surely her husband wouldn't have risked life and limb to blow-dry his hair in the tub? He was vain, not stupid.

Something wasn't adding up.

It would be quite some time before the deputy obtained statements from everyone. No time like the present, she decided, to slip out and have a quick look around.

On the pretense of heading for the powder room, Phaedra rose and wandered into the entrance hall. She lingered by a gilt-framed landscape hanging on the wall and risked a glance up the stairs. There was no sign of Detective Morelli.

At the far end of the hall, past the dining room on the left, she rounded the corner and retraced her steps to the morning room she'd visited earlier with Charlene. Relieved to see no one there, she went inside.

Charlene's desk stood near the fireplace. Its polished surface was empty save for a blotter and a stack of art books piled on one corner. With a quick glance at the door, Phaedra felt inside her reticule for the pair of short, lacy gloves she kept there and drew them on.

Wearing gloves not only lent authenticity to her Regency dress, they came in handy for a bit of impromptu snooping. It wouldn't do to leave fingerprints behind.

She opened each of the side drawers in turn, but they revealed only paper clips, pads of paper, keys to long-forgotten doors, an assortment of pens and pencils, and a box of personalized stationery.

She tried the middle drawer, but it was locked. With another glance over her shoulder to reassure herself no one was in the vicinity, she took out a paper clip and fiddled with the lock until it opened.

The drawer was empty except for a check in the amount of $2,500, stamped at the top with William Collier's name and address, signed and dated yesterday. The payee line was blank.

It might mean nothing or it might be a clue. The amount was larger than the typical utility bill. Then again, Marling was a large house. Perhaps Collier was being blackmailed? With his checkered past, it wasn't a stretch of the imagination to suppose that someone had dirt on him.

Phaedra took out her phone and snapped a quick photo of the check.

She closed the drawer. Who had taken Charlene's choker? Anyone in the drawing room could have yanked it from Tinsley's neck during the power outage. Phaedra frowned. Did the theft have anything to do with Collier's murder, or were the two things unrelated?

Her glance strayed to the portrait of William Collier over the fireplace. What secrets hid behind his smug smile?

As voices drew closer in the hall outside, Phaedra hurried to stand before the mantel and pretended to study the portrait.

Detective Morelli appeared in the doorway.

"Professor Brighton." He regarded her steadily, his expression unreadable. "What are you doing in here? You should be in the drawing room with the others."

"I don't handle waiting very well." She glanced at the painting of William Collier. "I decided to come back and have another look at Mr. Collier's portrait. Charlene showed it to me earlier."

"I see."

He didn't believe her, she realized, not for a minute.

"Is that why she brought you back here?" he asked. "To show you her husband's portrait?"

"No. She gave me a quick tour before we went in the drawing room to wait out the storm."

He indicated the sofa and pair of tufted Victorian chairs arranged around the fireplace. "I'd like to ask you a few more questions, if I may."

"Of course." She took a seat in one of the chairs and waited, hands clasped primly in her lap.

"You're a historical consultant on the program, correct?"

"Yes. I share my knowledge of the Regency time period wherever it's needed. Wardrobe, for instance."

His glance went to her hands. "Like those gloves?"

"Yes." Had he noticed that she wasn't wearing them earlier, at the top of the stairs? "Gloves were one of the few gifts a Regency-era man could give a single woman he wasn't engaged to marry."

50   KATIE OLIVER

He made no comment but retrieved his notepad once
again and flipped it open. "Who lives here at Marling besides
Mrs. Collier?"

"Her mother, Violet Lucas. She was in her room upstairs
all evening."

"The woman in the wheelchair." He tapped his pen
against the pad. "I spoke to her a few minutes ago. She said
something that left me a little puzzled."

"Oh? Did she see something?"

"No. She stayed in her room all evening, reading a book."

"What's puzzling about that?" Phaedra asked.

"You stated that the power went out around one thirty
p.m., correct?"

"Yes."

"According to Mrs. Lucas, her room never lost power. She
was quite certain because her reading lamp remained on the
entire time."

Phaedra frowned. "But that makes no sense. The power
definitely went out."

"I checked with the county electrical authority. There
were no reported outages in the area."

"So you're suggesting, what? That someone deliberately
cut the power to the first floor?"

"It's possible someone tampered with the breaker panel.
Probably the same person who stole the choker."

"I never tried the light switches upstairs," Phaedra admitted. "I just assumed . . ." She met his eyes. "Have you
checked the panel?"

He sighed. "Yes, Professor. Everything is just as it should
be. But circuit breakers can be switched on as well as off.
What else can you tell me about Mrs. Lucas?"

"As you've seen, she's wheelchair-bound. Her nurse visits
once a day."

"Nurse?"

"Violet is diabetic." She waited as he made a note. "She
has tremors, so the nurse administers her insulin shot."

"Anyone else live here?"

"Finch, the butler. He was Mr. Fortune's manservant for a number of years. He stayed on after Harold died."

His pen moved over the pad. "I imagine you've had time to observe the cast and crew in your capacity as a consultant. Have you noticed anything unusual?"

"Unusual? No. Just the typical chaos of a film set. Today was my first day."

"Any arguments on the set, that sort of thing?"

She thought of Dorothy Fortune. "There was an incident earlier today between Mrs. Fortune and Mr. Collier."

His glance focused. "About?"

"The Fortune inheritance. Dorothy was upset to lose Marling, her family's home for so many years, to her husband's nephew. She accused him of stealing the estate out from under her. Along with her daughters' chance to star in their own reality show."

"*Who Wants to Marry a Fortune?*" He nodded and made another note. "Did Dorothy leave after the argument?"

"As far as I know. I didn't see her again."

"How long have you known Charlene Collier?"

"Since high school. We were close until I left and went to UVA. We lost touch for a few years, but we reconnected when I returned to Laurel Springs to teach at Somerset University."

"Would you say she and William were happily married?"

Phaedra shrugged. "I hardly know. They weren't engaged long, a few weeks. Charlene barely knew him."

"And that bothered you?"

"Frankly, yes. It happened so quickly. He came to town after inheriting his uncle's estate and stopped in at Bertie's Café for lunch. Charlene worked the counter. He made a point of coming in every day, and less than a month later, he asked her to marry him."

"Must've been a dream come true for a hardworking waitress in a small-town café."

She didn't like the insinuation behind his words. "Charlene isn't a gold digger, if that's what you're suggesting. She turned him down. Her mother is disabled, and diabetic. Charlene has taken care of Violet for most of her life."

"That must've been difficult."

Phaedra nodded. "That's what changed Charlene's mind, in the end. That, and William's persistence." She met his eyes. "She could barely make ends meet. She can't have earned much at the café. Marrying Mr. Collier ensured Violet had the best care, and Charlene no longer had to scramble to pay for her medications."

"So, her reasons for marrying Collier were financial."

"Yes, but not in the way you mean. She wasn't trying to land a rich husband. She's practical. She's had to be. William offered her a way out."

"How did the Colliers behave toward each other? You must have formed some idea of the state of their relationship."

"They seemed to get along well enough. But we didn't talk about her marriage."

"Did they ever argue?"

She hesitated. Admitting that her best friend had exchanged words with her husband just a short time before his murder wouldn't do Charlene any favors. But nor could she lie.

Morelli leaned forward in his chair, his expression intent. "Professor Brighton, if you know something, you need to tell me. Did the Colliers have an argument on set?"

"I wouldn't call it an argument, exactly," she hedged. "Charlene informed William she'd loaned the choker to one of the bachelorettes to wear during filming."

"Tinsley Prentiss. And what was his reaction?"

"Anger. When the choker was stolen a short time later, he was furious." She paused. "He shouted and belittled her until he made her cry. Nick Ross told him to stop."

"Nick Ross? The actor playing Mr. Darcy?"

"Yes. We were all appalled by Mr. Collier's behavior. We couldn't sit by and watch. I also asked him to leave Charlene alone."

"And did he?"

"Yes. After telling me in no uncertain terms to mind my own business. Then he went upstairs to get ready to go out to dinner with Charlene."

"Was she angered by her husband's treatment?"

Phaedra regarded him in surprise. "No. She was upset by his reaction, but she wasn't angry."

"Did Mrs. Collier leave the drawing room at any time?"

Here it was. The question she'd hoped to avoid.

"Professor?" he prodded.

"Yes, she left to go in search of candles."

"After the power went out downstairs?"

"That's right. She said the power might be out for quite some time."

"How long would you say she was gone?"

Again, Phaedra hesitated. "I can't say for certain, but I'd guess about fifteen minutes."

Morelli jotted down the information but made no comment. She eyed him uneasily. Did he wonder, as she did, where Charlene went for those unaccounted fifteen minutes?

"All right." He closed the notepad and returned it, along with the pen, to his pocket. "That's all for now. You can go, but don't leave town. I may have further questions." He reached in his pocket and pulled out a card, extending it to her between two fingers. "Call me if you think of anything else. No matter how insignificant."

She nodded and took the card. Beneath the Somerset County Investigations logo, his name, Detective Matteo Morelli, appeared, along with his email and phone number.

Phaedra studied the card and lifted her eyes to his. "Matteo," she said, recalling his response to her name. "What do they normally call you?"

"Matt." He produced a bland smile. "But you can call me Detective Morelli."

Phaedra tucked the card in her pocket and stood. Score one to Morelli.

"I didn't know Mr. Collier well," she ventured after a moment, "but from our brief acquaintance I can tell you he wasn't a very nice person." She met his eyes. "He didn't endear himself to the crew, or to Dorothy Fortune, and thought nothing of humiliating his wife in front of a room full of people. But he didn't deserve to die like this."

"No one does. Thank you for your time. I'll be in touch."

Once again, she was dismissed.

After a moment's hesitation Phaedra turned away, glad to finally leave Marling behind after such a long, strange day.

Eight

The carriage house was dark as Phaedra let herself in at half past eight that evening. The rain had finally stopped, and the downed tree blocking Rolling Hill Road was gone. She switched on a lamp and dropped her briefcase, reticule, and keys on the hall table. The lamplight chased away the shadows to reveal Wickham, curled up on the sofa as he fixed her with a sphinxlike gaze.

He didn't jump down and twine himself around her legs in a lazy figure eight as he usually did, or close his eyes and purr throatily as she settled beside him and scratched behind his ears. He was plainly not in a forgiving mood.

"Still angry, are you?" Phaedra cocked her head and met his unblinking blue eyes. "Sorry I'm late. But I see Mom refilled your water dish, and there's kibble scattered on the kitchen floor, which tells me you had dinner. So you have no justification for being such a grouch."

That's a matter of opinion. Wickham leaped down from the sofa and stalked off.

With a sigh, Phaedra kicked off her slippers and went into the kitchen in search of something to eat. She'd had an apple and a piece of cheddar from the craft services table early in the afternoon, but nothing since, and she suddenly realized she was ravenous.

A rummage in the fridge revealed a carton of Greek yogurt, two days past its sell-by date, half a bottle of pinot, and a slice of leftover pizza. She ate the cold pizza standing up and washed it down with a bottle of water.

"Hey, Wicks," she called up to the loft as she washed her hands afterward. "Would you like to go out?"

He shot down the stairs and made a beeline for the kitchen door, waiting impatiently as Phaedra dried her hands.

"Silly question, huh?" she said. She received a curt tail twitch in return. "Go do your thing. Just don't bring back any nocturnal presents." She opened the door and he streaked out, vanishing into the darkened back garden.

She closed the door and picked up the mail from the kitchen counter. As she flipped through the usual combination of junk and bills, her cell phone rang. Lucy.

"Hi, Lu. What's up?"

"You tell me. I left you a couple of messages earlier. Imagine my concern when you didn't respond."

Phaedra glanced at her notifications, dismayed to see two missed calls, both from Lucy. "I'm sorry. I was busy all afternoon, and I never checked my messages."

"Confirming the cliché of the absentminded professor. What kept you so busy, exactly? Consulting? Schmoozing with Nick Ross, aka Mr. Darcy? Or did Karolina what's-her-name ask you to revise the entire script for historical accuracy? One can only hope."

"It's a reality show, Lucy. There *is* no script."

"Phaedra, everyone knows reality shows are scripted and edited to create drama where there is none. They have about as much to do with reality as a politician's campaign promises. So what's kept you so preoccupied? The truth."

Phaedra hesitated. "Something happened at Marling today. Something I'm not at liberty to discuss."

"Not at liberty to discuss?" Lucy echoed. "That sounds

serious. And more than a little evasive." She paused. "What's his name? How was dinner? Where did you go?"

"It's nothing like that, honestly. I wish it was." She hesitated. Lucy would normally be her first choice as a sounding board. But she'd promised Morelli she wouldn't discuss the case, and she couldn't go back on her word.

Bad enough she'd told her mother. It was a decision she already regretted.

"If you say so." Lucy didn't sound convinced. "After finally persuading you to get with the twenty-first century and create a Tinder account, I thought maybe you'd connected with someone. Found your own Mr. Darcy."

"Oh please. As if I'd ever find Mr. Darcy on a dating app."

"People do. Find matches online, I mean. Some even get married."

"Where's the romance?" Phaedra grumbled. "Swipe right, swipe left . . . there's no tenderness in Tinder."

"You'd prefer the good old days of quill pens and handwritten letters, I suppose? Sealed with wax and filled with the breathings of your heart?"

"Letters were a far more romantic method of communication." Phaedra sank down on the sofa. "Men courted women and treated them with respect. They were gentlemen, in every sense of the word."

"Not to mention those breeches and boots they wore."

"And there were no smartphones or dating apps," Phaedra went on. "No Ubers or speed dating or meaningless hookups."

"You say that like it's a good thing."

"It is."

"Don't forget the downside," Lucy pointed out. "A woman couldn't vote, or manage her own money. Nor could she choose her own husband. And if she had a child," she added, "odds were not in favor of her surviving the birth."

"Way to bring down the mood, Lu."

"Sorry. I like Mr. Darcy as much as anyone. But I prefer to deal with the facts and live in the present, not dwell in the past. You should, too. Give me cell phones and ATM machines over quill pens and carriages any day.

"The point is," Lucy added before Phaedra could protest, "there are plenty of great guys out there, real guys who'd give Darcy a run for his money—"

"Ten thousand pounds a year is nothing to sneeze at."

"—but you'll never meet anyone if you don't venture out of the lecture hall or leave the Humanities building once in a while."

"I was in love once," Phaedra reminded her. "Or I thought I was."

As a confirmed literary nerd by the time she was twelve, she didn't run with the popular crowd. So when handsome newcomer Donovan Wickes singled her out her senior year of high school, she was shocked. And very, very flattered.

Convinced she'd found a love most people only dreamed of, Phaedra ignored her friends, especially Charlene, who warned her Donovan was a player. They didn't understand. She thrived on drama and she welcomed the angst. She was Catherine to Donovan's Heathcliff, the Elizabeth to his Darcy.

Which lasted until he stood her up the night of senior prom.

The agony of waiting for him, of looking for his beat-up GTO to pull up out front, finally running upstairs to tear off her strapless gown when it became clear he wasn't coming, still seared her memory. She broke up with him the next day, applied to the University of Virginia, and threw herself heart and soul into academia.

"From what little I've managed to drag out of you over the years, even though I've never even met the guy, I'd say Donovan is serially incapable of committing to anything. Or anyone. At least you didn't do something really stupid. Like marry him."

"I know. And you're right." Phaedra felt weariness settle over her as the events of the day caught up to her. "But I don't trust my judgment when it comes to men. My track record isn't very good."

"I get it. I do. But we all make mistakes. And you can't let one mistake fifteen years ago keep you from finding that special someone."

"That special someone?" Phaedra echoed. "You sound like one of those online dating services. Listen, Lu, I love you for caring, but I can't do this right now."

"Why not?"

"Because it's been a really long day, and I'm meeting that new professor tomorrow to get him settled in and give him a tour. I'm not looking forward to it."

"You never know. He might surprise you."

"What do you mean?"

"He might be hot."

"Hot? A Shakespearean scholar?" Phaedra laughed. "Doubtful. He's probably so old he creaks when he walks."

"I guess you'll find out tomorrow morning."

"I guess I will. Good night, Lu. Thanks for the pep talk and the cold dash of reality in my face. I needed both."

"Happy to oblige. See you tomorrow."

Warm, rose-scented bubbles enveloped Phaedra as she sank gratefully into her freestanding tub a short time later and thought about Lucy's words.

"I don't live in the past," she said out loud. "Do I, Wickham?"

He ignored her. *Just because you let me out and gave me a treat*, his cool blue eyes seemed to say, *don't think for a minute you're forgiven.*

She sighed. All she wanted was a good man. A life partner with the attributes of Mr. Darcy, with honesty and selflessness and a gentlemanly regard for her well-being. A man who wouldn't lie. And looking good in a damp shirt wouldn't hurt, either. Was that so much to ask?

She rested her head against the raised porcelain back and closed her eyes.

Bliss.

Her bliss evaporated as the image of William Collier's

body, lifeless and still in the antique tub, barged into her thoughts like an uninvited guest.

She sat up with a splash of water. She could still see his arm, his stiffened fingers brushing the tile, could hear the slow drip of water from the faucet.

With a shudder she pulled the plug and climbed out of the bath. Sleep would prove elusive tonight.

Because every time she closed her eyes, Phaedra knew she'd see Collier's face, his eyes staring sightlessly up at the ceiling.

Nine

Mark Selden was late.

Phaedra glanced at her watch and pressed her lips together. Twenty-five minutes late, to be exact.

She sipped her coffee, already grown cold, and set the cup aside. She aligned her pencil with the top of her desk blotter. She glanced again at her watch. She had very few pet peeves—crunchy peanut butter, aggressive drivers, and science fiction among them—but tardiness topped the list.

Obviously, this particular Shakespearean scholar had better things to do than to bother showing up on time for a tour of his home for the upcoming academic year. Perhaps he's still on UK time, she thought peevishly. Perhaps he showed up five hours ago and he's already left for the day.

Perhaps he'd forgotten.

Whatever his excuse, there *was* no excuse.

Phaedra picked up her pencil and tapped it against the blotter in a staccato rhythm. She could be at home, measuring and proofing dough for Karolina's four dozen Bath buns, or outlining lecture topics for next semester.

She could be with Charlene, who needed comfort and reassurance following her husband's unexpected death. But

instead she sat here waiting for a man who obviously had not
a shred of concern for anyone but himself—

"Professor Brighton, I presume?"

She looked up. The plummy British accent, precise yet
mellifluous, was richly compelling.

"Yes. I'm Phaedra Brighton." She stood and rounded her
desk, a determinedly polite smile affixed to her lips and her
hand extended. "And you must be . . ."

"Mark Selden."

His hand closed over hers, strong and firm. "Apologies for
my lateness. I had an overseas call, and the drive-through
line at the local coffee shop was excruciating." He brandished a cardboard cup with his free hand as if to prove his
statement.

"It usually is." She met his eyes and found she couldn't
look away. The words of reproof she'd intended to unleash
on him died unspoken.

He wasn't handsome, exactly. But there was something.
Something compelling.

He's like a falcon, she thought. Regal. Intimidating. And
ready to pounce at any moment. From his sweep of dark
brown hair to his piercing eyes and hawklike nose, he per-
sonified nothing so much as a bird of prey. She could easily
imagine him striding along King's Parade, black gown flap-
ping behind him.

He met her curiosity with a frank, curious gaze of his
own. "I see you favor Regency attire."

"I like to immerse my students in the study of Jane Austen. Not only by examining her novels, but by understanding
who she was, how she dressed, and how she lived."

"Then I suppose it's fortunate I don't share your immersive philosophy. Otherwise I'd be sporting a doublet and
breeches right now."

He released her hand to unshoulder his shoulder bag and
glanced around the office. "Is there a desk I might claim for
my own? Dare I hope for an office?"

"Of course. Right this way. It's small, but it's yours."

She showed him to his office, a former paper closet, where a computer sat on his desk, and waited as he dropped his shoulder bag on the swivel chair. "Will I have access to a printer?"

"Yes. The copier and printers are just down the hall. We have a large format as well. Let me show you."

"Thanks." He shed his jacket and followed her out the door.

Phaedra preceded him inside the glassed-in media room and took a four-color poster from the hopper of the large format printer. "Oh, good, it's finished printing. I need to pin this up on the lobby bulletin board during our tour of the building. I hope you don't mind."

"Not at all." He clasped his hands behind him as he peered over her shoulder. "Ah. A Jane Austen literary festival."

She nodded. "We sponsor one every year. It's popular with students and locals alike. We offer book signings, writing workshops, food, music, and games." She didn't add that this year, the Humanities staff would largely be footing the bill themselves.

"Sounds intriguing. And does everyone dress in Regency costume?" His glance flicked over her. "Like yourself?"

"Most do, yes. The lit staff pitches in to portray various Austen characters. We have a Louisa Musgrove, an Elizabeth Bennet, a Captain Wentworth, and of course, a Mr. Darcy."

"Of course. One cannot host an Austen event without Darcy. After all, he's the undisputed rock star of Miss Austen's oeuvre."

Phaedra heard the amused condescension behind his words but elected to ignore it. "Our festival is similar to a Renaissance fair," she said, and led him down the hall to the main lobby. "Another of our quaint American customs."

He studied her. "You don't quite fit the image of a typical Austen heroine. You strike me as more of a Brontë character." He considered her. "Catherine comes to mind."

Her hand went involuntarily to one of her drooping, and

no doubt by now frizzy, ringlets. "I'm not sure I'm flattered or insulted. Now, if you'd said Jo March . . ."

"How do you see me?"

What a question. Yet he expected an answer.

"Do you mean, which Austen character do I see when I look at you?" she stalled. "Or any character?"

"Let's go with Austen. And please don't say Mr. Darcy."

A laugh bubbled out. "Oh, you're definitely not Darcy. No, I'd say you're more of a . . . Captain Wentworth."

"Interesting choice. Brontë?"

She didn't hesitate. "Mr. Rochester."

"'To women who please me only by their faces, I am the very devil when I find out they have neither souls nor hearts.'"

"Have any Shakespeare to throw at me?" she asked as they stopped before the elevators.

He didn't miss a beat. "'I am fresh of spirit and resolved to meet all perils very constantly.'"

"*Julius Caesar.*" She punched the button for the second floor.

"You know your Shakespeare." As they stepped off the elevator onto the second floor, he took in the dingy walls and threadbare carpet. "I see the Humanities budget is as much of an afterthought at Somerset as it is in most colleges."

Her first instinct, to bridle at the implied criticism, was unfair, and she bit back a retort. He was right. Their budget, slashed to the bone at the beginning of the academic year at the expense of the Econ department, wasn't likely to change anytime soon.

"We manage," she said instead. She could just about underwrite this year's festival herself, with the help of raffle ticket sales and staff donations; but what about next year?

He noticed things. Inconsequential but telling things, like the peeling paint and air-conditioning that struggled to cool the upper floors.

Phaedra stopped at the end of the hall and indicated a large glassed-in room. "This is our staff library-slash-lounge."

"It's hardly the Bodleian, but it'll do."

"There's a vending machine in the kitchen, and a soda machine at the end of the hall. You have to hit it twice."

They returned to the ground floor, and after pointing out the restrooms, she left him at the door to his new office.

"I'm sorry to leave so soon, but I've taken the afternoon off. I have a few personal matters to address." Phaedra fished out a card from her pocket and handed it over. "Here's my cell number if you have any questions."

"Thank you." He pocketed it with barely a glance. "I suppose I'll see you on Monday, then."

"Yes. It was a pleasure to meet you, Professor Selden."

"Mark, please. The pleasure was mine, Professor Brighton."

"Phaedra." She smiled. "We're pretty informal around here."

"Phaedra was the daughter of Minos and the wife of Theseus, if my memory of Greek mythology serves."

"What can I say? My mother was obsessed with Greek mythology when I was born."

"At least she didn't name you Mnemosyne."

"Good point."

As she returned to her own office to get her keys and purse, Lucy thrust her head inside the door. "Not leaving already, are you?"

"I am." She lowered her voice. "I came in to give the new professor a tour. Mission accomplished."

Lucy, her expression at once guarded and avid, came in and shut the door quietly behind her. "And? What do you think after meeting the great and learned Professor Selden? Is he ancient? Middle-aged? All of the above?"

"None of the above."

"I need specifics. Give me one word to describe him."

"Inscrutable. Intelligent. Observant."

"That's three words."

Phaedra sighed. "Okay, he's . . . not old. He isn't handsome, at least not in the conventional sense, but he's—oh, I don't know. Striking, I guess. Now, I really have to get going.

I need to stop by the grocery store before I start my baking marathon this afternoon."

"Make a few extra for me and Mari."

"Will do. See you Monday."

With a wave, she left. She was halfway across the lobby when Marisol rushed in, brown hair caught back in a pony-tail and her face flushed.

"Phaedra! Glad I caught you before you left."

"What's up?" Phaedra saw the *Laurel Springs Clarion* gripped in her assistant's hand with misgivings.

"See for yourself." With a dramatic flourish, Marisol un-furled the paper to display the front-page headline, MUR-DER AT MARLING. "Why didn't you tell us? It's no wonder you canceled our meeting last night."

"Let me see that."

She snatched the paper away and scanned the article with growing consternation. Along with recent photos of Bill Col-lier and Charlene, there were several inches of text about the murder and Collier's notorious past as a crooked televange-list. Like most *Clarion* pieces, it was slim on facts and long on lurid speculation.

Phaedra glanced at the byline and groaned. Clark Mul-linax. He wouldn't know the meaning of "journalistic ethics" if he looked it up in a dictionary. How had he got wind of Collier's murder? Detective Morelli would not be happy word had leaked out. Which begged the question—who had talked to the press?

"It happened early yesterday afternoon." Phaedra handed the paper back. "A tree fell on the roof, and when I went up to investigate, I found Mr. Collier in the bathtub."

"*Dead?*"

"Yes, dead. I called the police. Everyone on the property at the time was detained for questioning, and we were in-structed not to discuss the case with anyone."

"Well, someone obviously did. 'A source close to the fam-ily,' it says here." Marisol frowned. "Any ideas?"

"None." Her cell phone rang. "Charlene! I was just leaving. How are you holding up? Did you get any sleep?"

"Not really." She sounded both exhausted and wired at the same time. "They took Bill's body away to be autopsied right after you left."

"Oh, sweetie, I'm sorry. But an autopsy is typical in a case like this."

"A homicide, you mean." Charlene expelled a breath. "Detective Morelli questioned me for what felt like hours, and a couple of deputies are searching the house from top to bottom. He said the pathologist ordered a toxicology report, which makes no sense, because Bill was . . ." She sucked in a deep, shuddery breath. "Electrocuted."

Phaedra's curiosity quickened. What had the pathologist found when he conducted the postmortem? "Did you ask Morelli? What did he say?"

"He's not telling me anything."

"Perhaps I should come over. I can try and get some answers for you."

"Would you?"

"Of course. The police probably won't be any more forthcoming with me than they've been with you," she warned. "But I'll do my best to learn whatever I can."

"Thank you." She sniffled. "I feel so alone in all of this. I could really use a little support right now."

"You've got it. I'll head over there now."

"I'll be in the morning room. They took my cell phone, so I'm calling from the landline. Forensics went over the upstairs bathroom and took photographs and dusted for fingerprints and I don't know w-what all."

"They're doing their job. Which is a good thing. They want to find whoever did this as much as we do." Phaedra glanced at the newspaper under Mari's arm. "Did Detective Morelli mention this morning's article in the *Clarion*?"

"He's not too happy about it. He wanted to know who talked to the press, but no one owned up."

"Are any other people still being questioned?"

"Only Finch, and Tinsley. I heard one of the deputies say they intend to talk to Dorothy Fortune. She had an argument with Bill on the set yesterday. Oh, Phae," she moaned, "this is like a nightmare I can't wake up from."

After promising she'd be there as soon as she could, and reassuring her that everything would be okay, Phaedra ended the call and turned back to Marisol. "I'm headed to Marling."

Sympathy softened her face. "How's Charlene doing?"

"About like you'd expect. She needs a friend, and a shoulder to cry on. Take any messages, please, and if you get a chance, start printing the Austen festival fliers."

"I thought the festival was a no-go this year."

"The festival," Phaedra said firmly, "is happening. Even if I have to bankroll it myself."

"I can drum up some support. Put out an appeal for donations. Why don't you ask Nick Ross to contribute? He's been in a couple of BBC Austen films, hasn't he?"

Phaedra nodded.

"Maybe he'd autograph a few photos. Then you could hold an auction, and students could bid for the chance to have a picture taken with him."

"Great ideas. I'll see what I can do." She glanced at her wristwatch. "But right now, I need to get over to Marling."

"Poor Charlene." Marisol shook her head mournfully. "To be married such a short time, and then . . . this. Did you—did you actually *see* the body?"

"I did." She thrust the memory away. "But I'd rather wait until our next meeting to share the details. Besides which, I'm not supposed to discuss the case with anyone."

"Even though someone else already did?"

"Even so. Sorry." Phaedra turned resolutely toward the automatic doors. Charlene was her focus now. "See you later."

Ten

Filming was well underway at Marling as Phaedra parked the Mini half an hour later. Trailers crowded the muddy lot, and the hum of generators filled the air. A table with a coffee urn and rows of bottled water had been set up under the shade of an oak tree.

She opened the door and eyed the soggy ground with distaste. A muddied hem could be washed, but a quagmire like this meant ruination for her pale pink ballet slippers. Good thing she kept a pair of sneakers on the passenger seat for just such occasions.

She switched out her slippers for sneakers and hurriedly tied the laces. As she emerged from the car she saw several reporters with cameras and fluffy microphones loitering at the end of the gated drive, hoping for a photo or an exclusive interview. She grabbed her laminated badge and hung the lanyard around her neck.

Being a member of the production crew had definite advantages.

"It's Professor Brighton, the woman who discovered the body!"

"Any comments, Professor?"

"Who murdered William Collier? Care to speculate?"

Ignoring them, she made her way across the front lawn and into the thicket of cables, camera booms, and lights that comprised the outdoor set.

A Somerset County Sheriff's Department car parked in front of the house indicated the police were here. Phaedra reached in her reticule and pulled on her gloves, just in case an opportunity to investigate arose. She pressed the doorbell, hoping to avoid Detective Morelli, at least until she'd had a chance to speak with Charlene.

After all, she reasoned, *praemonitus praemunitus*. Forewarned was forearmed. She'd try to glean as much information from Charlene as she could before dealing with the police.

The door swung open. Finch, his face haggard and his eyes bleary, regarded her without surprise. "Ms. Brighton. Come in." He stepped back as she wiped her muddied sneakers on the mat. "Mrs. Collier is waiting in the morning room."

"Thank you. No need to show me the way." She eyed the mug in his hand. "Is that tea?" she asked hopefully.

"Yes. Would you like a cup?"

A cup of tea sounded like balm to the soul. "I'd love one. But if you're busy with other things—"

"There's a fresh pot of rooibos in the kitchen. And scones in the oven."

"That sounds heavenly. Why don't I come with you? Save you the fuss of bringing out a tray." Not only that, she could have a little look around while she was here.

He inclined his head. "Of course. This way, please."

She followed him across the dining room, past the table set for lunch, and into a connecting service hallway. To the left was a utility room, the "boot room," Finch informed her, with a wooden bench along one wall and a row of pegs above it, hung with sweaters and raincoats. An assortment of boots stood along the baseboard. She saw a breaker box mounted beside the door.

Was Detective Morelli right? Had someone tampered with that panel last night?

It wouldn't be difficult, Phaedra surmised as Finch headed toward a green baize door at the end of the hall that led to the kitchen. Her gaze lingered. The thief could've easily flipped the first-floor breakers and returned to the drawing room to grab the choker.

Which meant anyone from the household staff to one of the caterers could be the thief.

"Professor?" Finch said. "This way."

She shook off her thoughts, nodded, and followed him through the door and into the kitchen proper.

It was a large room, updated with new appliances and a spacious island, but a weathered brick fireplace still occupied the far wall. She could imagine an iron kettle suspended over the flames or a haunch of venison turning slowly on a spit.

Bertie stood in front of the stove, frying eggs and stirring a pot of something that smelled deliciously of thyme and onions. She looked up as they walked in and eyed Phaedra. "Something I can help you with?"

"Just getting Professor Brighton a cup of tea," Finch informed her. "Nothing to concern yourself with."

She turned away and resumed stirring. "You can take these eggs up to Mrs. Lucas. The toast just popped up."

Finch set two cups on the counter. "Why not? I do everything else around here." He went to retrieve the toast. "I remember Mr. Fortune had quite the fondness for fried egg sandwiches."

The plate in Bertie's hand slipped and smashed onto the floor. Red-faced, she bent down to sweep it up.

"Has anyone seen Kitty?" Jen asked, appearing in the doorway. "He just ran in here."

"I told you to keep that cat in the garage." Bertie let out a violent sneeze. "I'm allergic. I don't want it in my kitchen. It's not"—she sneezed again—"sanitary."

"I'll find him, Mrs. W.," Jen promised.

"See that you do." The oven timer dinged. "Get that, Finch," Bertie snapped, her eyes watering as she turned back to her pot. "Don't want the scones to burn."

"Anything else?" He grabbed a grease-stained mitt from a peg by the door and bent down to remove two trays of fresh-baked scones from the oven. "Since it seems I'm a sous-chef now, as well as a butler."

"They smell divine," Phaedra said.

"Cheddar and chive." Bertie didn't turn around. "For Mrs. Collier's tea," she added, pointedly.

Finch set the trays down and discarded the mitt to pick up a china teapot. He poured the deep red liquid into a mug and set it in front of Phaedra. "South African chai rooibos. I'd offer you a scone, but . . ." He rolled his eyes at Bertie's back.

"This is perfect." She wrapped her hands around the thick earthenware mug and took a sip. "I taste cinnamon, cloves . . . and something else."

"Cardamom."

She nodded appreciatively. As she lingered over another sip, her glance strayed to the floor, drawn by something gleaming in the corner near the kitchen door.

Something blue-green.

Her gaze sharpened. What was it? And how to examine it more closely without attracting attention?

"I should go," she told Finch. "Charlene's waiting. Thanks for the tea."

"You're welcome. After I deliver Mrs. Lucas's tea and toast," he added, shooting Bertie a dark look, "I'll be in the dining room if Mrs. Collier should need me. Polishing silver and awaiting the next round of questioning by the police."

"I imagine they're questioning everyone."

"Some," he confirmed cryptically, "more than others."

Phaedra set her mug on the counter and glanced down at her sneakers. "Oh, for . . . my laces have come untied again. They're always doing that."

"Then perhaps you should get a new pair of shoes," Bertie retorted.

"Perhaps I should." She knelt down to tie her shoe, her back to Finch. Quick as a flash, she palmed the blue-green stone, dropped it into her sneaker, and retied her shoelace.

Without a closer examination she couldn't be sure, but it looked like an aquamarine from the stolen choker. Charlene had mentioned that one of the stones was loose.

She straightened, picked up her cup, and followed Finch into the dining room.

"Thanks again," she said, lifting her mug in a salute as she reemerged into the main hallway.

He nodded and shut the doors.

In the morning room, Phaedra paused in the doorway. Charlene sat on the edge of the sofa, her body angled toward the fireplace and a cup of tea balanced precariously on her lap as she gazed into the flames.

"Do you mind company?"

Charlene looked up, relief suffusing her face as she set the cup and saucer aside. "Phaedra! I was beginning to think you weren't coming."

"Of course I came. Finch offered me tea and I couldn't say no." She set her mug down beside Charlene's. "Jen chased a kitten into the kitchen and Bertie had a sneezing fit."

"Oh yes. She has terrible allergies. Her eyes itch and sting something awful in the spring." She smiled wanly. "It feels like a lifetime ago since you left. Hard to believe it was only yesterday."

"A lot's happened since then," Phaedra said. "It's natural that you're feeling overwhelmed."

She closed the door and sat down beside Charlene, who lifted teary eyes to hers. "I'm sorry. I'm just so t-tired. I barely slept, and my thoughts are all over the place."

"That's understandable. You're grieving, and you're still in shock." Phaedra reached out to squeeze her hand. "If you feel up to it, I want you to tell me everything the police said."

"They haven't told me much. They keep asking about my argument with Bill yesterday, if we often argued. I told them no, not really, just the normal things that all couples argue about. And Detective Morelli asked me if the blow-dryer in the tub was mine."

Phaedra eyed her curiously. "Was it?"

"No. I told him I don't keep my personal things in that bathroom. And I've never seen that pink dryer before."

"Perhaps one of the Fortune girls left it behind. They had to clear out of here in a hurry."

"It's possible," Charlene agreed. "I said as much to Detective Morelli." Her gaze was troubled. "I don't think he believes me."

"Do you need a lawyer?"

"They haven't charged me with anything." Her shoulders sagged. "At least, not yet."

"While we're alone, there's something I want to show you." Phaedra walked to the writing desk. "I found something in the desk yesterday, in the middle drawer. A check for $2,500, signed by Bill."

"A check? That's strange. Bill always kept that drawer locked. And he rarely used that desk—it was more mine than his. Who was the check for?"

"The payee line was blank. The drawer was locked," Phaedra added, "but I had a MacGyver moment with a paper clip. I hope you don't mind."

Charlene shook her head.

Phaedra reached for the middle drawer with a gloved hand, hoping it was still unlocked, and gave it a tug. It slid open.

But the check was gone.

"It's not here." Good thing she'd taken a photograph of it. She pulled the drawer out farther, running her hand along inside to see if she'd missed it somehow. Her fingers brushed against something coiled and bumpy in the back of the drawer. It felt like a bracelet, or a string of pearls. "There's something back here."

Phaedra withdrew an intricately worked choker fashioned of blue-green aquamarines, diamonds, and seed pearls. A square aquamarine sat in the center, and a clasp in the back fastened the two ends together. The workmanship was exquisite.

"You've found it!" Charlene sprang up with a cry and joined Phaedra. "You found my missing choker!"

Eleven

Charlene stretched out her hand for the antique Georgian necklace.

"Best not touch it," Phaedra advised. "It's evidence."

"You think it might have something to do with Bill's death?"

"I don't know. Possibly."

She eyed the sparkling aquamarines in amazement. "But what on earth is it doing here? I checked every drawer and went over every inch of this house yesterday, and it wasn't here. Now it is. I don't understand."

Phaedra carefully set the choker aside on the coffee table and retrieved the aquamarine from her shoe. "I found this on the kitchen floor a few minutes ago, when Finch made me a cup of tea."

Charlene studied the square-cut blue-green stone gleaming in Phaedra's palm. "This definitely belongs to the choker," she said. "But why was it in the kitchen?"

"The thief must've carried the choker out the back door when the power was out, and it came loose. What puzzles me is that no one noticed it."

"As busy as the kitchen is, especially with Bertie and her staff here, someone should've seen it."

"The power wasn't restored until the police arrived," Phaedra said. "And there was a lot going on. Which might explain why no one noticed it last night." She frowned. "But I saw it right away. Which makes me wonder if the thief hid the choker in the kitchen until he or she could get it out of the house."

"Or pass it off to an accomplice," Charlene said.

"Exactly. But . . . that's odd." She studied the choker with a frown. "None of the stones are missing."

Charlene watched Phaedra draw the choker slowly through her gloved fingers. All of the stones were intact.

"You're right." She lifted a puzzled gaze to Phaedra. "It doesn't make sense."

"No, it doesn't. Unless—" She lowered the necklace. "I wonder."

"You think it might be a copy."

Phaedra smiled wryly. "You know me too well. Yes, that's exactly what I think."

"Then we should tell the police. Give them the choker and let them deal with it. After all, it's evidence, isn't it?"

"Yes, but . . ." Phaedra hesitated. "I'd like to take it to the jeweler's and have it authenticated first. See what I can find out before we say anything to the police."

Doubt was written on Charlene's face. "It feels wrong, not telling them."

"The choker belongs to you, and it probably has nothing to do with Bill's mur—" Phaedra caught herself. "With your husband's death. We don't even know if it really *is* the one he gave you. That's what we need to determine."

"I suppose you're right."

"There's only one way to find out. I'll stop by Bascom's on the way home and let you know what I learn."

"All right. But you'd better hurry." As the sound of male voices down the hall drew nearer, she added, "Someone's coming."

Phaedra slid the choker and the aquamarine into her reticule just as a knock sounded sharply on the door.

"Mrs. Collier?" Detective Morelli said. "Finch told me I'd find you in here. May I come in?"

Phaedra resumed her seat on the sofa as Charlene opened the morning room door to the detective.

He came to a stop as he saw Phaedra. He didn't look pleased. "Professor Brighton. What brings you here?"

"I called to check on my friend." She gave Charlene a reassuring smile. "And to offer my support."

"Did you speak to the press after you left here?"

"No, of course not. I was as surprised as anyone to see the headline on the *Clarion* this morning."

Skepticism was plain on his face, but he made no comment. "Would you mind leaving us now? I have a few questions for Mrs. Collier."

"Does she need a lawyer?" Phaedra asked, cocking her head in curiosity.

He met the challenge in her eyes with equanimity. "Not unless she thinks she needs one."

"Call me if you need me," she told Charlene. "Anytime, day or night."

"I will. And thank you." Her eyes met Phaedra's. "For everything."

"Close the door on your way out, please, Professor Brighton."

She nodded at Morelli but didn't reply, and shut the door with perhaps a touch more energy than was strictly necessary.

As she passed the dining room doors, still closed, she heard the rise and fall of voices. Chief among them was Finch's unmistakably dramatic baritone.

After ensuring no one was in the vicinity, Phaedra edged closer.

". . . have no idea why he insisted on bathing in that hideous old tub," Finch was saying. "With so many perfectly good bathrooms in this house, it made no sense."

"Habit." It sounded like Jen, the young woman who'd

helped serve drinks the night before. "Mr. C. liked his routine."

"Sometimes habit can be a dangerous thing."

Phaedra recognized the clipped female voice as Bertie's.

"Meaning?" Finch asked.

"Meaning that predictability makes a person vulnerable. A routine known by everyone in the household made it simple for someone—someone who knew his habits—to dispatch Mr. Collier."

"Are you suggesting one of us offed him?" Finch demanded. "That's ridiculous."

"Someone did. And you were his butler. You knew his habits better than anyone at Marling."

"And what about you? You and your staff had plenty of opportunity to do the deed, wandering around the house and grounds with your food trays—"

"I barely knew the man. Why would I, or any of my employees, want to kill him?" Bertie scoffed. "We're far too busy keeping the cast and crew fed. Besides which, Mr. Collier wrote the checks. Paid us all very well indeed. Why would I do away with my golden goose?"

Phaedra heard the morning room door open and stepped away from the dining room as Detective Morelli rounded the corner.

"Professor Brighton. Still here, I see. Listening at doorways now?" He glanced, rather pointedly, at the closed dining room doors. "Seems to be a habit of yours."

"I was just leaving."

"Before you go, I'd like to ask you another question."

"About what? I've told you everything I know."

"Refresh my memory. What did Mr. Collier do when he learned his wife had loaned the choker to Ms. Prentiss?"

"He reprimanded her, quite vehemently. He grew increasingly angry with Charlene until everyone began to notice. His reaction struck me as somewhat . . ."

"Excessive?"

"Yes. I stayed silent as long as I could. But when the

choker was stolen, and he blamed Charlene, I'd had enough. He shouted and belittled her until he reduced her to tears, and I told him to stop. I won't stand by and allow anyone to be bullied. And William Collier was a bully."

"All right." He sighed and made a notation on his pad. "Thank you for your cooperation. That's all for now."

He left and met with a pair of sheriff's deputies for a quick consultation in the entrance hall. They gave her a brief nod as they walked past with purposeful steps to the morning room.

What was going on?

Phaedra lingered. Was Charlene about to be charged with her husband's murder? She took out her phone, intent on calling her father to see if he could recommend a good lawyer, when Charlene hurried around the corner.

She made a beeline for Phaedra. "Thank goodness you're still here. I was afraid you'd left."

"What's happening? I just saw two deputies go into the morning room."

She drew closer and lowered her voice. "They're looking for the choker. The detective mentioned it when he questioned me earlier."

Phaedra shot a quick glance at Morelli, but he had his back to them as he tapped out a text on his cell phone. She resisted the urge to touch the choker in her reticule just to reassure herself it was still there.

"Do they think it's connected to your husband's murder?" she asked.

"He didn't say. And I didn't tell him we found it."

"Good. I'll stop at the jeweler's on the way home."

"I still think we should tell them."

"We will," Phaedra promised. "Just as soon as I talk to Mr. Bascom. He'll know if what we found is a fake or not."

"I suppose you're right."

"I'll call as soon as I learn something." Phaedra drew her into a quick, fierce hug. "I know it's difficult right now, but hang in there."

She promised to do her best, and Phaedra made her way across the entrance hall to the front door.

"Goodbye, Detective," she said, and paused with her hand on the doorknob. "I'm leaving now."

"Glad to hear it. While you're at it, try to keep out of trouble." He added pointedly, "And stay out of my investigation."

"I wouldn't dream of interfering."

With a bright smile, and the choker nestled safely in her reticule, Phaedra departed.

Twelve

Bascom's Jewelers, located halfway down Main Street, was quiet when Phaedra arrived. The old-fashioned bell over the door jangled as she thrust it open, and she nearly tripped over the owner's Saint Bernard lying in the aisle.

"Hey, Bosco." She bent down to scratch the dog's head. "Having an afternoon snooze?"

"Good afternoon, Phaedra." Mr. Bascom looked up from the loupe in his hand and smiled. "How's Malcolm?"

"He's fine. Mom loved the pearls you sold him. Says it's the best birthday gift he ever got her."

"Glad to hear it."

Phaedra straightened and went to the counter. "I wonder if I might trouble you to take a look at an antique choker for me."

He put aside the loupe and ring he'd been examining. "Let's see what you've got. An antique choker, you say?"

"Georgian. Could you take a look at this stone, too?" She carefully withdrew the necklace and the single stone from her reticule and laid them out on a piece of dark velvet cloth Mr. Bascom produced.

He picked up the stone between two fingers and held it up.

"It's a beautiful example. Aquamarines really do look like seawater, don't they?"

"Makes me long for the Bahamas."

He adjusted the angle of a balanced-arm light clamped to the counter and studied the aquamarine, turning it under his loupe. "It's a princess cut of excellent quality. The color and clarity are exceptional. I'd date the setting to 1819 or thereabouts."

"So the stone is authentic."

"Yes. You understand, of course, that carats make no difference to the value of these semiprecious gems. Everything depends on clarity and depth of color, regardless of the stone's size. Let's look at the choker. Is it a family piece?"

"No." At least that much was true. "It belongs to a friend who wants it authenticated and valued."

He drew the necklace slowly through his fingers as he inspected it under the light; next, he examined it through the loupe, paying particular attention to the stones and their settings.

Phaedra waited, resisting the urge to drum her fingertips against the counter, until at last he lowered the choker and set the loupe aside.

"The choker is a copy, I'm afraid."

"A copy," she echoed, her hopes that Charlene had found the missing heirloom evaporating. "You're certain?"

"Completely. It's an excellent copy, but a copy all the same. Its weight alone tells me the necklace isn't authentic. It's far too light for a piece of its design and substance. The stones are paste, and I'd date the scrollwork from the mid-1950s." He pointed to a worn spot on the clasp. "You can see signs of tarnish in several places. It's silver-plated metal."

"Yes, I see. My friend will be disappointed."

"I'm sorry I can't give you better news. It's not uncommon for a family to have a copy made of a valuable piece. That way the owner can wear the copy in public and keep the original safely tucked away. But the aquamarine is authentic, and not without value on its own."

He placed the choker and the stone into a velvet drawstring bag and handed them back to her.

"You've been very helpful. Thank you, Mr. Bascom."

"My pleasure. If she ever decides to sell the original, let her know I'd be interested in purchasing it."

"I'll let her know. Thanks again."

Phaedra slid the velvet bag into her reticule, her thoughts working overtime, and gave the jeweler a distracted smile as she headed out the door.

Once out of the dim environs of the shop and back on the street, she blinked in the afternoon sunshine. Mr. Bascom had confirmed her suspicions and raised several questions in her mind.

The choker she'd found in the desk was unquestionably a fake. But the aquamarine was real. Which begged the question . . . how had it ended up on the kitchen floor?

Obviously, the thief left with the choker via the kitchen door, or passed it to an accomplice, unaware the stone had come loose. But two things puzzled her. Why had no one else noticed the aquamarine lying on the floor?

Marling's kitchen was busy, with the cook and the caterer sharing the space, not to mention the catering and household staffs coming in and out. The theft happened early yesterday afternoon, which meant the stone had lain on the floor for quite some time. Yet no one had seen it.

Secondly, who stashed the fake choker in Charlene's desk drawer? Was the theft, along with the missing check for $2,500, somehow connected to Collier's murder?

She didn't know. But as she slid behind the wheel of her Mini Cooper and headed for the IGA, Phaedra was determined to get some answers.

Half an hour later, as she hefted a large bag of flour into her grocery cart in preparation for her weekend Bath bun bake-a-thon, Phaedra's cell phone rang.

"What are you bringing to the bookstore on Sunday?" her mother asked. "I'm making quiche, and those crab salad tea sandwiches you like so much."

The Spring Fling! With all the events at Marling, she'd nearly forgotten her dad's yearly open house at the Poison Pen. "Good timing. I'm at the IGA, so I'll add some dark chocolate and two pints of strawberries to my cart."

"Perfect. And perhaps you wouldn't mind bringing a liter of ginger ale, as well? I'm making my punch."

Phaedra suppressed a sigh and wheeled her cart toward the bakery section. "Okay."

"There was a new man at the Heritage Society meeting last night. Very charming."

"Single?" Of course he was, or her mother wouldn't have worked him into the conversation.

"As a matter of fact, he is. With such a dearth of suitable men, I thought you'd be glad to know I found an eligible prospect."

"I'm not interested in finding a man." She tossed a bag of brown rice into the cart. "If it happens organically, fine. But I won't be pushed into a relationship before I'm ready. And I'm not ready."

"Phaedra, I hate to burst your bubble, but you're not getting any younger. You're wasting prime childbearing years teaching a bunch of outdated classics to students. Novels that no one reads anymore."

She tamped down her annoyance and reminded herself they'd had this argument before. And they'd doubtless have it again. "The books on my class syllabus are read, and are still being read, and not only by my students. Take Austen's novels, for instance. Her books are classics precisely because they've stood the test of time."

"I won't argue the point. But you can be married and have a career, too. Plenty of women do both. I want grandchildren eventually, Phaedra. Preferably before they have to visit me in a nursing home."

"Then focus on Hannah. She wants to get married. I don't. And stop trying to fix me up with every stray man who comes along. I have no need of a husband."

"Well, then, I suppose inviting him to the Spring Fling was the wrong thing to do."

Phaedra counted silently to five. "Any other surprises?"

"Hannah and Charles might stop by. He's visiting his sister Karolina for the weekend, and Hannah's joining him." She paused. "She has *news*."

Phaedra suspected her mother hoped Charles had already popped the question and slid an engagement ring on Hannah's finger. "Sounds great. Anything else I should bring?"

"Just bring yourself. And please wear normal clothes. You won't be standing behind a lectern, so there's no need to dress like a Regency spinster."

She resisted the urge to take her mother to task and swallowed her irritation instead. "Bye, Mom."

"Goodbye, darling."

Phaedra let herself into the carriage house an hour later and lowered two grocery-stuffed tote bags onto the kitchen counter. Wickham eyed her in reproach from his position by the back door.

"I suppose you want out." She opened the door and he darted out. "You're getting crotchety in your old age," she called after him. Of course he paid her no mind.

She topped up his kibble with a half can of tuna and put fresh water in his water dish. That should improve his mood. Or not. Upstairs, she changed out of her Regency gown into jeans and an "Obstinate, Headstrong Girl" T-shirt and returned to the kitchen to get to work.

After mixing the dough for the Bath buns and setting it aside to rise, Phaedra let Wickham in. As he went to his food dish to devour his tuna, she settled at the dining room table with her laptop and notes. She slid on her tortoiseshell reading glasses and resumed work on her monograph, "Jane Austen: Her Literary Critics, Past and Present."

She soon immersed herself in the rhythmic tapping of the keyboard. The bleat of her cell phone startled her out of the world of curricles and calling cards and brought her back to reality with an unwelcome jolt.

Phaedra reached out to silence her phone and ignore the call, but changed her mind as she saw Charlene's name on the screen. She grabbed the phone to share the news that the choker they'd found was a fake. But the words died in her throat. She knew by her friend's silence that something was wrong.

"Charlene? What is it? Is everything all right?"

"No." The word erupted as a sob.

"What's wrong? Tell me what's going on."

"The postmortem results came back."

Phaedra waited, her heart beating far too fast. "And?"

"The pathologist noticed bruising on the back of Bill's neck. He examined the site more closely and discovered . . ." Her voice quavered. "A puncture mark."

"A puncture mark," Phaedra repeated, although she already knew about the medical examiner's discovery. "But William was electrocuted. I saw the blow-dryer floating in the water."

"Yes. But he was also injected with s-something. They can't confirm what it was until the toxicology report comes back, which might take weeks, but . . ." She sucked in a shuddery breath. "The pathologist thinks Bill may have been injected with insulin."

"Insulin! But he wasn't a diabetic."

"No. He wasn't. He was as healthy as a horse. Which makes this whole thing even more horrific. As if being electrocuted isn't h-horrific enough."

Phaedra sank back in her chair. "Do you mean to say that someone deliberately put your husband into a diabetic coma *before* they electrocuted him?"

"It looks that way. Whoever did it knew exactly what they were doing. Who would do such a thing?"

"Oh, Charlene—I can't even begin to imagine. I'm so sorry. I know this is all terribly upsetting for you."

She heard raised voices in the background.

"What's going on?" Phaedra asked.

"Hold on." Charlene covered the phone and had a muffled conversation with someone. After a moment, she returned. "They've found something. In the morning room."

"What? Tell me what's happening, please."

"They were searching the fireplace, and one of the deputies found something in the bottom of a vase on the mantel." She lowered her voice to an anguished whisper. "They've found a syringe and an empty vial of insulin."

"But that's a good thing," Phaedra reassured her distraught friend. "That means they're one step closer to finding out who did this to your husband."

"No. No, you don't understand." Charlene's voice was low but tight with anxiety. "The syringe and vial they found are identical to the ones I sometimes inject my mother with."

Phaedra's heart sank. "Did you tell Detective Morelli that you administer the insulin to your mother occasionally?"

"Yes. I told him I've done it for years. She has tremors and can't inject herself."

She heard more voices in the background, Morelli's chief among them, growing nearer. "What's going on? What are the police saying?"

"Oh, Phae . . . they want me to go with them for questioning. At the station." She sounded really rattled. "I think they intend to arrest me."

"Listen to me, Charlene." Phaedra spoke firmly as she reached for her keys and pushed back her chair. "You don't have to go. You can refuse. But if you do go, don't say anything—not one word—until I get you a good attorney."

Thirteen

Phaedra called her father, a retired criminal lawyer with a wealth of useful contacts. "Dad? Can you recommend a top-notch local lawyer to represent Charlene?"

He paused. "Well, good afternoon to you, too, pumpkin."

"Sorry." Phaedra let out a lengthy sigh. "I didn't mean to be so abrupt, but I'm concerned for Charlene. She's agreed to go into the police station for questioning."

"Has she been formally charged?"

"No. Not yet, anyway."

"She doesn't have to comply," Malcolm Brighton pointed out. "And she can refuse to answer questions without an attorney present."

"That's exactly what I advised her to do. Can you recommend a good criminal lawyer to represent her?"

"Tom Moore is the best criminal attorney I know," Malcolm Brighton said without hesitation. "Georgetown Law, top of his class. And I agree, Charlene needs someone like Tom in her corner. Give him a call and tell him I referred you." He read off Moore's cell phone number.

"Thanks, Dad. Do you think the fact that they've brought Charlene in for questioning means they think she's guilty?"

"At the very least, she's a person of interest. I understand you discovered Collier's body in the bathtub."

"Yep. Lucky me." Phaedra suppressed a tiny shudder. "It's not an image I'll forget anytime soon."

"Do the police have any leads? Any suspects besides Charlene?"

"They questioned everyone who was there, including me, but as far as I know they've only followed up with a couple of people. Myself, the butler, and Tinsley Prentiss, one of the bachelorettes." She frowned. "It all started with the choker."

"Choker? I thought Collier was electrocuted, not strangled."

"He was. Possibly," she amended. "I'll explain in a minute. Before I went upstairs and found the body, the power went out, and someone snatched an antique Georgian choker from Tinsley's neck. She'd borrowed it to film a scene."

"That's pretty brazen. Someone was determined, or desperate. Do the police think the theft is related to the murder?"

"I don't know. They're not saying." She filled him in on the theft and the tree crashing onto the roof. "I couldn't help but overhear the pathologist when he examined the body."

"You mean you were eavesdropping."

"Yes." Ignoring the disapproval in his voice for the moment, she added, "Which means I'm not supposed to know what I'm about to tell you."

He sighed. "Very well. Give me a dollar the next time I see you and consider yourself covered under attorney-client privilege."

"Done." She recounted Dr. Kessler's discovery of the puncture wound and his belief that someone had injected Collier beforehand with an unknown substance. "And the power upstairs may—or may not—have been on at the time."

"Interesting. So Kessler believes it's possible that Collier didn't actually die of electrocution."

"Right. Even though I found him in the bathtub with a plugged-in, bright pink blow-dryer floating on the water."

"Sounds like a title from the Poison Pen's cozy mystery section," he mused. "*Shampoo, Cut, and Die.*"

"Do me a favor and stick to selling books, Dad, not writing them," Phaedra advised with a wry smile.

"Will do." His voice sobered. "And I apologize for joking about something like this. There's nothing remotely funny about murder, especially not when it concerns your friend. Please give Charlene my sincere condolences."

"I will. And I'll pick up those paperbacks you put aside for me tomorrow."

"So your mother roped you into coming to the Spring Fling open house, did she?"

"Of course she did. Finger food, her infamous punch . . . and yet another unattached man on the menu. How could I miss it?"

He chuckled. "You know your mother too well. Is there anything else I can do for you?"

"No. This is great. I'll call Mr. Moore right now. And thanks again."

"You got it, baby girl."

"I'll drop your dollar off tomorrow," she promised, and smiled.

She hung up and dialed Tom Moore. After explaining the situation, he agreed to head over to the Somerset County Sheriff's Department and offer Charlene legal counsel.

"I'll probably see you there," Phaedra said as she reached for her keys. "She'll need a ride home."

"Provided they don't detain her. And I intend to do everything in my power to ensure they don't. See you shortly."

Phaedra arrived at the two-story brick courthouse complex a short time later and strode inside.

As she passed through security and reclaimed her shoulder bag, the elevator doors nearby slid open.

"Professor Brighton. Thought you might show up." Detective Morelli crossed the lobby and approached her.

"Why is that?" she asked, truly curious. "Do you have psychic abilities in addition to your detecting skills?"

"Nothing so dramatic. Tom Moore called to say he's on

his way to represent Charlene Collier. I figured you'd be right behind him."

"Is she here?" She slid her purse on her shoulder.

"Yes." He gestured to a long corridor on the left. "If you don't object, I'd like a word with you."

"Do I need a lawyer?"

"Not unless you have something to hide."

She followed him through a door halfway down the corridor and into his office.

"Have a seat."

Warily, she complied. "What's this about?"

"Your role in all of this."

"My role, as you put it, is simply that of a close friend. A friend who wants to ensure Charlene has the counsel she deserves."

"Sure you don't see yourself as something more? Maybe an interfering amateur sleuth?"

"Let me ask a question of my own." She clasped her hands around one jean-clad knee and met his gaze squarely. "Charlene says your men found a syringe and an empty insulin vial hidden in the morning room earlier today. Is that why you brought her in for questioning?"

"Last I checked you're not her lawyer. Or a cop."

But she wouldn't be deterred. "Perhaps you can tell me this, then. Did Bill Collier die of an insulin overdose?"

The question hung between them. As the silence stretched, she began to think he wouldn't answer.

"This is an ongoing investigation," he said finally. "We won't have specifics until the toxicology results come back. Which could be weeks. In the meantime, I'm not discussing the case with you."

"I'm not asking you to. I'm simply wondering if the two things are related."

"What two things?"

"The stolen choker. And Mr. Collier's death."

"You tell me."

"What? I don't understand."

He leaned forward, his expression grim. "Twice now I've found you alone in that morning room. What were you doing in there? Oh, I know what you told me," he added as she began to protest. "This morning, you claimed you were there to comfort your friend. The evening of the murder, you said you wanted to take another look at Collier's portrait while you waited to give your statement to the sheriff's deputy."

"And that's the truth. In both cases."

"You weren't looking at that portrait. You were looking for something else."

She didn't answer.

"Maybe you went in there to hide the evidence for your friend," he mused. "You said yourself you two are close. Maybe you owed her a favor or two. Or maybe you killed Collier yourself. After all, you were at Marling when he was murdered. You and he exchanged words. And you found the body."

"That's ridiculous! I was in the drawing room with Charlene when he was murdered. And why would I want to kill a man I'd just met? What possible reason could I have?"

He shrugged. "People kill for all sorts of reasons, Professor. Maybe you did it, and Charlene covered for you. Or vice versa. It's awfully convenient that you're providing each other's alibis."

She reached for her cell phone. "I'm calling my lawyer."

"That's up to you. But it'll go much easier if you just answer me truthfully. What were you doing in the morning room?"

They'd circled back to his original question. He was nothing if not persistent.

"I told you—"

"I know what you told me. Now, I want the truth. Because otherwise, I'm inclined to think you might've hidden that syringe and vial at some point. After all, you were the last person seen in front of that fireplace after the murder took place."

Phaedra eyed him in amused disbelief. "You're not seriously accusing me of murder."

"No. But I have enough to hold you for questioning. As it

stands right now, you're a person of interest. So unless you want to join your friend in the interrogation room, I'd suggest you cooperate."

After a moment's hesitation, she reached into her handbag and retrieved the small velvet sack containing the choker. "I found this in the middle drawer of Charlene's desk earlier today. It was thrust in the back."

She spilled the necklace out onto the detective's blotter.

He frowned. "Isn't that—"

"The missing Georgian choker? Yes. And no."

"Meaning?"

"It's a fake, a copy of the original. According to Mr. Bascom, our local jeweler, it was made sometime in the mid-1950s. The jewels are paste set into plated silver."

"And I suppose I'll find your fingerprints all over it," Morelli said, his expression thunderous. "As well as the jeweler's."

"Actually, no. I wore gloves. As did Mr. Bascom."

"Did it never occur to you to bring this find of yours to my attention?"

"I intended to," she replied, "but I wanted to authenticate it first. Charlene was convinced it was the choker, but I had my doubts."

"You did." His words oozed polite sarcasm. "And why was that?"

In for a penny, in for a pound . . . "Because I also found this." She shook out the single aquamarine from another, smaller pouch. "It was on the kitchen floor, by the back door. Unlike the choker, Bascom says the stone is authentic."

"Great work, Nancy Drew." Morelli flung his pencil down. "But I don't need your help, accidental or otherwise. You're interfering in a murder investigation. *My* investigation."

"How am I interfering? We don't know that the choker is even connected to the murder."

"*We* don't know that it's not." He leaned forward once again, resting his forearms on the desktop. "Sheriff Dobbs wants this case wrapped up. Somerset County draws a lot of tourism thanks to the spa and the Laurel Springs Inn. The town needs the economic shot in the arm this reality show will provide. Murder makes for bad publicity. For the town, and for the show."

"Understood. And you don't want my help. Got it."

"Look, I get that you're trying to protect your friend. I respect your loyalty to Charlene Collier. But right now she's a suspect, one with both motive and means. In the meantime, I'll keep the choker and aquamarine for evidence. If you don't object."

Sarcasm had crept back into his voice.

"What if someone set her up for her husband's murder?"

"Suspects are rarely framed in real life. This isn't an episode of *Murder, She Wrote*."

"You don't think it's all just a little too convenient?" Phaedra asked.

"What I think," Morelli said, his words deliberate, "is that you need to butt out and let me do my job. Or I'll charge you with obstruction."

They glared at each other.

"Are we done?" Phaedra stood abruptly and slid the strap of her purse over her shoulder.

"For the moment. Thank you for your time, Professor Brighton."

Fourteen

An hour later, Charlene emerged into the courthouse lobby with Tom Moore. Phaedra waited until Moore left and offered her friend a ride home.

"Thanks. I was afraid I'd have to call Finch, and I'd rather not." Charlene followed Phaedra across the lobby and back to Phaedra's Mini Cooper.

"Why? He seems pleasant enough. And he's employed by you, after all."

"I feel uncomfortable being driven around." She waited as Phaedra unlocked the car with a chirp of her key fob. "I never had a *car* before, much less a chauffeur."

"I understand." Once inside the car, Phaedra paused, seat belt in hand, and regarded her friend. "Are you okay? Do you want to talk about what just happened?"

"They asked a lot of questions. Mr. Moore instructed me not to respond to most of them."

"What did they ask you, exactly?" Phaedra backed the car out of the parking spot.

"They asked if I hid the empty syringe in a vase on the fireplace mantel. They asked if I've ever injected a diabetic

PRIDE, PREJUDICE, AND PERIL

patient with insulin. They asked for my whereabouts during the storm, if I'd left the drawing room for any reason."

"Did you mention you left for a few minutes, to get candles?"

"Yes. I had to. They grilled me about that. What time did I leave the room? How long was I gone? Where did I go? Could my mother confirm my visit to her room? And they wanted to know if I . . ." She shook her head wearily and added, "If I'd injected Bill."

"Oh, honey—I'm sorry you have to go through all of this."

"Bill's body will be released in a day or two. I need to make funeral arrangements."

"You have plenty of time to make those decisions." Phaedra reached over and laid her hand on Charlene's. "And of course I'll help you in any way I can."

"Thank you. I'll plan something simple, for the immediate family. Perhaps a graveside service." She leaned back and closed her eyes. "If you don't mind, I'd rather not talk about this anymore."

"Of course. I completely understand."

After dropping Charlene off at Marling, Phaedra returned to the carriage house and turned onto the private drive. Time to get baking and finish those Bath buns she'd promised Karolina.

But instead of measurements and ingredients, questions troubled her thoughts as she shut off the engine. Who killed William Collier? Had the same person who injected him tossed the blow-dryer into the bathtub, or were there two murderers? Was Charlene a serious suspect? Was *she*?

And then there was Nick Ross. He was in the drawing room that afternoon, and he'd stayed the night. But she dismissed the thought almost as soon as it occurred.

Ross and Collier were strangers. Granted, they'd exchanged words when Nick stood up for Charlene. But that hardly constituted a motive for murder. And Nick hadn't left the drawing room. At least, not that she knew of.

Deep in thought, she realized her phone was ringing inside her handbag. She grabbed it and glanced at the screen. Unknown caller. The area code indicated a local number.

Hoping she wouldn't regret the impulse, Phaedra answered. "Yes?"

"Ms. Brighton? This is Clark Mullinax, with the *Laurel Springs Clarion*. Would you care to comment on William Collier's recent murder?"

"I would not." Mullinax, the former editor of her high school newspaper, was the last person she wanted to talk to. "And it's Professor Brighton. I'm hanging up now."

"Please don't."

"Why shouldn't I?" Phaedra retorted.

"Because I have information you might want."

"I doubt that."

"My source claims one of the Fortune sisters was in a C-ville pawnshop earlier today, trying to unload stolen property. A valuable Georgian choker, to be exact."

Her fingers tightened on her phone. "How do you know about the choker? That information hasn't been released to the public."

"It's been released to me. Courtesy of my source."

"I don't believe you." But her heart kicked up a notch. "Surely whoever stole that choker has sense enough to dispose of it anonymously. Legitimate dealers require identification and keep serial numbers on file. All sales of precious metals and gems are forwarded to the police."

He chuckled. "Sell a lot of stolen merch, do you?"

"My father's a retired criminal lawyer. We discussed laws and statutes at the dinner table."

"I'm sure you did."

Ignoring the edge in his voice, Phaedra said, "Criminals usually break the stones down and sell to a fence. That's how it works."

"I'm guessing the Fortune kiddos aren't exactly accustomed to handling hot merchandise. They're rich girls, after all."

"Not anymore."

"No. But you're right. It was a risky move on Patsy's part. As soon as the owner went in the back to make a phone call—to notify the cops, no doubt—she got rattled, and skedaddled."

"How do you know it was Patsy Fortune?"

"My source says she wore a pair of expensive designer sunglasses, identical to Patsy's. And she drove a green Lambo. License plate, '4-Tune Grrl.'"

"Well, if it was really Patsy," Phaedra said, still doubtful, "she's incredibly stupid."

"Well we *are* talking about the Fortunes. Those girls might be beautiful and famous, and until recently, filthy rich. But now they're broke. No more lavish lifestyles or canoodling with stars like Nick Ross."

"Nick?" She remembered the glance Patsy and the actor had exchanged the day before. "And Patsy?"

"Yep. They were the talk of the tabloids a couple of years ago. She and her sisters never missed a photo op. Patsy was—still is—the queen of social media. But from what I hear, she's not particularly, shall we say, astute."

"Who's your source? Is it the same person who tipped you off about the murder and the stolen choker?"

"Oh, come on, Phaedra. Journalism 101. A journalist never reveals a source."

"You work for the *Clarion*, Clark, not the *Richmond Times-Dispatch*." While she'd hardly justify Clark as a journalist, she did give him a small measure of credit for refusing to reveal his informant.

"True. But at least I don't write for the *Coupon Clipper*."

"Maybe you should. They have more subscribers."

"Funny," Clark said sourly.

She couldn't resist one more dig. "When I'm looking for a garage sale or a used car, the *Coupon Clipper* is my first choice."

"You know, Phaedra," he said, his words measured, "you haven't changed a bit since high school. Not everyone's had your advantages in life—wealthy family, top-notch education, roots in the community. You're like a character in one of those Jane Austen novels you love so much. Privileged and clueless."

His accusation left her unable to speak. Disbelief gave way to anger. "That's unfair. And untrue."

"Prove it. Give me a quote about Collier's murder. Something. Anything. This is a big story, maybe the biggest story in Laurel Springs' history."

"Hyperbole becomes you."

"Come on, Phaedra. This is a stringer's dream. All I need are a few juicy insider quotes and I can sell the story to the *Times-Dispatch*. Or even the *Washington Post*."

She unbuckled her seat belt. "I'm not interested in being your ticket to fame and notoriety. And even if I were, the police don't want anyone talking to the press."

"I promise I'll keep your name out of it."

She remained stubbornly silent.

"Our readers have a right to the truth."

"Sure they do. All three of them."

A wounded silence greeted her.

Phaedra sighed. "I'll think about it, okay? I'm hanging up now." Before he could pressure her further or offer any more journalistic aphorisms, she ended the call.

As she got out of the car, she noticed the sun sinking and shadows lengthening across the yard. She frowned. Where had the day gone? She locked the car and headed for the front door, her feet crunching across the gravel driveway.

Was Mullinax right? Did Patsy Fortune try to sell the stolen choker in a Charlottesville pawnshop?

Was she really privileged and clueless?

Clark's words, so blunt and unexpected, burned in her memory. *Don't let him get in your head*, she told herself. How could someone who'd known her for a hot minute back in high school have the slightest idea who she was *now*?

And why, she wondered peevishly, was Detective Morelli so determined to pin William Collier's murder on Charlene instead of finding the real culprit? He was wasting time chasing after the wrong suspect, while the real murderer's trail got colder by the minute.

Her steps slowed as she neared the front door and paused to dig out her house key. In the early-evening hush she heard the croaking of the peeper frogs from the pond in the woods behind the carriage house, and she smiled.

Spring was here.

Her smile faded as another, less welcome sound reached her ears. A thud, followed by several rhythmic thumps, came from inside the house. She glanced around but saw no cars parked on the street nearby or in her driveway.

She waited, shifting uneasily from one foot to the other, but all was quiet.

It's nothing, she reassured herself. *There's no one in the house. You're jumpy because you have murder on the brain.* She extracted her house key with an unsteady hand and reached for the front doorknob. She saw no sign of a break-in. No scratches or damage to the lock . . .

. . . but the door was ajar.

Alarm bells sounded in her head. Someone was definitely inside. Who? A burglar?

Maybe Collier's killer?

You're being ridiculous. Stop it, right now. Phaedra dragged in a calming breath that did nothing to calm her and, heart thwacking rapidly in her chest, eased the door slowly wider.

With a yowl, Wickham streaked out past her feet. She bit back a scream as he raced across the yard and disappeared into the hedges. Shaken, she reached once again for the doorknob to risk a cautious peek inside.

As her fingers closed over the cool brass knob, footsteps thudded down the stairs that led up to her loft bedroom.

And the footsteps headed straight toward the front door.

Fifteen

Phaedra looked around wildly. Spying a spade peeking out from beneath the hydrangeas planted on either side of the steps, she dived down, grabbed it, and brandished it in front of her as the steps pounded ever closer.

The door flew open.

"Hannah!"

"Phae?"

Still clutching the spade, Phaedra sagged against the doorjamb, her heart beating double-time as she glared at her sister. "What are you doing here?"

Hannah fisted her hands on her hips. "Well, hello to you, too." She eyed the spade. "That's your weapon? Good thing I wasn't a real intruder."

"It's all I could find." Phaedra tossed the spade aside. "I didn't know you'd be here."

"You'd know if you ever checked your text messages. Charles dropped me off on the way to his hotel. I didn't think you'd mind if I crashed here tonight."

"Of course I don't mind. I just wasn't expecting to find anyone inside the house. You gave me a real scare."

"You? What about me? Your cat darned near gave me a

heart attack! That yowl he let out . . . it sounded like someone being strangled."

Phaedra gave a shaky laugh. "That's Wickham. Always a drama queen." She held out her arms and enveloped Hannah. "All's well that ends well. How've you been? I've missed you."

"Same." She squeezed Phaedra and drew back. "I'm doing okay, other than losing a year of my life just now. Would've been here sooner but there was a wreck on I-64."

"You look great."

With her petite build and unruly caramel-brown curls pulled back in a hair elastic, Hannah resembled one of those rosy-cheeked, nesting Matryoshka dolls.

"Oh, please. I'm a mess. The humidity did a number on my hair. I couldn't do anything with it, hence the hair elastic."

"Come in." Phaedra led the way inside, spotting a rolling suitcase at the top of the stairs. "Ah, the mystery is solved."

"What mystery?"

"The thumps I heard outside, the ones that sounded like someone lugging a dead body . . . it was you, dragging that suitcase upstairs. Why didn't you stay at the hotel with Charles?"

"I figured I'd stay here. Catch up on all the latest." She followed her sister's lead and sank down onto the comfy, slipcovered sofa. "Plus, I forgot to book a room. Do you know there's not a hotel room available anywhere from here to Charlottesville?"

"The wine festival." Phaedra nodded. "Everything books up weeks in advance." She couldn't resist adding, "I'm sure Charles would've gladly shared his room with you."

"He's a consul at the British embassy, Phae. You know this. We *work* together."

"So? Doesn't mean you can't have a relationship. You're not opposing counsel in a lawsuit. You're two adults who like each other. Have you asked him out yet?"

Hannah's cheeks went pink. "No, I haven't asked him out. I can't."

"Why not? You like him. He likes you. Seems fairly straightforward to me."

"That's just it. It's not. I don't know that he likes me. He's polite and very sweet, but he's that way to everyone. What if I ask him out and he gives me a horrified look and says no? I'll die of mortification. I'll see him every day at work." She made a face. "It'll be . . . awkward."

Phaedra got up and went into the kitchen—small, but recently redone with top-of-the-line appliances—and filled the kettle. "I don't see the problem. He's made it plain he likes you. He stops by the embassy kitchen every morning to say hello—you told me so yourself. Start small. Ask him out for coffee, or tea. Brits like tea. No big deal."

"Easy for you to say."

"Why? Because I'm thirty-four, single, and definitely *not* in want of a husband?"

Although she made light of her single status, it was an undeniable fact, and the knowledge both liberated and depressed her. She had a career she loved, drove an aging but reliable Mini Cooper, and considered herself intelligent, loyal, and independent.

She switched on the kettle and took two cups down from the cupboard. But every now and then, especially after a difficult day, she longed to come home and share her thoughts with someone over a cup of tea or glass of wine, to sit across from that same someone at dinner and argue over which television program to watch.

But she'd never admit as much to Hannah.

Hannah followed her into the kitchen, retrieved a lemon from the fridge, and began slicing it into thin rounds. "Don't let Mom pull that you-should-be-married routine on you." She fanned the slices out on a plate and carried it to the table. "You're smart. You have a great career. And you're happy. That's all that matters."

Was she happy? Phaedra wondered. Her life was full, no question, and filled with things she was passionate about—teaching, writing, and sharing knowledge of Jane Austen and the Regency period.

But success alone was no longer enough. She wanted more. Not marriage, necessarily. Not yet.

She wanted a deep and lasting relationship with a man who'd rise to her challenges, who'd cheat at Scrabble and make her laugh, who'd cherish and value her just the way she was.

Did such a man exist? Or did he exist only in the pages of a Jane Austen novel?

"Yes, I'm happy." Phaedra warmed the Brown Betty pitcher with a vigorous swish of hot water, emptied it out, and spooned in loose green tea. "Happy you're here. Happy this day is over."

"Rough one?"

Phaedra sighed and sat down across from her. "I suppose you'll hear about it soon enough."

"Hear about what?"

"There was a murder yesterday, at Marling. And I was there."

Hannah gasped. "A murder? In Laurel Springs? What happened? Who was murdered? And what were you doing there?"

"The victim was William Collier, former CEO of Longbourn Pharmaceuticals. Ring any bells?"

"Collier, Collier . . ." She frowned, and after a moment her face cleared. "He's that Fortune guy's nephew, right? The one who inherited everything when Mr. Fortune kicked the bucket and left his wife and daughters with nothing."

"He left them enough to live on," Phaedra corrected. "If they invest wisely and live prudently."

"Invest wisely? Live prudently?" Hannah let out a snort. "You're joking, right? The Fortune girls are social influencers. They hang out with celebrities and Russian oligarchs. Every five minutes they're posting selfies on yachts or private jets, and they drive cars that cost more than most people make in five years."

"Not anymore."

"True. Well, I can't blame the network for scrapping their pilot. But their loss is Karolina's gain. Yours, too," Hannah pointed out. "You can add 'historical consultant' to your already impressive resume. Plus, you get to hang out with Nick Ross."

"I've barely seen him. He stays in his trailer most of the time. But to get back to Collier, he was murdered. Someone tossed a blow-dryer in the bathtub."

"Who found him?"

"I did." As Hannah's eyes widened, she added, "It's a long story. He and Charlene recently got married."

"Married? But they just got engaged, like, five minutes ago."

"I know. Now Charlene has to plan his funeral."

After filling her sister in on the hasty civil marriage, the theft of the choker, and the murder, Phaedra poured their tea. "The police seem to think Charlene did it, since she had the strongest motive."

"I assume all of that lovely money goes to her."

"Yes. They took her in for questioning today, as a matter of fact. Dad recommended a good lawyer, Tom Moore, and he's agreed to represent her. Beyond that, and trying to track down the real killer, there's not much else I can do."

"Are you crazy?" Hannah set her china cup down with a sharp clink. "You're not a cop, or a private detective. You're a professor! Going after the murderer could get you killed."

"I'm not going after anyone. I'll be careful. I'll just ask a few discreet questions, listen and observe, and keep a close eye on everything that happens on the set."

"I don't like it, Phae. It's risky. And it could be very, very dangerous."

Phaedra stood up and retrieved three Bath buns and set them out on the table. "I know. But like I said, I'll be discreet. And careful." She nudged the plate toward her sister and sat back down. "Have one. I made them myself."

"Thanks for the warning."

"Just try one."

"Eating your baked stuff is an exercise in trust. Half the time you get distracted and forget to add something crucial. Like eggs, or salt. Or baking powder."

"Baking powder is vastly overrated." She took a sip of tea and suppressed a yawn. "Time for me to say good night. You can have the bed. I'll take the sofa."

"No, I'll sleep down here," Hannah offered half-heartedly. "I don't mind."

"You traveled half the day, you're tired. You get the bed. Don't argue. Besides," she pointed out, "your suitcase is already up there, which tells me you had no intention of sleeping on the sofa in the first place."

"You know me too well." A sheepish grin teased Hannah's lips as she lifted a bun and bit into it. Surprise and pleasure flickered over her face. "Wow. This is actually good."

"Don't sound so surprised."

"It's so good, I might even want the recipe."

"I might even give it to you." Phaedra stood to put her cup and saucer in the sink. "I'll wash up in the morning. I'm glad you're here."

"I'm glad I'm here, too. Sounds like you need my wise, sisterly advice more than ever." She yawned. "And we'll both need a good night's sleep to get through tomorrow. You know Mom. She'll be in full-on social butterfly mode, schmoozing and networking at the open house."

"Ugh. Don't remind me. See you in the morning."

"Good night." Hannah put her cup in the sink beside Phaedra's, knelt down to give Wickham a gentle scratch behind his ears, and made her way upstairs to bed.

Sixteen

The Poison Pen bookstore teemed with activity as Phaedra and Hannah arrived early the next afternoon. Cars crowded both sides of Main Street. As Phaedra wondered if she'd ever find a place to park, a spot opened up in front of the bookstore, and she squeezed the Mini in.

"Good thing this car is small," Hannah observed from the passenger seat. "Otherwise we'd be hoofing it for three blocks, lugging this stuff." She glanced back at the liters of ginger ale and a plastic-wrapped tray of chocolate-covered strawberries.

"The place looks good," Phaedra said as she got out of the car and studied the Victorian row house. "Festive. And not a cloud in the sky today."

The store's flag, featuring a black quill pen atop a bright red splotch of blood, snapped jauntily in the breeze. Boxwood topiaries flanked the double doors, and a banner hung in one of the turreted front windows.

"Spring Fling Open House," Hannah said out loud. She waited, a tote laden with several liters of ginger ale over her arm, as her sister maneuvered the tray of strawberries from the back seat and nudged the door shut with her hip. "Are all these cars here for Dad's bookstore?"

"Possibly, but I doubt it. Lots of people are in town for the wine festival this weekend." She joined her sister. "Are you ready?"

"Ready as I'll ever be."

Holding the tray, Phaedra led the way up the sidewalk and ascended the wide wooden steps to the porch fronting the house. Their parents lived above the bookstore.

"You're here! Come in, come in." One of the narrow, glass-fronted doors swung open as Nan Brighton ushered them inside. "I'll take that."

She relieved Phaedra of her tray and set it down on a table already covered with a tantalizing assortment of goodies ranging from tiny biscuits with ham and pepper jelly, pimento cheese, and crab salad sandwiches, to plates of cookies and sliced lemon cake. Nana's antique punch bowl held pride of place in the center. It was empty.

"No punch?" Phaedra asked, secretly relieved.

"I haven't made it yet. Just waiting for the ginger ale to arrive. But we have plenty of nibbles and noshes," her mother added in satisfaction.

"It looks fabulous."

"Darla brought her pimento cheese, and Wendy's bringing cucumber sandwiches, and I made those little ham biscuits everyone loves. Oh, and your father made the most delicious Parmesan crisps. They're addictive." She gave Hannah a quick hug and drew back to fix her with a bright, inquisitive eye. "How are you, darling? Where's Charles?"

"He's on his way."

"You didn't come along together?"

Hannah handed over the tote. "Nope. I stayed at Phae's last night."

"Oh? Why didn't you stay here, in your old room upstairs? You know you're always welcome."

And here we go, Phaedra thought as she left her sister to

it and made her way across the slanting wooden floors to find her father. Poor Hannah. Mrs. Bennet truly had nothing on Nan Brighton when it came to determined matchmaking.

The floors creaked under her feet as they always did, and the pleasant, faintly musty smell of old books greeted her, as familiar as a childhood friend. There was no rhyme or reason to the bookstore. Just shelves and shelves of books, most of them mysteries and crime novels, interrupted here and there by a cushioned window seat or a comfy armchair. Across the hall, Fitz, her mother's pug, lay snoring on the braided rug near the cash register.

"I envy his ability to sleep through all this," Phaedra's father greeted her from behind the counter. "Glad you could make it."

"I wouldn't miss it. Looks like a full house."

"It's been like this for the last couple of hours. I'm gratified by the turnout. Wendy said she'd stop by later."

Her mother's sister, Phaedra's aunt, owned the popular Laurel Springs Inn bed-and-breakfast.

He came around the counter and drew her aside. "How's Charlene? Did she get in touch with Tom?"

"Yes. He went to the courthouse and represented her during the questioning."

He nodded. "He's the best. He rarely loses a case."

"Here you two are," Hannah grumbled as she squeezed past a knot of women to join them. She directed an accusing frown at her sister. "Thanks for sneaking off. Mom's practically got me and Charles married off already, and we're not even dating."

"It's your own fault," Phaedra said.

"How do you figure that?"

"You told her you had news before you left D.C. You know Mom. She heard 'news' and jumped straight to *engaged* without passing go."

Hannah exhaled. "No wonder she asked if I preferred filet mignon or flounder amandine."

"She's already planning your wedding menu."

"Excuse me, Malcolm." A silver-haired woman, arms laden with paperbacks, smiled at Mr. Brighton. "Do you have any good mystery recommendations? I'm looking for a classic whodunit."

"Of course, Mrs. Evans. Right this way." He led her toward the back of the store. "I have the perfect Ngaio Marsh title in mind for you . . ."

The bell jangled over the front door, and Hannah rose on her tiptoes to see who it was. Panic chased over her face. "Oh no. It's Charles."

"Isn't that a good thing?"

"Not if Mom gets to him before I do." She shot off, weaving her way through the crowd.

Phaedra was about to follow suit when the bell over the front door jingled again.

"Mr. Selden," her mother caroled. "Welcome! How good of you to come."

Selden? Phaedra froze. No, surely not. It couldn't possibly be. What was the newest addition to the university's English department faculty doing here?

"Call me Mark, please," came the polite, British-accented reply.

It could be. It was. A quick glance at the man with thick, dark hair and hawklike nose confirmed it.

Mark Selden was here. And her mother knew him by name.

Before she could slip upstairs or make a quick exit via the back door, or maybe hide behind one of the high-backed Victorian armchairs, her mother bore down on her with Mark in her wake.

"Phaedra! There's someone I want you to meet." She came to a stop before her daughter and beamed at Selden. "This is Mark Selden, the charming man I told you about."

"Hello." She affixed a polite smile to her lips and extended her hand. "We've already met."

"So we have." He clasped her hand briefly and turned to Nan. "Professor Brighton gave me a tour of my new home at Somerset University only yesterday."

Her mother looked as if she'd died and gone to heaven. "So you'll both be working together? How wonderful! You're a professor as well, Mark?"

"Shakespeare and comparative literature."

"Well, we're very glad you're here. Aren't we, Phaedra?" She barely paused before tapping her lower lip thoughtfully. "I'll arrange a dinner party for you one evening soon. Introduce you to a few key people."

"I'm sure Professor Selden is far too busy to commit to any social obligations, Mother," Phaedra said firmly.

"On the contrary," he said. "I look forward to it."

"Nan? Nan, are you here?"

"There's Wendy. Finally." After inviting Mark to help himself to a plate of food and recommending he try the shrimp puffs, Mrs. Brighton excused herself and hurried off to greet her sister.

"You don't have to do this, you know," Phaedra informed Mark.

"Do what?"

"Stay. Mingle with the locals. Endure my mother."

"I think your mother's charming. And the locals seem harmless enough." He glanced at the shelves of mysteries. "I like your father's bookstore. Very atmospheric. And a perfect place to spend a rainy afternoon. Did you spend a lot of time here, growing up?"

"Here, in the bookstore? No. Dad practiced law in Charlottesville until he retired a few years ago and moved back here. He grew up in Laurel Springs. And this," she added as she swept her arm out to encompass the shelves and the slanting wooden floors, "was my grandmother's house. She left it to Dad when she died. Retirement didn't agree with him, and he loves a good mystery, so he decided to open a bookstore."

Mark nodded. "And does he sell anything besides mysteries? Any Jane Austen novels, for instance?"

"He stocks a few classics, and genre stuff. But he sells mostly whodunits. And first editions."

"I see. Do you have any first editions at home?"

"Only two. I can't afford them."

"Which ones? No, don't tell me. Let me guess."

She folded her arms against her chest and shrugged. "Have at it."

"Let's see." He frowned. "You have a first edition of *Persuasion* and another of *Mansfield Park.* You have paperback copies of all six novels, highlighted and annotated with copious handwritten notes. You prefer tea over coffee, you detest dating apps, and you have a . . ." He frowned. "A Yorkshire terrier named Mr. Darcy."

"A cat," she corrected, tightly. "Wickham."

"Like the bad boys, do you?"

"And the first edition is *Pride and Prejudice.*"

His smile was smug. "I rest my case."

Oh, the arrogance of the man. "And I suppose you have a complete, leather-bound set of Shakespeare's works—"

He shrugged. "Of course."

"—and a plaster bust of the Bard sitting on your desk. No doubt wearing a backward baseball cap and sunglasses, the better to show your students what a hip sense of humor you have."

His smile faded. Bingo.

"Jane Austen is overrated," he said after a tense silence. "Were it not for the never-ending parade of costume dramas and 'I Love Darcy' coffee mugs, her books would no doubt be forgotten, gathering dust on a bookshelf very much like one of these."

And with that, he turned away.

Phaedra watched him go, expecting he'd head for the buffet and fill a plate with food, but he didn't. He strode past the table, nodded briefly at her mother, and left the bookstore.

Seventeen

What on earth did you say to him?" Nan demanded as she joined Phaedra at the table a moment later.

She picked up a plate. "You might ask yourself first what he said to me."

Before her mother could pursue the matter and plague her with more questions, Hannah returned with a young man in tow.

"Have you met Charles?" she asked Phaedra as she joined them.

"No, I haven't had the pleasure." She turned her attention to the man standing next to her sister. "Hello. I'm Han's sister, Phaedra."

"Charles Dalton." He smiled and extended his hand. "We work at the British embassy together."

He had a thatch of coppery hair and a ready smile, and Phaedra liked him at once. "I hope you're enjoying your time here in Laurel Springs."

"Very much so. I haven't seen much of it, truthfully, aside from the inside of my hotel room. Although," he added hastily, "it's a very nice hotel room."

"Did you get a plate of food yet, Charles?" Mrs. Brighton

asked. "No? Well, best hurry. Those shrimp puffs are going fast!" She turned to Phaedra. "Did you bring along any of those Bath buns you made for Karolina?"

"No. She's using them in a scene tomorrow. They're all boxed up and ready to deliver first thing in the morning."

"I'll see Karo later this evening," Charles said. "To say goodbye. I'd be happy to pick them up and take them to her, save you a trip in the morning."

"Would you?" Phaedra flashed him a grateful smile. She faced a full day at the university tomorrow, with a first-year undergraduate lecture on British Romanticism, essays to grade, and emails to answer, not to mention the monograph research she'd hoped to complete.

"Of course. I'll stop by later and pick them up."

Nan beamed at Charles, then focused her attention on Hannah. "What's your news, darling? When we talked last, you hinted that you had something to share. Do tell us."

"Oh, my news can wait. This is Dad's day."

"Don't be silly. Your father is perfectly happy to share the spotlight with you. Aren't you, dear?" Nan called out to him. He nodded vaguely and continued what looked to be a serious conversation with his sister-in-law.

"Mom, really, it can wait." A flush crept slowly up Hannah's neck as several people turned to regard her with interest.

"Don't be shy, Hannah," Charles chided her. "Go ahead. Share the good news with your family."

Phaedra cut a glance at her mother. Excitement danced in her eyes, along with visions of wedding gowns and registries and china patterns.

"Well. Okay, then." Her sister took a deep breath. "I've been named one of the top twenty new chefs to watch by *Washingtonian* magazine."

In the fraction of a second before everyone began clapping and calling out congratulations, Phaedra saw disappointment register on her mother's face. But she rallied and plastered on a convincing smile as she turned to Hannah.

"Well, congratulations," she exclaimed, and swooped down on her daughter to offer a hug. "I'm so proud of you."

"We all are," Phaedra added. After congratulating her sister, she excused herself and wormed her way through the crowd to the front of the bookstore, where her aunt was still deep in conversation with Dad.

". . . might have to sell the inn," Wendy told him in a low voice. "I can't make ends meet since the divorce."

"You can't sell the inn." Phaedra knew dismay showed plainly on her face as she came to a stop before her aunt. "Where will I go? Will I have to move?"

The carriage house she called home stood directly behind the Laurel Springs Inn, backed by woods and bounded by a privacy hedge. The prior owner, a former chef at the inn, refurbished it and sold it back to Wendy, who turned the cozy one-bedroom house into a rental property.

"This isn't about you, Phaedra," her father said, and frowned. "Your aunt is facing a very difficult decision."

She opened her mouth to defend herself but realized he was right. "You're right. I'm sorry," she told her aunt. "Of course my first concern is you."

"It's okay, sweetie." Wendy drew her in for a hug. "And no, you won't have to move. Not yet, anyway. If things change I'll let you know." She drew back. "I hear you're a consultant on that new reality show. Congratulations! I bet you have some stories to tell."

"Oh, I do." Phaedra paused. "I was at Marling for the first day of filming. But a storm chased everyone inside, and . . ."

"And you found William Collier's body in a bathtub." Wendy shuddered. "I read about it in the *Clarion*. What a terrible thing."

"It was quite a shock." Phaedra winced. "Sorry, poor choice of words."

"Yes, he was electrocuted, wasn't he?" She lowered her voice and leaned forward. "Murdered. That's what the *Clarion* said, anyway."

Phaedra nodded. "The police are investigating. They have

a few suspects. And you," she added, steering the subject away from Collier's murder, "have a new hairstyle." This was Dad's day, and she didn't want it spoiled with talk of bodies in bathtubs and floating pink blow-dryers.

Wendy fluffed her short, stylishly cut brown hair with a self-conscious motion. "You like?"

She studied her aunt, a former catalog model who was still slim and attractive in middle age, with a critical eye. "I do. It suits you."

"I had it balayaged."

"What the heck is balayage?" Malcolm asked. "Sounds extremely complicated."

"It's . . . oh, never mind." She patted him on the arm. "Why don't you run along and fix yourself a plate and let us girls talk in peace?"

"Good idea. Those ham biscuits are calling my name. And they're almost all gone." He glanced at Phaedra. "Don't forget to take those paperbacks I put aside for you when you leave," he reminded her. "Two Agatha Christies and a Mary Roberts Rinehart."

"I won't. And thanks." She waited as he threaded his way toward the table, stopping every few feet to talk to a customer, before turning back to her aunt. "Now what's this about selling the inn? You can't be serious."

"I'm afraid I am. Since the divorce, I'm struggling to pay the bills. And I know what you're about to say," Wendy added. "Yes, we're booked up right now. That's just spillover from the wine festival, and it's only temporary. Bookings are down twenty percent from this time last year."

"I'm sure things will pick up. Have you thought about offering themed events?" Phaedra suggested. "A roaring twenties weekend, for instance, or a *Titanic* tea, or a murder mystery weekend? People love that sort of thing."

Wendy shook her head. "I'm sure they do, but it costs money to pull something like that together. Money I just don't have."

"Oh, stop moaning about money," Nan scolded her sister

as she joined them. "Take out a loan. The house is nearly paid for, isn't it?"

"It is. But the taxes are killing me."

For the first time, Phaedra noticed shadows under Wendy's eyes, and she reached out to lay a reassuring hand on her aunt's arm. "Is there anything we can do to help?"

"No, I'm fine. I'll figure something out." She leaned over and pecked her niece on the cheek. "Your mother's right. It's time I stopped complaining and got back to work. Tell your father I'll drop by later this week."

Well, Phaedra reflected as her aunt departed and the crowd thinned, it had certainly proven to be an interesting afternoon. Good news, bad news . . . and without even trying, she'd managed to offend Mark Selden.

Guilt prickled her. She hadn't intended to do that.

After saying goodbye to her father, busy ringing up sales at the cash register, she found her sister and Charles lingering at one end of the buffet table.

"I'm leaving," she told Hannah, who was nibbling on a slice of lemon cake. "Looks like this shindig is winding down. Are you ready to go?"

"I think I'll stay awhile longer."

"I'll bring Hannah home," Charles offered. He smiled over at her. "We're leaving for D.C. first thing in the morning. In the meantime, she's promised to give me a tour of downtown Laurel Springs."

"That should take about five minutes." Phaedra waved her fingers. "See you later, then. Have fun. Nice to meet you, Charles."

"You're not leaving, are you?" her mother demanded as she waylaid Phaedra on the way to the front door.

"I need to let Wickham out." It was her standard excuse and they both knew it.

"Don't you want some leftovers? The biscuits are gone, but there's still some cake, and a few cookies—"

"No, thanks. I have to fit into those Regency gowns you hate so much. And before you ask, Hannah's not leaving with me." She glanced over at her sister, sharing a private joke with Karolina's brother. "She and Charles have plans."

"Really?" Her mother followed her gaze and perked up considerably. "Well, I'm glad to hear it. Looks like the two of them are getting on famously." The possibility of a wedding and all it entailed shone, once again, in her eyes. "Goodbye, then, darling. I'll call you later."

Free at last, Phaedra let herself out and headed down the steps and back to the car.

As she reached in her handbag for the key fob, she noticed a vintage white Bentley idling at the curb across the street. A woman emerged from the passenger side, a pink scarf fluttering at her neck, and gave the driver a brief nod. A pair of sunglasses hid her face, but Phaedra recognized her dark auburn hair and red lips instantly.

Dorothy Fortune.

After losing her home and her late husband's estate to William Collier, how could his widow afford the luxury of a chauffeured Bentley? Puzzled, Phaedra watched as Dorothy walked away at a brisk pace, heels clicking against the sidewalk, and entered . . . Woofgang's Gourmet Doggy Bakery?

Odd. As far as she knew, the Fortunes didn't have a dog.

Her puzzlement deepened as she returned her attention to the Bentley. It pulled smoothly back into the flow of traffic, slowing as the stoplight on the corner changed from yellow to red.

Phaedra squinted. Wasn't that Jasper Finch behind the wheel?

She couldn't be entirely sure; like Dorothy, the driver wore sunglasses. But he certainly looked like the Fortunes' former butler. Was he, perhaps, moonlighting as a driver for Dorothy Fortune?

He must be. How else could Finch afford to drive a Bentley on a butler's salary? But then again, how could a woman of seriously reduced circumstances such as Dorothy afford a car and driver?

It was most perplexing.

Phaedra's fingers tightened around the key fob as another thought occurred to her.

She remembered the check for $2,500 she'd found in Charlene's desk drawer, and the blank payee line. The next day it was gone. Had William Collier left it there for Finch?

Could the Fortune's former butler be supplementing his income with blackmail?

Eighteen

Charles dropped Hannah off at the carriage house that evening and took the Bath buns, promising he'd deliver them to Karolina on his way back to the hotel.

"I like him," Phaedra told her sister after he left. "He's sweet, and thoughtful, and he's a man of his word. Ask him out."

Hannah turned a pretty shade of pink. "Turns out I won't need to. He invited me to go for a drive next Saturday, to Middleburg. And don't say it."

"Don't say what? I told you so? Fine. I won't say it."

The next morning, cradling a mug of Keemun, Phaedra studied the half dozen Empire-waist gowns hanging at one end of her bedroom closet. Nothing appealed. With so few dresses, each in weekly rotation, one thing was clear.

Her Regency wardrobe needed a major overhaul.

Phaedra puckered her brows. Custom-made, historically appropriate clothing didn't come cheaply. In high school and college she'd stitched up her own costumes; now, with lectures to deliver and papers to grade, not to mention a murder to solve, she didn't have the time, or desire, to sew her own gowns.

She chose a day dress of cream and primrose stripes, tied beneath the bust with a primrose ribbon, and paired it with a shawl of fringed muslin. Not only would she look the part of a demure Austen heroine, her bare arms wouldn't get goose bumps in the chilly confines of Lecture Room 3.

After twisting her hair into a knot and securing it at the nape of her neck, she was ready to face the day.

She carried her mug downstairs and set it in the kitchen sink. Wickham looked up from his favorite spot on the back of the sofa, where he surveyed the front yard, the driveway, and a small slice of the street.

"See you later, Wicks." She rubbed him between the ears, and he purred extravagantly, pushing his head closer, seeking her massaging fingers. "Shameless boy."

As she retrieved her keys, reticule, and briefcase and opened the door, Phaedra was glad Cupid's arrow had found her sister Hannah.

At least love was working out for one of them.

Her nine o'clock lecture on British Romanticism ended at eleven, and Phaedra remained to answer questions from the undergraduates. It was nearly noon when, questions answered and hunger beginning to gnaw at her stomach, she gathered her notes and books and returned to her office.

Lucy was in a closed-door meeting in her office with one of her students, and Marisol was nowhere to be seen. She saw the pop quiz she'd asked Mari to copy earlier on the corner of her desk, exactly where she'd left it.

"Thanks, Mari," she grumbled. "Like I don't have enough to do today."

Yanking off the Post-it note she'd stuck to the quiz—hunger always made her irritable—Phaedra threw it away and went into the copier room to duplicate the document herself. As the machine hummed and whirred and began spewing stapled pages into the hopper, she thought about all the other things awaiting her attention.

Emails to answer. Calls to return. Lectures to outline. Turning the unquantifiable aspects of teaching and learning into metrics for people who tracked such things, people who were neither teachers nor students, in order to determine her department's rate of success or failure.

"We're not making widgets on an assembly line, after all," she grumbled. "We're teaching."

The "paper bin empty" message flashed, and with an aggrieved sigh, she tugged the drawer open.

"Sorry." The voice behind her was politely British. "Did you say something?"

She whirled around. "Professor Selden." Heat crept up her neck. "I . . . no. Just refilling the paper bin."

He said nothing, but waited, a sheaf of papers in hand.

She grabbed a ream of copier paper from the shelf and tore it open.

"Better put in another," Selden said, and reached out to hand her a second ream. "One won't last an hour round here."

With a nod she tore off the paper wrapper and shoved it in on top of the stack. "Two reams. That should do it." She closed the drawer and turned to go.

"Professor Brighton?"

She paused, her heart executing a clumsy little dance step inside her chest, and turned back with what she hoped was cool indifference. "Yes?"

"Aren't you forgetting something?"

Phaedra stared at him. His eyes, she noticed, were as green as an English meadow. Why had she never noticed before?

He lifted the copier lid and plucked her original pages from the glass and held them out.

"Yours, I believe?"

"Oh. Yes. Thank you." Getting a stern hold of herself, she snatched the quiz and bent down to retrieve her copies from the side hopper.

"Good day to you," she said with as much dignity as she could muster, and turned away.

All the way to her office, Phaedra's cheeks burned with vivid pink flags of embarrassment. Good day to you? What was she thinking? She'd done everything but curtsy and inquire after his family's health!

She closed the door, her face hot with mortification, and slid behind her desk. She punched in Lucy's extension.

"Professor Liang."

"We need to hold a meeting of the Jane Austen Tea Society," Phaedra said without preamble, "to discuss this month's book. What night this week is good for you?"

"Tonight?"

"Can't. I have essays to grade. How about Friday? Poison Pen reading room, nine p.m.?"

"That works. My Friday night social calendar is wide open, sadly. I'll let Mari know."

"If she can't make it, maybe you and I can meet for a drink. Catch up." Phaedra reached in her desk drawer for a trail bar. "Is Monday over yet?"

"Not even close. What's wrong?" Lucy asked. "Bad day?"

As she unwrapped her fruit-and-nut bar, Phaedra filled her in. "So, not bad, exactly," she finished, and took a bite. "Just busy."

"How was the open house? Sorry I couldn't make it."

"It was great, and don't worry about it. The turnout was unexpectedly high. But that was probably due more to the wine festival than anything else." She paused. "Mark Selden stopped by."

Dead silence.

"Lu? Are you there?"

"Did I just hear you say Professor Selden came to your father's bookstore?"

"He likes to read mysteries, I guess. I don't know. My mother probably invited him."

"Did you talk to him?"

"Briefly. I insulted him, so he insulted me back. Then he left."

"What are you, in fifth grade?"

There was a knock on the door. "Hold on." One of Phaedra's first-year students from Women Writers of the Nineteenth Century waited outside to meet with her. "I have to go; my twelve o'clock is here. Talk later?"

"You bet we will," Lucy said grimly. "I want details. How about we have that drink at Josie's, tomorrow night, and you can fill me in. Seven?"

She hesitated. Lu wanted details about her relationship with Mark, even though there was no relationship, and thus, nothing to tell. "We should probably invite Mari."

"I'm pretty sure she has a date. But I'll ask her."

"OK." Phaedra knew argument was useless. "I'll see you then."

On her way home that evening, Phaedra turned onto Main Street and circled the block until she found a place to park in front of the newest addition to the street, Woofgang's Gourmet Doggy Bakery.

Time to conduct a follow-up investigation on Dorothy Fortune's recent visit.

An electronic chime sounded as she pushed the door open a moment later and entered the shop. It looked like a typical bakery, with gleaming wood floors, a few café tables and chairs scattered here and there, and a glass display case filled with an assortment of colorful treats.

Gourmet doggy treats.

"Welcome to Woofgang's."

A slim young woman put aside her cell phone and eyed her from behind the counter. Phaedra recognized her instantly as Patsy Fortune, middle Fortune daughter. The girl who'd allegedly tried to sell Charlene's stolen antique choker.

Well, well. Phaedra pursed her lips thoughtfully. No wonder Dorothy had visited the gourmet dog bakery. Her daughter worked the counter.

"May I help you?" Patsy's blond hair was drawn back into a tight, glossy ponytail high on her head. With her expertly applied cat's-eye liner and flawless skin, she belonged behind a department store cosmetics counter.

"Just looking, thanks."

"There's a special on Savory Sweets this week. Peanut butter, banana, or cheddar, and they're grain-free. Dogs love them."

"I bet they do. Actually, they sound pretty good." Phaedra smiled. "I must be hungrier than I realized."

Her smile was not returned. Patsy, like Queen Victoria, was plainly not amused.

"I'll just have a look around," Phaedra said.

With a shrug, Patsy returned to her phone.

She leaned down and pretended to study the bins of bone-shaped dog treats, doggy donuts, and decorated canine cookies, amazed at the color and variety. She'd better buy something for Fitz. Otherwise, Patsy might get suspicious.

Covertly, she eyed the Fortune girl. She was tall, and so thin one hip bone jutted out as her thumbs skimmed over the phone's keypad.

"I'll take a half dozen of the peanut butter savories," she decided. "And half of the cheddar cheese."

Patsy put her phone down and grabbed the stainless steel scoop. She slid the treats into two separate cellophane paw-printed bags, closed them with a twist tie, and set them on top of the display case.

"That'll be fifteen dollars."

Phaedra paused, one hand thrust in her reticule. "I thought they were on sale."

"They are. Normally, they're twenty a dozen."

Good grief. She took out her charge card and slid it across the counter. Good thing she had a cat and not a dog.

"A friend of mine recommended this place," Phaedra said as Patsy took her card and turned away to slide it through the reader. Time to test the waters. "In fact, you might know him."

She didn't turn around.

"He's a reporter for the *Clarion*. Clark Mullinax. Ring any bells?"

Patsy shrugged. "Yeah, I guess. So?"

Phaedra took the card she held out and met her eyes. "He says someone saw you in a pawnshop in Charlottesville on Saturday."

That got her attention. "A pawnshop? Me? You've got to be kidding."

"That's what he says."

"Well, he's mistaken. A pawnshop? Seriously?" She sniffed. "I get my clothes from other sources. Designer friends. Exclusive boutiques. I wouldn't be caught dead in a secondhand dress. Ugh."

"Pawnshops don't sell clothes," Phaedra pointed out gently. "They buy and sell . . . other things. Like jewelry."

"Oh. Well, whatever. I wouldn't know because I don't go to places like that. Why are you asking me all these questions, anyway? Who are you?"

Before she could formulate a suitable answer, Patsy's eyes narrowed on the cream-and-primrose-striped gown and the reticule dangling from Phaedra's neatly gloved hands.

"I know who you are. You're that college professor who wears old dresses and bonnets. I saw you do an interview on channel 29."

"Who I am doesn't matter. It's who you are that does."

"What does that even mean?" She picked up her phone once again.

"You're Patsy Fortune, the most famous Fortune sister. You're a social media influencer, a fashion brand. A trendsetter. Or at least, you were." Phaedra paused to let that sink in. "But if what Clark's source says is true, you could be facing a whole doggy-biscuit-load of trouble."

"I told you, I don't know what you're talking about." Patsy regarded her imperiously. "I think you should leave."

Phaedra didn't budge. "His source saw you enter a pawnshop in Charlottesville. You went inside to sell something."

She paused. "An antique Georgian choker, to be exact. A stolen antique choker."

The color drained from Patsy's face.

Bull's-eye, Phaedra thought.

She quickly recovered. "Is that what Clark said? He's lying. And his source is lying, too."

"Why would he lie?"

"He sensationalizes everything he writes. It's what he does. Everyone knows that."

"Maybe. But he wouldn't print something he knows to be untrue. It could come back to bite him, and the *Clarion*, in the form of a big, fat lawsuit. I don't think his editor would want that."

She crossed her arms against her chest and glared at Phaedra. "If this source is telling the truth, then why hasn't Clark's so-called story run in the paper? I'll tell you why. Because it's a pack of lies."

"Again . . . why would he make something like that up?"

The door chimed, and a middle-aged couple entered the bakery.

"Be right with you," Patsy called out. She turned back to Phaedra and lowered her voice. "Look, I don't have time for this. I'm working and I need this job. If I tell you something, will you go away?"

Heartbeat spiking, Phaedra nodded. "Promise."

"I sold some clothes to an upscale used clothing boutique in Charlottesville. Designer stuff, mostly. I needed the money."

"Okay. So why did Clark claim someone saw you selling Charlene's choker in a pawnshop?"

"Clark's been after me for months. He follows me around like a puppy dog. He's asked me out eleven million times, and every single time my answer is the same. No. My guess? He's mad because I turned him down. He knows my family's down on its luck, so he's stirring up trouble at the worst possible time."

"Seems a little extreme to me. To go to such lengths."

"Not for Clark." She leaned closer, resting her elbows on

the glass-topped counter. "He said he'd run the story in next weekend's edition if I don't go out with him."

Phaedra stared at her. "But . . . that's unethical. It's also blackmail." She frowned. "You're not giving in to his demand, are you?"

"Heck no. I told him I'd call the police, and he backed right down. I can handle Clark. Believe me, he's all bluster." She straightened. "Now, if you'll excuse me? I have customers. Real customers."

Phaedra nodded, gathered up her treat purchases, and left the shop.

Darkness settled over the street as she returned to her car and slid behind the wheel. She glanced at the bakery store window, where Patsy, all smiles now, scooped heart-shaped cookies from a bin and slid them into a paw-printed bag for the couple.

Was she telling the truth? Had Clark fabricated the story about the stolen choker and used his position at the *Clarion* to threaten her? And if so, why involve Phaedra?

She frowned. When Clark called, the first thing he'd asked for was a comment on William Collier's murder. Did he hope she'd reward his faux news tidbit with inside information about the Collier murder case . . . information he could parlay into a *real* story?

She didn't know. But someone was definitely lying.

The question was, who? Patsy? Or Clark?

Nineteen

After letting Wickham out, Phaedra took her reading glasses and the paperbacks her father had given her and settled on the sofa to take a look at his latest finds.

She opened Agatha Christie's *The Murder at the Vicarage*, the first published appearance of elderly amateur sleuth Miss Marple, and began to read. Halfway through the second chapter, the phone rang.

Charlene.

"It's good to hear from you," Phaedra said, putting the book aside. "How are you managing? Is there anything I can do?"

"Nothing. But thanks for offering. You're the only one who has." She paused. "Bill's funeral is Sunday at one o'clock, at St. Cyprian's Episcopal Church."

"Not here in Laurel Springs, at Grace Episcopal? It's right off Main Street."

"Having the funeral out of town will limit the attendance of people who didn't know him. At least, that's what I hope." She drew in a measured breath. "The reception will be here at Marling. I hope you'll be there."

"Of course I will. Count on it."

*   *   *

Josie's was surprisingly busy for a Tuesday evening as Phaedra arrived. She paused just inside the door. The wine bar's marriage of industrial and rustic struck a note of warm sophistication that was at once relaxing and invigorating. She waved at Josie, the middle-aged owner serving drinks behind the bar, and wove through the crowd to a table by the window where Lucy had already ordered a bottle of pinot.

As Phaedra sat down, Lucy leaned forward to fill her glass. "Mari can't make it, so let's talk turkey."

"About?"

"The new Shakespeare prof. You said he showed up at your dad's bookstore on Sunday?"

"Yes, but he didn't stay long."

"And?"

"He said the bookstore was atmospheric, in that plummy British accent of his, and dismissed Jane Austen as overrated. Oh, and he accused me of being an oversexed spinster with a cat."

Lucy set her glass down abruptly. "He didn't."

"No, he didn't," she admitted. "Not exactly. But that's what he meant."

"Do you think maybe you, I don't know—overreacted?"

Before Phaedra could respond, Marisol joined them and sat down amidst a flurry of hellos and what'll-you-haves.

"Chardonnay, please," she told the approaching waitress, and hung her purse strap over the back of her chair. "Sorry I'm late. My date canceled at the last minute. What did I miss?"

"Nothing," Phaedra said, a little too quickly.

"O-kay," Marisol said, drawing out the word to signal her skepticism. She lowered her voice. "Were you talking about . . . the murder?"

"No!" Seeing the girl's startled glance, Phaedra reached out to touch her arm. "Sorry. But what happened at Marling has to stay between us three."

"I get it. And I haven't told a soul. But we've never discussed a murder case before," Mari pointed out. "Laurel Springs isn't exactly a hotbed of crime."

"Don't sound so disappointed." Lucy finished her pinot and reached for the bottle. "Shut up and drink, both of you. You have some catching up to do."

As Phaedra dutifully sipped her wine, her gaze wandered past the other tables, most occupied, and checked out the bar. More people arrived, and patrons waited two- and three-deep at the far end of the pendant-lighted bar to place drink orders or slide into seats at one of the high-backed chairs.

That's when she spotted him. Mark Selden.

He stood with the dean of Somerset University and a professor of economics she knew only by sight, a glass of red in one hand. He wore khakis with a collared shirt and a polite expression. Thankfully, he'd turned away toward the bar without spotting her.

"Isn't that our new Shakespearean scholar?" Mari asked, following her gaze. "He's got all the girls in Advanced Calculus wanting to switch majors to English."

"From calculus to Chaucer," Lucy said. "Why not? Speaking of leaps into the unknown, have you talked to him yet, Phaedra? Audited one of his classes? Asked him to be the Darcy to your Elizabeth?"

"No, to all three." She moved to stand up. "I'm going to the ladies."

"No she's not. She's going up to speak to Darcy," Mari said. "Aren't you, Phae? Admit it."

"Sorry to disappoint, but I really do need the ladies. Back in a few."

"I'll get the last round." Lucy reached into her purse for her phone. "As much as I love you both, I have an eight o'clock lecture tomorrow morning."

Phaedra stood and moved resolutely through the crowd, skirting the edge of the bar area, and kept her expression neutral and her eyes averted as she drew closer to the farthest end of the bar.

"Have you met Professor Brighton yet?" Dean Carmichael asked Selden.

"The Austen scholar? Yes. She gave me an abbreviated tour of the campus on Saturday."

Phaedra's steps slowed, and her fingers tightened on the strap of her purse.

"She's attracted no small amount of notoriety," Carmichael said. "Likes to dress in period clothing when she lectures. She calls it immersive learning."

"I call it immersive nonsense," the economics professor said with a shake of his head. "Theatrics. Deliver the lecture and get on with it."

"Nonetheless, you can't deny that her classes are popular." The dean turned to Selden. "What do you think, Professor? Do you approve of such unusual teaching methods?"

"I think innovation has its place in education," he replied, "if applied judiciously. And the fact that Professor Brighton's classes are popular indicates her methods obviously work."

Phaedra could scarcely believe it. He'd actually stood up for her to Carmichael. Maybe he wasn't so bad after all.

"But it's not a method I'd use," he added. "In my opinion, the woman's little more than a caricature. She looks as if she stepped straight out of one of those ridiculous costume dramas."

Sudden heat burned her face. Not only was he just as bad as she'd initially thought. He was worse.

She thrust her way through to the ladies' room, her eyes stinging with anger and mortification.

Mostly anger.

Thankfully, the bathroom was empty. When she finished, she paused at the mirror to reapply her lipstick, smacked her lips together, and pushed the door open.

She'd sweep past and ignore him. No. She'd pause, and wither him with a stare of such hauteur and scorn that he'd never dare insult her again.

Phaedra risked a covert glance at the bar as she sidled by on her way to their table. She longed to give Professor Selden, in Regency parlance, the cut direct, and leave him with no doubt of her true feelings.

But it was too late. He and his company were gone.

"Your Shakespearean dreamboat took off," Marisol said as Phaedra returned to her seat. "Leaving a lot of very disappointed women behind."

"Well, I'm not one of them." Phaedra took a final sip of her pinot and reached for her wallet.

"You're not leaving already," Lucy protested. "You haven't even finished your drink."

"It's been a long day, and I have a lot on my agenda tomorrow. I'll take care of the bill on the way out."

"Phaedra . . ."

She saw the questions in Lucy's eyes and, having no desire to answer them, fixed a bright smile to her lips and bid them both a cheery good night.

Late Thursday afternoon, Phaedra called a meeting of the English department heads to discuss funding and planning for the upcoming Jane Austen literary festival. Turnout, as she'd expected, was somewhat sparse.

Professor Selden was noticeably absent.

"We need money." Phaedra's opening salvo was blunt and succinct. "Dean Carmichael's budget for the department includes very little in the way of operational funds for the festival." She nodded at Marisol, who was chewing on the cap of her pen. "Mari has some excellent ideas to raise money. Would you share those with us?"

"Of course." She laid her pen aside. "Nick Ross is in town with the new reality show, *Who Wants to Marry Mr. Darcy?* If he agrees to autograph a few photos, maybe put in an appearance at the festival, we could sell raffle tickets. Students could bid for a chance to take a picture with him in period costume."

"I'm sure he's far too busy filming." Althea Browning, the resident Brontë expert, frowned at Marisol over the top of her reading glasses. "Raffle tickets alone won't raise enough money. We need something more. Something splashy, like an auction. Offer a few big-ticket items for bid."

"We don't have money for big-ticket items, Althea," Lucy Liang pointed out. "That's the problem."

"Well, then, we could offer something more modest, but still nice. A gift certificate, for instance. Perhaps dinner for two at that new French restaurant."

"Maybe a bake sale?" Professor Morgan suggested.

"Those are great ideas," Phaedra said. "I can enlist my sister's help for the bake sale. She's a professional pastry chef. We'll have to pay for the ingredients, but I can cover that. Marisol, why don't you call the Sans Souci and see about purchasing a dinner certificate for two?"

"On it."

The conference room door opened, and Phaedra looked up to see Mark Selden. His shirt, she couldn't help but notice, sported a damp splotch that looked suspiciously like coffee, and he wore khakis. He never wore khakis on campus.

Judging from their crumpled state, he'd plucked them from the clothes hamper.

"Thank you for joining us, Professor," she said as he closed the door and took a seat at the end of the table.

"My apologies. I was on a call."

"We were just discussing fundraising ideas for the Jane Austen literary festival. Any suggestions?"

If she'd hoped to put him on the spot, her attempt failed. He rose to the challenge without hesitation.

"I do have one, actually. Your father owns the Poison Pen, a popular local bookstore, correct?"

"Yes."

"Perhaps he'd consider donating a first edition or two," Selden suggested. "I'm sure there'd be a frenzy of bidding if we auctioned off a first edition of *Pride and Prejudice* or *Persuasion*."

"Good idea." She kept her voice neutral. Selden's idea wasn't just good; it was excellent. And she knew her father would readily agree. "Thank you," she added stiffly. "All right. Next up, planning. Are we reprising our Austen roles from last year?"

Several nods and a murmur of agreement went around the conference table. "Dee can't be Elizabeth Bennet this year," Althea said. "She's out for knee surgery. Probably won't be back until the fall term."

Secretly, Phaedra was relieved. While Dee was the right age to portray Elizabeth Bennet, her wire-rimmed glasses and frizzy brown hair made her look more like Miss Bates than Miss Bennet. And her acting ability was truly cringe-worthy.

"Any volunteers to replace Dee?" she asked, and glanced expectantly around the table. There were no takers.

"What about you, Mr. Darcy?" Phaedra smiled across the table at Alan Roberts, who played the role every year. "Are you ready to court Miss Bennet once again, despite the inferiority of her circumstances?"

He inclined his head. "I shall do my utmost to overlook her parental shortcomings."

"Good," Phaedra said over a ripple of laughter. She glanced at Mark Selden and away again. "I'll talk to my father about donating an Austen first edition and speak to Mr. Ross to see if he'll autograph a few photos. Perhaps he'll give us a donation as well, or agree to give the winner of the raffle a personal tour of the set."

"That's a great idea," Marisol enthused. "I'd buy tickets for that."

"I'll do my best to make it happen. In the meantime, we'll focus on finding a new Elizabeth Bennet. Anything else before we adjourn?"

Mark Selden raised his hand. "I have a suggestion."

"Another one?" She crossed her arms loosely against her chest. "I'm sure I speak for everyone when I say we can hardly wait. Please, share it with us."

"Since we find ourselves without an Elizabeth Bennet, why don't you take the part?" He held her startled gaze, then glanced over at Alan. "Mr. Roberts obviously has the pride aspect well in hand. He requires a match worthy of his esteemed consideration. A woman," he added evenly, "who's unfairly prejudiced against him." He met her eyes. "Despite knowing almost nothing about him."

Her voice, when she found it, was composed. "And you think I'd be that woman."

He shrugged. "You already dress the part."

She drew her shawl closer around her shoulders and gave him a tight smile. "My Regency clothing is a teaching tool, Professor Selden. As I believe I've explained."

"So you have. But this isn't only about appearance, is it? It's about character. Miss Bennet stubbornly clings to her preconceived notions about Darcy, no matter how wrongheaded they are. You could assume her persona quite easily."

"And you'd make an excellent Mr. Darcy," she shot back. "Opinionated, arrogant, and full of his own self-importance. What a shame the part's already assigned."

Selden said nothing. But he didn't need to. His smirk, and the dangerous glint in his eye, said it all.

Phaedra thrust her chair back and stood. "If we can't find another Elizabeth, of course I'll consider stepping in." She pressed her lips together. "But I have every confidence we'll find someone more suited than myself."

She swept up her notes and strode, inwardly seething, out of the conference room. She'd make it her mission to find someone for the role of Elizabeth Bennet. She didn't have time in her daily academic schedule to take on one more thing.

And she wasn't about to concede even one tiny victory to Professor Mark Selden.

On Friday, Phaedra returned to Marling.

With no scheduled lectures or meetings, she donned jeans, sneakers, and a pink oxford shirt and headed for the *Who Wants to Marry Mr. Darcy?* set. Today's filming location, according to the call sheet Kyle handed her, was behind the house, in the gazebo overlooking the rose garden.

She shaded her eyes and glanced at the blue sweep of sky overhead, scrubbed clean after the previous day's rain. Virginia weather could be notoriously fickle, but today was postcard perfect. She couldn't think of a better place to enjoy the sun-warmed breezes than here at Marling.

Even better, there was no sign of Detective Morelli.

Time, Phaedra decided, to do some investigating. She'd start by asking Jasper Finch a few questions about his relationship with his former employer.

She went up the front steps of Marling and lifted the knocker. After a longish wait, the door jerked open. It wasn't Finch, as she'd expected, but Bertie Walsh. She wore an apron tied at her waist, and her expression could only be called unwelcoming.

"Yes?" she snapped.

"Good morning." Phaedra thought quickly. She didn't want Charlene to know she was here, at least not yet, and she couldn't ask for Finch. Doing so would raise too many questions. She blurted out the first thing that popped in her head. "I wonder if I might use the ladies' room."

"I suggest you use one of those." She gestured at the row of portable bathrooms near the unit location parking lot and moved to close the door.

"Wait, please." Phaedra thrust her sneakered foot in the doorway. "They're too far away. I'll never make it. Too many cups of tea this morning," she added with an apologetic wince. "I won't be long, I promise."

"Very well." Bertie scowled and edged the door wider. "Powder room is on the right." She jerked her head at a door down the hall, just past the staircase. "Let yourself out when you're done. I have lunch to make and a crew to feed, and no time to play butler."

"Thank you, so much—" But Bertie had already turned and trundled away down the hall, back to the kitchen.

Phaedra glanced into the drawing room. It was empty.

While the cast and crew filmed at the gazebo, no one was around, only the caterers and a few of the household servants. She heard the distant murmur of voices from the kitchen. Where, she wondered, was Finch?

With the police gone and everyone else in the kitchen, she wanted to sneak another look in the morning room, see if she'd overlooked a possible clue. Just outside the dining room doors, she heard voices, and froze.

A pair of caterers entered the room, talking as they set up the table for lunch.

". . . think it was an inside job." The voice was female, and firm.

"The theft?" Her companion was male. "So you're a cop now, Jen?" He chuckled as he set down a platter on the table with a thump.

"I'm serious." Jen lowered her voice, and Phaedra leaned closer to the doorframe to catch her words. "One of the maids said Mr. Collier accused Finch of trying to steal that choker only last week."

"Finch? What would the butler want with that old choker?"

"Money, obviously. It's valuable. He probably planned to break the stones down and fence 'em."

"Really." The word was imbued with skepticism. "Since when are you an expert on criminal activity?"

"That's how it's done. Everyone knows that."

Everyone, Phaedra thought, but Patsy Fortune.

"Oh, come on, Jen. Finch already has a Bentley. Not to mention a cushy job. Why risk it by stealing a bauble from his employer? What did he say in his defense?"

"He swore that Mrs. Collier told him to take it to the jeweler's to get a loose stone repaired. But Mr. C. didn't buy it. He threatened to call the police."

"Obviously, he didn't. Otherwise Finch would be in jail right now."

"Mr. C. didn't call the police because he never got the chance." She paused. "He was murdered the next day."

Twenty

Phaedra's eyes widened. She drew back as someone else entered the dining room.

"I might have known," Bertie snapped. "There's plenty to be done, yet here you two are, dawdling. Get back to work!" she ordered. "You're not paid to talk about things that don't concern you."

"Sorry," they mumbled, and departed.

Phaedra knew she should leave before someone saw her, but she wanted to speak with Finch more than ever. Not only because she suspected him of blackmail, owning a Bentley on a butler's salary; now she'd learned William Collier had accused him of stealing the choker . . . the day before he was found dead in the tub.

Which gave Jasper Finch an excellent motive for murdering his employer.

"Phaedra! How lovely to see you."

With a guilty start, Phaedra looked up to see Violet Lucas, Charlene's mother, wheeling toward her from the far end of the hallway with impressive speed.

"Hello, Violet. Where did you come from?"

"The elevator just off the kitchen. By the service stairs. I can't use those, you know." She chuckled.

Service stairs. Interesting. Perhaps the murderer had used them to slip upstairs without being seen. "You're looking very well."

Violet's complexion, although mapped with wrinkles, glowed with health, and she wore a purple dress with a lavender scarf looped into a bow at her throat. A smile blossomed on her lips.

"Why, thank you, dear." Mrs. Lucas maneuvered her wheelchair into place before Phaedra, her violet-blue eyes sparkling. "And why shouldn't I, when I'm fortunate enough to have the best of care?" She leaned forward and lowered her voice. "I suppose under the circumstances I should act the part of the grief-stricken mother-in-law, but . . ." Her eyes glinted. "I can't say I'm sorry he's gone."

Phaedra hardly knew what to say in the face of such blunt honesty.

"Oh, don't look so shocked. You didn't like him, either, I'll wager. Nobody did. He was a nasty bully of a man. In the short time they were married, he made poor Charlene's life a living hell."

"He seemed to have a talent for rubbing people the wrong way," she admitted.

"A talent? He had an absolute gift for verbal cruelty." Her lips turned up in a grimace of a smile. "The police shouldn't ask who hated Bill enough to murder him. Far simpler to ask, who didn't?"

The front doorbell chimed.

"Should I get that?" Phaedra asked.

"Finch will answer it." She leaned back. "Forgive me, I've neglected my manners. Are you looking for Charlene? She isn't here, I'm afraid. May I offer you a cup of tea in the meantime? Or coffee?"

"Actually, I was just about to leave."

"Oh. What a pity. Well, another time, then. I'll tell Charlene you stopped by."

"Where is she, by the way?" Phaedra asked.

"She didn't say, but she was in a fluster when she left." Violet drew her white brows together. "I do hope she's all right. This business with Bill has her terribly upset, you know."

"I can imagine."

A harried-looking Finch materialized, casting Phaedra a questioning glance as he passed, and answered the door.

"Detective Morelli. Come in." His obsequiousness was a tad overdone, but if Morelli noticed, he gave no sign as he stepped inside the entry hall. "I regret that Mrs. Collier is not at home at the moment."

"I'll wait."

"It may be some time before she returns."

"I'll be in the drawing room."

"Very good, sir. I'll bring coffee." Finch sketched a bow and retreated.

"Well, if you'll excuse me, Ms. Brighton," Violet said, turning her wheelchair away, "I'll bid you goodbye. I'm suddenly feeling a bit tired."

She scooted back down the hall with amazing agility and disappeared around the corner. To the elevator, Phaedra presumed.

"Snooping again, Professor?"

Detective Morelli ambled toward her, a manila folder in his hand. Today he wore jeans and a dark blue shirt.

"Like you, I stopped by to see Charlene." She glanced at the folder and lifted her brow. "I hope you didn't want to talk to Mrs. Lucas."

"Not yet."

"That sounds ominous."

He didn't take the bait. "Learn anything new?"

"Nothing much," she said. "I had a tip that Patsy Fortune tried to sell Charlene's stolen choker in a pawnshop in Charlottesville on Saturday."

She didn't add that Patsy had denied stealing the choker. If Morelli wouldn't share information, neither would she.

"And who was the source of this tip?" he asked.

"I don't actually know."

"Don't know, or not saying?"

"I don't know. The informant spoke to Clark Mullinax, and he's not disclosing his source."

"Clark Mullinax, at the *Clarion*?" Morelli all but laughed. "Let me stop you right there. Number one, fifty percent of Mullinax's stories are just that. Stories. Number two? I'd give Patsy Fortune credit for a little more intelligence than trying to unload hot merchandise in a pawnshop. The serial numbers of every piece of jewelry and precious gem they buy are tracked. We keep a list on file for two years."

"I know that. But maybe Patsy doesn't. And what if Clark's source is right?" Phaedra ventured. "It might be worth following up."

"Do you know how many pawnshops there are in Charlottesville? I'm not wasting one minute of the department's time chasing after a tip from Clark Mullinax."

"But—"

"Nice to see you again, Professor Brighton. Now, if you'll excuse me?" He turned away and headed for the drawing room to wait for Charlene.

She glowered after him for a moment and let out a sigh. Much as she hated to admit it, he was right. Patsy was a smart cookie. She'd never take the stolen choker to a pawnshop. If she even had it.

With no reason to linger, Phaedra left and paused on the front steps. She really did need to talk to Finch.

She remembered Violet's remark that Charlene was flustered when she'd left. Why? Where had she gone? And why did Violet vanish the minute Detective Morelli arrived?

Charlene's mother made no bones about the fact that she couldn't stand William Collier. Did she have something to hide?

Phaedra descended the front steps and rounded the house

as she headed for the gazebo. It was too beautiful to stay indoors. Besides which, she'd promised to ask Nick Ross to sign a few photographs for the Jane Austen festival fundraiser.

With barely a week until the festival, today was as good a time as any.

"Quiet on the set!" the director called out as she approached the shoot.

Nick and Tinsley, a sound boom hovering directly above them, stood in front of the gazebo, both dressed in their Regency finery. Birds twittered and swooped from the tree branches, and the lake glinted in the sunshine behind them.

The two of them might have been the only ones in the world . . .

. . . except for the film crew encamped nearby.

Phaedra watched for a few minutes. A path wound around the back of the house, past the gardens and the terrace, and she followed it, curious to see where it led. As she skirted the walled kitchen garden, Finch emerged from the house and strode across the lawn. Where was he going?

The garage, she realized. Formerly the carriage house, the building housed the family's vehicles as well as the butler's living quarters. She followed him.

As she drew closer she saw Finch, shirtsleeves rolled up to the elbows, leaning over the hood of the Bentley, whistling as he began to polish it with a chamois cloth. Perspiration dampened his forearms.

"That's a beautiful car," Phaedra ventured as she approached. "A Bentley, isn't it?"

He nodded and draped the cloth over one shoulder. "My pride and joy."

"I can understand why. They're pricey, aren't they?"

His smile faded. "Somewhat, yes."

"A couple of hundred grand? I'd say that's quite expensive." She walked slowly around the car and admired it. "But unquestionably impressive."

"Why are you here? Shouldn't you be at the gazebo?"

"I'm not needed at the moment." She crossed her arms loosely against her chest. "Just wondering how a butler can afford a car like that."

"It belonged to Mr. Fortune." His gaze slid away. "Mr. Collier left it to me in his will."

"Did he? That's very generous."

"He appreciated my loyalty, staying on after Mr. Fortune died."

She nodded. "I'm sure. Makes me wonder, though . . . why *did* you stay on? From what I understand, you and Bill Collier couldn't stand each other. He wasn't a very pleasant employer, was he? He belittled you on a regular basis. Insulted you. Yet you stuck around."

His eyes narrowed. "Not that it's any of your business, but I needed the job."

"Even after he accused you of attempting to steal his wife's antique Georgian choker?"

Finch flung the chamois aside. "I didn't steal that blasted choker," he growled.

She took an involuntary step back. Fury suffused his face and darkened his gray eyes to black, and just for a moment, her resolve faltered. But she refused to back down. "One of the maids overheard you and Mr. Collier. He said you stole it."

"One of the maids?" He snorted. "All those girls do is gossip and make up lies to entertain themselves, as if they don't have enough work to keep them busy. Useless, all of them." He bent down to retrieve the polishing cloth. "One of the stones was loose, an aquamarine. Mrs. Collier asked me to take the choker to the jeweler's, get it repaired."

"And did you?"

"That was my intention, yes. I went in the morning room to retrieve it from the desk where Mrs. C. said she'd left it. Collier walked in just as I picked the damned thing up and accused me of stealing. I was only doing what his wife asked, and I told him as much, but he wouldn't hear it. He threatened to call the police."

"When did this take place?"

"I don't remember what day it was," he said testily. "A week or so ago, I suppose."

"The day before Mr. Collier was murdered?"

"Yes. Yes, I suppose it was." He paled. "Wait a minute. You're not suggesting . . . You can't honestly think *I* murdered him?"

"You had an excellent motive."

"I won't deny that the thought of throttling my employer crossed my mind on more than one occasion." He fixed her with a steely glare. "But I didn't murder William Collier. And I didn't steal that choker. Ask Mrs. Collier if you don't believe me." His phone rang. "Yes, Bertie, what is it?" he snapped.

He listened for a moment, scowled, and put the phone away. "Now, if you'll excuse me, I'm needed at the house."

She watched him go, his legs eating up the distance with angry strides. Perhaps she'd misjudged him. She fully intended to check his story. In fact, she'd compare notes with Charlene just as soon as she returned.

She struck out for the gazebo. Time to find Nick Ross and persuade him to help with the Jane Austen literary festival fundraiser. She hoped he'd be amenable.

Because if he refused to help, the festival would be over before it started.

Twenty-One

When Phaedra returned, filming had wrapped and Nick was nowhere in sight.

As the crew hauled equipment back to the unit lot, the bachelorettes headed back to Marling for lunch in groups, chatting and laughing. Tinsley Prentiss lagged behind the others.

"Any idea where Nick's got to?" Phaedra asked as she fell into step alongside her.

Tinsley barely glanced up. "He went to his trailer."

"That's a beautiful dress." Her gown, of deep green silk, had a square neckline and puffed sleeves that barely covered her shoulders. "I'd love to borrow it sometime."

"You'd have to speak to the wardrobe supervisor." Looking straight ahead, she quickened her pace. Her lips were set in a grim line.

"Tinsley, wait, please." Phaedra laid her hand on the bachelorette's arm. "What's wrong? Are you upset with me?"

"No, I'm not upset with *you*," she retorted, and drew her arm away. "I'm furious with Nick. He's taking this whole Mr. Darcy thing a little too far."

"What do you mean?"

"We were supposed to have our first official date this evening, for the show. A romantic candlelight dinner in the dining room, just the two of us." Her lower lip wobbled. "But he just informed Karolina he's not up to it, and begged off."

Phaedra shrugged. "Perhaps he has a headache."

"The only headache he has," she bit off, "is that mysterious girlfriend of his."

"Girlfriend? Do you mean one of the bachelorettes?"

She brushed away an angry tear. "I don't know who she is, but it's not one of us. He sneaks off at every opportunity to call and text her. He's not even supposed to have a phone! But he's the star," she added with a sniffle, "so he gets away with things none of the rest of us can."

"Maybe he's calling a family member. Or his agent."

Tinsley shook her head. "No, it's a woman. I'm sure of it. I'm convinced he's having an a-affair."

"But . . . what about the show? He signed a contract. From what I understand, he's not allowed to date anyone, other than the bachelorettes, for the duration of filming."

"Oh, officially, he plays by the rules. But he's an actor, Professor, and a very good one. Deception comes second nature to a man like Nick Ross."

"You care for him, don't you?" Phaedra said softly. "Oh, Tinsley . . . you've fallen for him."

"I have," she admitted, tears falling freely now. "I love him. And it hurts, Phaedra. I never knew being in love could hurt so much."

After reassuring Tinsley that everything would work out for the best and advising her to be patient and give the relationship time to unfold, Phaedra left to find Nick Ross's trailer. She crossed the side lawn and headed at a brisk pace for the unit lot.

Mr. Darcy, indeed. Although the fictional Darcy might be socially inhibited and too proud for his own good, he'd never behave in such an ungentlemanly fashion as Mr. Ross. She had half a mind to tell the bachelor exactly what she thought of him.

But.

Phaedra's steps slowed. Like a journalist, she had to consider the facts. Tinsley suspected Nick was seeing another woman on the sly. That didn't make it true. It was possible she'd gotten the wrong end of the stick and Ross had done nothing wrong. After all, Phaedra reminded herself, neither of them knew the actor well, and she'd known Tinsley for only a short time.

And without Nick's cooperation, fundraising for the Jane Austen literary festival would suffer a serious blow. With no autographed photos of the star to raffle, no chance to win a tour of the set with the handsome actor, ticket sales would be paltry, at best.

Be practical. Like it or not, you need Nick Ross to come through. The future of the lit fest depended on his support . . . and her powers of persuasion.

She waved down the location assistant, Judy Friend. "Judy, hi. Is Nick Ross in his trailer?"

"Yes," she replied, glancing at a large motor home on the far edge of the lot. "But he asked specifically not to be disturbed."

"Oh. Well, I suppose it'll have to wait, then."

Judy nodded. "He has dinner with the bachelorettes at the house around six."

"Thanks. Guess I'll speak with him later."

Phaedra eyed Ross's trailer. This might be her only chance to speak with the actor alone. She needed his help to raise enough money for the festival. And one way or another, she'd get it.

Gravel crunched under her feet as she crossed the unit lot to his trailer with purposeful steps. Nothing indicated it belonged to the star, other than its sheer size.

As she drew in a breath and climbed the steps leading up to the door, she reminded herself of Elizabeth Bennet's words. *My courage always rises with every attempt to intimidate me.* She would *not* be intimidated.

She rapped smartly on the door. "Mr. Ross? It's Phaedra Brighton, the historical consultant."

Dead silence, then she heard footsteps approach and stop on the other side of the door. "What is it?"

"I need to ask you a question."

"No interviews. Speak to my agent. She'll set something up."

"I don't want an interview. I just need a quick word. May I come in?"

As the silence lengthened, she feared he wouldn't answer, but after a moment the door swung inward, and Mr. Fitzwilliam Darcy himself stood before her in all his glowering, antisocial glory.

"You have five minutes," he growled, and stood back to gesture her inside. His eyes were as dark as his tousled mop of hair.

She brushed past him, swallowing the urge to bob a curtsy, all too aware of his fitted trousers and boots and the cravat loosened at his neck, and stopped just inside the door.

The trailer was surprisingly roomy. There was nothing of a personal nature in the sitting area or kitchenette to provide even a small clue as to the man who stood before her. A script lay spine-up over the arm of the sofa, and a bottle of kombucha stood on the coffee table.

"I'd like to ask a favor, if I may," she said, steadying her qualms and tipping her chin up as she faced him.

"Of course you would." He sighed and rested one shoulder against the doorjamb. "Everyone does. Go on."

"When I'm not consulting on the show, I teach at Somerset University. I'm a Jane Austen scholar and a professor of nineteenth-century British literature."

Nick inclined his head. "I'm sure Karolina appreciates your expertise. What is it you need from me, exactly?"

"Every year we sponsor an Austen literary festival on the campus. It's popular with students and locals alike. This year our budget's been slashed, and we're struggling to fund the event."

"And you want me to donate money."

"No, although donations are always welcome. I wonder if you'd consider autographing a few photos of yourself—as Mr. Darcy, of course—that we could raffle off to ticket holders." She paused. "And perhaps you'd put in an appearance at the festival and select a winner in a separate drawing for a tour of the set. With yourself as a personal guide."

His dark brows drew together.

She expected him to dismiss her request out of hand, to tell her politely but firmly that he was too busy and the answer was no.

"I see no reason why I can't do any of those things. Depending on my filming schedule, of course. I'll discuss it with my agent, and she'll arrange things with Karolina. And I'd be happy to make a donation as well."

Relief swept over her. "That's very generous! Thank you, so much."

He straightened. "You're welcome. Now, if you'll excuse me . . ." He glanced pointedly at the script.

"Of course," she said. "I've taken up enough of your time. Thank you again."

"A pleasure."

He sketched a polite bow, waited as she brushed past him once again, and shut the door after her.

Pleased with achieving her mission, Phaedra paused at the top of the steps to release a breath of relief. Marisol would be thrilled. With Nick Ross as a draw, raffle tickets would sell out in record time. The Jane Austen literary festival was officially back on track.

As she descended the stairs, she heard Nick's voice from the other side of the trailer door.

"—can't be a next time. Don't you understand? We nearly got caught. I can't risk it. I have far too much at stake."

Phaedra didn't move. Was Ross talking to his mystery girlfriend, the woman Tinsley claimed he was seeing on the sly? It certainly sounded that way.

"I know, love," he went on, his voice imbued with regret,

"and I'm sorry. That bloody reporter . . . no, I don't like it any more than you do. But it can't be helped. Perhaps if we put our heads together, we can figure out another way . . ."

He moved away from the door, his voice fading. Phaedra, afraid he'd glance out the window and see her, scooted down the steps and hurried across the gravel.

Perhaps Tinsley was right. Maybe Ross did have a secret girlfriend on the side.

Who was the mystery woman? She must be quite special if he was willing to put his *Who Wants to Marry Mr. Darcy?* contract, and possibly his career, at risk.

When she arrived back at Marling, Charlene hadn't returned and Detective Morelli was gone. Concerned for her friend, and wondering where she was, Phaedra pulled out her phone and called Charlene. The call went straight to voice mail.

"Phaedra here," she said after a lengthy beep. Charlene must have a lot of messages. "Is everything okay? I'm leaving Marling, and I need to talk to you. Give me a call when you can. Thanks."

With nothing more to do, she returned to her car, slid behind the wheel, and drove home.

At nine o'clock that evening, Phaedra flipped the "Open" sign on the Poison Pen's door to "Closed."

"If you leave before we return," her father said as he came downstairs in a suit and tie, "lock up. Your mother and I have dinner reservations at Orsini's."

"I've heard great things about that place. You're looking very handsome, by the way." She pecked him affectionately on the cheek. "Our meeting should be over before you get back. But I'll stick around until you do."

Nan Brighton sailed down the stairs in a sleeveless jade green dress and heels, a silk pashmina draped over her shoulders. "Have fun at your meeting, darling. And please—"

"I'll wash up and put everything away when we're done. We have a lot to discuss tonight."

"I'm sure you do," she conceded. "Now that there's been an actual murder in Laurel Springs."

"Any progress in finding the killer?" Malcolm asked.

"Not as far as I know," Phaedra said. "Not that Detective Morelli ever tells me anything."

"Matt Morelli?" Surprise widened her father's eyes. "He's the officer assigned to the case?"

"Yes. Why? Do you know him?"

"He came out to investigate when someone broke into the bookstore last month and stole those first editions. You remember."

She did. "Were they recovered?"

"Sadly, no. The case is still open. Morelli was very thorough. Good man."

That, Phaedra thought, was subject to debate.

"He's certainly attractive," Nan remarked. "Perhaps I'll invite him over for Sunday dinner. You, too, Phaedra. I'll do a roast and all the trimmings."

"Stop it, Mother."

"Stop what? I can't invite a perfectly nice young man to join us for Sunday dinner?"

"Time to go, Nan," Malcolm said, and glanced at his watch. "We don't want to lose our reservation."

"Have fun, you two," Phaedra called after them as her father opened the door and ushered her mother onto the porch. "Don't do anything I wouldn't do."

He winked. "I promise I'll have her home by eleven."

"See that you do." She waved goodbye and closed the door, locking it behind her. After switching on the outside lights, she made her way upstairs.

Time to get ready for a much-needed reconvening of the Jane Austen Tea Society.

In the kitchen, Phaedra fixed a pot of Darjeeling, steeping the leaves in a Blue Willow pot, and arranged a plate with a few of her mother's lemon poppy seed cookies and another with brownies. She took down cups and saucers, spoons and napkins, and set out the creamer and sugar bowl.

She'd just arranged everything on a tray when her phone rang. A smile lit her face. "Hannah! How's everything? How's Charles?"

"Fine. We're driving out to Middleburg tomorrow."

"Yes, I remember. And afterward?"

"Dinner at the Red Fox Inn."

"Nice. The man has excellent taste."

"Oh, Phae . . . I like him. A lot. He's so thoughtful and sweet." She sighed. "He has two tickets to see a famous Shakespearean actor, Tyrell something, at Ford's Theatre."

"Tyrell Blackmoore." Phaedra added a few more brownies to the plate. "I didn't know Charles liked Shakespeare."

"He doesn't. Someone at the embassy gave him the tickets. They're hard to come by, and Charles was too polite to turn them down. Do you know anyone who might want them?"

She thought, briefly, of Mark Selden. "Possibly." The doorbell rang downstairs. "Listen, Lu and Mari are at the door. I have to run."

"Okay. I'll call Sunday, let you know how it went."

"Great. Talk then. Bye."

She carried the tray downstairs and set it on the hall table as the doorbell rang again. "Coming."

"You certainly took your time," Lucy complained as Phaedra opened the door. She shrugged off her sweater and hung it on the hall tree. "We've been standing out here for five minutes."

"You're exaggerating," Marisol pointed out. "It was four minutes."

"Sorry," Phaedra apologized. "Hannah called, and I was getting everything ready for our meeting. Come on back."

She took the tray and led them down the hall to the reading room in the back of the bookstore and lowered it onto a table that ran the length of the room. Formerly a library table in her father's law office, it was perfect for researching, reading, lingering over a cup of coffee with the newspapers . . . or comparing notes with her friends.

Her parents had converted the glassed-in sunporch to

year-round use with the addition of heat and air-conditioning. Customers used it during business hours, while the family enjoyed it on Sundays, when the bookstore was closed. Darkness pressed against the windows.

Marisol went straight to the tea tray. "What goodies do you have for us tonight, Phaedra?"

"A fresh pot of Darjeeling, lemon poppy seed cookies, and brownies."

"Did you make the cookies? Or the brownies?" Marisol asked doubtfully.

"Neither. They're Mom's contribution. The only thing I made was tea, so help yourselves with impunity."

"Thanks." Lucy filled a cup with the fragrant hot tea. "Although I'd prefer copious amounts of wine."

"Another lackluster date?" Phaedra teased.

"At this point, I'd settle for lackluster. No date, and no prospect of one in the foreseeable future."

They settled at one end of the table with cups, saucers, and plates. "So what's on the agenda tonight?" Marisol asked as she bit into a cookie. "We finished *A Vindication of the Rights of Woman* last week. Interesting, but not much fun. What's next?"

"Something a little different," Phaedra answered. "Dad gave me a few classic cozy mysteries recently."

"Oh, I adore cozy mysteries." Marisol beamed.

Lucy raised her brow. "You adore everything."

"At least I'm not a literary snob. I didn't like *Vindication*, so what?"

"It's a groundbreaking treatise on feminism and the rights of women."

"It is. It's also *boring*."

"I have a suggestion," Phaedra said. Lucy and Mari often clashed over books, but tonight she wanted to stay on topic. "Instead of reading classic literature, why don't we mix it up a little, read *The Murder at the Vicarage* by Agatha Christie?"

"Sounds like more fun than Wollstonecraft," Marisol agreed. "That's the first Miss Marple book, isn't it?"

Phaedra nodded. "She inspired every female amateur sleuth from Tuppence Beresford to Jessica Fletcher."

"Okay," Lucy grudgingly agreed. "But I get to choose the next book."

"Deal."

"So what are we discussing tonight?" Marisol took another bite of her cookie.

"A real crime," Phaedra answered, "right here in Laurel Springs."

Lucy leaned forward, intrigued. "You mean William Collier's murder?"

"Yes. I thought we'd discuss suspects and share any theories we come up with. But before we start, I have good news of an unrelated nature. I talked to Nick Ross today about the Austen lit festival fundraiser."

"You actually talked to him?" Marisol's eyes, round as the Blue Willow saucer at her elbow, fastened on Phaedra.

"I did. He couldn't have been more accommodating. He agreed to sign a few photos of himself in character as Mr. Darcy, and he'll give a tour of the set to the raffle winner. Provided his filming schedule permits and Karolina allows it."

"That's great. It really is." Lucy set her cup down and touched a napkin to her lips. "Now, just for tonight . . . let's talk murder."

Twenty-Two

Phaedra rolled the flip-top blackboard to one end of the table and picked up a piece of chalk.

"Okay," she said as she finished writing a list of names, "let's start with possible suspects. Least likely to most likely." She read each name on the list out loud, tapping each one with her finger.

"Nick Ross. Dorothy Fortune. Tinsley Prentiss. Violet Lucas. Jasper Finch. And lastly, although I don't think she did it, Charlene. All of them had reason to kill Mr. Collier."

"Why is Charlene on the list?" Lucy asked. "If you think she didn't do it."

"I'm ninety-nine percent sure she didn't. But she left the drawing room for fifteen minutes when the power went out, to look for candles and check on her mother."

Marisol frowned. "You don't seriously think she snuck upstairs and tossed a blow-dryer in her husband's bath. Do you?"

"It's possible, but unlikely. Charlene wouldn't kill anyone, especially not in such a cold-blooded manner. And the blow-dryer wasn't hers. She'd never seen it before."

Phaedra didn't add that the pathologist believed the cause of death was injection by an unknown substance. She couldn't share what she wasn't supposed to know.

Guilt flickered through her. Eavesdropping on Detective Morelli's conversation with Dr. Kessler wasn't her finest moment. He'd hit the roof if he knew. But she'd gleaned valuable information . . . information the detective never would have shared with her otherwise.

She pointed to the first name on the list. "Nick was in the drawing room the afternoon of the murder. He and Collier had never met. But they exchanged words when Nick came to Charlene's defense."

"What happened?" Marisol asked.

Phaedra recapped the confrontation between the two men and added, "I doubt Nick slipped off to kill his host. He wouldn't risk it, not for someone he'd just met. And he only left the room for a few minutes.

"Next up," she went on, "Dorothy Fortune. She lost everything to Collier when her husband died. Her money, her home. And her daughters lost their chance at television fame and fortune."

"Isn't she the most likely suspect?" Marisol asked. "Mrs. Fortune has the strongest motive of anyone."

"True. But she wasn't in the house at the time of the murder," Phaedra pointed out. "At least, not that I know of. She couldn't kill Collier if she wasn't there. She and Nick stay at the top of the list as least likely suspects."

"What about Tinsley Prentiss?" Lucy asked as Phaedra touched the name under Dorothy's.

"She's one of the bachelorettes. Charlene allowed her to wear the choker for a scene. But a storm blew in and chased everyone into the drawing room. When Mr. Collier saw Tinsley wearing it, he was furious."

"Why?" Lucy asked.

"It was his wedding gift to Charlene. He told her, in front of everyone, that she had no right to loan it out, how dare she, et cetera, until he reduced her to tears."

"What a jerk!" Marisol made no secret of her disgust. "Why did she marry someone like that?"

"Money? Desperation? Or just poor judgment." Lucy shrugged. "Take your pick. But it sounds like he was angry with Charlene, not Tinsley."

"He was." Phaedra took a sip of her tea. "But he went on to humiliate Tinsley when he insinuated she intended to steal the choker."

"Was this before or after the choker was stolen?" Lucy asked.

"Before."

"Interesting. Is it possible he knew something we didn't? Maybe Tinsley had an accomplice. Or maybe she really did steal it."

"It's possible, I suppose. At any rate, she was angry at Bill for embarrassing her in front of the crew and the other bachelorettes."

"Angry enough to kill?" Marisol ventured.

"Maybe? But again, she never left the drawing room." Phaedra put a question mark beside her name. Although she didn't say it, Tinsley's background in medicine meant she knew the properties of insulin and how to administer shots.

The measured click of toenails coming toward them down the hardwood hall heralded the arrival of Fitz, Nan's pug. He stood in the doorway to the reading room and regarded them with doleful eyes.

"Hey, Fitzie," Marisol called out. She reached for her plate. "Would you like a cookie?"

Normally more than willing to accept a treat and a scratch behind the ears, he didn't move and didn't wag his tail. Instead, he stared fixedly at the windows enclosing three sides of the former sunroom. A low growl emanated from his throat.

"What's wrong, boy?" Phaedra followed his gaze to the leftmost window, where an overgrown rhododendron bush all but obscured the lower half of the glass. Their own ghostly reflections, three women grouped around a table littered with cups, plates, and notepads, looked back at them. "There's nothing there."

His fur bristled, and he growled again, louder and more insistently this time.

"He sees something," Lucy said.

Marisol met Phaedra's eyes. "Maybe someone's in the yard next door. A neighbor taking out the trash, or something."

"He knows the neighbors. And trash pickup isn't until Tuesday." She turned back to the dog. "Come on, Fitz. Let's turn on the back lights."

She'd barely rounded the table when the dog erupted into a frenzy of barking and bolted past her into the room. He hurled himself at the far left window, barking and snarling, toenails scrabbling as he struggled for purchase on the narrow windowsill.

"There's definitely something out there," Lucy said, pushing her chair back. She crossed to the window and pressed her face against the glass.

"Do you see anything?" Marisol asked uncertainly.

"No. It's too dark."

"I'll turn on the porch light," Phaedra said. "Be right back."

She hurried down the hall into the entrance foyer, Fitz panting at her heels, and flipped the switch for the backyard lights, then cautiously edged the front door open. The yard, the street, the front porch . . . all was quiet and still.

Fitz darted past her and squeezed out the door.

"Fitz!" she cried, and dived after him. "Bad dog! Come back here!"

But the pug had other ideas. He made a beeline for the side yard, racing around the corner of the house with his short legs flying, until he stopped at the gate that enclosed the backyard. It hung open.

After a quick, thorough sniff, he plunged through the gap and headed for the exterior of the sunporch with Phaedra close behind him.

Her heart flailed in her chest as she rounded the corner. *I should've grabbed an umbrella from the stand*, she thought wildly, *or a fallen branch*. One never had a weapon to hand when one needed it . . .

A bloodcurdling screech followed by a yowl of outrage pierced the night as something black streaked across the grass and leaped over the back fence, Fitz in hot pursuit.

Twenty-Three

"What happened?" Marisol cried as she and Lucy hurtled around the corner. "Are you okay?"

"It was a cat," Phaedra said, her breath coming in ragged spurts. "Feral. Fitz . . . went after him."

"'This is a cat,'" Lucy intoned in the manner of an emergency broadcast announcer. "'This is only a cat. Had there been a real intruder, you would have been instructed to scream and chase the intruder into the backyard . . .'"

She began, helplessly, to laugh, and the others joined in until they were clutching one another and gasping for breath.

"The front door's wide open." Phaedra's mirth fled at the thought. "You guys go back in. I have to get Fitz."

"Sure, send us inside to get murdered by whoever was out here." Lucy turned back. "Come on, Mari."

As they left, Phaedra called to the pug until he trotted obediently back, and she knelt down to rub his head. "Good boy. Let's go inside and get you a treat. You've earned it."

Ten minutes later, with order restored and Fitz devouring a savory cheddar biscuit from Woofgang's, Phaedra led them back into the reading room and they resumed their seats. "Okay. Where were we?"

"The next suspect," Marisol said. "Violet Lucas."

"She's Charlene's mother, right?" Lucy asked. "The sweet old lady in the wheelchair?"

"Yes. She's another long shot, but she was in her room upstairs when the murder took place. And she told me herself that she couldn't stand Mr. Collier. She said he was a bully who made Charlene's life a living hell."

"So she has motive," Lucy said.

"Yes. She also said the power stayed on in her room." Phaedra scribbled a note at the bottom of the board.

"I thought the storm knocked it out," Marisol said.

"It did, eventually," Phaedra told her. "When the tree fell on the roof."

"But the power had to be on when Collier was electrocuted," Lucy pointed out.

"Yes. It was out downstairs when he left the drawing room. But he was found in the east wing, and the wiring is different there. As for the rest of the house . . . Detective Morelli believes someone deliberately cut the power to the first floor just before the choker was stolen."

"Probably the thief," Lucy agreed. "And whoever did it knew exactly where the circuit box was."

"Good point. That rules out the cast and crew." Phaedra tapped the fourth name. "Which brings us to Jasper Finch. He's the Fortunes' former butler, now employed by Charlene Collier."

"Why is he a suspect?" Marisol asked.

"He was in the drawing room on the afternoon of the murder."

"Along with some of the crew, the caterers, Nick, and all of the bachelorettes," Lucy pointed out.

"None of them had a motive to kill Mr. Collier. But his butler did." She crossed her arms and began to prowl the room. "Collier accused Finch of stealing the choker the day before the murder. He threatened to call the police, but Finch swore he took it on Charlene's orders, to have a loose stone repaired."

"That's easily confirmed," Lucy said. "All you have to do is ask Charlene if it's true."

"I tried to ask her today, but she wasn't home. I left a message." Phaedra returned to the blackboard. "Finch ran Collier's bath that evening, so he was probably the last person to see his employer alive."

"Other than the murderer," Lucy pointed out. "Unless Finch tossed that blow-dryer in the tub."

"Collier treated Finch pretty badly, which made me question why he stayed on after Harold died. So today, I asked him. He said he needed the job. Which is reasonable. Until I found out he owns a Bentley."

"Pretty expensive wheels for a butler," Marisol said.

"Exactly. He claims Collier left it to him in his will, but he's been driving it for quite some time."

"Maybe he doubles as a chauffeur."

"He drives Charlene occasionally," Phaedra confirmed. "I can check with her on that. I'm thinking—"

"Blackmail." Lucy leaned back in her chair. "Finch stayed on because he had something on Collier."

"My thoughts exactly. As to the choker, I recently received a tip that someone else has it," Phaedra said. "The only problem is, the source is somewhat unreliable."

"What source is that?" Lucy asked.

"Clark Mullinax of the Laurel Springs *Clarion*."

Eye rolls followed on the heels of her answer. "What did he say?" Mari questioned. "And who is he pointing his finger at? Does he have enough facts to publish a story?"

"Not really," Phaedra admitted. "Which is why I doubt he's telling the truth. He claims Patsy Fortune tried to sell the choker in a Charlottesville pawnshop."

Lucy folded her arms under her chest and eyed Phaedra with skepticism. "And he knows this how? Did he see her?"

"He says his source did. But he won't tell me who the source is."

"Why would Patsy get mixed up in something like that?"

Marisol asked, her brow puckered in puzzlement. "She has . . . well, had, gobs of money, and she's pretty well known around here. I can't believe she'd steal a choker, and I really can't believe she'd try to sell it in a pawnshop."

"I agree," Phaedra said. "I think it unlikely she'd do something so reckless. Patsy strikes me as pretty savvy. When I asked her about Clark's accusation, she denied it. She says it's his attempt to coerce her into having dinner with him. If she refuses, he'll run the story."

"That sounds exactly like Clark." Marisol shook her head. "He's hit on me before. He's irritating, and persistent. But basically harmless."

"If you call blackmail harmless," Phaedra said.

"I think we should leave Patsy off the list for now," Marisol said.

"But what if she's lying?" Lucy pointed out. "Maybe she didn't take the choker to a pawnshop, but maybe she *did* steal it. The Fortunes aren't exactly swimming in money right now."

"True," Phaedra agreed. "But she wasn't in the house that afternoon, so it's unlikely she took it. Doesn't mean she didn't have an accomplice, though." Phaedra put Patsy's name at the end of the list with a question mark after it.

"There's one more name you might want to add to the list," Marisol said. "Bertie Walsh."

Phaedra regarded her in surprise. "Bertie, the head caterer? Why?"

She finished her cookie and patted her mouth with a napkin. "I stopped by the café for lunch today. It was the Friday special, the Pastrami Plate." She smiled dreamily. "Pastrami on rye with Thousand Island dressing, piled with sauerkraut, and a big garlic dill pickle on the side—"

"How do you stay so skinny?" Lucy interrupted. "You eat like a dockworker."

"It's called working out."

"Okay, you two, we're getting off track." Phaedra tapped Bertie's name. "Back to our suspect."

"Sorry." Marisol pushed her plate aside. "I don't know if anyone's noticed, but there's a 'For Lease' sign in the café window."

Phaedra nodded. "It's been there for a while. I heard the building's under new ownership."

"I heard the same. I was curious, so I asked the waitress. She said ownership changed hands recently, and the new owner refused to honor Bertie's lease." She paused. "She has to vacate the premises by the end of next month."

"That sucks," Lucy said. "If she can't find another property to lease, she's out of business and out of luck. Even so, I fail to see a connection. How does losing her lease make Bertie a murder suspect?"

"Because," Marisol said, leaning forward and resting her elbows on the table's edge, "the new owner, who refused to honor her lease? William Collier."

After a brief silence, they all began talking at once.

"That definitely gives Bertie a motive." Phaedra scrawled the woman's name on the board. "Not only did she face losing her business location, she had to go to work for the man who took it away from her. Bill Collier."

"If that's not a motive for murder," Lucy said as she pushed her chair back and stood, "I don't know what is."

Twenty-Four

Phaedra rinsed the last plate and set it in the dish rack when she heard the key in the front door.

"We're back," her father called up.

"In the kitchen." Phaedra took down cups from the cupboard and reached for the kettle of hot water. "Can I interest either of you in a cup of tea before bed?" she asked as her parents appeared in the doorway.

"None for me, thanks," Malcolm said. "I ate far too much. It was an excellent meal."

"I'll have a cup." Her mother sat at the table and eased off her heels. "I've wanted to do that all evening."

"How was your meeting?" Malcolm asked Phaedra. "Did you figure out who the murderer is?"

"No. But we came up with a suspect list and a few theories." She set a cup of chamomile tea in front of her mother. "Cookies? There are a few left."

Nan shook her head. "I couldn't possibly. Your father insisted we share dessert afterward."

"None for me, either." He patted his stomach. "I'll take Fitz out for a walk before I turn in."

"I'll take him," Phaedra offered. "You look tired." She

didn't mention Fitz's pursuit of the backyard intruder who'd turned out to be a feral cat.

"It's dark out there, pumpkin. I'll do it."

"I'll just take him around the corner to the church and back."

She took the dog's leash down from a peg by the door and called out, "Who wants to go for a walk?"

Fitz barked from his dog bed down the hall and trotted into the kitchen.

"It's chilly," Nan said as Phaedra clipped the leash onto the pug's collar. "Grab a sweater from the hall tree."

"Will do. Come on, Fitzie. Let's go."

He waddled down the stairs after her, curly tail wagging in anticipation, and waited impatiently while Phaedra shrugged one arm, then the other into a dark blue sweater she found.

She opened the door and followed Fitz across the porch and down the front steps, casting a wary glance around her. All was quiet. Releasing a breath she hadn't realized she'd held, Phaedra turned left onto the sidewalk and let Fitz lead the way. It was Friday night, and Main Street teemed with passing cars and foot traffic as couples who'd just finished dinner or closed their tab at Harper's Pub spilled out onto the sidewalks for a late-evening stroll.

Phaedra and Fitz rounded the corner onto Church Street, and the traffic and noise fell farther behind. Rows of houses, most dark and fronted with parked cars, came to a stop at the end of the street, where the tall white spire of Grace Episcopal Church rose into the sky. Elms and sycamores cast the yards into deep shadow.

She thought of Charlene, who faced her husband's funeral in two days' time. No matter how awful William Collier was, his wife believed there was good in him. Whether he'd truly changed or merely hoodwinked his bride into believing he'd changed didn't matter.

He didn't deserve to die. Murder was such a horrible, senseless crime.

"Come on, Fitz," Phaedra urged as they neared the end of the street. "Do your thing. It's chilly out here."

Streetlights illuminated the darkness at regular intervals behind them as they reached the entrance to the church lot, and she stumbled over a weedy fissure in the sidewalk.

As Fitz nosed around the church's sign and sniffed at the azaleas planted around it, her cell phone rang. Gripping the leash with one hand, she reached in her pocket and glanced at the screen.

"Charlene! Where were you? I left a message earlier. Hours ago."

"Sorry I didn't call back sooner, but I'm worried sick. And I don't know what to do." Her voice broke.

"Calm down. Tell me what's upset you. What's going on?"

"It's my mother. I'm . . . oh, Phaedra, I'm afraid she may have murdered Bill."

For a moment Phaedra was too stunned to respond. "What on earth makes you say that?"

"That detective came to see me today. I wasn't home, but he left and came back. Finch said he waited for me all afternoon."

"Morelli." She remembered speaking to him at Marling, seeing a folder in his hand, and suddenly she knew what it had contained. "What did he say?"

"The toxicology report came back. There's no doubt, no doubt at all. Bill didn't die of electrocution. He died of an insulin overdose."

No wonder she hadn't called sooner. "What makes you think your mother did it?"

"Because she hated him."

Phaedra let out a shaky laugh. "Lots of people hate other people. It doesn't mean they act on it—"

"No, you don't understand. He ruined her life. Both our lives."

"What? How?"

"My mother lost her life savings to him, years ago. When he was a televangelist. She never missed his program, and once she got taken in by his so-called ministry, she sent him every penny she had. She truly believed his prayers would make her walk again."

"Oh no."

"Of course, nothing of the kind happened. He conned her, just like he did so many others. She lost our cottage, and we moved into an apartment. Every day she struggled to make ends meet. The cost of insulin kept going up. She had to have it. As soon as I could, I went to work. I took every shift I could get." Bitterness crept into her voice. "That's why I never went to college. We needed every penny to pay for her medication."

"I had no idea. I'm so sorry." She paused. "Charlene, tell me something. Why did you marry that man? After all he did to you and your mother? Why?"

"He wanted to atone for his past mistakes. He knew he'd wronged my mother, wronged me. He begged me to let him make things right. I really do believe he meant it." She paused. "I was tired of being alone, tired of working double shifts and never having a moment to call my own. I wanted a home, Phaedra, a real home of my own. And Bill offered me that."

"What does Morelli say?"

"He doesn't have enough evidence for an arrest yet. But he suspects me, Phaedra. I know he does. The syringe the police found in the vase was one of my mother's. If my fingerprints were on it, I'd be in jail right now."

"Until that time comes, try not to worry," Phaedra said. "Leave everything to me. I'll get to the bottom of all this, I promise."

Charlene hitched in a breath. "Thanks, Phae."

"Just hang in there, okay? I'll see you soon."

She ended the call and dropped the phone back in her pocket. "Come on, Fitz. Time to head home."

But the pug was buried up to his nose in one of the azalea bushes and wouldn't budge. Growls rolled out of his throat.

"Come *on*." Phaedra gave the leash a gentle tug, but Fitz hunkered down and dug his paws in. Whatever he'd found in that bush, he wasn't about to give it up. "Fitz, enough! Let's go. Now."

Something rustled in the bushes. Fitz dived on it and yelped as a black shape erupted from the azaleas with an inhuman shriek. A cat, she realized with a start. Probably the same feral cat Fitz chased from her parents' backyard.

With a bark, he charged after the cat and nearly tugged Phaedra's arm out of its socket. "Fitz, stop!" she shouted. Determined to give chase, he ignored her and barreled ahead. She barely kept a grip on the leash.

As the dog abandoned the sidewalk and dragged her toward the street, a car parked along the curb switched its headlights on, momentarily blinding her. The sound of an engine filled her ears, and she looked up.

She glimpsed a white hood and a large grill, gleaming momentarily under the streetlight as the driver gunned the engine . . .

. . . and hurtled straight toward her.

Acting purely on instinct, she snatched Fitz and spun on her heel. *Run*, her brain screamed as she raced to the sidewalk, eyed the thick privet hedge, and dived over it.

She hit the grass hard, barely aware of the explosion of pain in her arm in her frenzy to escape the oncoming car. Fitz whimpered and squirmed in her arms.

"It's okay," she gasped. "It's okay." Trembling, she clutched the dog tightly against her chest. Tiny branches scratched her face and raked her sweater. The throaty rumble of the engine grew louder.

She hunched into a ball and waited, her breath coming in short, labored gasps. The roar of the motor filled her ears. She heard a shout, and the vehicle suddenly veered away, narrowly missing them as it brushed the hedge, sending a shower of leaves down before it careened around the corner with a squeal of tires and vanished down Baxter Street.

Phaedra sat up, dazed. Maybe the driver was drunk. After all, Harper's Pub was practically across the street. But even as the thought occurred she dismissed it.

Whoever was behind that wheel had tried to run her down. Deliberately. And they'd nearly succeeded.

Shaken, she set Fitz down and scrambled to her feet in time to see taillights rapidly vanishing into the night. She didn't get a license number. And she couldn't be sure . . . but she thought she recognized the car.

It looked suspiciously like a white Bentley.

Twenty-Five

Phaedra leaned over, dragging in breaths as she tried and failed to gather her thoughts and calm her racing heart. "Good boy," she gasped as her arms went around the pug. "Good Fitzie."

Feet pounded toward her from the corner of Main, and another shout rang out. "I saw that car come at you. You all right?"

She couldn't answer. She couldn't breathe, couldn't think or form the words to reply. She straightened, pushing the hair out of her face, and met the man's concerned gaze.

He wore jeans, a lightweight sweater pushed up to his elbows. And his eyes were brown.

Espresso brown.

"Are you injured?" He hadn't recognized her, probably because his attention was focused on his phone as he thumbed the screen. "Did that car hit you?"

"Morelli?" she croaked. Was he really standing there, or was she imagining it? "What . . . what are you doing here?"

For the first time, he looked up. "Professor Brighton?" Confusion skimmed his face. "What . . . I could ask you the same thing."

"I was walking Fitz when we nearly got run over." She shifted from one foot to the other and winced. "Your turn."

"I met up with a couple friends at Harper's." He indicated the pub on the other side of Main Street. "When I left, I heard tires squealing, and I looked up just in time to see a white vehicle fishtailing around the corner."

"Did you manage to get a tag number?"

"A partial. The vehicle had already turned."

He pressed the phone to his ear. "I'm calling an ambulance."

"No." Her voice was unsteady but firm. "Please don't do that. I'm okay."

"You need to get checked out. You're banged up. You were almost hit by a car."

"I'm fine," she insisted. "Just a few scratches and a bruise or two. No concussion, no broken bones." A wave of dizziness swept over her, and she reached out instinctively to steady herself on his arm.

"You're not okay." He tucked her free hand firmly into the crook of his arm. "You're shaking like a leaf, and I'm walking you back home. No arguments."

"'Shaking like a leaf'? Is that the best you can do?" she mumbled.

"Sorry, Professor Brighton, but a cliché is the best I can come up with right now."

She managed a smile. "I'll overlook it this once. But only if you call me Phaedra."

"Phaedra it is." He glanced down at Fitz. "Cute dog. Yours?"

"My mother's. My parents live down the street." She gave the pug's leash a gentle tug. "Come on, Fitz. Our adventure is over. Let's get you home."

"What, no argument?" Morelli asked. "No telling me you're a big girl and you can take care of yourself?"

"I am, and I can. But right now?" A tremor rippled through her. "I appreciate the company."

They began walking, Fitz trotting alongside them. The

detective's arm was warm and solid under the curve of her fingers.

"You want to tell me what happened?" he asked as they rounded the corner and turned onto Main Street.

"Someone raced toward me in a car, sideswiped the bushes about two seconds after I jumped over, and came way too close to running me down."

"Any idea who? Was it a man, or a woman? Did you get a license number? Make, model?"

She shook her head. "It happened too fast. It was a white sedan; that's all I can say with certainty. I couldn't see the driver; the headlights shone in my eyes." That much, at least, was true. She didn't add that she was ninety-nine percent certain the car was a Bentley.

Bentleys were unheard of in Laurel Springs. College students, retirees, and families drove minivans and economy cars, maybe a pickup truck or an SUV. No one could afford a car that cost more than the average person made in a year.

Except for Jasper Finch. He'd told her himself that William Collier left him the car in his will. Which meant there was a good chance he'd been behind the wheel.

She frowned. Her earlier suggestion, that Collier's accusation of theft gave Finch a motive for murder, had enraged him. He'd taken a threatening step toward her. For a moment, real fear had seized her.

Was he angry enough to try and run her over?

"Thoughts?" Morelli asked. "Any ideas who might do something like that?"

"None," she replied. "Like I said, I couldn't see the driver. It could've been anyone."

"In my experience, a person doesn't attempt to run another person down for no reason."

She was silent.

He stopped and turned to face her. "You've been poking around, haven't you? Asking questions. Rattling cages. Putting yourself in danger."

"I've been at my parents' all evening," she retorted,

"drinking tea and talking with my friends." Her eyes widened. Fitz! He'd barked and lunged at the window, then raced outside and hurtled through the side gate, the *opened* side gate, to chase a cat from the backyard.

They'd assumed the intruder was nothing more than a feral cat.

But what if they were wrong? What if the intruder, a *human* intruder, had crouched in those rhododendron bushes to spy on them?

What if tonight's meeting of the Jane Austen Tea Society *had* rattled someone's cage?

"What is it?" His voice sharpened. "Talk to me."

"It's nothing. Probably nothing," she amended. She told him about Fitz, and the cat he'd chased in the backyard, but left out the details of her meeting with Lucy and Marisol. Discussing *The Murder at the Vicarage* was one thing; collectively theorizing about William Collier's murder case was quite another. "I wonder . . . Maybe someone was hiding in those bushes."

"Who? And why would anyone eavesdrop on a bunch of women having a tea party?"

She felt a headache beginning. "There are so many things wrong with that statement, I don't even know where to begin." Relief washed over her as they reached her parents' house and headed up the sidewalk to the porch. "Thanks," she said curtly. "You can go now."

"I'm not going anywhere until I get some answers."

"What answers? I've told you everything I know."

"I need to report this, Phaedra." His eyes, so dark and intense, searched hers as he drew closer. "Don't you get it? Someone tried to kill you tonight."

She opened her mouth to protest, to deny what he said, but she couldn't. He was right. Instead, she said, "You didn't have to walk me back."

"I know I didn't." He cocked an eyebrow as if he expected her to object. "I wanted to. Is that a problem?"

"No. I'm glad you did." She turned away self-consciously

and opened the door. "Why don't you come in? You can interrogate me over a cup of tea."

The house was quiet. The only light was a lamp left on in the hall table.

"No interrogation. And I'm not a tea kind of guy. But I wouldn't say no to a coffee."

Phaedra preceded him up the staircase to the second floor and led the way into the kitchen. "My folks must've gone to bed." She unclipped Fitz's leash and returned it to the peg by the door. As he padded off to his doggy bed down the hall, she began making a pot of coffee.

"This is the second time," Morelli remarked.

"The second time what?"

"The second time I've seen you out of that Regency getup you usually wear." His gaze cut to her jean-clad legs. "I approve."

"My 'Regency getup,' as you so inelegantly call it, is a teaching tool. It brings Jane Austen's world alive in a way that lectures can't." She emptied water into the coffee maker. "And my students enjoy it."

He slid onto one of the breakfast bar stools. "You sound like a very devoted professor."

"I try. Are you a devoted cop?"

"I try." He watched as she filled the basket with ground coffee.

"Was your dad a cop, too?"

Morelli shook his head. "Second-generation Italian restaurant owner. We had a pizza place in Chicago. South Side. I worked the counter every weekend and every summer. One Friday night, a couple of gang members came in, hopped up on something. My little brother Leo mouthed off to one of them."

Phaedra's finger went still on the brew button. "What happened?"

"They shot him. He hung on for a couple days, but he didn't make it. The shooter was underage, like Leo, and got off on a technicality." He met her gaze. "So I decided to become a cop."

She pressed the button to start the coffee maker, and the scent of fresh-ground Guatemalan filled the kitchen. "I'm sorry." The words were woefully inadequate. Deciding a change of subject was in order, she said, "I understand you know my father. He speaks highly of you."

He lifted an eyebrow. "I'm surprised he remembers me."

"He said you responded when the bookstore was burglarized. A couple of first editions were stolen."

"Yes. Never recovered them, unfortunately." He glanced around the room, taking in the island, the row of copper pots and pans hanging overhead, a shelf of well-thumbed cookbooks over the farmhouse sink. "Is this where you and your friends had tea earlier this evening?"

"No." Her wariness returned. His question was casual. Offhand. But deliberate. "Downstairs."

"In the bookstore?"

She turned away to take down two mugs. "That's right. In the reading room, in the back of the house."

"Mind if I go downstairs and take a look?"

Phaedra set the mugs down with a thump, sloshing coffee over the sides, and turned around. The last thing she needed was Morelli snooping around. "Maybe later. The coffee's almost ready—"

But he was already out of his seat and halfway down the stairs.

"Damn it," she muttered, and hurried after him.

When she entered the former sunroom a moment later, floorboards creaking under her feet, Detective Morelli stood in front of the blackboard. He didn't turn around as she hovered in the doorway.

"I can explain," she began.

"No need. I can figure it out on my own." He studied the list of names. "Nick Ross. Dorothy Fortune. Tinsley Prentiss. Violet Lucas. Jasper Finch. And your friend Charlene . . . all suspects in William Collier's murder."

"We were kicking a few theories around, that's all," she

said lightly. "Normally, we try different varieties of tea and discuss books. Jane Austen, literary fiction, nonfiction. But tonight we . . . branched out. We're reading an Agatha Christie novel for our next meeting, and the subject just naturally came around to murder."

"Naturally." There was no mistaking his skepticism, or his disapproval. He tapped the blackboard. "And this?"

"We put our heads together to try and figure out who the culprit is, using a process of elimination."

"This isn't some kind of parlor game, Ms. Brighton. This is an open murder investigation. It's not a mystery for you and your chums Bess and George to solve."

She opened her mouth to protest, but he cut her off. "Your intruder must've seen the blackboard through the window and realized what you three were up to. Obviously, he or she didn't like it."

"You don't honestly think he—or she—was the same person who tried to run me down tonight."

"Do you have a better theory? Yeah, I think so. Someone wanted to send you a message."

"Well, message received." Phaedra pulled out a chair and sat down hard as the events of the evening sank in. "Loud and clear."

"Good. You want my advice? Stop snooping. Stick to teaching and keep yourself and your friends out of trouble."

"How can I do that?" She pushed herself away from the table. "Especially now? We're onto something, Lucy and Mari and me. The fact that someone's determined enough to hide in the bushes, and try to run me down, proves . . ."

"It proves they're dangerous, and determined enough to finish the job properly next time." Morelli stepped back as she stood and brushed past him into the hallway. "Look, I'm not trying to scare you."

"Sure sounds like it to me." She led the way back upstairs to the kitchen, wordlessly set out sugar and cream, wiped up the spilled coffee, and poured out two fresh mugs.

He resumed his seat and took the mug she handed him. "You need to understand how risky it is, getting mixed up in a murder case."

"I'm not mixed up in anything. I've asked a few discreet questions, that's all."

"Don't forget rifling through drawers and taking potential evidence. Which I could have you charged for, by the way."

"But you haven't."

"No, I haven't. Not yet."

"Charlene didn't kill her husband." She sat down beside him. "And I'm not trying to interfere in your investigation. I just want to get to the truth."

"Again, that's my job. Not yours." He set his coffee down and shot her a sideways glance. "The tox report came in today. I thought you'd want to hear the results."

"And I thought you wanted me to stay out of your investigation."

"I do." His lips turned up slightly. "But I think we both know that's not happening."

She remembered the folder she'd seen in his hand earlier that afternoon. "Charlene said her husband died of an insulin overdose."

He nodded. "His hemoglobin was through the roof. He was injected with eighty-four units. Enough to treat two insulin-dependent diabetic patients for an entire day."

"But he wasn't diabetic."

"No. His sugar level fell rapidly after the injection, and he slipped into a coma within a short time."

"So he was already unconscious when the killer threw that hair dryer in the tub."

"Looks that way."

Phaedra frowned. "I still don't understand why you're telling me this. I know you went to see Charlene earlier, but . . ." Suspicion chased across her face. "You can't honestly think she had anything to do with this."

"I'm telling you the results of the tox report as a courtesy,

Professor, because you're Mrs. Collier's closest friend, and I thought you should know. But it doesn't look good for her right now."

"No, it doesn't. But Charlene didn't do this. She was in the drawing room with me practically the entire time."

"You said she disappeared from the drawing room for fifteen to twenty minutes. That's a problem, because it means she had time to go upstairs and kill her husband."

"No." Her mouth settled into a stubborn line. "I'll never believe it."

"Let's look at the facts. Your friend had motive—to get her hands on that money, for one thing, and to put an end to the frequent verbal abuse from her new husband, for another. You said it yourself. He was a bully."

"He was," Phaedra admitted. "He seemed to get a kind of malicious pleasure out of criticizing Charlene. But she wouldn't see murder as a solution."

"She had means," Morelli continued, "access to her mother's syringes and insulin, as well as the ability to administer her injections. And she had opportunity, when the storm struck and the power went out. When Collier went upstairs, she followed a short time later on the pretext of getting candles, injected him, and returned downstairs."

"What about Finch? He went upstairs to run Collier's bath. He was the last person to see her husband alive."

"The timeline doesn't fit. The pathologist said someone attempted to electrocute Collier after he was injected, not before. Which means Finch would've had to draw his bath, ready a syringe, and administer the injection, all within a few minutes."

"Unless he had a syringe prepped beforehand."

He shook his head. "He stated during questioning that he's never administered a shot in his life. He's also deathly afraid of needles."

"He could be lying."

"He could," Morelli conceded. "But the evidence so far leads back to Charlene Collier. She had access to her mother's syringes and insulin, not to mention years of experience administering her shots. And she had an excellent motive."

"Then why throw the blow-dryer in the tub? Why bother, if she'd already injected him with enough insulin to fell a horse? It makes no sense."

"It takes time for a nondiabetic patient to die from an insulin overdose. It doesn't happen immediately. My guess? Her husband didn't die fast enough, so she grabbed the hair dryer and threw it in to speed up the process." He paused. "There's another possibility."

"Which is what, exactly?"

"Maybe Collier wasn't electrocuted at all. If the power really was out upstairs, maybe she tossed that blow-dryer into the tub to throw us off."

Twenty-Six

As Phaedra set out Wickham's food dish the next morning, one question preoccupied her. Why would a mild-mannered butler attempt to run over a college professor he barely knew?

She didn't know, but after shaking off her near-death experience, she was determined to find out.

She made a cup of Earl Grey to go and watched, one hip resting against the kitchen counter, as Wickham devoured his Salmon Surprise, nudging aside the kibble underneath. He permitted her a quick scratch behind his ears before he retreated into the living room and leaped up on the sofa.

"What do you think, Wicks?" she asked as she followed him to his perch. "Is Finch the murderer?"

He regarded her with a disinterested blue gaze. *How should I know? I'm just a cat. But even I know you need proof before you start throwing around accusations.*

"I need to get a closer look at that Bentley," she mused. "If the butler really *did* do it, there should be signs. Scuff marks on the driver's-side tire. Scratches."

Wickham yawned. *Whatever. Good luck. Oh, and don't*

forget to stop by the grocery store and get a few more cans of Gourmet Tuna Treasure on the way home.

She texted Charlene to say she was on the way and slid her phone into her jeans pocket. No reticule today, she decided. No Empire gown or ballet slippers or fumbling in a tiny drawstring purse for her phone if she encountered a problem.

Today she meant business.

She wasn't expected until nine, which gave her ample time to drive to Marling, park in the unit lot, and skirt the back of the mansion to the garage. Finch would be in the main house, doing whatever butlers normally did, leaving her free to focus on the task at hand.

Finding proof he'd tried to run her down with the Bentley last night.

Along Main Street, the town of Laurel Springs readied itself for another day. Shop owners flipped window signs from "Closed" to "Open," calling out greetings to one another as they swept the front steps and set out chalkboards advertising the day's specials and sales.

Already, shoppers and tourists wandered the sidewalks, on the hunt for bargains, breakfast, or a copy of the morning newspaper. The sidewalk tables in front of Bertie's Café filled up quickly on Saturday mornings.

Phaedra slowed the Mini to a stop at the corner of Main and Maple, and as she left the shops behind, her certainty that Finch used the Bentley to run her down the night before grew. What she couldn't understand was why. Why would he want to harm her?

Only one answer made sense. Finch had crouched in those rhododendrons last night, not a feral cat as they'd thought. He'd seen the evidence board, and his name listed as a potential murder suspect.

No wonder Fitz had attacked the window with such canine ferocity. He knew someone was lurking out there.

She had another, more chilling thought. If Finch hid under that window, he must have followed her when she took Fitz for a walk around the corner. Had he returned to the car on Church Street, watching and waiting for the chance to mow her down?

The thought was disquieting, to say the least.

The light changed, and she turned left onto Maple Avenue with renewed determination. It took more than a dive into a hedge and a few scrapes and bruises to discourage her from getting answers.

At the thought of the Bentley zooming toward her, headlights shining in her eyes, fresh anger gripped her. She and Fitz might've been seriously hurt. Or worse. Her fingers tightened on the wheel.

Finch owed her answers . . . and one way or another, she intended to get them.

Phaedra slowed as she turned onto Rolling Hill Road. She glanced over at Dixon's farm stand. In the fall, the chalkboard boasted apples, pumpkins, and butternut squash for sale, along with jars of homemade apple and pumpkin butter, chrysanthemums, and cider doughnuts dusted with cinnamon sugar.

Now, baskets of sun-ripened tomatoes rubbed shoulders with pints of strawberries and colorful bunches of wildflowers. Normally, she couldn't resist the enticing display of flowers, fruit, and produce, and stopped in often to say hello to Emmylou Dixon, the owner. But today the tomatoes and berries would have to wait.

Twenty minutes later, she parked in the unit lot at Marling and got out of the Mini. She had fifteen minutes to spare before Charlene expected her.

More than enough time to visit the garage.

With any luck, Finch was in the house. As she rounded the far corner of the mansion, her glance moved past the walled kitchen garden and the glistening expanse of dew-covered grass to the former carriage house. Hopefully, the Bentley was parked outside. If not, she'd have to find another way.

Her luck held. She could see the garage door was wide open, and the car gleamed inside. The butler was nowhere to be seen. Phaedra quickened her pace, staying close to the garden wall until it ended. Sending up a silent prayer that no one would see her, she darted across the lawn toward the garage.

No shouts rang out; no one commanded her to stop or demanded to know what she was doing.

She slipped into the cool, dim interior of the garage. The pungent smell of motor oil and gasoline lingered, and she smothered a sneeze. A set of steps at the far end of the garage led up to Finch's apartment.

Suppose he was up there? What would she say if he came down those stairs and found her here? She needed a plausible explanation, fast.

She glanced at the silver bracelet clasped around one wrist, a gift from her father on her sixteenth birthday. She'd say she'd lost a charm. Would Finch notice she wasn't wearing it yesterday? Or wonder how one of her charms ended up on the garage floor?

Maybe she should've thought this through a bit more carefully.

She crossed the floor, skirting the grease stains, until she reached the steps that led to the apartment upstairs.

"Finch?" she called out. "Are you up there?"

No answer.

Relieved, Phaedra returned to the Bentley. A quick glance along the driver's side confirmed that several small but deep scratches marred the front fender and wheel well, scratches she hadn't noticed before.

Scratches left from a close scrape with a privet hedge, perhaps?

Despite the surge of anger the sight roused in her, Phaedra knew she had to keep her emotions in check and tread carefully. A few scratches didn't prove anything. It certainly didn't prove that Finch had tried to run her down last night. He could've backed into one of the hedges lining the drive. He could've been involved in a fender bender.

He could be completely innocent.

But if her instincts were right and he was behind the wheel last night, Finch was a potentially dangerous man with murderous intentions.

She edged down the length of the car, crouching low, searching for any other signs of damage. But the car was pristine. No mud, no indication of recent use.

A couple of damp spots on the driveway outside told her that he'd washed the car, and recently. Even the whitewalls were spotless. She pursed her lips. Soap and water might wash away dirt, but it couldn't hide those scratches . . . or Finch's guilt.

Her thoughts skittered to a stop as a sound reached her. Footsteps. Stealthy footsteps. They came closer, shoes plainly visible now as she froze behind the rear tire.

Black wing tips, topped with cuffed black trousers.

"Professor Brighton," Jasper Finch said icily as he rounded the Bentley and loomed above her. "What the devil do you think you're doing?"

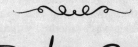

Twenty-Seven

Phaedra scrambled to her feet. She pasted a smile on her face and decided to brazen it out.

"Finch. Good morning. You startled me."

He didn't answer her smile.

"I suppose you're wondering why I'm here," she added.

"The thought crossed my mind, yes."

She lifted her wrist to display the bracelet. "I lost a charm from my bracelet yesterday. The Eiffel Tower. Silly, I suppose, but it means a lot to me. It was a birthday gift from my aunt Wendy. From Paris." She always talked too much when she was nervous. "I think I might've dropped it around here somewhere. But I don't see it."

He said nothing. Disbelief was evident on his face, along with something else. Suspicion.

"Well," she added as she began to edge away, "it's obviously not here. I must've dropped it somewhere else. Sorry. I'll just head back to the house now. Charlene is expecting me—"

"Not so fast." Quick as a shot, he wrapped his fingers around her wrist in a surprisingly viselike grip. "I'd suggest you tell me why you're skulking around out here. And I'd suggest you try the truth this time."

She summoned up a show of indignation. "I told you, I'm looking for a charm that fell off my bracelet yesterday—"

"You weren't wearing a bracelet yesterday. I'd have noticed." His eyes bored into her. "You're an intelligent woman, Professor. But you're not a very good liar."

Although Phaedra could see the back of the house across the lawn, the sight didn't reassure her. She'd left her car in the unit lot. Charlene didn't know she was here.

No one knew she was here except Finch.

Despite a tendril of fear unfurling deep inside her, Phaedra met his eyes with defiance. "Let go of me, and I'll be more than happy to explain."

He scowled, but after a moment he released her and folded his arms against his chest. "Very well. Start explaining."

When all else fails, tell the truth. "I wanted another look at the Bentley."

"Why? And make it good. Because if I don't like your answer, I'm calling the police." He reached for his phone.

"That isn't necessary." She rubbed her wrist, imagining Detective Morelli's reaction if he learned she'd been . . . well, snooping. "I've done nothing wrong."

"I disagree. You're on private property, loitering around this vehicle without permission. I'd call that suspicious. Not to mention you're trespassing."

"I'm not trespassing," Phaedra retorted. "Charlene invited me for tea. Ask her if you don't believe me."

"I have no doubt she did. In fact, I was brewing the tea myself when I glanced out the kitchen window and saw you. But that doesn't explain why you're out here. One doesn't normally take tea in the garage."

His gaze was implacable. Nothing else to do but put her cards on the table. After all, she reasoned, with the house in plain sight across the lawn, he wouldn't dare to harm her.

Would he?

"Last night, I took my mother's dog for a walk," she said. "On Church Street."

"How nice. Your point?"

"My point," she went on, anger gathering inside her in the face of his indifference, "is that someone tried to run us down. Someone in a white Bentley, like yours."

His eyes widened, then narrowed, but he said nothing.

"I grabbed the dog and dived over a hedge and narrowly missed getting hit." She lifted one of her arms and showed him the scratches.

"That must've been terrifying," he conceded. "But surely you're not suggesting that I—"

"—tried to run me down? Yes. That's exactly what I'm suggesting. What I don't understand is why."

"That's absurd." He looked at her as if she'd lost her mind. "I can assure you, Professor Brighton, this car never left the garage last night. I put it away myself after dinner."

"I know what I saw. This Bentley was parked halfway down Church Street, just across the street from Harper's Pub."

Something flickered across his face. Surprise, mingled with . . . doubt?

"I'm telling you, you're mistaken," he insisted. "Why in God's name would I want to run you down?"

"I hoped you'd tell me. Unless you'd rather tell the police, when Detective Morelli arrives."

"What time did this so-called incident take place?"

"Around ten thirty." Phaedra took out her phone. "Morelli ran out of Harper's to see if we were okay. He saw the whole thing."

Finch's expression grew guarded. "He was there?"

"Yes. He got a partial on the license plate, so I imagine you'll get a call when the DMV database turns up a match."

He glared at her. "All right. It's true I was at Harper's last night. I had the night off. I have every Friday night off."

"Which explains why your car was parked on Church."

"It doesn't explain a damned thing," he snapped. "I didn't take the car last night. A friend picked me up here at Marling and dropped me off just after midnight. The Bentley never left the garage."

"Then how do you explain the scratches on the fender and the wheel wells?" she challenged. "They weren't there yesterday."

"I have no idea! Nor can I explain why the gas tank was low this morning. When I put the car away yesterday evening, it was perfect. There were no scratches, and the tank was half full. I remember because I intended to fill it up this morning."

Phaedra was silent. Was he telling the truth? She was almost inclined to believe he was. "Can anyone confirm your story? Your friend, for example?"

"Of course. The bartender, too, I imagine. Harper's is always busy on Friday nights."

"Does anyone else drive the car?"

"No. I take Mrs. Collier out if she needs to run errands. She doesn't drive. She doesn't have a license."

"Someone took it." Phaedra eyed him. "If not you, then who?"

"It's hard to say. There's an extra set of keys on a hook in the kitchen. Anyone could've borrowed it."

"You told me the car was yours. That Harold left it to you in his will."

"I lied," Finch said, testily. "He left it to Collier, not me. I've always wished it was mine," he admitted, "that much is true. But it isn't. It was Collier's and now it's Charlene's. A woman who doesn't even drive." He let out a disgusted snort. "Isn't that always the way? Now, any more questions before you leave and I return to my duties, Professor?"

"I do have one question. Maybe you can tell me how an aquamarine from Charlene's stolen choker ended up on the kitchen floor."

"An aquamarine? I have no idea."

"I found it by the back door," Phaedra said. "The day after the murder." When he remained silent, she added, "Odd place for it, don't you think? I couldn't understand how it got there. Or why no one had noticed it. Until I remembered the oven mitt."

"Oven mitt?" His expression gave nothing away. "I'm sorry, but I'm not following."

"Bertie asked you to remove a tray of scones from the oven. You took down an old oven mitt from a peg by the door and used it to pull them out."

"That greasy old thing? It's ancient. Been hanging there as long as I can remember." He fixed her with a belligerent glare. "I fail to see your point, Professor."

She glanced back at Marling, reassured by the sight of several of the bachelorettes drifting outside to have their morning coffee on the terrace.

"Then let me lay it out for you." Her words were cool. "I think you killed the power and grabbed the choker from Tinsley's neck. Next, I think you hid it inside that oven mitt, where no one would find it, not even the police. And finally, I think you passed it on to an accomplice via the back door early the next morning."

"An accomplice?" He shook his head, amused. "Your imagination does you credit."

"I didn't imagine finding Charlene's choker in the back of her desk drawer in the morning room afterward." She was pleased to see his smirk falter. "I took it to the local jeweler, along with the stone, and he confirmed something I'd wondered about."

He hiked up his brow. "Oh?"

"He said the aquamarine I found on the kitchen floor was real. But the choker is a bona fide . . . fake."

"All very interesting, I'm sure. But this has nothing to do with me. Tell it to the police."

"I will. I'm sure they'll be interested in my theory."

"That I stole the choker and passed it off to an accomplice in a carefully orchestrated heist?" He shook his head. "Preposterous."

"Is it? After all, you know Marling better than anyone," she mused, eyeing him thoughtfully. "You could've easily slipped into the boot room and flipped the breakers, plunging the first floor into darkness. You returned to the drawing room, grabbed the choker and dropped it into your pocket, and hid it—"

"In the oven mitt," he finished, and let out an indulgent chuckle.

"The only thing I can't figure out is where the fake choker came from. No one had access to that locked drawer but Bill, and Charlene. And you."

He blanched but remained stubbornly silent.

"Why not save yourself a world of trouble and tell me the truth?"

"I've told you the truth." He narrowed his gaze. "Mrs. Collier wanted that loose stone repaired. You know the rest. Collier caught me, accused me of attempted theft, and threatened to have me arrested."

"But he didn't call the police. Why?"

"He confirmed my story with Charlene and let the matter drop."

"But that's not the end of the story, is it?" Phaedra met his glare. "I think you handed the necklace off to someone and replaced it with a replica. A very good replica, good enough to fool anyone who didn't examine it too closely."

"That's ludicrous. Why would I do such a thing? Why take the risk?"

"That's what I don't understand." She drew her brows together. "Not only why, but who? Are you and this mystery person planning to break the gems down and sell them on the black market, split the difference? Is that it?"

"I've told you." His words were shards of glass. "You're spinning fantasies. And wasting my time! Now, if you'll excuse me, I have things to do back at the house—"

"Perhaps the police will have a theory of their own."

The silence was absolute. Phaedra held his scowl despite the rapid uptick in her heartbeat. Finch was a potential thief . . . perhaps even a murderer. What was she doing? Was she crazy, confronting him like this?

Probably. Unquestionably. She didn't know how he might react, what he might do. But it was too late. She'd thrown down the gauntlet, and the next move was his.

"Yes, I took it." His words were vehement.

"Why?"

"Because that choker belongs to Mrs. Fortune. It was never Collier's to give. Harold gave it to his wife, Dorothy, as a wedding present. She had a copy made to wear in public but kept the original in a safe in the morning room, behind a landscape painting that hung over the fireplace mantel."

"Where the portrait of Bill Collier is now."

"Yes." He grimaced. "Hideous thing. When he took the landscape down to hang his portrait, he found the safe, but he didn't have the combination."

"Did you give it to him?"

"No. I didn't have it, and I wouldn't have given it to him if I had. It was a simple three-number combination. He figured it out after a couple of tries."

"And took the choker."

"Which he gave to Charlene as a wedding present and passed off as a family heirloom." He snorted. "Family heirloom, my behind! He stole it. That choker belongs to Mrs. Fortune, and Collier had no right to take it."

"Why didn't Dorothy pursue the matter in court?"

"Too costly. He would've dragged it out for years. Thanks to Harold, she didn't have the money to fight him. What Collier did was wrong, and I told Patsy as much."

"I see." She paused. "And she wanted the choker back."

"Yes, for sentimental reasons. Or so she said. She claimed she wanted to return it to her mother."

Hearing the note of bitterness underlying his words, Phaedra raised her brow. "But she didn't."

"No. She lied."

"So you cut the power and grabbed the choker from Tinsley's neck."

"One good yank and I knew it would come loose. I dropped it in my pocket and hid it in the oven mitt, where no one would notice it, and handed it off to Patsy the next morning. And she gave me the fake."

"So you could 'find' it in Charlene's desk drawer."

"Yes. If I'd known Patsy wanted it for herself, to break the stones down and keep the money . . ." He glowered. "I never would've done it. I put my job on the line to steal that choker and nearly got arrested for my trouble, and all she wanted was to line her own greedy pockets."

"You were angry." Phaedra's expression was thoughtful. "You wanted to get back at her for lying to you, so you called Clark Mullinax and said she tried to sell the stolen choker at a Charlottesville pawnshop."

"Yes." He looked at her then, realizing the enormity of his confession, and his eyes darkened with anxiety. "I could lose my job for this. I could go to jail. You won't tell that detective, will you?"

"I should. Regardless of your reasons, you broke the law. But whether I come forward or not . . . that depends on you."

Twenty-Eight

On me?" His eyes narrowed. "What do you mean?"

She studied him. "How'd you like to be my eyes and ears at Marling?"

Before he could answer, the intercom filled the garage with Bertie's belligerent voice.

"Finch! You're needed in the dining room. What are you doing out there?"

He pressed the button. "On my way."

"Well, hurry. These dishes won't clear themselves."

Phaedra lifted her brow. "There's no escaping her."

"The woman's relentless," he grumbled. "Mr. Fortune installed the intercom years ago, to aid communication between myself and the house. It was rarely used until Mr. Collier upgraded the system. Now that it's wireless there's no getting away from her." He glared at the speaker. "One day I'll take a hammer and smash it to bits."

Bertie flung the kitchen door open as they neared the house. "About time." She focused her ire on the butler before turning to Phaedra. "Where did you come from?"

"Not that it's any of your concern," Finch replied, "but Professor Brighton wanted to see the Bentley."

"Oh?" Suspicion darkened her gaze. "Why is that?"

"It's a classic automobile." Phaedra favored her with a winning smile. "Finch keeps it in immaculate condition. Truly, it belongs in a car museum."

"Might as well be, for all the use it is to Mrs. Collier. Which reminds me—have you gone to the grocery store yet?" She addressed this last to Finch.

"No, I have not. I'll go when I've cleared the breakfast dishes. And let me remind *you*," he countered as she opened her mouth to object, "I answer to Mrs. Collier. Not you." He brushed past her and stalked inside.

Scowling, she followed him down the hall. "We're short-handed, with Cook out today. But do you care? Evidently not . . ."

As Phaedra debated whether to wait or go in search of Charlene, she came down the hall with a tea tray in hand.

"Finch told me you're here," she said. "Let's go in the drawing room and sit down."

When they were settled and sipping Earl Grey, Phaedra shared the harrowing events of the night before. "Luckily, Detective Morelli was nearby. He walked me home."

"How horrible! I'm relieved you and Fitz are all right." Charlene set her cup into its saucer with a rattle of china. "Who would think such a thing could happen here in Laurel Springs?"

"At least neither of us was seriously hurt." Phaedra sipped her tea. It was deliciously bracing, if a little lukewarm. She set her cup aside and leaned forward, lowering her voice. "I can't be positive, but the car . . . it looked like a Bentley."

"*Our* Bentley?" Charlene was aghast. "You must be mistaken. Why, Finch would never do such a thing."

Phaedra, not wishing their conversation to be overheard, indicated the double doors that opened into the entrance hall. "May I?" At Charlene's nod, she rose and shut the doors, relieved to see no one in the vicinity.

"I agree." Phaedra resumed her seat. "In fact, Finch told me he wasn't behind the wheel. He said the car stayed in the garage all evening. Did it?"

"Yes, as far as I know."

"Charlene, think carefully. It's important. Did anyone leave the house last night around nine or nine thirty?"

"I don't know." She laid a hand on her throat in distress. "I went upstairs at nine and locked the bedroom door. I couldn't stop worrying about Mother, wondering if she did it. Trying to convince myself she didn't. After I called you—it must've been nearly eleven—I was still upset, and I took a sleeping pill."

Phaedra took a sip of tea and swallowed her disappointment. She'd hoped Charlene might provide a lead. "Finch said you asked him to take the choker to Bascom's to have a loose stone repaired. He claims that's what he was doing when Bill caught him and accused him of stealing."

"Yes, that's true. I talked to Bill and smoothed things over. He had a temper," she added, unnecessarily. She paused. "You saw Detective Morelli last night? Has he . . . Did he say anything to you? About the investigation?"

"Only that the toxicology report came in, and it confirmed your husband was injected with insulin."

Charlene reached for the pitcher of milk and tipped it into her cup with an unsteady hand. "Do you remember when I went upstairs to get more candles? And to change?"

"Yes. When you came back, you still wore the same clothes. And you said you didn't get a chance to talk to Bill." She hesitated. "I did wonder about that."

"I meant to do both, but when I came upstairs, I saw Mother. She . . ." Charlene set her cup down. "She'd wheeled herself to Bill's bathroom door, and she was in a state."

Phaedra's breath quickened. "What was she doing there?"

"Exactly what I asked her. She said she was scolding him. That was her exact word, 'scolding,' for his rudeness to me in front of our guests. She heard him shouting and wheeled herself down the hall to confront him, but the door was shut."

"What did she do?"

"She demanded he open the door. But he didn't answer.

Which only made her angrier. I took her back to her room and tried to calm her down. But I can't help wondering. Did she confront him before I came up? Was she angry enough to grab a syringe and inject him? Or grab that hair dryer in a fit of rage and toss it in his bathtub?"

"I can't honestly see Violet doing either of those things," Phaedra reassured her. "And with her tremors, she'd have difficulty jabbing him in the neck with a needle. He'd have heard her wheelchair on the bathroom tiles. Had time to react."

"I suppose." She didn't sound convinced.

"Unless the police bring charges, you have nothing to worry about. And there's no reason why they should. Don't upset yourself needlessly."

"It's all so distressing. The funeral service is tomorrow. I dread it. The notoriety, the curiosity, the reporters . . . I just want it to be over. All of it."

On Sunday morning, Phaedra put on her only black dress and stepped into a pair of low-heeled black pumps. A strand of her Nana's pearls completed the outfit.

Her fingers paused on the clasp. Her heart ached for Charlene, who'd gone from a bride to a widow in the space of a few weeks. Picking up her keys as she headed for the door, Phaedra resolved to do whatever she could to help her friend get through the service.

And perhaps she'd ask a few discreet questions at the reception afterward. One of the caterers or household staff might know who'd borrowed the Bentley on Friday night. She might even manage to slip into Finch's apartment above the garage and have a quick look around.

"I'm leaving, Wickham," she called up the stairs. "I'll see you in a few hours."

Wickham did not deign to answer, or to show himself.

"Be that way, then. Bye."

The sky was clear and the temperature mild as she emerged

from the carriage house and locked the door behind her. *At least it's not raining*, she thought as she slid behind the wheel of the Mini. Funerals were sad enough without the addition of dismal weather, muddy ground, and dripping umbrellas.

Forsythia, dogwood, and redbud trees bloomed in profusion along the highway as she left the outskirts of town and began to look for the church. After a few miles she spotted it and slowed down.

St. Cyprian's Episcopal Church presented an unassuming fieldstone face to the road, its simple white spire topped with a wrought iron cross. A small cemetery adjoined the churchyard.

Phaedra turned into the lot and saw perhaps fifteen other vehicles. Charlene hadn't wanted a large turnout, and she'd gotten her wish, but at least a respectable number of mourners had shown up to pay their respects.

Retrieving her clutch and dropping the keys inside, Phaedra headed for the entrance, where the Episcopalian flag, with its distinctive red St. George's Cross against a white background, fluttered in the breeze.

Inside, the subtle scent of incense and fresh-cut flowers greeted her. She took a seat on the end of a middle pew as the organist played "A Mighty Fortress Is Our God." Charlene sat in the front row with an elderly woman beside her. The woman's face was composed but lined with grief.

The casket was closed.

The Reverend Frances Marsh, a middle-aged woman who spoke with intelligence and compassion, led the service.

An hour later, as pallbearers escorted the casket down the aisle and through the front door, everyone rose to the uplifting strains of "Joyful, Joyful, We Adore Thee" and filed into the cemetery for the burial.

Phaedra offered words of condolence to Charlene and her mother-in-law, and at their invitation, she joined them at the graveside service.

The cemetery was located behind the church, under the sheltering branches of an ancient oak. Many of the older stones dated back to the late 1700s. A newly dug grave covered with a canopy awaited the arrival of the mourners.

If you could call them mourners, Phaedra thought. They made a small group, perhaps seventeen people, all dressed in black and all appropriately somber. Although their faces were arranged in expressions of sorrow, no one displayed a trace of true emotion or loss.

Only William's mother, the elderly woman with Charlene, betrayed genuine grief. Incomprehension clouded her face as she wept, and she paused several times to blot her eyes with a handkerchief. She leaned heavily on her daughter-in-law's arm.

Phaedra recognized Marling's household staff, among them Finch and Mrs. Williams, the housekeeper, as well as several men she didn't recognize. Businessmen, she surmised, probably top brass from Longbourn Pharmaceutical. The Fortune family was conspicuously absent.

Clark Mullinax loitered across the street with a handful of other reporters, cameras and microphones at the ready. Phaedra glanced at the Reverend Marsh and bit back a smile. Despite her kindly nature, she had no doubt the reverend would toss any journalist bold enough to disturb the service right off the property.

Most of the cars from the church parking lot lined Marling's drive as Phaedra arrived a short time later for the post-funeral reception. Bertie and her staff circulated with trays of sherry as Phaedra walked into the entrance hall, and Finch quickly took his place beside the front door.

He directed her to the drawing room, where small groups gathered to converse in subdued voices. Several people assembled at one end of a table set out with light luncheon fare. Not seeing either Charlene or her mother-in-law, Phaedra picked up a plate and joined them.

As she deposited a slice of roast turkey and a roll on her plate, Reverend Marsh approached her.

Phaedra introduced herself. "It's a pleasure to meet you, Reverend Marsh. It was truly a lovely service."

"Thank you. Please, call me Reverend Fran. Everyone does." She speared a slice of roast beef and added a generous dollop of potato salad to her plate. "I can't resist potato salad," she confessed. "It's my weakness."

They settled on the sofa with their plates. "It must be a challenge to find words of comfort and hope in such an unfortunate circumstance as this," Phaedra ventured.

"On the contrary, such times are when comfort and hope are most needed. Did you know Mr. Collier?"

"No. But I've known Charlene since high school. I met her husband after they married."

"It's a terrible thing," the reverend said, and sighed. "To be wed and widowed in such a short time. My heart goes out to Mrs. Collier, and to William's mother. But I firmly believe God's grace will guide them. Are you married, Professor Brighton?"

The change of subject startled Phaedra. Reverend Fran was nothing if not direct. "No."

"I am. I married rather late in life, but I recommend it highly. I believe we all have a helpmate out there, or a soul mate if you prefer. The trick is to find him or her before it's too late. Not always easy."

Phaedra managed a wry smile. "You sound exactly like my mother."

"Well, your mother is a wise woman. You should listen to her." Reverend Fran put her plate down and stood. "Now, if you'll excuse me, I'd best mingle. I enjoyed our talk."

"So did I. Thank you."

As the reverend joined a group by the doorway, Bertie approached with a tray. "Sherry, Professor?"

"Yes, thank you." Phaedra took one of the small, fluted glasses and took a sip. She stood, glass in hand, and made her way across the room.

"If you ask me, he didn't deserve to be remembered," a

man said in a low voice as she passed by. "He was a tyrant and a swindler without an ounce of human decency."

"And those were his *good* qualities," another man joked. A ripple of discreet laughter followed.

"You can't deny that he knew how to amass a fortune," a woman in a chic black trouser suit and heels pointed out.

"And how to take a Fortune's fortune away," someone else quipped.

Phaedra was about to step in and point out the insensitivity of such comments when William's mother, Inez Collier, approached her.

Her face was pale and she looked extremely frail. "I can't seem to locate Charlene, and I'm feeling a bit overwhelmed. I don't know any of these people."

"Perhaps some fresh air first?" Phaedra suggested.

"Yes. Please."

"Let's go out to the terrace and sit down. Can I get you anything? Some water, perhaps?"

"No, thank you." She laid a hand, slightly trembling, on Phaedra's arm, and they went to the morning room, through the French doors, and onto the flagstone terrace.

"Have you eaten?" Phaedra inquired as they sat down. "I'd be happy to go inside and get you a plate."

Mrs. Collier shook her head. "I'm not hungry. I just—" She groped in the pocket of her Chanel blazer for a tissue and pressed it to her eyes. "This is all so difficult."

"Are you alone? Is your husband here?"

She shook her head. "Henry passed away several years ago. He wouldn't have come to the funeral at any rate. He and William were estranged. His health," she added, almost as an afterthought.

"I'm sorry. This must be difficult for you."

"You have no idea." Lost in memories no one else could share, she gazed off into the distance. "I can't believe anyone would kill my son." Her gaze focused on Phaedra. "Do the police have any leads, do you know?"

"No, I don't. But they're actively investigating, and I'm sure they'll find the culprit."

"I wish I shared your certainty. But so many murders go unsolved. Of course, finding out who killed William won't bring him back, but I need to know who took him from me."

"I understand. And I hope that person is found."

"I've lost them all, you know." Her voice was barely audible. "My husband, my son . . . his father. All gone."

Thrusting the crumpled bit of tissue back into her pocket, Inez Collier stood abruptly. "Excuse me, but I need to find Charlene. Thank you for your kindness."

Before Phaedra could offer to accompany her back inside, she crossed the terrace into the house.

Phaedra was about to follow when she decided to take the path that led past the kitchen garden to the back entrance. Here was her chance to question the staff about the mysterious vanishing Bentley.

Which, as luck would have it, was parked outside the garage.

She let herself in the kitchen, relieved to see no sign of Bertie, and closed the door quietly behind her.

"Excuse me, but this is the kitchen, ma'am," one of the caterers—Derrick, according to his name badge—informed her as he entered with an empty tray. "I'll show you to the drawing room."

"Thanks, Derrick, but I'm looking for an aspirin. Terrible headache," she added apologetically.

He set the tray down. "Oh. Well, wait here. I'll see what I can do."

"Thank you."

As he left, Jen came in bearing a tray of empty sherry glasses and slid the tray onto the counter. She opened the dishwasher and began putting the glasses in the upper rack, and glanced over at Charlene. "Help you, miss?"

"Derrick's gone to find me an aspirin," Phaedra said. "I was just admiring the Bentley parked out back. It's a beautiful car, isn't it?"

She shrugged. "I suppose. I'm not into cars. Only Finch ever drives it, as a rule. He takes Mrs. Collier around sometimes."

"No one else drives it?"

"No, ma'am. Although"—she nodded at a key rack by the pantry door—"there's a set of spare keys over there."

"Do you know if anyone borrowed the car on Friday night?"

"Friday night? Why do you ask?"

"Just curious. I thought I saw it on Church Street when I was walking my dog. It's such a distinctive car."

"It is, isn't it? No going incognito in *that*." She frowned. "Now that I think about it, I noticed the keys were missing when we cleared the dessert plates."

Phaedra's heart leaped. "Did Finch take the car?"

"I don't think so. No, he didn't, because he went out to his apartment over the garage after dinner. He left later, but a friend of his picked him up. He didn't take the car. I'm sure of it."

"But someone did."

"Someone must have," she agreed. "The keys were definitely gone."

Before Phaedra could question her further, Bertie arrived with Derrick trailing behind her.

"Here's your aspirin, Professor," she said, thrusting a pill into Phaedra's palm. "Now, I must ask that you leave the kitchen. Servants and catering staff only."

"Of course." She accepted a glass of water from Jen and pretended to swallow the aspirin, thanked them, and beat a hasty retreat.

Bertie Walsh followed her to the doorway and watched, arms crossed, until Phaedra made her way down the hall and returned to the drawing room.

Violet caught her eye and patted the empty chair beside her, and soon engaged her in conversation. Phaedra smiled and nodded and pretended to listen, but her thoughts were elsewhere.

Someone took the keys to the Bentley on Friday night. And that someone, according to Jen, wasn't Finch.

Who, then? Was it a servant? Derrick? A bachelorette? Whoever it was, Bertie plainly didn't like her questioning the catering staff. Why? Who was she protecting?

Even more puzzling was Inez Collier's earlier remark, just before she'd returned to the house.

She'd said she lost her son, and her husband, Henry. But why had she mentioned losing "his father" as well? It almost sounded as if William wasn't Henry's son, but someone else's.

Her investigation, such as it was, had done little to answer her questions.

Instead she only had more.

Twenty-Nine

On Monday, Phaedra sailed past Marisol with a jaunty "good morning" and into her office, dropping her briefcase, reticule, and a stack of glossy photographs on her desk.

She'd barely slid into her chair when the phone rang. "Professor Brighton, English department."

"Professor? Detective Morelli here."

She swallowed her surprise along with a quick sip of the tea Marisol handed her. "Hello, Detective. To what do I owe the honor?"

"I ran the partial on the plate of the car that tried to run you down. The DMV database returned a few matches. Your vehicle description of a white vintage model sedan narrowed the field quite a bit."

"And? What did you come up with?"

"A few possibilities. But only one that makes sense." He paused. "A Bentley. Registered to William Collier."

Phaedra was silent. Damn Morelli for being so efficient.

"No comment, Professor? You're usually not at a loss for words. Was it a Bentley that came at you that night? They have a very distinctive grill. Seems like you would've recognized it right away."

"It was dark," she said sharply, "and the headlights were shining in my face. It happened very quickly. I wasn't thinking clearly. I wasn't thinking about anything except not getting run over."

"Any idea why anyone at Marling would attempt a hit-and-run on you?"

"No, of course not."

"You don't think maybe your questions upset someone in the house? Someone who decided to come after you?" When she didn't answer, he added, "The same someone who hid in the bushes outside your father's bookstore that night?"

"I don't know. It's possible, I suppose."

"I think it's more than possible. Someone from that house tried to run you down. The question is, who? And why?"

Phaedra pushed her tea away. She no longer wanted it. "A lot of people are at Marling right now. The bachelorettes, Nick Ross, the production crew, the caterers and household staff—"

"And let's not forget the family. Mrs. Collier and her mother, for instance."

"Violet can't drive. Obviously. And Charlene doesn't have a license."

"Which leaves a couple of other possibilities. Jasper Finch, for instance."

Her heart began to beat apace, but she said nothing.

"I just spoke to Jake at Goodall's repair shop. They're working on a white Bentley right now, polishing out scratches on the left side of the hood and the front wheel well." Morelli paused. "You wouldn't know anything about that, would you, Professor Brighton?"

"Are you accusing me of something?" Phaedra asked levelly. "If so, just say it."

"I'm not accusing you of anything. I'm asking a question. And I'd appreciate a straight answer."

With a sigh, she admitted she'd seen Jasper Finch at Marling on the morning she went to see Charlene. "When I arrived, I saw the Bentley parked outside the garage. I decided to take a closer look."

"And?"

"And . . ." She hesitated. "Finch showed up and asked me what I was doing. I told him what happened."

"That someone tried to run you down."

"Yes. I was angry, and seeing those scratches on the car didn't help. I suspected the Bentley was involved. Which had to mean Finch was behind the wheel."

"If Jasper Finch really did attempt to run over you, confronting him wasn't the smartest idea."

"I agree. But he swore he didn't take the Bentley out that night. He parked it in the garage at Marling earlier that afternoon." She told him about the extra set of keys hanging on a hook in the kitchen. "Which means anyone could have taken that car."

"Or Finch could be lying."

"Maybe," she admitted. "But it's easy enough to check his alibi. He was at Harper's Pub on Friday night."

"So was I. I don't recall seeing him."

"Ask the bartender. Finch bought a couple of rounds for his friend, and he ran up a tab."

"I'll check it out. Oh, and regarding your tip from Clark Mullinax . . . there's no record of Patsy Fortune selling any jewels or precious stones in Charlottesville. Guess his source was mistaken."

"I guess so. Still, it was worth a shot."

"Do me a favor in the future, Professor," Morelli said evenly, "and stick to teaching."

"Why don't you do us both a favor and find whoever murdered Charlene's husband?" she nearly snapped. "Instead of harassing me?"

Fortunately, her only response was a dial tone. Morelli had already hung up.

Marisol appeared in the doorway. "Annoying call?"

"You could say that. Thanks for the tea, by the way."

"You're welcome. She eyed the stack of photos on the desk curiously. "What's that?"

"This," Phaedra announced with satisfaction, "is Mr. Fitzwilliam Darcy. In full, glorious color."

"Are those the photos of Nick Ross? Ooh, let me see." Marisol crossed the room in three steps and eagerly picked up the top photograph. Nick, from his neatly tied cravat to his gleaming Hessian boots, was the epitome of an elegant Regency gentleman. "Look at that haughty expression," she exclaimed. "And those dark, stormy eyes!" She clutched the photo to her breast. "He's perfect. Can I keep it?"

"No." Phaedra plucked the photo from her and returned it to the pile. "Please don't crush Mr. Darcy."

"I wouldn't dream of it. How did you get the photos done so quickly?"

"Nick had a few extras in his trailer from a recent photo shoot." She lifted a manila envelope from inside her brief-case. "These headshots are autographed."

"Even better. Once word gets out, those raffle tickets will sell like crazy. Good work, Phaedra."

"Thanks. And speaking of . . ." She eyed the stack of papers waiting to be graded on Marisol's desk.

"Okay, not-so-subtle hint taken. I'm on it." She returned to her seat in the outer office and pulled the essays toward her. "Have you found an Elizabeth Bennet to replace Dee yet?"

"Still looking. No one's volunteered." Phaedra, notes in hand, looked up and studied Marisol with an assessing gaze. "What about you?"

"What about me, what?"

"You'd make a perfect Elizabeth."

"Oh no." She dropped her red pen and shook her head firmly. "No way. You convinced me to play Marianne Dash-wood last year and stuck me with Professor Bryce."

"Of course you were paired together. He was Colonel Brandon. Who was deeply in love with Marianne."

"I bet Colonel Brandon never got grabby with Miss Dash-wood," she said darkly. "Every chance he got, Bryce tried to put his hand on my—"

"Good morning, ladies."

Phaedra looked up to see Mark Selden standing in the outer doorway. He wore a dark blue suit and an open-collared shirt, and her heart gave a leap. He really was attractive.

"Good morning," she replied. "You're looking very professorial today."

"It's my first official lecture here at Somerset. Wish me luck."

"Oh, you won't need it. I've no doubt your bardolatry will serve you well. But good luck anyway."

"Bardolatry?" Marisol echoed, eyeing the two of them in puzzlement. "What's that? Some kind of pagan religion?"

"It means someone who idolizes Shakespeare," Selden said, his eyes leveling on Phaedra. "The term originated with the philosopher Voltaire, who detested the Bard. It's usually derogatory in nature."

"I'm sorry." Phaedra fiddled with her staple remover. "That was uncalled for. The fact is, I owe you an apology, not only for what I said just now, but also for my behavior during the fundraising meeting. And for . . . other things."

"There's nothing to apologize for."

Marisol excused herself and discreetly departed for the faculty lounge on the pretext of getting a coffee.

"Please, come into my office." Phaedra waited as he preceded her inside. With trembling hands she shut the door and leaned back against it. "I don't know why, but you seem to bring out the worst in me, and I'm sorry."

"Sorry that I bring out the worst in you? Or sorry it makes you behave badly?"

"Either? Both." She sank down in the chair behind her desk and sighed. "I really am sorry."

"I'd be a churl not to accept such a heartfelt apology." He perched on the edge of the seat in front of her desk. "Consider it forgotten. I think it's fair to say we both got off on the wrong foot."

"I agree. Let's try and behave more kindly to each other in future."

"Austen couldn't have said it better herself." He caught sight of the photos stacked on the corner of her desk. "May I?"

She nodded. "Nick Ross graciously provided photos for the fundraiser. And he autographed a few for the raffle."

"He makes an excellent Darcy," he said as he studied the picture. "Handsome and forbidding in equal measure." He set the photos aside. "Now all we need is Elizabeth. Any luck thus far?"

"No." She slumped against the back of her chair. "Looks like I'll be assuming the role. Unless you have any other candidates in mind," she added hopefully.

"I think you should go for it, Professor Brighton. You'll make the perfect headstrong, obstinate girl."

"Phaedra, please. And I'm hardly a girl."

"Alan Roberts is hardly a young man. Doesn't seem to bother him."

"You're right. It's all in a spirit of fun, after all." Phaedra straightened. "That's settled, then. I'll find a properly demure ball gown—white, of course—stick a few pearls and tiny flowers in my hair, and go as Elizabeth at the Pemberley ball."

"Sounds captivating. It almost makes me wish I could be Darcy."

Phaedra laughed. "Be careful what you wish for, Professor Selden."

Her words proved prophetic. After weeks of selling raffle tickets, sourcing and sewing costumes, lining up vendors, and scheduling and confirming a variety of speakers and workshops, the English department was ready for the opening of the two-day Jane Austen literary festival the following Saturday.

"This year," Phaedra announced as she surveyed her office, "will be the best festival ever."

"You say that every year," Marisol reminded her.

"This time I really mean it." She threw her hand out to encompass her surroundings, which boasted a profusion of costumes, flyers, and ticket rolls. "We have autographed photos of Nick Ross, a tour of the *Who Wants to Marry Mr. Darcy?* set with Mr. Darcy himself, numerous speakers—from fan fiction writers to noted Austen scholars—Regency-themed food, and a staff ready to recreate Darcy and Elizabeth, Wentworth and Anne, Emma and Knightley . . ."

"I can't believe you roped me into playing Marianne again this year," Marisol grumbled.

". . . and Marianne and Colonel Brandon," Phaedra finished. "What more could one want?"

"How about wanting to strangle Mr. Darcy?"

Lucy Liang stood in Phaedra's doorway, her arms jammed beneath her chest and a grim expression on her face.

"What do you mean, Lucy? What's happened?"

"Food poisoning happened. As in, Alan ate something last night that's violently disagreed with him."

"How violently?"

"He's in the hospital as we speak, getting intravenous antibiotics."

"Oh no." She closed her eyes. "No, no, no. That means we're without a Mr. Darcy for the festival tomorrow."

"Your sympathy knows no bounds," Lucy said. "What about poor Alan?"

"You're the one who wants to strangle him," Phaedra pointed out. She sighed. "But you're right. Send flowers and sign the card 'with best wishes for a speedy recovery from the English department,' et cetera." She reached for her reticule and withdrew a credit card. "Put it on this."

Lucy grabbed the card from her, turned, and strode away.

"What'll we do about finding a replacement?" Marisol asked. "It's not like we have an understudy waiting in the wings. And we don't have much time to look."

"We don't have *any* time to look." Phaedra felt a headache coming on. "We have to find someone, and quickly." She began to pace around the confines of the office. "Someone with presence. Someone with dark hair."

"Someone who can fit into Alan's costume."

Phaedra sighed. "That, too."

She glanced up as Mark, briefcase in hand, left his office and headed for the lobby with easy, confident strides. His hair was dark. He definitely had presence.

And like Mr. Darcy, he was British.

"I have an idea," she said, and hurried around her desk.

"I know what you're thinking." Marisol stood and followed her to the doorway, where Selden had nearly reached the lobby. "And you're right. But he'll never do it."

Phaedra didn't answer. She quickened her pace and caught up to him as he reached the lobby doors. "Mark? Wait, please. I need to ask a favor."

He turned and paused as the door whisked open. "Of course. What is it?"

Marisol followed and lingered in front of the soda machine down the hall. It was painfully obvious she was eavesdropping.

"There's been a change in the schedule," Phaedra said. "For the Austen literary festival tomorrow."

He waited, mild puzzlement on his face. "Oh?"

"It's Alan," she went on. "Professor Roberts. He's down with food poisoning, and he's in the hospital."

"Oh. Well, that's too bad. I'm sorry to hear it." Selden's glance went from Phaedra to Marisol and back again. "But I'm not sure why you're telling me this."

"It's a problem. A huge problem," Phaedra added, "because Alan is our Mr. Darcy for the Austen literary festival. He's never once missed a year."

Comprehension dawned, replacing puzzlement with alarm, Mark stepped back. "No. Oh no."

"Don't say no before you hear me out," she implored. "Will you take over the role in his absence? All you have to do is wear the costume, and it's only for two days!"

"Only two days?" he echoed. "That's the entire weekend. I'm driving to Charlottesville for the Shakespeare festival at UVA tomorrow."

"At least think about it, please. I have Alan's costume, and I think you can wear it without any alterations." She regarded him with a frown. "Although he's a little heavier than you, and a little shorter, so we'll need to take in the waist and lengthen the trousers . . ."

She was babbling, but convincing him to assume the role of Mr. Darcy was imperative. He had to say yes.

"No. I'm sorry, but I can't do it."

"What if I throw some Shakespeare at you? 'We know what we are, but know not what we may be.'"

"Ophelia, *Hamlet*." He added grudgingly, "Good quote. And irritatingly appropriate."

"So? Will you do it?"

"No."

"Please," she cajoled, desperation rising as he turned to go. "For the good of the English department. For the good of liberal arts students everywhere."

"The festival, not to mention the liberal arts, will survive very nicely without my presence this year, I assure you. Now, if you'll excuse me—"

Phaedra refused to give up. Mark Selden was her only hope. "I think you should go for it, Professor Selden." She folded her arms against her chest. "You'll make the perfect proud, condescending aristocrat."

His scowl deepened. "I see what you did there. Turning my own words against me. But the answer's still no. Good evening, Professor."

The lobby doors swished open as he stepped forward.

Desperate to sway him, she remembered Hannah's recent offer. "What if I said I could get tickets to see Tyrell Blackmoore at Ford's Theatre?"

He paused. "I wouldn't believe you. The man is a legend. Tickets have been sold out for months."

"Yes. But I have a pair in my possession, box seats. *And* a meet and greet afterward with Mr. Blackmoore himself. Are you interested?"

His face, skepticism yielding to cautious hope, told her he was very interested. "Possibly."

"Well then, they're yours."

"What's the catch? Why am I even asking? As if I don't already know."

"Two days of your time at the festival, dressed as Mr. Darcy. Looking haughty and aloof, of course . . . but approachable enough to mix and mingle with your fans."

"My fans?"

"Darcy's fans," she corrected. "Pose for pictures, sign books, wander around and look forbidding. Should be easy enough." At his glower she coaxed, "It'll be fun."

"Fun," he echoed. "Somehow, I doubt it."

"Let's go." She took his arm and led him back across the lobby.

"Wait. What are you doing? I was nearly out the door. I'm on my way home!"

"Not yet. First, you need to come with me to try on your costume and learn how to tie a proper cravat."

"You're mad," he protested as she all but dragged him toward her office. "This is ridiculous."

"We're all mad here. Haven't you heard?" She ushered him inside. "Now, I need you to take off your shirt."

Mark came to a dead stop just inside the door. "I beg your pardon?"

"Your shirt," she repeated, turning away to rummage, frowning, through a garment rack by her desk. "Remove it, please." She grabbed a hanger from the rack and held out a shirt. "And try this on."

"But—"

"And once you've done that, I'll teach you to tie a cravat."

"You're not only mad," he grumbled as he snatched the shirt from her. "You're certifiable."

thirty

On Saturday morning, students, Austen fans, and costumed faculty thronged the Somerset University campus in search of workshops, book signings, and a glimpse of their favorite Austen characters as the fifth annual Jane Austen literary festival got underway.

Even the weather had cooperated, providing clear, rain-washed skies and mild temperatures. Phaedra smoothed her white silk skirt and touched a hand to her pinned-up hair. An artfully arranged tendril escaped here and there, and her mother had woven in a few tiny pearls and bits of baby's breath.

"Perfect," Nan had declared as she finished and gave her daughter a hand mirror. "You're the picture of Elizabeth Bennet at the Pemberley ball."

Phaedra admired her reflection and laid the mirror aside. "I just hope I have a better time of it than Elizabeth did on the night of the ball."

"You will." Her mother had spoken with assurance. "Not even Mr. Darcy will be able to resist you."

Now, as Mark Selden, looking handsome but patently uncomfortable in his costume, approached her, she thought of her mother's words and blushed.

He executed a bow. "Miss Bennet."

"Mr. Darcy." Her cheeks warmed as his gaze lingered just a touch too long on her face. "How are you finding our little festival thus far?"

"Tolerable, I suppose."

"But not exciting enough to tempt you?" she teased.

"That," he ventured, "remains to be seen."

"This is amazing," Marisol said as Phaedra and Mark posed for a female fan's photograph. "Look at the turnout!"

"Didn't I tell you it'd be the best year yet?" Phaedra glanced around her. A breeze filled the welcome banner stretched across the main concourse. "We sold every ticket. And every single raffle ticket."

"Did you see the teacup cupcakes?" Marisol pointed out a booth selling the confections. "So cute! They're baked right into little fluted silicone teacups."

"I got the idea from Hannah," Phaedra said. "She made them for a cream tea at the British embassy last year. They were a big hit."

"Your sister works at the embassy?" Mark asked.

"Yes. She's the pastry chef. You would have met her," she added tartly, "if you'd stuck around a little longer at the Spring Fling."

"Small world. My friend Charles is a consul there."

Phaedra stopped and stared at him. "Charles Dalton?"

He nodded. "We went to school together, years ago. Summer Fields. We were both Year 3 monitors."

"I can't believe it. Charles gave me the tickets for Tyrell Blackmoore. He got them from one of the diplomats at the embassy."

"I'm surprised. Charles hates Shakespeare."

"He was too polite to say so. Hence, the tickets."

"His manners are always regrettably impeccable."

She fell into step alongside Selden and regarded him quizzically. "What about your manners, Mr. Darcy? I must say they're impeccable, as well. You've stepped into the role quite convincingly."

"One can't study Shakespeare without making a study of Elizabethan drama. Passion, intrigue, greed, ambition . . . all of the themes he and Marlowe and Jonson wrote about are found in Austen's works, as well."

"True." They paused to pose for another photo. "I have Charles's sister Karolina to thank for getting me an interview for the consulting job on *Who Wants to Marry Mr. Darcy?*"

"Ah yes. Karo." He said nothing more, and his expression did not invite questions.

Was there history between them? Phaedra wondered. She smiled and inclined her head as festivalgoers waved and giggled and nudged one another as they passed. Obviously, there was. No one else but Charles dared refer to Karolina as Karo.

"Is Nick Ross honoring us with his presence?" Mark asked after a moment.

"Yes, later this afternoon. He's drawing the winner for a tour of the *Who Wants to Marry Mr. Darcy?* set. They're filming by the river this morning, taking advantage of the weather."

"Will he make it back in time, I wonder? You'll have a lot of disappointed people if he doesn't." Posters of the actor in full Darcy regalia were everywhere.

"He promised he would. If he doesn't . . ." She eyed him thoughtfully. "I suppose you'll have to take his place at the dunking tank."

He followed her gaze to the "Dunk a Hunk" booth, where half a dozen steps led up to a bright blue tank filled with water, bridged by a collapsible seat.

"You *cannot* be serious." An expression of slowly dawning horror settled over his face.

"It'll be fun. You sit on that seat, and people try to take you out by hitting the target with a ball." She pointed to a round paddle on one side of the tank. "If they hit it just right, you go for a swim." Her lips dimpled into a smile. "Just like that famous British actor in the movie. Clingy white shirt and all."

He'd just opened his mouth to protest when Phaedra let out a peal of laughter. "Your face! I've never seen you look so discombobulated. You're far too easy to tease, Mr. Darcy."

"I'm glad I amuse you." He paused as a passing fan, an older woman dressed in costume, took their photo. As she hurried off, beaming with pleasure, a buzzing sound emanated from his person. "Excuse me." He reached in his pocket and withdrew a cell phone.

A tiny frown marred Phaedra's brow. "You know the rules. No cell phones allowed by those of us in costume. Verisimilitude is of the utmost importance."

"So is this call. Now, if you'll excuse me?" He turned away and lifted the phone to his ear.

She watched his departure with annoyance. She'd established the festival rules only that morning—no cell phones, no rudeness, staying in character from beginning to end. Trust Professor Selden to break all three rules at once.

He never did anything by halves.

A moment later he returned, his cell phone gone and his lips set in a tight line. "My pardon for the interruption, Miss Bennet." He held out his arm. "Shall we?"

Without reply, she curled her fingers around his sleeve and fell stiffly into step beside him.

"Is everything all right?" she ventured after a moment.

"Fine."

"I didn't mean to come across as a stickler for rules earlier. It's easier to preserve the fantasy for our guests if we leave our electronic devices at home."

He stopped and turned to face her. "I understand. But sometimes, real life intrudes. Whether we like it or not."

"I've offended you."

"You flatter yourself if you think me so easily offended. Everything isn't always about you, you know. You give yourself too much credit."

"And what about you?" Anger warmed her cheeks. "I suppose you think you're above such petty things as rules."

"As usual, you assume too much. I think no such thing."

"I think you're not taking this festival seriously."

"I'm sorry you feel that way." His words were clipped. "But I have a lot going on at the moment. My number one concern is my gram. She's . . ." He plowed a hand through his hair in a motion of frustration. "She's not doing well."

"Oh." Phaedra's anger deflated. "I'm so sorry. I didn't know."

"No, of course you didn't. How could you?"

"Well, you can tell me now. Please."

He paused for a moment before slowly saying, "I spent my summers with her. She all but raised me after my parents divorced. My father expected me to earn a law degree and become a judge, like him, but Gram convinced him that I was more suited to studying Shakespeare than statutory law." He looked away. "She was recently diagnosed with early-stage dementia."

Phaedra reached out to touch his arm. "Oh, Mark . . . how awful. I'm so very sorry."

"I'd already arranged to move back to the States and accepted the faculty position at Somerset when I found out. I didn't want to leave, but she insisted I go."

"I was surprised you gave up your place at Welford Academy in Hampshire to come and teach at Somerset," she admitted. "Welford is a highly regarded boys' school."

"I wasn't making much of a difference there. And I didn't have much choice. My father's health is poor. He lives in Charlottesville, and I needed to be nearby."

"I'm sorry to hear it. And I apologize. I—well, I was wrong about you."

He glanced at her. "That wasn't so hard, was it? To admit you were wrong?"

"You should have told me." Defensiveness crept into her voice. "If you had, I would have understood."

"Instead, you jumped to the worst possible conclusion, as you so often do where I'm concerned." He paused. "I ask you to remember one thing, Miss Bennet."

"What's that?"

"To quote a famous literary gentleman, 'My good opinion once lost, is lost forever.'"

With a curt inclination of his head, he turned on one booted heel and strode away.

Late in the afternoon Phaedra made her way to the Austen Tea Shoppe booth. The crowds had thinned, but the festival still teemed with activity. Spying an empty table on the quad nearby, she collapsed into a chair. Her feet hurt, she'd eaten nothing but a lemon buttercream teacup cupcake and a few sips of tea, and there was no sign of Mark Selden anywhere.

"I'm exhausted." Marisol dropped into the chair across from her. "I finally gave Professor Bryce and his wandering hands the slip. Where's your Mr. Darcy, by the way? I haven't seen him in ages."

"He isn't 'my' Mr. Darcy. As to where he is, I have no idea. We posed for a photo a couple of hours ago, but I haven't seen him since." Phaedra glanced around and frowned. "He didn't leave, did he? He promised he'd help secure everything after closing."

Lucy, wearing her normal street clothes, sat down and handed them each a bottle of water. "If you're talking about Professor Selden, he left a while ago."

"Left?" Phaedra echoed. "But he knows we're all staying until five to clean up. Why would he bail on us?"

"Maybe he doesn't like cleaning up," Marisol offered. "Or picking up trash. He is Mr. Darcy, after all."

"Well, whatever the reason," Lucy said, "he's gone."

Phaedra fell silent as the others talked and joked and compared notes on the day's experiences. Why did Mark leave so abruptly? Had she offended him that badly?

Was his good opinion lost? Mark had quoted Darcy's words to her, and she'd felt the sting of his anger like a slap. No wonder he'd been such an excellent Mr. Darcy.

True, in the beginning his enthusiasm was lacking, but she'd called him on it and he quickly adapted, and as the day went on he seemed to enjoy personifying the haughty fictional hero. His British accent didn't hurt, either.

She told herself she didn't care if Mark Selden was annoyed with her. She didn't like him, anyway. He was arrogant and aloof. Rather like Darcy himself.

"You're awfully quiet." Lucy nudged her. "What's up? You're a million miles away."

"Just thinking of all the things we need to do when the festival ends tomorrow. Costumes to return, booths to deconstruct, posters and banners to take down . . . I always forget about that. And I dread it."

"Are you sure something else isn't on your mind?" Lucy questioned. "Or should I say, someone else?" Curiosity glimmered in her dark eyes.

"Of course not." Phaedra pushed her chair back. "What a ridiculous idea."

"Ridiculous." Lucy arched a perfectly groomed brow. "If you say so, Miss Bennet."

Thirty-One

On Monday Phaedra delivered back-to-back lectures in the morning and faced a full schedule of student consultations in the afternoon. She had no time to dwell on Mark's abrupt departure from the literary festival on Saturday or his non-return on Sunday.

And she was glad. Being busy made it that much easier to keep her distance from him.

Tuesday found Phaedra at Marling, ready to resume her consulting duties for *Who Wants to Marry Mr. Darcy?*

She stood at the head of the dining room table and smiled at the bachelorettes ranged along both sides, their faces fixed expectantly on hers.

"Are any of you familiar with the language of fans?" she asked.

Amidst a sea of blank looks, Tinsley lifted her hand. "It's when a woman used her fan to flirt with a man, right?"

"Exactly." She picked up a fan lying closed on the table in front of her and unfurled it. "By holding a fan in a certain way, a lady conveyed a message to a gentleman observing her. Opening and closing the fan quickly meant 'You are cruel.' But drawing the fan across the cheek," she added, "signified 'I love you.'"

"How romantic," one of the girls gushed.

"Very," Phaedra agreed. "Unfortunately, none of it is true. Fans went out of fashion after the French Revolution and sales declined. 'Fan etiquette' was a marketing ploy designed to boost sales . . . and it worked, for a time. Female spies also used 'peeping fans' during the Napoleonic Wars to conduct discreet surveillance at social gatherings."

As she demonstrated the proper way to furl, unfurl, and flutter a fan, urging the bachelorettes to do the same, Finch entered the dining room with a silver tea tray and set it down on the sideboard. Bertie followed, carrying a second tray filled with dainty cucumber and watercress sandwiches.

"Thank you," Phaedra said as they left. "Next, we'll practice proper tea etiquette." She put her fan aside and went to the sideboard to retrieve the silver teapot. "During the Regency era, tea was served at breakfast, after a dance, and after dinner."

"They certainly liked their tea," Renee observed.

Phaedra said nothing. Her glance strayed to the nearest window, where a flash of pink and the swish of a blond ponytail caught her attention.

Was that Patsy Fortune?

She gazed intently out the window but saw no one.

"Professor Brighton?"

With a guilty start, Phaedra turned around. "I'm sorry. Yes, Tinsley?"

"Suppose a Regency lady didn't like tea?"

"Hot chocolate might be served, or coffee, or perhaps a tisane. Chamomile was a popular aid to digestion or calming the nerves. It still is."

"Did people ever get sick from ingesting herbs?" another young woman wondered.

"Not usually, although one had to be careful," Phaedra said. "Pokeweed, found here in the Blue Ridge, is a highly poisonous plant. But people once brewed tea from the fruit or the leaves to treat rheumatism and dysentery."

For once, the bachelorettes were completely focused on something other than Nick Ross. Phaedra bit back a smile.

"There was a great demand for tea in the early nineteenth century," she went on, "which led to the production of cheaper, counterfeit teas."

"Counterfeit?" Tinsley echoed.

"Yes. Most tea came from England, and it was costly. With the lower classes demanding tea as well, counterfeit tea filled the gap. If you were lucky, you'd end up with nothing more than previously brewed leaves . . . weak, but harmless. More unscrupulous sellers sold blackthorn leaves colored with verdigris to resemble tea leaves."

"Isn't verdigris poisonous?"

Phaedra nodded. "Yes, but only in large doses. Drink enough over time, however, and you'd likely die."

"Poisoned tea!" someone exclaimed. "How awful."

Voices echoed from the far end of the hallway. "Finch, is that for my mother?" Charlene asked.

"Yes," the butler replied. "It's her tea tray."

"I'll take it. I'm going upstairs, at any rate."

"The tray is heavy, Mrs. Collier," he said doubtfully. "Perhaps it's best if I take it."

"It's fine. I've got it. Thank you, Finch."

Charlene passed by the dining room a moment later, tray in hand, as Finch hovered a few steps behind her.

"Where were we?" Phaedra asked as she turned back to her class.

"Tea etiquette," one of the bachelorettes piped up.

"Right. Let me demonstrate how to pour, and drink, our tea."

Halfway through the demonstration, satisfied the bachelorettes had mastered pouring and holding their teacups, Phaedra set out the plate of cucumber and cress sandwiches on the dining room table when a piercing scream reached their ears.

She instructed everyone to wait and hurried out of the dining room to the entry hall.

"Finch!" Charlene cried from the top of the stairs. Her face was twisted in anguish, and she'd gone deathly pale. "Get up here. Something's wrong with my mother."

He rushed down the hall and headed up the stairs, a dish towel flung over one shoulder, as Phaedra followed behind him. "What is it? What's happened?"

"I'm not sure." With a shaking hand she indicated a cup and saucer lying on the floor near Violet's feet, tea forming a brown stain on the carpet. "She took a few sips of tea. Then she suffered a tremor and dropped the cup."

"Perhaps her blood sugar is low," Phaedra suggested.

"No. She had her insulin shot not half an hour ago. She was fine until just now . . . Phae, is she having a stroke?"

"I don't know. Let's not jump to conclusions. We need to get her to a hospital, right away."

"Can't . . . breathe," Violet murmured. "Terrible headache. Heart beating . . . oddly."

"I'm calling 911." Finch took out his cell phone and relayed Violet's symptoms to the dispatcher. "Yes, just now. She had a few sips of tea and suffered a tremor. Difficulty breathing, irregular heartbeats." He listened for a moment. "We're at Marling, Rolling Hill Road. Thank you. And please hurry."

A short time later the EMTs arrived. After taking Mrs. Lucas's vitals and asking a few brief questions, they loaded her onto a collapsible gurney and carried her downstairs to the waiting ambulance.

"May I ride along?" Charlene asked as she hovered nearby, her face ashen.

"Of course."

"I'll call as soon as I know something," she told Phaedra.

"Just focus on your mother," Phaedra told her, and squeezed her hand reassuringly.

Charlene climbed in to sit beside her mother, and a moment later, the ambulance departed.

"What an awful thing," Phaedra said as she and Finch turned back toward the front steps.

"Terrible." His face was drained of all color as he held the door open and waited for her to go inside.

"Finch. Is everything all right?"

Bertie bustled toward them, an oven mitt on one hand. "What happened to Mrs. Lucas? We saw the ambulance take her away."

"She had a bad tremor and dropped her teacup," Phaedra told her. "It could be a stroke, but at this point we don't know. Charlene's gone with her to the hospital. She'll call when she has an update on Violet's condition."

"Poor woman. I do hope she'll be all right." Bertie made her way toward the staircase. "I'll go upstairs and clear away the mess."

"Best leave it," Phaedra said.

"Leave it? But the tea will stain the carpet."

"Leave it, Bertie, please. That'll be all."

Hearing the determined note in Phaedra's voice, the woman narrowed her eyes but turned away without further argument and returned to the kitchen.

"Why don't you want it cleaned up?" Finch asked in a low voice.

"Because the teacup may be evidence."

"Evidence? Of what?"

Phaedra hesitated. "It's possible Mrs. Lucas might have been poisoned."

"Poisoned?" Finch's eyebrows shot up. "What on earth makes you think such a thing?"

"It's just a thought. I'm probably wrong. But until we hear from Charlene, no one should touch that teacup or clean up the spill. Everything in Violet's room could be potential evidence and has to stay just as it is."

"But I made that tea," he protested, affronted. "English breakfast, unsweetened, with a slice of lemon. Just the way Violet likes it. And I promise you, I didn't put any poison in there."

"I'm sure you *didn't*," she reassured him, even as she wondered if he was telling the truth. "I hope I'm wrong. I can't imagine anyone in this house hurting Charlene's mother. Can you?"

"No, of course not. But it's no secret that she and Mr. Collier couldn't stand each other."

"Who else was in the kitchen when you made the tea?"

He frowned. "The usual people. Bertie, Jen, a couple of the catering staff."

"No one else?"

He shook his head.

"Do me a favor?" she asked. "Tell the bachelorettes our lesson is canceled." She headed for the stairs.

"Where are you going?"

"To Violet's room, to stay put until I hear from Charlene."

"So you really *do* think Violet was poisoned."

"I don't know what to think. But if there's even a chance someone put something deadly in her cup, I have to make sure the evidence doesn't disappear."

Thirty-Two

An hour later Phaedra's phone rang, and she put the book she'd found aside to answer it. "Charlene? What's going on? Is your mother all right?"

"She's resting. They tested her blood gases and glucose levels. Her blood sugar is normal, and she's not having a stroke."

"Thank goodness for that. What does the doctor say?"

"He won't know until the results of the blood gases come back. He asked what foods she ingested this morning."

Phaedra's fingers gripped the phone. "Does he think she might have food poisoning?"

"It's possible, although he seems to think it's something else." Charlene paused. "I need to go. The nurse just came in. I'll call you later."

"Thanks for the update. We're all thinking of Violet."

She returned to her book but couldn't focus on the words. Her gaze went to the tea tray sitting atop the elderly woman's dresser. There was nothing on the tray but a silver teapot and a spoon on a linen napkin.

Had Violet's tea contained something deadly?

And if so, was enough tea left behind for forensics to test?

Phaedra glanced down. Although most of the brown liquid had spilled onto the carpet, there was a small amount remaining in the teacup.

She hoped her hunch was wrong. After all, who would want to poison Charlene's mother? Finch had made the tea. He said the cup contained her usual, English breakfast tea and lemon, and Phaedra was inclined to believe him. He had no motive to harm Violet.

No one did.

The sound of footsteps on the stairs brought Phaedra to her feet. She went to Violet's door and saw Bertie, a tray in hand, coming down the hall toward her.

"Since the others are eating downstairs, I brought your lunch up," she said briskly, and handed the tray over. "Ham and cheese on rye, potato salad, and an oatmeal-raisin cookie." She turned to go.

"Wait, please." Phaedra set the tray aside and turned back to the door. "You were in the kitchen when Finch made Violet's tea earlier, weren't you?"

A guarded look came over her face. "Yes."

"Who else was there?"

"I'm sure I don't know. I have enough to do without taking notice of who comes in and out of the kitchen."

"Finch said Jen was there, and a couple of your catering staff."

"That's right. Jen helped bake the cookies while Derrick and Rob made sandwiches and plated the lunches."

"Anyone else there that you can think of? It could be important."

"No." She turned away, paused, and turned back. "Well, now that you mention it, there was someone. Patsy came by."

"Patsy Fortune?" Phaedra remembered glimpsing a blonde in hot pink darting past the dining room window.

"Yes. She came in the back door, wanted to talk to Finch."

"About what?"

"She didn't say and I didn't ask." She rested her hands on her hips. "I assume it was a personal matter. I told her he was in the kitchen garden, getting thyme for the beef stew. I prefer fresh herbs," she added. "Far superior to dried."

"What did she do?"

"She went out to find him, and I went to the dining room to set the table for lunch."

"When did this take place?"

"Just after Finch made Mrs. Lucas her tea."

Phaedra felt her heartbeat pick up. "So the tea was unattended for a few minutes."

"Yes. But no one in the kitchen touched that tea. Everyone was busy. And I'd have noticed. I run a very tight ship." A truculent expression settled on her face. "Is that all? I have things to do."

"Just one more question. Does Patsy often show up here at Marling?"

"Every now and then. Finch worked for the Fortune family for a good many years. I wouldn't say he and Patsy are friends, exactly, but they keep in touch. She was here the night of the storm," she added. "One of the maids saw her in the upstairs hall just before the power went out."

Phaedra stared at her. She couldn't believe what she'd just heard. "Patsy was *here*? Did the maid tell the police about this?"

"I've no idea. You'd have to ask Maggie. She gave a statement to the sheriff's deputy like the rest of us. She probably didn't think it was important enough to mention."

"Why on earth not? Patsy was here the night Mr. Collier was murdered!"

She shrugged. "Patsy and her sisters live in the old caretaker's cottage. Like I said, she wanders in to see Finch now and again. No one pays any mind. This was their house not so long ago, after all. Now, if that's all? I've work to do."

"Yes, that's all. Thank you for the tray."

Bertie didn't reply as she lumbered off.

Phaedra turned back into Violet's room, all thoughts of the elderly woman's tea and who might have tampered with it replaced with Bertie's startling news.

A maid had seen Patsy Fortune upstairs on the afternoon of the storm . . . just before William Collier's murder.

Which meant Patsy could've snuck in and thrown the blow-dryer in Collier's tub.

The Fortune girl would know where to find the dryer, particularly if it belonged to her. And she'd know that the wiring in that particular bathroom wasn't modernized.

Phaedra sank down on the edge of a chair by the fireplace with a frown. Everything came back to motive. Patsy Fortune had good reason to kill William Collier. He'd stolen everything away from her and her family . . . their money, reality show pilot, even their home. She had a motive, and opportunity. It wasn't a stretch to imagine she'd murdered William Collier.

But how did she manage to get upstairs without being seen? With everyone in the kitchen or the drawing room late that afternoon, surely someone saw Patsy. The entrance hall and stairs were in plain view of the drawing room.

Suddenly, she remembered Charlene telling her Violet insisted she'd seen the Marling ghost upstairs during the storm. Charlene had dismissed the claim.

But suppose Violet didn't imagine seeing Elizabeth Marling's ghost? What if she'd seen a young woman, very much alive, at the end of that long, shadowy hall?

What if she'd seen Patsy Fortune?

Patsy must've slipped into the kitchen unobserved. Bertie said no one paid much mind to her comings and goings. It would've been an easy matter for her to use Violet's elevator or the back stairs to reach the second floor.

Not only that, but the elevator opened across from the bathroom where William Collier was murdered . . .

. . . the bathroom where Violet claimed she saw Elizabeth Marling's ghost.

Her phone rang. Although she didn't recognize the number, she answered. "Hello?"

"Phaedra? It's Mark Selden."

Surprise suffused her face. "Mark? Where are you?"

"Blockley. In Gloucestershire."

"Yes, I know it. My parents did a walking tour of the Cotswolds a few years ago." She paused. "What are *you* doing there?"

Silence. "I had to come home," he said after a moment. "Gram died."

Suddenly, the pieces fell into place. His defensiveness at the festival, the phone call he'd taken, his abrupt departure. It all began—and ended—with his grandmother.

A myriad of emotions swirled through her. "Alzheimer's?" she ventured.

"That, and pneumonia. She died, Phaedra, and I wasn't there. I didn't get back in time to see her before . . ." He blew out a shaky breath. "I didn't get to say goodbye. To thank her for all she did for me, growing up. To sit beside her and hold her hand."

She thought of all the words she could say . . . kind but essentially useless words like *I'm sorry, is there anything I can do* . . . and instead said the first thing that came into her head. "Oh, Mark—I had no idea. Please," she added earnestly, "don't blame yourself. She wanted you to come here. When you offered to stay, she insisted you go."

"That's . . . very kind. Thank you." After an awkward silence, he cleared his throat. "Well, I'd best ring off. Goodbye."

"Goodbye, Mark. And . . . thank you for letting me know."

As she hung up, her heart ached for him. For his loss, and for the blame he'd assign himself for not getting back in time to see his gram before she died.

She'd barely disconnected when her phone screen lit up with a call from Charlene.

"How is Violet?" Phaedra asked. "Have you got the test results back? Will she be all right?"

"Yes. She should be fine. But the next twenty-four hours are critical."

Concern puckered Phaedra's brow. "Why is that?"

"The blood gases test. It revealed traces of tetrahydrozoline. A common ingredient in eye drops."

"Eye drops? What would something like that be doing

in . . . oh my God." Phaedra drew in a sharp breath as her gaze darted to the brown stain on the carpet. The tea.

"If she'd ingested a little more, her heart would have failed," Charlene said, her voice unsteady. "And here's the scary part. The chemical wouldn't have shown up in a normal toxicology report."

"So whoever did this would literally have gotten away with murder," Phaedra finished slowly. "Violet's tremor saved her life."

"Yes. They're keeping her at the hospital overnight. I'm staying with her."

"Of course. Is there anything you need me to bring you? A change of clothes, or toiletries?"

"I don't want to inconvenience you—"

"Don't be silly. It's no trouble. I'll bring a nightgown and robe for your mother, too." Phaedra added, "Has anyone notified the police that she was poisoned?"

"Yes, the hospital did. Don't be surprised if Detective Morelli shows up."

"I expect he will. I've been in Violet's room the entire time, making sure no one touches that teacup."

"Thank you. I'm sure the police will want to test it."

"As soon as they let me go, I'll head to the hospital and bring you an overnight bag."

"Thanks again, Phae. For everything."

"No problem. See you soon." Phaedra stood up and returned the phone to her back pocket, and as she did, the doorbell rang. She waited in the hallway outside Violet's door, listening for the sound of Finch's footsteps as he crossed the entry hall and opened the front door.

"Detective Morelli. Come in."

A moment later, Finch led him upstairs and down the hall to Mrs. Lucas's room. The detective came to a stop as he saw her.

"You again." He didn't sound surprised. Or pleased.

"Sorry." She shrugged. "Dastardly deeds just seem to follow me around."

His glance took in the cup and the stain on the carpet. "You haven't touched anything, I hope."

"No. No one has, except Mrs. Lucas, of course. I stayed to make sure no one cleared away the mess."

"Good." He took out his phone. "Morelli. Send a crime unit to Marling," he said into his phone. "No, no body this time—attempted poisoning. Thanks."

"I'm headed to the hospital to take Charlene a change of clothes," she told Morelli. "I'll be down the hall in her room, packing an overnight bag."

"Not so fast. I have a few questions first."

She pressed her lips together. "Of course you do."

"Tell me what happened."

She told him Finch had made the tea, Charlene brought it up, and Violet drank a small amount before experiencing a severe tremor. "Luckily, she dropped the cup, as you can see. There's still some tea inside."

"So the only fingerprints on the cup are Finch's, Mrs. Lucas's, and Charlene Collier's. Correct?"

"As far as I know. Yes."

"What about yours?"

"I told you, I didn't touch anything."

"Okay. I'll get your full statement later. You can go, Professor."

She hesitated in the doorway. "I can't imagine who'd do this. No one had reason to poison Violet."

"Someone did. And there's always a reason. We may not see it yet, but it's there."

Phaedra considered sharing her suspicions about Patsy Fortune but decided against it. With no evidence, just a hunch and the word of a maid who might be mistaken, there seemed little point.

"Charlene loves her mother," she said. "She's devoted most of her life to caring for her."

"Yes, she has."

"She wouldn't poison Violet. It makes no sense."

He went to the window and glanced out. "Maybe it does."

He turned to face her. "After years of caring for her mother, giving up her education and her personal life and working double shifts to make ends meet, Charlene finally finds love. Or something approximating love."

Phaedra waited, a wary expression on her face as he shook a few tiny breath mints from a container in his pocket into his palm.

"She marries Collier," he went on, "and the arguments with her mother start. Violet hated the man. And she never missed an opportunity to remind her daughter of that fact."

"Charlene understood her reasons for hating Collier," Phaedra pointed out. "Violet lost her life savings to him. And their home. And you're right, she didn't approve of their marriage, and Charlene knew it. But her reasons for marrying him were hardly selfish. He offered financial security, not only for Charlene, but her mother. She could finally have the medical care and attention she needed. The care Charlene couldn't afford to provide on her own."

"She's a veritable saint," Morelli said dryly. "But even saints have a breaking point. And Charlene reached hers."

"No." Anger bubbled up inside her. "Charlene didn't do this. She wouldn't. And I'll prove it."

"And how do you plan to do that?"

"Find whoever actually *did* do it."

"I've warned you before to stay out of this investigation. You're still not hearing me. If you persist in interfering, I'll charge you with obstruction."

"Whoever poisoned Violet may have murdered Bill Collier," she said, choosing to ignore him. "But you refuse to see anyone else as a suspect. As far as you're concerned, Charlene is guilty."

"Charlene Collier has motive for both crimes, Professor Brighton, not to mention means and opportunity. Finch stated that she insisted on taking Violet's tea tray from him and carried it upstairs. Which means she had opportunity to lace her mother's cup with tetrahydrozoline. All I need is physical evidence to link her to one scene or the other." He glanced at the carpet. "And thanks to you, that teacup should do the trick."

Phaedra met his eyes with dismay as the full impact of his words hit her. Her actions, guarding the teacup in an effort to help identify the culprit, had backfired. She should've let Bertie clear the damn thing away.

But she hadn't. And now, because of her interference, Morelli had physical evidence, Charlene's fingerprints on that cup. Evidence he could use to link her with an attempted murder.

Instead of helping her friend, she'd made things a hundred times worse.

"Thank you, Professor," Morelli added, dismissing her.

She swallowed a sharp retort, turned on her heel, and left to go and pack a bag for Charlene and Violet.

thirty-three

Late Saturday afternoon, as tourists crowded the sidewalk in search of handmade quilts and ice cream cones, Phaedra inched the Mini Cooper forward. Traffic on Main Street moved at a snail's pace.

No, she amended silently. Snails moved faster.

She drummed her fingers against the steering wheel with mounting impatience and glanced at the canvas bag of groceries on the seat beside her. Cans of gourmet cat food for Wickham, tomatoes and blackberries from Dixon's farm stand, and her guilty pleasure, one of Emmylou's ginormous, home-baked chocolate chip cookies.

Good thing, because at this rate, she'd need a little sustenance to appease her growling stomach.

Patrons filled the outdoor tables at Brewster's, a new small-batch brewery and restaurant, and shoppers crowded the sidewalks looking for clothing, antiques, or one-of-a-kind items. Even Woofgang's Doggy Bakery was busy.

Her foot came down hard on the brakes as a car cut in front of her. "Tourists," she muttered.

The right lane ground to a stop, and the traffic, already snarled, came to a standstill as one car after another signaled a lane change. Phaedra craned her head to see what the problem was.

A jingling harness and the clip-clop of hooves up ahead answered her question. A horse-drawn carriage blocked the right lane as passengers disembarked from their leisurely tour of downtown Laurel Springs. Although popular with visitors, locals were less enthusiastic.

Fifteen minutes and three light cycles later, she arrived at the carriage house. She dropped her keys and mail on the hall table and lugged the groceries into the kitchen. Daylight was waning, she was tired, and she desperately needed a glass of pinot and something savory to nibble on.

"I'm starving," she complained as she kicked off her shoes and headed for the kitchen.

Wickham looked up from his spot reclining atop the sofa. *I'm here*, his unblinking eyes seemed to say, *waiting for my dinner. You're not the only one who's hungry, you know. Where've you been?*

"Sorry, Wicks," she said as she removed the contents of her reusable canvas bag. She studied the cans of cat food. "Tuna Supreme or Salmon Divan?"

Surprise me.

She set down a dish of kibble topped with an entire can of salmon on the kitchen floor and smiled as Wickham darted over to devour his meal. After tossing together a salad of baby spinach leaves and dried cranberries drizzled with balsamic vinaigrette, she poured herself a well-deserved glass of wine.

Poor Mark. Caught between his grandmother's untimely death and his father's failing health. No wonder he'd been subdued during the literary festival. Remorse washed over her as she sprinkled a few flaxseeds on the salad. Sometimes, she really was clueless.

She carried the bowl and her glass to her desk and sat down. Time to do a little research on Patsy Fortune.

She reached for her laptop and typed the youngest Fortune sister's name into the search engine, and hundreds of hits popped up. Most were photos taken at charity balls and galas, fashion shows, or ringside at the racetrack or football field on the arm of her current boyfriend du jour.

Patsy was certainly a busy girl. Whether sunning on a private yacht in Barbados, schussing down the Alps in Verbier, or partying all night in a private nightclub, she carried her public persona off with style.

Phaedra's cursor hovered over a photo of Patsy taken last Christmas in Marling's drawing room with Taffy, her tiny Yorkie-poo. What happened to Taffy? Was she, like Patsy Fortune's jet-set lifestyle, gone?

She sipped her wine and studied the young man beside Patsy more closely. He was attractive, no surprise there, but she didn't recognize him. Which meant he wasn't a celebrity or sports figure. And he showed up only in more recent photos. Who was he?

A few clicks revealed his name was Kevin Garber. He and Patsy dated for eight months, attending a few galas and private parties together, but kept a low profile. Why? Phaedra wondered. Perhaps Patsy had finally found real love and didn't want to share the relationship with the public.

She searched for more information, finding very little, until her persistence was eventually rewarded.

Patsy's former boyfriend was a paramedic. Which meant he'd know all about poisons.

"Interesting," she murmured.

After Harold Fortune's death, photos of the pair disappeared. Phaedra frowned. Did the relationship simply run its course? Or did Patsy discover that Garber had more interest in her money than her?

Her suspicion turned once again to the Fortune girl. She'd lied about the choker and persuaded Finch to steal it, ostensibly to return it to its rightful owner . . . her mother. More lies. She'd been seen upstairs at Marling at the time of Collier's murder, and again on the morning that Violet's tea was poisoned.

Plus, Patsy lived in the caretaker's cottage on the property, which gave her access to the house and grounds, not to mention ample opportunity. Sharing close quarters in a tiny cottage with her mother and four sisters would be enough to induce anyone to murder.

Phaedra took a thoughtful sip of wine. Did Finch, like her, suspect that Patsy had murdered Collier? Did he threaten to go to the police with his suspicions?

And when Patsy entered the kitchen and saw Finch fixing a cup of tea, did she assume it was his? Phaedra sat up straighter as a new thought occurred.

What if the attempt on Violet's life was a mistake?

What if Patsy Fortune never meant to poison Violet? What if her intended victim was Finch?

After a leisurely Sunday breakfast of tea and toast the next morning, Phaedra marshaled her thoughts and took her theory to Detective Morelli at the Somerset County Courthouse.

He listened, leaning back in his desk chair with an impassive expression. "It's possible Patsy Fortune is involved," he conceded. "But I need more than theories to arrest her, Professor. I need hard evidence."

"Such as?"

"Such as Patsy's fingerprints on Violet's teacup. There weren't any. Only Finch's, and Violet's. And Charlene's."

So they were back to Charlene as the main suspect. Phaedra waited with impatience as he shook out some mints from the container in his pocket.

"Can't you go to the cottage at Marling and talk to Patsy? Search the place? Then you might find the evidence you need."

"I can't obtain a warrant without probable cause."

"What about the maid who said she saw Patsy upstairs on the night of the murder?"

"Again, I need proof, something to physically link her to the location. And I don't have it. Without compelling evidence, the judge would toss the case out of court. There were no prints on the syringe we found, and none in the vicinity of the crime scene. Whoever murdered William Collier did a thorough job of covering their tracks."

She stood and slung her purse strap over her shoulder. "This is a waste of time. You're not interested in identifying anyone else as a suspect. Only Charlene."

"I'd be interested if I had a viable suspect. But I don't." His expression settled into hard lines. "If you had some actual proof to offer, Professor Brighton, then that would be different."

"Fine. You want proof? That's just what I'll get." She went to the door. "Goodbye, Detective."

"Where do you think you're going?" he demanded as he pushed himself up from his chair. "I've told you to stay out of this investigation so many times I'm tired of hearing myself say it."

"That makes two of us."

"Stay away from Marling, Professor. You'll end up in the middle of a dangerous situation if you don't bow out. I'm warning you for the last time."

"Good to know," she said.

And she left.

Halfway to Marling, Phaedra's phone rang. Her mother. Still fuming over her conversation with Detective Morelli, she let the call go to voice mail. Nan Prescott Brighton and her latest attempt at matchmaking would have to wait.

"His name is Arthur Fassbinder," she'd gushed when Phaedra stopped by the bookstore last week. "Such lovely manners! I showed him your photo, and he's very interested to meet you."

Such lovely manners was Mom-speak for unattractive, or strange, or both. "What does he do?"

"Something technical to do with computers."

Which meant he worked in a gaming store at the mall and spent his free hours playing Dungeons and Dragons.

"Sorry, Arthur," she said as she turned onto Route 250, "but I think I'll pass. Remaining a spinster is looking better and better every day."

Passing up the unit lot, which was quiet on this nonworking Sunday afternoon, Phaedra parked the Mini in front of Marling and went up the front steps.

She lifted the polished brass knocker and let it fall. As she waited, she pondered how best to approach Finch. She needed to talk to him but couldn't risk questioning him in the house, with so many eyes and ears all around.

Perhaps she could say she had car trouble and ask the butler to take a quick look under the hood. Then, at least, they could talk in privacy.

She heard footsteps, and the door opened. "Professor Brighton," Finch said, a trace of surprise on his face. "The production is shut down today. As I'm sure you know. What brings you to Marling?"

"Car trouble," she said. "On the way over the engine started making a strange knocking sound. Could you come out and have a look?"

"I'm about to serve Mrs. Collier her afternoon tea." In a lower voice he added, "I can't leave the tea unattended for even a minute. You do understand."

"Of course," she whispered back. "But I really do need your help with something."

His face, she noticed as he hesitated, was pale and haggard, as if he hadn't slept well.

"Did you fill the tank recently?" he inquired in a normal tone. "Cheap gas is notorious for knocking. I suggest you drive it to the nearest station. Now, if you'll excuse me . . ." He moved to close the door.

"No, I'm sure it's something else," she insisted. She leaned forward and whispered, "Please come outside. We need to talk, in private. It's important. Vitally important."

"I see." He cleared his throat and cast a nervous glance over his shoulder. "Very well, then, Professor, I'll have a

look under the hood. Take it around to the garage, and I'll
see you after I deliver Mrs. Collier's tea tray."

"Thank you." She flashed him a quick thumbs-up and returned to her car.

"What's this all about?" he demanded twenty minutes
later as he strode across the lawn to the garage, where she
waited, leaning against the front fender of the Mini. "What's
so important you dragged me from my duties?"

"It's about Violet's poisoned tea." She lifted the hood and
waited for him to join her, where they'd be hidden from any
prying eyes at the house. "I think it may have been meant
for you."

Thirty-Four

Me?" Finch blanched. "What makes you say that?"

She explained her theory, that Patsy had murdered Mr. Collier and suspected Finch knew.

He rested one hand against the top of the hood. "Let me get this straight. You think Patsy poisoned Violet by mistake. And that I was her intended victim." He shook his head. "Interesting theory. But Patsy didn't kill William Collier," he said firmly. "And even if she had, I wouldn't go to the police with the information. Whoever offed the bastard did the world a favor."

"How can you be so sure she didn't kill him?"

He leaned over the engine and pretended to look it over. "It's true she was upstairs late that afternoon, not long before the murder. And it's true the maid saw her at the end of the hall. Violet did, too."

Phaedra nodded. "She told Charlene she saw the ghost of Elizabeth Marling. Why didn't you tell the police you saw Patsy?"

"Because she didn't go upstairs to murder Collier." He straightened and met her inquiring gaze. "She had . . . shall we say, an assignation, with Nick Ross."

Her eyes widened. So Clark Mullinax was right. Nick and Patsy, once an item, were involved. "I see."

"They met in Gstaad a couple of years ago and played it off to the media as a holiday romance, but they continued seeing each other in secret. Until recently."

"When Nick landed the role as Mr. Darcy on the show."

"Yes. It changed things between them. Nick told Patsy their relationship was over, that he couldn't jeopardize his contract or his career by seeing her any longer."

"And I'm guessing she didn't take it well."

"That's putting it mildly. She lost it. She called him constantly, texting and leaving messages, until he was forced to block her."

Phaedra nodded slowly as she remembered Nick's phone conversation the day she'd left his trailer. He'd mentioned "that bloody reporter" and the need for discretion. She frowned, deep in thought.

Was the reporter Clark Mullinax of the *Laurel Springs Clarion*? Had Clark found out about Patsy's secret relationship with the Welsh actor and threatened to go public?

She'd bet money he'd blackmailed Patsy with the information in an attempt to coerce her into agreeing to a few dates with him.

Her frown deepened into a scowl. He'd played games, not only with Patsy, but her, sending her to Woofgang's on a wild-goose chase with questions he knew would rattle the youngest Fortune sister.

"That sneaky little weasel," she muttered.

"Who? Nick?" Finch asked, perplexed.

She shook her head. "Someone else. So did Patsy give up? Has she stopped seeing Nick?"

"Far from it. She spies on him during filming, leaves him notes, even hangs around the kitchen in hopes of seeing him. Karolina barred her from the production site, but the Marling grounds are extensive, and Patsy knows every shortcut and private path."

Suddenly, her conversation with Tinsley the day the bachelorette had been so upset with Nick made sense.

"Well, I guess I got it all wrong." Phaedra sighed. "I was so sure Patsy was the murderer."

"She has her faults, but she isn't a killer." He slammed the hood shut and reached for a rag to wipe his hands. "But someone is. And that someone left a note under my door last night."

"A note? What did it say?" she asked, her interest quickening.

"It was short and sweet. It said, 'You're next.'"

"Did you keep it?"

"I was so rattled I left it on my dresser and locked my bedroom door. I barely slept all night. At some point early this morning, I finally dozed off. When I woke, the note was gone."

"Who would do that? Why? Tell me everything you know," she urged him.

After eyeing her warily, he admitted he'd threatened Collier. "I'd long suspected Harold Fortune was being blackmailed, but I didn't know who, or why. When he died and left everything to Collier, I had my answer."

"Why would Bill Collier blackmail Mr. Fortune?"

"I don't know. Harold was a very wealthy man, so I imagine he had his share of enemies, and secrets. But I've no idea what they were."

"So you confronted Mr. Collier."

He nodded. "The day he accused me of stealing the choker and threatened to call the police. I was outraged. I told him if he called the police, I'd tell them he coerced Harold into changing his will." He cleared his throat. "And I told him I knew the rest of it."

"The rest of what?"

"That's just it." Perspiration dampened his forehead. "I was lying. I wanted to frighten him, make him think I had something big on him, so he'd back off."

"Well, it worked. But you frightened someone else, too.

Someone who must've overheard, and thought you knew more than you did."

"Yes." He mopped his brow with the rag. "But who?"

"Someone who isn't afraid to threaten you," she said, her words grim. "Someone who won't hesitate to make good on a threat. Someone," she added, studying the placid, sun-warmed exterior of Marling, "who may have murdered William Collier."

After visiting Charlene, Phaedra was relieved to learn that Detective Morelli hadn't put in an appearance in several days.

"It's been quiet," Charlene said as they took their tea on the terrace in the late-afternoon sun. "Too quiet. It makes me nervous."

"Believe me, if the police had something, they'd be here. The fact that they aren't tells me they don't have a case."

"Or they're in the process of building one."

Phaedra did her best to reassure and distract her with tales of her mother's tireless matchmaking attempts, Arthur Fassbinder being the latest.

"At least you can laugh about it," Charlene said, and smiled as she sipped her Formosa oolong. "And you know she means well."

"So did Mrs. Bennet."

"I think poor Mrs. Bennet is unfairly maligned," Charlene ventured thoughtfully. "She spoke her mind, after all. She didn't give a fig for popular opinion, she put up with a husband who paid little attention to her, and she cared deeply about her daughters' financial security."

"And embarrassed them at every opportunity," Phaedra added. "Just like my mother." She rose to her feet. "But I hear what you're saying, and you're right. Mom's intentions are good. And I love her for it. I just wish she'd stop throwing every stray man she meets in my path and face the fact that I'm not interested in marriage."

"You know what they say," Charlene reminded her.

"Once bitten, twice shy?"

Charlene's lips curved into a smile. "Never say never."

On the way back to Laurel Springs, Phaedra drove on auto-pilot. The miles slipped by, but she barely noticed the lush green of the fields and horse farms or the faded clapboard barns as they passed by her window. Troubling questions filled her thoughts.

Who overheard Finch's conversation with William the day before his murder? Whoever it was had a connection to both Harold and Collier. What was the common denominator? What did they think Finch knew?

Every question led to more questions. Was the eavesdropper the same person who wrote the note to Finch? It seemed likely.

Her phone rang. The unmistakable bass line of "Under Pressure" filled the cabin. With a sigh, she took the call on the hands-free phone and kept her attention on the road. "Hi, Mom. What's up?"

"You haven't listened to my message, have you?" Nan Brighton accused.

"No, sorry, I haven't. I've been at Marling to see Charlene. I'm on my way home now."

"You're never home." She sniffled. "How is Charlene? The police haven't arrested her yet, I hope? Poor girl. To lose her husband, and then be suspected of murdering him!"

"No, they haven't arrested her yet, because they don't have a case. Mom, why are you sniffling? Do you have a cold? You sound funny."

"Do I?" Sniffle. "That's probably because I'm . . ." She blew her nose. "Devastated."

Phaedra felt tightness in her forehead that usually pre-saged a headache. "What happened?" she asked, although she already knew.

At least once a year, her mother decided that her husband,

Malcolm, took her completely for granted, announced that she needed a break, and packed her suitcase.

The separation typically only lasted a few days, or at most a week. Which was good.

Because every time she left their father, she arrived on Phaedra's doorstep and threw her life into a tailspin.

"You don't have anything to eat in this place, by the way," Nan pointed out with another sniff. "A half bottle of pinot, a container of yogurt past its sell-by date—"

"Like me," Phaedra said.

"—and one very sad-looking apple. What do you *live* on?"

"The vending machine, mostly. Takeout. Ramen noodles." She could almost see her mother shuddering.

"I have a delicate constitution. I require healthy food to sustain me. Antioxidants. Probiotics. Things like salad, and veggies, and fresh fruit. A steak would be divine. Oh, and perhaps a bottle of cabernet. Some dark chocolate . . ."

"I'll stop by the grocery on the way home," Phaedra gritted, and ended the call before her mother could add anything more to the list, like champagne, or truffles.

As she drove to the IGA, she wondered if Mrs. Bennet turned up on Elizabeth and Darcy's doorstep at Pemberley whenever she and Mr. Bennet had a disagreement.

She parked and tucked a canvas tote under her arm before entering the grocery and grabbing a shopping basket.

"Professor Brighton? I almost didn't recognize you in normal clothes."

Phaedra looked up to see Karolina Dalton standing in front of the parsnips in the produce aisle. "Oh. Hello, Karolina." She reached for a bag of carrots and a stalk of celery and put them in her basket. "I always dress down when I'm not teaching. How is Charles?"

"Fine. Busy." She studied a rutabaga with a critical eye. "Which reminds me, we film the finale next week, when Darcy chooses his bride. You'll be on set, I hope?"

"Of course." She heard the producer say more words,

words like "budget" and "wardrobe" and "important ball-room scene," but her thoughts were elsewhere.

What, she wondered, did William Collier have on Harold Fortune? Did Jasper Finch know more than he was letting on?

Which turned her thoughts to Detective Morelli. He hadn't returned to Marling to continue his homicide investigation. Why? Had he dismissed Charlene as a suspect?

Or was he putting the final touches on his case against her?

"—you agree? After all, it's imperative everyone executes their dance steps perfectly."

"Yes," Phaedra said, tuning back in to Karolina's words, "I agree completely. Don't worry, we'll go over the steps of the quadrille until the bachelorettes can perform it in their sleep."

Mollified, Karolina gave her a nod and joined the checkout line to pay for her parsnip and rutabaga.

Soup, Phaedra thought. Or Charles's sister was on some kind of root vegetable diet.

Vegetables. Which brought her back to the task at hand, grocery shopping for her mother. She tossed a bagged salad into the cart, followed by a few Gala apples, a bottle of cabernet, and some dark chocolate. Only a few more items and she could leave.

Steaks. Brie. And a package of those English water biscuits her mother liked so much.

Her basket heavy on her arm, Phaedra headed for the checkout lane and paused in front of the latest tabloid magazines for a glance at the headlines. WHO WILL NICK PICK? EXCLUSIVE PHOTOS FROM THE *WHO WANTS TO MARRY MR. DARCY?* SET!

She picked up a copy and flipped through the glossy pages to the article. *Which lucky bachelorette will say "yes" to Nick Ross?*

Which, indeed? Although the first episode had aired, next week marked the filming of the two-hour season finale, and no one, not even the cast and crew, knew which of the remaining two contestants Ross would choose.

Tinsley? Or Renee?

Oh, what the hell. Phaedra added the magazine to her basket. One needed one's comforts during a marital breakup, after all. Even if said breakup was nothing more than a tempest in a teapot.

More importantly, she reflected as she unloaded everything onto the belt, she had to find William Collier's murderer. It was imperative to prove Charlene's innocence, and soon.

Before Detective Morelli put her best friend behind bars.

Thirty-Five

How was your weekend?" Lucy asked Phaedra as she entered the teachers' lounge on Monday morning and headed straight for the coffee maker.

"Do you want the polite answer or the truth?"

"The truth, of course. You never drink coffee, only tea, so I'm assuming it was bad."

Phaedra sloshed Columbian into a cup and added a liberal splash of half-and-half. "Mom's taking a vacation from Dad. Again. She's my new roommate as of late yesterday afternoon, for who knows how long this time."

"Oh." Lucy made a face. "Talk about cramping your style. And your love life."

"I don't have a love life. It's everything else that's pushing my buttons." She pulled out a chair at the table and slumped over her cup.

"Such as?"

"She can't sleep on the sofa; it's too hard on her back. Which means I slept on the sofa. Or, more accurately, I didn't sleep on the sofa. Not a wink. She snores, Lucy, and not even a pillow over my head drowned out the sound. Imagine a buzz saw on steroids. She rearranged my furniture last night and organized my kitchen cupboards this morning and now I can't find anything. And she and Wickham despise each other."

"Wickham isn't exactly easy to love," Lucy said.

"He's a cat," Phaedra snapped. "Cats aren't meant to be lovable."

"Neither are nineteenth-century English professors, evidently."

Phaedra let out a lengthy sigh. "Sorry. I'm just so tired, and I have a full teaching schedule today."

"Perhaps doughnuts will help."

They looked up in surprise as Mark Selden entered the lounge, a box of the aforementioned doughnuts in hand, and slid them onto the kitchenette counter.

"I asked them to throw in a couple of maple glazed, two each of the blueberry, jelly, coconut, and crullers, and some cake doughnuts iced in violent shades of pink and purple. Very interesting to look at, but I'm not sure I'd eat those."

"You're a god among men," Lucy enthused, and hurried over to inspect the box. "I take back all the things I said about you."

He turned to Phaedra. "Professor Brighton? What would you like?"

"Two days' sleep." She yawned. "Barring that, I'll settle for a cake doughnut."

"Violent pink or violent purple?"

"Purple, definitely." She eyed him suspiciously. "Why are you in such a chipper mood? It's Monday."

He handed her a doughnut. "Why does everyone act as though Monday is the equivalent of an eight-hour root canal? I've never understood it." He poured himself a coffee and leaned back against the counter. "It's a new day, a new week. A new start."

Lucy licked a trace of maple glaze from her fingers and pushed her chair away from the table. "Too much optimism in here for my liking. I have a meeting in ten. See you both later."

She left, and Phaedra, knowing full well Lucy didn't have a meeting, stood up, too. "I'm glad you're back." Her traitorous heart began to beat faster, and the words she wanted to say to him, words like *I missed you*, and *I'm sorry*, wouldn't come.

"Thank you. I'm glad to be back."

"Well. Good. See you later, then. And thanks for the doughnut." She crumpled her napkin and tossed it in the wastebasket, and made it halfway to the door with a bright, false smile on her lips when he spoke.

"I'm sorry for the way I acted," he said. "For leaving so abruptly."

Phaedra paused. "You've already apologized," she reminded him. "And there's nothing to apologize for. You lost your grandmother. She meant a lot to you."

"She did. She does. But the Austen festival . . . it means a lot to you, as well. I realize that now." He paused. "I regret not telling you the truth before I left. I should have. And I'm sorry I made such bollocks of my Darcy role."

A tiny smile, a real one this time, bloomed. "Oh, but you didn't. You were the perfect Mr. Darcy. Aloof, unapproachable, and forbidding."

"And now?"

She met the uncertainty in his gaze, and her own evaporated. "A great improvement, I'd say. Except for one thing."

"Oh?" He drew his hawkish brows together. "And what's that?"

"You have powdered sugar on your chin, Mr. Darcy."

With a prim curtsy, she left.

The week passed quickly. Although Phaedra needed to convene a meeting of the Jane Austen Tea Society, her workload and her mother's continued presence in the carriage house prevented it.

"You can tell your father I'm not going back home until

he apologizes," Nan informed her daughter on Thursday evening.

"He told me he has nothing to apologize for," Phaedra said. "And he's right. You're being ridiculous, Mother. You've both reached an impasse, and I've reached the limits of my tolerance. You need to leave. Tonight."

"You can't throw me out." Outrage bloomed on her face. "Phaedra, honestly. I'm your mother!"

"Yes. And your place is with Dad, not me. You need to go home."

So saying, Phaedra went to the hallway closet, yanked it open, and dragged out her mother's suitcases. "I'll help you pack. I'll even drive you home, or call an Uber. But you're not spending another night here."

"Fine. I won't stay where I'm not wanted." Nan Brighton stood, grabbed one of the suitcases, and marched upstairs with her luggage thumping behind her. The sounds of slamming drawers and closet doors soon floated down.

When she returned twenty minutes later, Phaedra waited, car keys in hand, to take her home.

"I'm sorry, Mom," she said after stowing the suitcases in the back seat and sliding behind the wheel, "but this has gone on long enough."

"I don't expect you to understand. You're the apple of your father's eye. It's always been you and him against the world. While I, who only want the best for you and your sister, am shut out. Your father cares more for his books and you and H-Hannah than he ever has for me."

"That's ridiculous, and you know it." Phaedra glimpsed the hurt in her mother's eyes, and her voice softened. "Dad misses you. Terribly. He told me so." She glanced over and gave Nan a tentative smile. "And I know you miss him, too. Even if you won't admit it."

A frosty silence greeted her words.

With a sigh, Phaedra pulled away from the curb and took her mother home.

* * *

Rehearsal for the season finale of *Who Wants to Marry Mr. Darcy?* was underway in the ballroom at Marling when Phaedra arrived the following Monday.

The pocket doors separating the ballroom into two smaller rooms had been opened and the rugs rolled up and pushed aside, so the bachelorettes and their partners might practice their dance steps unimpeded.

Chandeliers sparkled overhead and the pine flooring gleamed below as the dancers nervously took their places. The ladies and gentlemen faced one another in a row of four couples.

Phaedra clapped her hands. "Lead couple, come forward and take your marks, please."

Nick Ross and Tinsley Prentiss, wearing T-shirts and loose-fitting sweatpants, obediently took their places on their respective masking-taped marks.

"Be sure to chalk the soles of your dancing slippers for the final dress rehearsal," she reminded them. "We don't want anyone taking a tumble."

"I'm not much of a dancer," Tinsley admitted. "Chalked soles or not."

"Practice makes perfect. Normally at a fashionable ball, we'd start with a minuet," Phaedra said. "But in the interest of time, we're dispensing with that and going through the figures of a quadrille."

"Which is . . . ?" Renee asked, displaying even more unease than Tinsley.

"A country dance. The lead couple performs the first set, then the next couple in line takes their turn, and so on, with each couple moving to the bottom of the line, until the first couple returns to the top."

"Leaving plenty of time for those not dancing to converse," Nick said, and gave Tinsley a roguish smile. "And perhaps flirt a bit."

Tinsley turned a becoming shade of pink.

As Phaedra directed the pair to bow to each other, she heard footsteps, and saw Karolina, dressed in her customary yoga pants and T-shirt, standing in the doorway. She acknowledged Phaedra with a brief nod.

She turned away to guide Nick and Tinsley through the first set of steps when she realized Karolina wasn't alone.

"So this is where you disappear when you're not at your desk," Mark Selden said, his voice echoing in the cavernous ballroom. He, like Karolina, was dressed down in jeans and a cashmere T-shirt.

"No classes this morning?" Phaedra asked.

"Not until this afternoon. Karo invited me to drop by, so . . ." He smiled at her. "I decided to take her up on it."

Karo, Phaedra noted, her good mood deflating. Obviously, the two were on close terms. And why shouldn't they be? Mark and Charles went to school together, after all. They'd known each other for ages.

Karolina slid her arm through his with the ease of long familiarity. "I'm so glad you did," she purred. She turned back to Phaedra, a gleam in her eyes. Triumph?

"The choreographer arrives this afternoon," she told Phaedra. "Do what you can in the meantime." She smiled up at Mark. "Now, Mark, I want you to meet the rest of the crew. Then we can have lunch in my trailer . . ."

At the Austen literary festival, Phaedra had wondered if there was history between Mark and Karolina. Now, watching them leave, their voices dissipating down the hall, she had her answer.

What surprised her was how much the knowledge hurt.

"Professor Brighton? Can we go over the first steps again?"

Startled out of her thoughts, she returned her attention to Tinsley and Nick and nodded briskly.

"Of course. Let's begin with *en avant et en arrièrre*. Step forward with your right foot . . ."

*   *   *

That night, she fell into a restless sleep and dreamed she was dancing with Mark Selden. Except he wasn't Mark; he was Fitzwilliam Darcy.

Forbidding. Disapproving.

"Why are you so aloof?" she asked as they executed the steps of a cotillion. "Your coldness vexes me."

"I am sorry, Ms. Brighton. But I've warned you before. 'My good opinion once lost, is lost forever.'"

Suddenly, he was no longer Mark as Darcy, but Detective Morelli. "You know I can't answer your question, Professor. This is an ongoing investigation."

Someone tapped Morelli on the shoulder. "May I cut in?" Curious, Phaedra turned to see who the interloper was, and the flirtatious smile on her face froze.

William Collier, his tuxedo dripping water and his skin waxy pale, held out his arms to her. "I'm always cold now, Professor Brighton."

She woke with a start and sat up, heart galloping in her chest, until her breathing calmed and reason gradually returned. What a crazy dream.

What time was it? She groped on the bedside table for her phone and lifted it. Four fifteen a.m.

"That's what I get for eating chocolate before bed," she muttered. As she hesitated, debating whether to try and go back to sleep or get up, her phone vibrated with an incoming call. She didn't recognize the number but answered it anyway. "Hello?"

She heard muffled sounds of the phone being dropped and another moment of fumbling as the caller retrieved it.

"Hello?" she said again, more sharply. "Who is this?"

"Professor Brighton? It's Finch. I'm at Marling." His voice was pitched low, his words rushed and urgent. "Sorry to call at this ungodly hour."

"Finch?" Dread settled over her. "What's going on?"

"The police just left. Mrs. Collier's been arrested."

Thirty-Six

That detective banged on the front door," Finch added, "and woke the entire household."

"Morelli?" Phaedra threw the covers back.

"Yes. He and his men had a warrant to search upstairs. I tried to stop them, but there was nothing I could do."

"No, of course not. One can't argue with a warrant." Her lips settled into a grim line. "This wasn't a spur-of-the-moment thing, Finch. This is Detective Morelli's doing. It takes time to obtain a warrant from the magistrate."

No wonder Morelli had stayed away from Marling. He'd been busy at the Somerset County Courthouse.

She thrust her feet into a pair of fluffy slippers. "Did they turn anything up during their search? They must have found something if they've arrested her."

"Unfortunately, yes. They went upstairs to her bedroom. Frightened her half to death, barging in like that in the early hours. I stood in the doorway while they conducted the search." He paused. "They went straight to Mrs. C.'s dresser. Where she keeps her jewelry box."

"And?" she prompted.

"They found a bottle of eye drops, Professor. Hidden under a pile of Violet's old brooches."

Eye drops. "Tetrahydrozoline," Phaedra murmured. "The ingredient in Violet's poisoned tea."

"Mrs. C. swore she had no idea how it got there. She told the police the bottle wasn't hers, that she'd never seen it before."

"Someone put it there, Finch. Someone in the house."

"Someone who wanted her arrested," he agreed. "Well, they got their wish. Morelli charged her with attempted murder, read her her rights, and took her away to the station in handcuffs. She wanted me to let you know."

"Has she called Tom Moore? Her lawyer?"

"She said he'd be her first phone call."

She thanked him, ended the call, and immediately speeddialed Charlene. As she'd expected, there was no answer. The police had already confiscated her phone.

"Damn you, Matteo Morelli," she muttered. "You've arrested the wrong person."

Something soft brushed against her ankles.

"Good morning, Wickham." She knelt down and stroked him, comforted by the reassuring vibration of his purr. "Sorry for waking you so early."

A generous serving of albacore would do wonders to improve my mood. Leave out the kibble, and I might even be inclined to forgive you. He wove himself once more around her feet, paused to eye her inquisitively, and darted down the stairs to await her in the kitchen, confident she'd follow.

She did. After putting on a pot of coffee, because she was in desperate need of caffeine this morning, she spooned a generous helping of chunked albacore tuna over Wickham's kibble and set it down before him.

He sniffed appreciatively and settled in to savor his breakfast in a leisurely fashion.

She glanced at the clock. Nearly five a.m. The court didn't open until eight o'clock, which gave her plenty of time to drink her coffee, formulate her thoughts, get dressed . . .

. . . and visit Detective Morelli at the county courthouse.

* * *

"Professor Brighton. I wondered when you'd show up."

Detective Morelli stood up from his desk as Phaedra all but catapulted into his office shortly after eight.

"Don't," she warned him as she strode inside, "say a word. Just listen. I'm running on caffeine and adrenaline right now, and I have a few things to say to you."

He sank back into his seat. "I'm sure you do."

Ignoring his weary gesture at a chair, she approached his desk and leaned forward, her eyes snapping with righteous indignation. "I know you arrested Charlene at zero dark hundred this morning. What I don't understand is why. Why are you so determined to pin William Collier's murder on Charlene?"

"Because she's our prime suspect," he shot back. "She had motive. She had means. And she certainly had opportunity. But I didn't arrest her for Collier's murder."

Phaedra lowered herself into the chair, her eyes never leaving his. "No. But you can't believe Charlene tried to poison her mother. The very idea is absurd."

"I disagree. I think your friend murdered her husband, and Violet had the bad luck to see her leaving the bathroom afterward."

She opened her mouth to argue, but the memory of Charlene's words echoed once again in her head.

What if Morelli was right? Phaedra wondered. What if Violet hadn't seen a ghost outside that bathroom, or Patsy Fortune, but her own daughter?

"I think Violet confronted her daughter," Morelli continued. "They exchanged words, and Charlene begged her mother to keep silent." He reached for his coffee cup, took a swig, and, with a grimace, pushed it away. "Which Violet did . . . until her conscience got the better of her, and she threatened to go to the police."

"No," Phaedra said sharply. "I'll never believe it."

"Believe it or not, your choice. Either way," he said as he

leaned back in his chair, "I have enough evidence to prosecute. Physical evidence that links Charlene to the attempted poisoning of Violet Lucas. I may not be able to get her for her husband's murder. But I've got her for attempted murder."

"You've wanted to pin Bill's murder on Charlene from the beginning," she accused. "From the first night you started your investigation. But you had no evidence. No fingerprints, no nothing. Now, conveniently, you do." Her eyes blazed with fury.

His own eyes narrowed. "What are you suggesting, Professor?"

"Oh, come on, Detective. It's obvious someone set Charlene up. Finch said your men went straight up to her bedroom after waving a warrant around and made a beeline for the jewelry box on her dresser. Where they conveniently found a bottle of eye drops with Charlene's fingerprints all over it."

"No one planted evidence, Professor Brighton, if that's what you're suggesting. I don't operate that way."

"Maybe not. But someone tipped you off. And that same someone deliberately put the bottle in her jewel box. Don't you think, Detective, that if Charlene really did try to poison her mother, she'd dispose of those eye drops? Why keep them, with a million other places in Marling to hide them? And why hide them in her jewelry box, of all places, where they'd be sure to be discovered?"

He didn't have an answer.

"Who was it?" she asked suddenly. "Who tipped you off?"

"An anonymous caller. And even if I knew who it was, you know I can't give you a name."

"Fine." Phaedra surged to her feet and went to the door. "Thanks for your time."

"Where do you think you're going?"

She turned back. "To visit Charlene."

"She's in a holding cell at the moment. No visitors."

"Then I'll go and see her lawyer, Mr. Moore." Determination marked her expression.

"You're wasting your time, Professor," Morelli said, and

thrust his chair back. "He won't tell you any more than I will. You've heard of attorney-client privilege? Do yourself a favor and let justice run its course."

"That's exactly what I plan to do. Charlene is innocent, and you know it as well as I."

"Professor Brighton," he warned, "I've told you before. Stay out of this."

"I can't do that. If you won't find the real murderer, I will."

Phaedra marched out of his office, fueled by anger and determination, and moved at a brisk pace down the hallway toward the lobby. Tom Moore would have arrived by now to consult with his client. If she couldn't speak with Charlene, then speaking to her lawyer was the next best option.

Her hope was rewarded as she spied the attorney heading across the lobby toward the exit doors, a briefcase gripped in one hand. Moore was the epitome of old Virginia charm, with his neatly groomed white hair and goatee, and an Italian suit that probably cost more than she earned in a year.

"Mr. Moore!" She waved and hurried forward.

He paused and glanced up, and as he caught sight of her, he smiled. "Professor Brighton. This is an unexpected pleasure."

"Hello, Tom. Have you spoken with Charlene? How is she? When will she be released? Is there anything I can do?" The questions tumbled out in a breathless rush.

He held up a hand. "I have it under control, I assure you. The wheels of justice may turn slowly. But they *are* turning. Why don't we step outside where we can talk more privately?"

She nodded, and together they exited the building, the automatic doors swishing shut behind them, until Moore stopped under a magnolia tree several yards from the entrance.

"To answer the first of your questions," he began, "yes, I've spoken with Mrs. Collier. She's upset, as you can imagine, but holding up well. Or as well as can be expected," he amended.

"Can you get her released?"

His white brows furrowed. "At the moment, the answer is no. She's been charged with attempted murder, and the police have evidence—her fingerprints on a bottle of eye drops found hidden in her bedroom."

"Those eye drops don't prove anything, surely? People use them every day to treat allergies or relieve redness. And the bottle was found inside her jewel box—someone planted it there. I know Charlene. If she really did try to poison her mother," Phaedra finished grimly, "she wouldn't be stupid enough to keep the bottle around, much less hide it in her jewelry box."

"I agree. The evidence against Charlene is purely circumstantial. It proves nothing, aside from Mrs. Collier's occasional need to relieve itchy eyes due to allergies or irritation. If Detective Morelli's case makes it to court, it won't hold up. It'll collapse like an overbeaten soufflé."

Phaedra allowed herself a glimmer of hope. "So the case against Charlene isn't strong. Does that mean you can get her released?"

"All in good time, my dear, all in good time," he assured her. "When I return to my office I plan to rectify the situation, and I'll begin by securing Charlene's release on her own recognizance. She's never been charged with a crime, and she isn't a flight risk, so I see no reason for the judge to refuse the request.

"And in answer to your final question," he said, lifting his wrist to glance at his watch, "no, there's nothing you can do." When her face fell, he reached out to pat her arm. "But you can continue to stand by her and be her friend. That, my dear Professor, is the best thing you, or anyone, can do for Charlene Collier right now."

Phaedra returned to her car and headed to Marling. There was nothing more she could do to help Charlene. Besides which, Karolina expected her on the set.

She scowled. *Karo* wouldn't accept anything less than death as an excuse for missing today's final dress rehearsal. She had a grim satisfaction in knowing that Mark had a lecture to give and midterm examinations to prepare. No hanging around with his former flame today.

Her fingers squeezed the wheel in a brief spasm of frustration. Why did she always do this?

Why did she fall for the men who charmed her, who skillfully wore down her defenses, brick by carefully placed brick . . . only to leave her high and dry?

Every time Donovan Wickes let her down, whether ditching her for his friends at the last minute or standing her up for the senior prom, he had a perfectly valid excuse. It wasn't his fault. Time got away from him. The girl in chemistry wouldn't leave him alone. He never meant to hurt her. It would never happen again.

But it did, until Phaedra broke up with him. And every relationship since started off with promise but ended in disappointment.

Is it me? she wondered. *Do I expect too much?* Could any man live up to the Darcy standard?

"I won't settle," she promised herself as she parked near the unit lot, already crowded with vehicles on this, the penultimate day before the last episode wrapped. She was older now, and wiser. And she deserved better.

If she ended her days alone with only Mr. Darcy and half a dozen cats for company, so be it.

She thought of Charlene. If not for her friend, who'd handed her Kleenex and distracted her with endless games of gin rummy after her breakup with Donovan, Phaedra would never have found the courage to attend university. She wouldn't have a teaching career she loved.

She owed Charlene a debt she could never repay. Which was why, she reminded herself as she got out of the car and headed purposefully across the lawn to Marling, she'd do whatever it took to help her now.

Even if she had to catch William Collier's killer herself.

*   *   *

The sky blazed with a pink-and-orange sunset as Phaedra finally returned to the Mini. With their dance steps mastered, the bachelor and bachelorettes had executed the quadrille flawlessly in their Regency finery as the ballroom chandeliers glowed overhead.

Hopefully, they'd do the same during filming of the final episode tomorrow.

"Any idea who Nick will choose?" she asked Tinsley during a quick lunch break outdoors. "He certainly looks at you in a special way."

Her cheeks turned pink. "Probably thinking what a bad dancer I am," she joked. "And to answer your question, I have no idea who he'll choose. We're filming two different endings so neither of us knows."

"And even if you did, you couldn't tell me."

She gave a rueful smile. "At least he's not seeing that woman any longer. No more mysterious phone calls."

"Glad to hear it." Phaedra hoped Patsy had given up her obsession with Ross and moved on. After weeks of filming, she fervently hoped Nick and Tinsley found happiness together.

She hoped somebody did.

Backing out of her parking space, she turned onto the drive that led to the house and decided to take a quick detour to the garage. She had questions about William Collier, questions that only Finch could answer.

Inez Collier's comment at her son's memorial service still puzzled her.

If her husband, Henry, wasn't William's father, then who was?

She followed the access road and turned onto the driveway that led to the garage. It would be dark soon. With dinner service over, Finch would be back in his apartment for the night, and they could talk in private.

Twilight, or *l'heure bleue*, as the French called it. A brief time between daylight and evening when the first stars began to twinkle and shadows lengthened across the grass.

She parked several yards from the garage door. Her conviction that Finch knew more than he was letting on grew. He'd alluded to "something big" when he'd threatened Collier, and someone in the house had overheard. Who?

Whoever the eavesdropper was, Finch's threat had rattled him or her badly. Badly enough that they'd left a threatening note under his door.

Why? What was Collier's secret? Did it have something to do with his real father's identity?

She shut off the engine. Encroaching darkness rendered the hunched shape of the Bentley, parked inside the garage, indistinct. Phaedra glanced up. The windows of Finch's apartment were dark.

Where was he?

A sound reached her ears as she climbed out of the car and shut the door. It was the rumble of a car engine.

She frowned. Why would the Bentley's engine be running with no one around? And why was no exhaust coming out of the tailpipe? A vague feeling of unease gripped her. She walked nearer and came to a stop just outside the garage door.

A tube ran from the exhaust pipe and into the car.

And someone was slumped behind the wheel.

"Finch," Phaedra cried, hurtling to the driver's-side door as she tried to tug it open. The door was locked. She leaned down and pounded on the window with her fists. "Finch!" she screamed. "Can you hear me? Open the door!"

He didn't respond. His eyes were closed, and his left shoulder had slumped against the door panel. His face was flushed.

"Carbon monoxide poisoning," Phaedra muttered as she reached for her cell phone and dialed 911.

"Please hurry," she told the dispatcher as she explained what had happened. "He may still be conscious. I tried to open the car doors, but they're locked."

"EMTs are on the way. Stay calm and repeat the address, please."

She ended the call and waited outside the garage, pacing in the cool evening air in a frenzy of adrenaline and indecision. Should she call Morelli? No, she decided. Not yet. Finch might merely be unconscious.

But even as the thought occurred, she knew it was only wishful thinking.

William Collier's murderer had struck again.

Thirty-Seven

Finch was pronounced dead fifteen minutes later.

"Carbon monoxide poisoning," she told Detective Morelli as he arrived and began questioning her. She heard his questions but couldn't focus. Finch was dead. It hardly seemed possible.

The household staff had gathered on the driveway, talking in hushed voices as attempts to save the butler's life were abandoned.

He studied the tube that led from the exhaust to the interior of the car. "Looks like a suicide."

"It's not." Phaedra's voice was dull but firm with conviction. "He was murdered."

His eyes sharpened. "What makes you say that?"

In halting words she told him about the butler's threatening note, *you're next*, and his attempt to blackmail William Collier, boasting that he knew "something big."

"Which was what, exactly?"

"Nothing. He wanted to frighten Collier, to stop him from calling the police when he thought Finch was stealing Charlene's choker. But someone overheard him. Someone who . . ."

She felt bile rise up in her throat. "Someone who murdered him, and made it look like suicide."

"Why didn't you tell me any of this before?" he demanded.

"Because I knew you'd be angry," she retorted, "just like you are now. And because you were fixed on Charlene Collier as the murderer right from the b-beginning." Her voice wobbled as the enormity of what had happened hit her.

She hadn't known Jasper Finch well, but despite his tendency to lie and a questionable moral code, she liked him. He didn't deserve this.

Detective Morelli nodded at the medical examiner, Dr. Kessler, who'd just arrived, and took Phaedra by the arm as he drew her aside. "Let's sit for a moment. You're in shock. Finding a dead body is never easy, even for a cop."

"I found William Collier's body," she reminded him as they sat on a wrought iron bench nearby. "And yes, it was horrible, the stuff of nightmares. But it didn't affect me like this." After a moment, she sighed. "I'm a regular murder magnet."

"A murder magnet," he repeated. "I like that."

"I almost made you smile."

"I smile," he protested. "I do," he added at her raised eyebrow. "Just not on the job."

"When will Charlene be released?" she asked. "Surely, tonight proves that she didn't kill her husband. Someone else did . . . someone who's still out here." She looked back at the house with a tiny shudder. "Or in there."

"Could be a copycat killer," he pointed out.

"That's a stretch and you know it."

He sighed. "Her attorney secured Mrs. Collier's personal recognizance late today. Provided she signs a statement agreeing to appear in court when the time comes, she'll be released without bail."

Relief, strong and sweet, swept through her. Charlene was coming back. Phaedra doubled her determination to find the real killer and clear her best friend's name.

They stood as Dr. Kessler appeared. He gestured Morelli over, and Phaedra followed them into the garage.

"Carbon monoxide poisoning, Doc?" the detective said.

"Yes. But it wasn't a suicide."

"I told you," Phaedra whispered. "He was murdered."

"What makes you think it wasn't a suicide?" Morelli asked Kessler.

"As I'm sure you recall, I presumed that the previous victim, Mr. Collier, was electrocuted in the bathtub. After being rendered unconscious beforehand."

"With an insulin overdose." The detective nodded.

"Correct. He presented excessive sweating and dilated pupils, inconsistent with electrocution. I'm seeing the same symptoms here. Which led me to examine the victim's neck, where I found a puncture wound." He paused. "I can't be sure until the postmortem, of course, but I'd postulate that this man, like Collier, was injected with insulin. Most likely before he was poisoned by carbon monoxide."

The ME turned away as Finch's body was transferred to a collapsible rolling stretcher and loaded into the rear of the county coroner's van. The household staff reluctantly dispersed and headed across the lawn, back to Marling.

Phaedra turned to Morelli. "Finch loved that Bentley." Her throat tightened as she glanced at the car. "Just like William Collier loved bathing in his claw-foot tub."

Morelli's silence told her that he knew she had more to say. And she did.

"The murderer knew what things each victim loved. In Collier's case, his bath, and in Finch's, his beloved Bentley."

But she was no closer to knowing why. What prompted Collier's murder? And why kill his butler? What did Finch know, or more to the point, what did the killer *think* he knew?

She remained convinced that Collier's father—his real father, whoever he was—played a significant part in all of this. But she kept her theory to herself. She'd been wrong before.

It was past time, she decided, for an emergency meeting of the Jane Austen Tea Society.

Declining Detective Morelli's offer to escort her home, Phaedra assured him she was fine and drove back to the carriage house.

Thank goodness Tom Moore had secured Charlene's release. The charge against her was still pending, but at least she'd be out of jail. In the morning, Phaedra would call and stop by Marling for a visit.

After tomorrow night's wrap party at Marling, the cast and crew of *Who Wants to Marry Mr. Darcy?* would go their separate ways.

Wickham greeted her at the door in a state of high dudgeon. *It's dark, in case you haven't noticed*, his narrowed blue eyes seemed to say, *and here I am, alone again. And ravenous, too, I might add.*

"I know you're hungry, Wicksie," she crooned, dropping her handbag on the hall table and kneeling to stroke behind his ears. "Sorry I'm a little late."

He stalked away with a twitch of his tail.

With a sigh, she rose. "You think you're mad at me now? Wait till we go to the vet for your core vaccines tomorrow."

Vaccines? We'll see about that. Right now? I demand that you feed me.

In the kitchen, she reached into the cupboard for a can of his favorite, Mixed Seafood Grill, and dumped it into his bowl, sans kibble.

"There," she said as he attacked his food. "Not another word out of you, mister."

After sorting through the day's mail and making herself a soothing cup of peppermint tea, Phaedra sank into a seat at the table.

"I'm sorry, Finch," she whispered, wrapping her fingers around the mug. The warmth calmed her. "I'll figure this out. Find whoever did this. I will."

She'd call an emergency meeting of the Tea Society to update Lu and Marisol and share her latest theory. Three heads, after all, were better than one. A yawn escaped her.

Tomorrow, she decided. After she visited Charlene, dropped Wickham off at the veterinarian, and put in an appearance at the wrap party at Marling.

Wickham finished his dinner and sauntered to the kitchen door. *I'm ready. Kindly let me go out and do my thing.*

"Your wish is my command." She stood and opened the door, and he shot outside.

The night sky was clear, but the backyard was dense with shadows. She heard rustling as Wickham made his stealthy nocturnal prowl through the herbaceous border that ran along the base of the fence.

Goose bumps prickled her skin, and not just because of the cool evening air. Who was the predator at Marling? Who stalked the halls and crept up from behind, ready to plunge a syringe into an unsuspecting neck?

Maybe packing up Wickham in his carrier and spending the night at her parents' house, as Morelli had suggested earlier, wasn't such a bad idea. In the wake of Finch's murder, the thought of being alone tonight unsettled her.

"C'mon, Wicks," she called out, suddenly wanting nothing so much as to close and lock the door. "Time to come in."

He lifted his head, eyes glinting in the moonlight, and resumed his explorations.

"Be that way, you stubborn cat."

With an aggrieved sigh she turned back to the screened door and flung it open, wincing as it let out a rusty squeak of protest. *Note to self: oil those hinges.* As she paused she noticed something else. A square of white paper, stuck inside the crossbar. It looked like . . . a note.

With shaky fingers she unfolded it and read the crudely pasted letters. The message contained two words.

You're next.

Thirty-Eight

The note drifted to the ground. Her heart thudded like a timpani in her chest as she bent down to retrieve the note, dropped it again.

Don't lose the damned thing, she told herself. It's evidence. Holding it gingerly by one edge, she went inside and put it on the kitchen counter.

"Wickham!" Her voice rang out sharp and clear in the chill night air as she retraced her steps and thrust her head around the screen door. "Inside. Now." As if sensing her mood, he streaked across the yard and darted into the kitchen. She closed and locked the screen and the back doors and flicked on the outside lights.

What to do, what to do?

She could go to Mom and Dad's and spend the night in her old room. Or she could stay here, lock up tight, and hope for the best. Neither solution was ideal.

"Morelli," she decided. "I'll call Morelli."

Reassured by the thought of his calm rationality, she grabbed her phone and called him.

No answer.

Of course he's not answering, she reminded herself as she

tossed the phone aside. *He's not in his office. He's at Marling, questioning suspects, calling in a crime scene team, doing everything necessary to investigate Finch's homicide.* And she didn't have his direct number.

Well, if she couldn't reach Morelli, she'd lock every door and window. She double-checked the front door, and as she slid the dead bolt into place, her gaze darted to the open treads of the staircase. Her old phobia seized her. What if someone was up there?

What if whoever had left that note outside lay in wait upstairs, concealed in a closet or under the bed?

"You're being ridiculous," she muttered, even as she switched on every lamp in the living room, dining room, and kitchen.

Before trying Morelli's number again, she eyed the stairs warily. She had to go up there. Just to be sure whoever had left that note hadn't slipped inside the house.

Weapon. I need a weapon first. Grabbing a bottle of unopened merlot from the mini wine cooler under the counter, she returned to the living area. "Wickham?" she called softly. "Are you here?"

He leaped up onto the sofa and settled onto his haunches. *Of course I'm here. Where else would I be? Now quit being a scaredy-cat and go upstairs.*

Phaedra released a shaky breath. "You're right. I'm overreacting, aren't I?"

He eyed her reproachfully and began to groom one paw. *You think?*

Halfway across the living room to the stairs, she heard a car door slam outside. Footsteps pounded up the walkway to the house.

Someone rapped, hard, on the front door.

She stood immobile, her heart thrashing as she wondered frantically what to do. Maybe she could make a run for it out the back door. Go to the neighbor's and scream bloody murder—

"Professor Brighton? Are you in there?"

For the second time that night, relief left her weak-kneed and as giddy as Ebenezer Scrooge on Christmas morning. Phaedra threw the bolt and flung the door open.

"Detective Morelli," she said. "Am I glad to see you."

"Everything okay?" he asked, his eyes filled with concern as he stepped inside. "I drove by on my way back to the station and saw the lights on."

"Yes. And no." She closed the door, led him through to the kitchen, and began making a pot of coffee. As she took two mugs down from the cupboard, she filled him in on the threatening note.

"Where is it?" he asked.

She indicated the note lying on the counter. "I'm afraid I touched it. I opened it to read it."

He withdrew a pair of latex gloves from his pocket and pulled them on, studied the folded paper. "Just like the one you said Finch received."

"Yes." *And we saw what happened to him*, she thought. "Has it turned up yet? His note?"

"No. We searched his apartment, and the crime team's dusting the garage and vehicle for fingerprints. If anything's there, we'll find it."

"I hope so. Poor Finch."

"Got a sandwich bag and some tweezers? I need to take this to CSI, see if they can find any latents." At her blank look, he added, "Fingerprints."

Over coffee for him, tea for her, she told him everything she'd gleaned about the case. "I made a lot of wrongheaded assumptions," she admitted. "I suspected Finch, and Patsy Fortune, even Violet." She sighed. "Now, we're back to square one."

"*We*," he said as he set his mug down, "are not a team, Professor. The perpetrator of these crimes is clever. Dangerous. Whoever it is won't hesitate to make you the next victim. I don't want that. I don't want you anywhere near this case." His eyes seared into hers. "Understood?"

She glared back at him, more than ready to defend her

right to do everything in her power to clear Charlene's name. Ready to hash it out right there over their cups of Columbian and chamomile. But his eyes, as dark and inky brown as a shot of espresso, held hers, and any words of protest she intended to utter died unspoken on her lips.

"Don't you get it?" He reached out to lay his hand atop hers. "I don't want you hurt. Or worse. I care about what happens to you, Phaedra. I care about *you*."

She didn't withdraw her hand, didn't want to. Her skin tingled under the warm spread of his fingers. "I . . ."

Her phone rang. Of course it did. "My mother," she apologized, the romantic moment deflating as the unwelcome sound of "Under Pressure" filled the kitchen. She drew her hand reluctantly away and answered the call.

"Phaedra! Thank goodness you picked up," Nan Brighton exclaimed. "Is everything all right?"

"Yes. Why wouldn't it be?" She held a finger up to signal Morelli as he finished his coffee and pushed back his chair. "One minute," she mouthed.

He nodded briefly and retreated to the living room.

With a sigh, she tuned back in to her mother's voice.

"—your father and I just saw that new movie everyone's talking about, you know the one—"

"Yes. And?" Phaedra prompted.

"Well, we drove by the carriage house on the way home, and there was a car parked out front, blocking the end of the driveway. Malcolm said it looked like an unmarked police car. Not only that, every light in the place was blazing. Have you been robbed? What's going on?"

"Nothing, Mother, I promise you. A . . . friend stopped by to check on me, that's all."

"Oh. Well, if you're sure."

"I'm sure."

"I'll talk to you later, then. Good night, darling."

"Good night, Mom."

"Sorry," Phaedra apologized as she ended the call and hurried out to the living room where Morelli waited by the front door. "Mom drove past with my father just now, and they saw the car and all the lights on, and got worried."

"That's good. They keep tabs on you."

"I guess that's one way of looking at it." She glanced over at the stairs. "Before you go, would you . . . ?"

"Of course." He conducted a quick, thorough search upstairs and returned a moment later. "All clear."

"Did you check behind the shower curtain? And under the bed?" She was only half joking.

"I did." He reached for the door. "I'll assign a patrol car to cruise the neighborhood tonight." He withdrew a card and handed it to her. "My number. Office, and cell phone. In case you lost the first one."

"Thank you." Her earlier fear had eased, and she felt steady once again, due in no small part to Matteo Morelli's presence. "And thanks for looking in on me."

They lingered at the door for one brief, fraught moment before Morelli's phone pinged with a message.

"The CS guys found something," he said as he looked up from the screen. "A syringe in the toolbox. Maybe this one will turn up some fingerprints."

"I hope so. Whoever this is needs to be stopped. Before . . ."

Before someone else ended up dead.

Thirty-Nine

I have to go," Morelli said. "Are you headed back to Marling tomorrow?"

"Yes, to say goodbye to the cast and crew. The wrap party's tomorrow night."

"Do me a favor," he said, his eyes leveling on hers as he pocketed his phone. "Keep that card and your phone by your bed tonight."

"I will."

"If anything spooks you, I mean *anything*, call me."

She promised she would and stood on the front steps as he returned to his car, started it up, and left.

With a sigh, she went back inside, shut and locked the door, and carried Morelli's card upstairs, where she put it on her nightstand.

Seeing it comforted her, made her feel less alone. Good to know that help, in the reassuring form of Matteo Morelli, was only a phone call away.

As she got ready for bed, she paused in front of the bathroom mirror, toothbrush in hand. Morelli had said he'd driven by the carriage house on his way to the station.

But the station was on the other side of town. Nowhere near her place.

She rinsed her mouth, straightened, and smiled at her reflection. *Busted, Detective.* Her smile lingered long after she climbed into bed and snapped off the light.

"Your breakfast, Mrs. Collier."

Bertie crossed the terrace with a tray of tea, toast, eggs, and pastries and deposited it on the table where Phaedra sat with Charlene the following morning.

"Thank you." Puzzlement creased Charlene's brow. "Where's Cook today?"

"Busy," Bertie said, as uncommunicative as ever. "I helped serve breakfast to the cast and crew this morning. I'll serve lunch when they've finished filming, then I'm done here."

She didn't sound particularly sorry, Phaedra noticed. "You're not catering the wrap party tonight?"

"The production company made previous arrangements."

"You and your crew are invited, I hope?"

"We are. Can't say as I'll go." She glanced at Charlene. "Anything else?"

"No, that's all."

As she departed, Phaedra reached out to squeeze Charlene's hand. "I'm glad you're back. I missed you."

"It's not over yet. I'm out on my own recognizance, but I'm still facing a charge of attempted murder."

"Which will be dropped," Phaedra assured her. "Finch's murder proves someone else is responsible. And Morelli knows it."

"He has to prove it." Charlene's words were resigned as she poured them each cups of tea. "Which is another matter altogether. Lemon?"

Halfway through their toast and Darjeeling, Mrs. Williams appeared. "You have a visitor, Mrs. Collier. It's Mrs. Fortune. Shall I bring her out?"

Charlene exchanged a quick, surprised glance with Phaedra and nodded. "Please."

A short time later, the housekeeper returned with Dorothy Fortune, who was wearing a yellow dress with a pink-and-yellow Pucci scarf tied jauntily at her neck.

"Good morning, Mrs. Collier." Harold's widow nodded at Phaedra. "Professor Brighton."

"Please, join us," Charlene invited her. "There's plenty."

"It looks delicious." She eyed the pastries with a touch of longing as she sat down. "But I'm determined to lose these last fifteen pounds if it kills me." She colored. "Poor choice of words. I do apologize."

"Quite all right. Tea?" Charlene prompted.

"No, thank you. I only came to welcome you back. And to bring you this." Resting an expensive leather handbag on her lap, Dorothy withdrew a set of keys and laid them beside Charlene's plate. "Keys to the cottage," she added. "My daughters and I are moving out."

"Oh! I'm sorry to hear it."

"Don't be. Ellery—my eldest—purchased a small horse farm just outside Yancey Mills with the money Harold left her. Never said a word. But then, Elly always could keep a secret. She and I and three of her sisters will be helping out on the farm."

"Congratulations. That's wonderful news," Phaedra said. "You mentioned four of your daughters. They're not all joining you?"

Dorothy fiddled with the clasp of her purse. "Patsy's rented an apartment above that ridiculous dog bakery where she works. She moved in yesterday."

Yesterday. The day before the last day of filming, Phaedra thought. After tonight's party, Nick Ross and his fiancée would leave for an extended honeymoon, and when the final episode ran, "Mr. Darcy" would be officially engaged.

It sounded like Patsy had moved on . . . literally and figuratively.

"Good for her," Phaedra said as she met Dorothy's eyes.

"Thank you." Dorothy's smile warmed her face but wavered as she glanced at the platter of fried eggs. "Seeing those eggs reminds me of Harold."

"Harold?" Charlene asked, puzzled.

Mrs. Fortune's eyes misted as she extracted a tissue from her purse and dabbed at her eyes. "A moment of sentiment. I apologize. My husband stopped at Bertie's café every morning on his way to work. I wouldn't have eggs in the house; they were bad for his cholesterol. He loved her fried egg sandwiches."

Charlene reached out to touch her hand.

"In the end, it didn't matter. He sickened gradually and died of heart failure." She leaned forward. "He was as healthy as a horse all of his life. I've often wondered . . ."

"What?" Phaedra encouraged.

She lowered her voice. "I don't believe Harold's death was entirely . . . natural."

"You mean . . ."

"Foul play," she said flatly. "There was no autopsy, no need since he died of natural causes. So they said. But I've always had my doubts." She bustled to her feet. "Well. I must go. Do come and visit us on the farm."

Phaedra stared after her in puzzlement.

Mr. Fortune had quite the fondness for fried egg sandwiches.

That's what Finch told Bertie, the morning Phaedra found the aquamarine on the kitchen floor. When Jen burst in, frantic to find her missing kitten, the comment was forgotten.

"Charlene," Phaedra asked with a frown, "what can you tell me about Bertie?"

"Bertie? I worked for her for years, waitressing at the café. You know that."

"Yes. But what do you know about her personal life? Was she ever married? Did she have family nearby?"

"There's not much to tell. She was married for a short

time, but the marriage ended in divorce. She lived with her sister above the café. Kay was her only family. She was a diabetic, like my mom."

"Was?"

Charlene nodded. "She passed away several years ago. She couldn't afford the rising cost of insulin, so Bertie wrote to the pharmaceutical company begging for help, for free samples or a discount. They ignored her letters and emails. She found a cheaper alternative in Canada, but Kay had a bad reaction and died."

Phaedra returned to the carriage house just before noon, thoughts spinning around like Catherine wheels in her head. Maddening. Illuminating. Whirls of confusion interspersed with questions.

The sky, so clear this morning, had turned cloudy, and the westerly wind carried the smell of rain. Hopefully, any bad weather would hold off until after tonight's party.

"Wickham," she called out as she entered the carriage house and shut the door behind her. "Time to go."

Wickham, fully aware that a visit to the vet loomed, was nowhere to be found.

She glanced at her wristwatch. Thirty-five minutes until his appointment at the Laurel Springs Animal Clinic. Which gave her time to do a quick online investigation before coaxing Wicks into his carrier.

Upstairs, she opened the laptop on her desk under the eaves and typed "pharmaceutical companies, insulin" into the search engine bar. There were only four manufacturers of insulin in the United States.

And one of them was Longbourn Pharmaceuticals.

William Collier was the former CEO of Longbourn. Did Roberta Walsh go so crazy with grief that she blamed Collier for her sister Kay's death, and killed him?

It made a twisted kind of sense. As head caterer for *Who*

Wants to Marry Mr. Darcy?'s cast and crew, Bertie had access to Marling's kitchen, as well as the rest of the house and grounds. Before that, Harold Fortune was a loyal customer at her café.

And Charlene had mentioned that Bertie suffered from allergies.

Eye drops contained tetrahydrozoline, the same chemical found in Violet's tea. Bertie had mentioned seeing Patsy in the kitchen the morning that Violet's tea was poisoned. Had she attempted to divert suspicion from herself? Did *Bertie* poison the tea? Why?

He sickened gradually, Dorothy had said that morning, *and died of heart failure.*

What if Harold's fried egg sandwiches contained something more than eggs, mayonnaise, and toasted bread? Over time, a few drops of tasteless, colorless tetrahydrozoline would lead to a virtually undetectable death.

Was that the "something big" Finch had hinted at?

Phaedra stared, unseeing, out the window. Charlene said Bertie occasionally administered insulin for Kay. And like any professional caterer, she always wore food preparation gloves.

What better way to hide her fingerprints?

She glanced at her watch. No time to pursue her suspicions any further right now. *And pursue what, exactly? All I have are a bunch of half-baked theories and wild suppositions.*

Unfounded though her fears might be, she had to warn Charlene. Bertie Walsh may have killed two men already, Harold Fortune and William Collier, and for the same reason . . . their connection to Longbourn Pharmaceuticals.

She'd likely murdered Finch as well.

Phaedra returned downstairs to retrieve the cat carrier and, with a great deal of begging and a little bribery in the form of a sardine, coaxed Wickham inside and dropped him off at the veterinary clinic.

First things first, she decided as she returned to the Mini and started the engine. Call Charlene and warn her.

She hesitated. Perhaps she should tell her in person.

Before she could decide, Karolina called. Never one for pleasantries, she barked, "Where are you?"

Phaedra, accustomed to her rudeness, bit back a retort. "I'm in Laurel Springs, leaving the vet's."

"We're having lunch in the dining room here at Marling in half an hour. I expect you to be here."

"I'm running errands. I'll be back in time for the wrap party tonight."

"Lunch. Noon. Don't be late." She hung up.

"Obstinate, headstrong witch," Phaedra muttered, and headed for Marling. Maybe a change in plan was for the best. After lunch with the bachelorettes and the crew, she could share her concerns with Charlene, pick up Wickham at the veterinary clinic, and return to the carriage house in plenty of time to get ready.

Morelli called. "Professor Brighton. Everything okay?"

"Yes. Thanks." She paused. "Sorry if I overreacted last night."

"Overreacted? Someone threatened your life. That's enough to rattle anyone. Where are you?"

"On my way to Marling," she said, and filled him in on her latest theories. "I think Bertie overheard Finch tell William Collier that he knew 'something big.' He didn't. But she must've assumed that he knew she'd poisoned Harold."

"And so she poisoned Finch's tea," he said slowly. "Which turned out to be Violet's tea instead."

"And when that plan went south, she murdered Finch."

He didn't dismiss her theories out of hand, as she'd expected, or tell her to butt out.

"Be careful," he said when she finished. "And promise me you won't do any investigating between courses."

"And here I hoped you'd finally decided to let me help with the case. It's a perfect opportunity—"

"Phaedra. Promise me." His words were grim. "Roberta Walsh is a potential murder suspect who may have killed three people. If your theories pan out, she's a dangerous and very devious woman."

"Oh, all right," she grumbled. "I promise."

No need to tell him that her fingers were firmly crossed.

Forty

"A toast," Nick Ross pronounced, thrusting himself to his feet at the head of the dining room table and raising his wineglass. "To Karolina."

Over the sound of clinking glasses and murmurs of "hear, hear" echoing around the table, he added, "And to a wonderful cast and crew, and bachelorettes beautiful enough to induce even a confirmed bachelor into marriage."

His dark gaze went straight to Tinsley.

Officially, no one knew who Nick-as-Darcy had chosen to be his bride, but Phaedra had a hunch it was Tinsley Prentiss. The bachelorette hadn't divulged the carefully guarded secret, but her glowing pink cheeks and lingering glances with Nick across the table gave her away.

"Shall we go outside?" Charlene asked her.

Phaedra nodded. As Bertie supervised the clearing of the table, they slipped through the French doors onto the terrace, and the cast and crew dispersed to get ready for the night's party.

"We can talk privately here," she added as they sat down at the wrought iron table. "You said you had something to tell me."

Phaedra filled her in and added, "There's no physical

proof yet. Bertie's too shrewd to leave fingerprints behind. But if anyone can find evidence, Detective Morelli will."

"It makes perfect sense," Charlene agreed, her lips pursed thoughtfully. "All of it. There's something a little . . . off about Bertie. I've always thought so." She leveled a steady gaze on Phaedra. "Is there anything else you'd like to share?"

"Right now, that's everything I know. Well, suspect," she corrected.

"That's not what I meant."

When Phaedra looked at her blankly, Charlene laughed.

"It's plain enough, to me anyway, that you like him."

"Like him? Who?"

"Detective Morelli."

She let out an incredulous laugh. "That's ridiculous. I can't stand him."

"Oh, come on, Phae. Every other word out of your mouth is 'Morelli' this and 'Detective Morelli' that. You're sweet on him. Admit it."

"Charlene, stop, please," she begged, and pushed herself to her feet. "You're way off base." The blush heating her cheeks gave the lie to her words. "I have to run or I'll never get back in time to pick Wickham up at the vet's and get dressed for tonight's soiree."

She followed Charlene back inside, where Mrs. Williams requested her help in the dining room.

"Go ahead," Phaedra told her. "See you tonight. I'll let myself out."

As she neared the front door, her phone rang, and she paused to answer it. "I stopped by and left a surprise for you in the kitchen," her mother said. "Some bubbly, to celebrate the end of the first season of your show."

"That was sweet of you. Thanks."

"Along with that cashmere shrug you like so much. It's draped over one of the dining room chairs."

"Shrug?" she echoed.

"You know the one." Impatiently. "Heathery gray, shot with tiny flecks of silver. It'll go perfectly with your new dress."

Phaedra thought of the deep purple slip dress she'd bought expressly for tonight's wrap party. "That does sound perfect. Thanks."

"It gets chilly at night, you know. And it looks like we're in for a storm this evening. Which shoes are you wearing? Something strappy and silver, I assume?"

"Yes."

"Good. Who's your date tonight?"

"My date?"

Her mother sighed. "Honestly, Phaedra, where is your *head* today? Who are you taking with you to the wrap party? Who's your plus-one? That delicious Shakespearean scholar?"

Phaedra hadn't seen Mark Selden since the rehearsal yesterday. When "Karo" gave him a grand tour of the set.

"I haven't asked anyone," she said. "I'm going solo."

"Of course you are." Nan sighed again.

Any minute now, Phaedra thought, she'll say I have no compassion for her poor nerves. "You never know, Mom. Maybe I'll fall in love with one of the crew. Run off with the cameraman. Oh, wait, no—he's married."

"Phaedra," her mother said crossly, "you're not funny in the least." She broke off with an exclamation. "Goodness, is that the time? I have a Historical Society meeting tonight, and I need to get ready."

"Did you lock the front door?"

Tiny pause. "Of course I did, darling. Don't I always?"

"No."

But her mother had hung up. With a sigh, Phaedra tucked the phone away, opened the front door, and returned to her car to head back to Laurel Springs.

"Here we are, Wicks. Home at last."

He mewled unhappily from within his carrier, making no secret of his displeasure.

It was verging on dusk when Phaedra arrived at the carriage house. Her errands to the grocery, post office, hardware store, and finally the veterinarian's consumed the better part of the afternoon. The Tea Society meeting would have to wait until tomorrow.

She set the carrier down. The front door was closed but unlocked.

"I swear, Mom," Phaedra grumbled as she hipped it open and brought Wickham inside, "I'm taking your key away."

Her gaze scanned the cozy yet familiar space. Her tea mug and spoon sat in the sink, and the *Tea Time* magazine she'd been reading last night was still open on the table. Her mother's surprise, a magnum of champagne, cooled in a silver bucket of ice on the kitchen counter.

Phaedra smiled. Mom's cashmere shrug hung over a chair in the dining room as she'd promised. Her gaze went to the open treads of the stairs rising up into the darkened bedroom above, and her smile faded.

Stop, she told herself firmly. There's no one here.

She let Wickham out of the carrier and set out a dish of kibble and tuna on the floor. Thunder grumbled in the distance, and the room had grown dark. A cold front must be moving in. The temperature had already dropped.

"Good thing Mom loaned me her shrug, eh, Wicks?"

He didn't spare her a glance but devoured his dinner. He finished, and with a baleful, blue-eyed glare, he stalked away and darted under the living room sofa. He didn't like storms. Again thunder sounded, a little closer this time, reminding her of the night she'd found William Collier's body sprawled in the claw-foot tub.

I'm always cold, he'd told her in the dream.

Shaking off the memory, Phaedra went to the kitchen drawer and scrabbled around until she found a flashlight. Just in case the power went out. On the heels of that thought, lightning speared the darkening sky, and the wind began to pick up.

Snapping on lights as she went, she made her way to the staircase, flashlight in hand. Time to get ready for the party. She'd laid out her new slip dress on the bed that morning, along with a pair of strappy silver heels.

The outfit made quite a change from her usual ballet slippers and demure gowns. Too bad Morelli wouldn't be around tonight to see her transformation.

At the top of the stairs, she paused. The loft contained a bedroom and small bathroom, and both were empty. She eased out a breath and took a few steps into her room. She'd shower, dress, and get the hell out of here.

She froze. Had a floorboard just creaked?

She waited, but all was silent. Only the growl and mutter of thunder outside, and the smell of ozone that presaged lightning. Why was she so jumpy?

The front door was unlocked. Anyone could've come inside.

But no one did, she scolded herself. Everything was as it should be. Books littered her desk under the sloping eaves, and a thick omnibus volume of six Austen novels, large enough to double as a doorstop, sat atop her most recent research notes. Her laptop was still open.

She frowned. The screen should've been dark, but it wasn't. Her search for "pharmaceutical companies, insulin" lit the screen. As if someone had recently looked at it.

You're next.

She shook off a growing uneasiness and paused inside the door to reach for the phone in her back pocket. She'd take it out and call Detective Morelli—

A stair tread let out a whisper of protest behind her, and the air stirred infinitesimally. Phaedra whirled around just as something hard and heavy and cold slammed down into her shoulder.

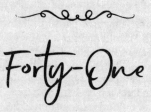

Forty-One

The magnum of champagne, she realized, pain exploding down her arm. Sitting in a bucket on the kitchen counter.
Bertie.

Her phone sailed out of her hand and slid under the desk. Phaedra backed, slowly, into the bedroom, her thoughts feverish. She needed a weapon. Something. Anything.

"No phone, Professor?" Bertie, brandishing the champagne, advanced into the room. "Pity."

"How did you know—"

"The front door was unlocked?" The older woman edged closer. "I heard you on the phone before you left Marling. I knew you had errands to run. I left after you and parked a few blocks away." She glanced around. "Charming place. I always wondered what it looked like inside."

"Well, now you know. And Detective Morelli knows you murdered Bill Collier. And Finch. And Harold Fortune," Phaedra added.

Bertie shrugged. "Knowing and proving are two entirely different things. William was Harold's son, by the way, the result of an affair with his brother's wife, Inez. That was Harold's dirty little secret."

"And William found out," Phaedra said slowly, "and blackmailed him." Phaedra paused. "How did you do it? How did you kill Harold and get away with it?"

"Fried egg sandwich," she said, and smiled at the memory. "Every morning I made him one to go. We were busy, so adding a drop or two of tetrahydrozoline to his fried egg was simple. It wasn't enough to kill him. Not right away. But over time . . ."

"Why did you murder William Collier?" The desk, Phaedra thought. If she could just move closer to the desk . . .

"Why?" Bertie snorted. "He was a monster, a heartless, rapacious little monster. He deserved to die."

"Because of your sister," Phaedra said. Keep her talking, and formulate a plan.

"Kay was diabetic," Bertie acknowledged. "The cost of insulin skyrocketed, so I wrote to Longbourn for financial aid. Harold ignored my letters. William did, too. Longbourn produces insulin. But you already knew that." Her glance cut to the laptop. "Didn't you?"

Phaedra shook her head. Bertie had on gloves, she noticed; food preparation gloves.

She's going to kill me.

"Thanks to greedy pharmaceutical companies like Longbourn, Kay couldn't afford the insulin she needed. We found a cheaper alternative, but it didn't work as well. She died."

"I'm sorry," Phaedra said, and meant it. "It shouldn't have happened. But you could hardly blame Bill. He had a company to run. A company he inherited."

"Oh, but I did blame him. He inherited Longbourn; he could've instigated change. Real change. He could have made insulin more accessible, more *affordable*, for everyone. But he didn't. And for that, he deserved to die. Ironic that an overdose of insulin did him in, don't you think? Kay needed it but couldn't afford it. He didn't need it and died from too much." She gave an ugly bark of laughter.

"And you let Charlene take the blame."

"Why not? She doesn't deserve all that money any more than Collier did."

"There's one thing I haven't figured out." *Keep her talking.*

"Only one?"

"Did you electrocute Mr. Collier? Violet said the power never went out upstairs."

"It didn't. Until that damned tree fell on the roof." She scowled. "I was just about to toss in the hair dryer when it hit and knocked out the electricity. Not just in the bathroom, but the entire east wing. As it turned out, though," she added, her eyes never leaving Phaedra's, "it didn't matter. The insulin I injected in his neck did the job. But enough talk." She set the magnum down atop the dresser by the door. "You won't feel a thing. You'll slip into a coma, and I'll leave nothing behind. No evidence. No fingerprints. Just another dead body." She slid her hand into her pocket.

Phaedra edged nearer the desk. Her heart thundered, and perspiration dampened her skin despite the chill in the room. Outside, wind lashed the trees and thunder rumbled overhead. Lightning arrowed across the sky.

"You don't need to do this," she said, and swallowed her fear. "This time, you'll be caught."

"Is this the part when you tell me I'll never get away with it?" Bertie chuckled as she withdrew the syringe. "But I did get away with it, Professor. Three times. Soon to be four."

"Morelli suspects you murdered Collier. And Finch. All he needs is evidence." She thought of the syringe CSI had found hidden in the toolbox in Marling's garage. "And he's got it."

"He's got nothing." She prepared the syringe, inserting the needle into the rubber cap of the insulin vial and pushing the plunger down. "Let's not make this difficult, Professor. Clean and quick, that's my motto." She stepped closer. "A syringe makes the perfect murder weapon. So much quieter than a gun, and far less messy."

Phaedra's phone chose that moment to blare out the opening bass notes of "Under Pressure." How appropriate, Phaedra thought wildly, and used Bertie's momentary confusion to snatch up the Jane Austen omnibus volume from her desk. She smashed it into the woman's face. Bertie let out a grunt of mingled surprise and pain as the syringe flew out of her hand across the floor and rolled under the slipper chair.

Phaedra dived after it, but strong fingers clawed at her arm.

"Give that to me!" Bertie hissed.

Straining with determination, Phaedra stretched, groping under the skirted chair with one arm until her fingertips brushed the syringe. Just a little farther, and she'd have it—

Bertie's body slammed atop hers, momentarily knocking the breath from her lungs.

Gasping, she reached past Phaedra and grabbed the syringe. "Got it," she gloated, brandishing the needle and pushing herself to her feet. "Your turn to die, Professor, among the books in the carriage house you love so much."

"Amongst," Phaedra gasped as she struggled for breath and inched away. "I . . . prefer . . . the British . . . usage."

"Too bad your fine education can't save you now." Bertie loomed over Phaedra, syringe in hand and a gleam in her eye. "You put up a decent fight, which is more than your predecessors did. Now," she added, preparing to inject her, "the time has come to say good night, Professor."

With a bloodcurdling yowl, Wickham leaped from the top of the dresser and landed on Bertie's shoulder, claws extended. She shrieked and flailed her arms and whirled in a panicked frenzy.

"Get off me, you beast!" She'd gone deathly pale and her skin broke into a sweat as she spun and batted ineffectually at the cat. "Help me!" she screamed. "Get this creature off me!"

A cat phobia, Phaedra realized, dazed, and pushed herself to her feet. Bertie had a full-blown terror of cats. The thought barely registered when her phone shrilled out "Under Pressure" once again.

She dived under the chair and grabbed it. "Mom! Are you there? Mom?"

But the call dropped and there was only a dial tone.

Bertie flung the cat away. Scratches covered her arms and face. She snatched the syringe from the floor and advanced, enraged, on Phaedra. "No one . . . to help you, Professor?"

"I wouldn't say that. Hands up, Mrs. Walsh."

Startled, Phaedra looked up to see Detective Morelli, her mother crowded in behind him, blocking the bedroom door. He leveled his Glock squarely on Bertie.

"Roberta Walsh, you're under arrest," he said, lowering the gun but keeping it trained on her, "for the murder of Jasper Finch, and for the attempted murder of Phaedra Brighton."

"You can't prove I killed him!" she taunted. "You can't prove a thing."

"We recovered the syringe used to inject Mr. Finch," he replied. "Your partial print was on it." He motioned her toward the door. "That's evidence enough to lock you up."

"I won't say another word without my lawyer."

He Mirandized her, produced a pair of handcuffs, and snapped them around her wrists. A pair of deputies came upstairs and led her away.

Nan Brighton brushed past them and enfolded her daughter in a bone-crushing embrace. "Oh, my darling, darling girl! Thank God you're all right. You frightened the life out of me! I was so afraid . . . that crazy woman . . ."

"Mom, it's okay," Phaedra reassured her. "I'm fine. Except for a little soreness in my shoulder." She winced. "Thanks for the champagne, by the way."

"Now you really do have something to celebrate." Her mother eyed her anxiously. "Are you sure you're all right?"

"Positive. But how did you know? To call Detective Morelli?"

"I didn't call him; he called me. The forensics people found Bertie's print on the syringe. I told him you'd gone to

Marling, but Charlene said you'd left hours ago, and Bertie was nowhere to be found, and I couldn't reach you on the phone, and your detective figured out the rest."

Phaedra flushed as Morelli reappeared in the doorway. Had he heard? She fervently hoped not. "He's not 'my' detective," she hissed at her mother.

Her face fell. "He's not? But I thought . . ."

"You thought wrong." She turned to Morelli. "Thank you, Detective. You saved my life."

He shrugged. "Looks like you did a pretty good job of it on your own. Roberta Walsh is a dangerous woman."

"Try 'unhinged.' She murdered William Collier and Harold Fortune, all because they owned the pharmaceutical company that produced her sister's insulin. Insulin she could no longer afford. And she killed Finch because she was convinced he figured out that she'd murdered Harold Fortune, too." She began to tremble. "She killed poor Finch for nothing. And she nearly injected me. Just like she injected Collier, and Finch. If not for you—"

"But she didn't," he reminded her. "That's all that matters." He turned to go. "I'll need you to come in and give your statement tomorrow morning."

"Of course."

"Detective Morelli," Nan called after him. "Are you free next Sunday? I'd like to invite you to dinner. To thank you."

"No thanks necessary, ma'am. Just doing my job."

"Call me Nan, please." She headed out after him. "Are you sure you won't reconsider? It's the least I can do. And my roast beef is exceptional, if I do say so myself . . ."

Phaedra sighed. As her mother's voice faded away down the stairs, she went to the window. A pair of Somerset County SUVs, light bars flashing a lurid red and blue, sat in the driveway, and the crackle of a police radio reached her ears.

Something silky-soft brushed against her ankles, followed by plaintive mewing.

"Wickham!" She bent down to stroke his fur. "My hero."

I should say so, his blue eyes accused. *If I hadn't landed on that murderous woman, you'd be a goner. I think this calls for a treat, don't you?*

"You've definitely earned a full can of Salmon Surprise tonight."

Forty-Two

I hereby call this meeting of the Jane Austen Tea Society to order," Phaedra announced.

Late-morning sun slanted into the reading room at the Poison Pen, where she, Lucy, and Marisol sat with cups of tea and a plate of freshly baked blueberry scones.

"It's a little late for a meeting." Lucy spread a tiny bit of butter on her scone and indicated the Thursday morning edition of the *Laurel Springs Clarion* on the table. "Considering you solved the mystery and caught the murderer single-handedly."

AUSTEN SCHOLAR SOLVES LOCAL MURDERS, the headline boasted. A photo of Phaedra in Regency attire, cradling Wickham in her arms, ran alongside the story.

"Good thing your dad closed the Poison Pen today." Marisol poured cream into her tea. "You're all anyone can talk about. Well, go on. Read us the story."

Phaedra cleared her throat. "'Somerset County police arrested Roberta Walsh, owner of Bertie's Café, and charged her with one count each of murder and attempted murder.

"'She will be tried for the murder of Jasper Finch, former

butler at the historic Marling estate, and for the attempted murder of Professor Phaedra Brighton.

"'Citing the efforts of Brighton, a Somerset University instructor and Jane Austen scholar, Detective Matt Morelli stated, "We intend to prosecute Mrs. Walsh to the full extent of the law."

"'Walsh is also a suspect in the death of former Longbourn Pharmaceutical owner Harold Fortune and his nephew, William Collier. Brighton, attacked in the bedroom loft of her home late Wednesday, fought Walsh off with a large volume of Austen novels and the help of her Himalayan cat, Wickham, who attacked the intruder.

"He's normally quite friendly," Brighton stated.'"

Lucy snorted. "Friendly? Wickham? So much for truth in journalism."

"Maybe he's not exactly cuddly," Phaedra admitted, "but he's never clawed anyone before."

"Thank goodness he did," Marisol said.

"Rest assured, Wickham knows he's a hero." Phaedra chuckled. "He's—pardon the pun—milking it for all it's worth."

"Seriously, Phae," Marisol said, her expression earnest as she leaned forward, "I'm really glad you're okay. You could've been killed."

Phaedra's throat thickened as Marisol stood to give her a quick hug, and she blinked away the unexpected rise of tears. "Thanks." She glanced at Lucy. "To both of you. You know what they say . . . there's the family you're born with. And the family you make. And you guys are my family."

After exchanging an awkward hug with Phaedra, Lucy followed Marisol to the door. "You know how I feel about sentiment. Besides which, I have classes to teach. See you both later."

They'd just left when footsteps echoed down the hallway. "Phaedra?" her mother called out. "You have a visitor."

Her voice contained a note of excitement, which could only mean the visitor was male. And single. Curious, Phaedra set her teacup down and turned around.

Mark Selden stood in the doorway. He held a book and a small bouquet of wildflowers.

"Mark! This is a surprise. What brings you here?"

"I believe congratulations are in order." He handed over the wildflowers with a flourish. "To the heroine of the day."

"Thank you." She regarded the bouquet containing larkspur, wild ginger, and dwarf iris with delight. "They're beautiful. But I'm hardly a heroine."

"I beg to differ. You single-handedly foiled a very dangerous woman and nearly got killed in the bargain. I'm just . . . I'm very glad you're all right."

"Not half so glad as I am," she admitted. "Would you like a cup of tea? We have blueberry scones."

"No, thanks. As tempting as that sounds, I can't stay. I have plans."

"With Karolina?" she asked, immediately wishing she hadn't.

"No." He regarded her quizzically. "With classes, and a stack of essays waiting to be graded." He hesitated. "Phaedra . . . Karo and I, we're friends. Nothing more."

"But I thought—"

"We dated, once. Years ago. It was a mistake. A big mistake."

"I see." To hide the fact that her heart suddenly felt as light and untethered as a helium balloon, she indicated the book in his hand. "What's that?"

"This?" He lifted the volume and studied the spine as if surprised to find it in his hand. "It's an illustrated first edition of *Pride and Prejudice*. Published in 1894 and one of only 250 copies released in England."

She drew in a sharp breath. "May I see it?"

"Of course." He held it out. "It was my mother's."

Reverently, she ran a finger down the brown buckram spine. "Illustrated by Hugh Thomson." Phaedra lifted her eyes to his. "This . . . this is amazing."

"I want you to have it."

"Oh, Mark." She struggled to find words in the face of

such unexpected generosity. "I can't accept this. It's worth hundreds—no, thousands—of dollars!"

"It was £4,000, the last time I had it valued."

She shook her head and held it out to him. "I do appreciate the offer. Thank you. But I can't possibly take it."

"Then I'll have to put it up for auction and present you with a check for whatever amount it brings."

Her eyes searched his. "Why are you doing this?"

"By way of apology. I abandoned you in the middle of the literary festival. I left you holding the bag, and I was a lousy Darcy, to boot."

"You were a perfect Mr. Darcy," she protested.

"But I'm doing it mainly because the Jane Austen literary festival needs funds, funds it won't get from normal academic channels. Consider this book"—he placed his hand atop hers on the cover—"a means of securing the festival's future—should you ever need to use it."

For the second time that day she felt tears threaten and blinked them away. Mark's gesture had taken her completely by surprise. "In that case," she said, lifting her eyes to his, "how can I possibly refuse?"

"You can't." He gave her a sideways smile. "I'll see you tomorrow?"

"Yes. And this time, *I'll* bring the doughnuts."

Acknowledgments

While writing a book is a largely solitary adventure, publishing a book truly does take a village.

Many thanks to the amazing team at Berkley Prime Crime/Penguin Random House: Michelle Vega, Sareer Khader, the art department who gifted me with the most gorgeous cover, and to everyone else who contributed to the making of this book. Thanks also to my agent, Nikki Terpilowski, for her unwavering belief in me.

Special thanks go out to Marilyn Brandt for her gracious kindness; to Lynn Folliot for her support and online friendship; and heaps of gratitude to Debi Smith, indie author extraordinaire and sender of the absolute best surprise packages. *Mahalos*. Thank you for your friendship, both online and in real life.

And finally, thanks to you, the reader. I hope you enjoyed *Pride, Prejudice, and Peril*. I look forward to sharing Professor Phaedra Brighton's next adventure.

Don't miss the next scintillating entry in
the Jane Austen Tea Society Mystery series,

A Murderous
Persuasion

by Katie Oliver

Coming in Fall 2022!

Ready to find
your next great read?

Let us help.

Visit prh.com/nextread

Penguin
Random
House